DRIFT
and
HUM

DRIFT
and
HUM

The Great Canadian – American Novel

ROBERT O. MARTICHENKO

Drift and Hum

By *Robert O. Martichenko*

© 2015, Karmack Publications LLC

Drift and Hum Disclaimer

This book is a work of fiction. Names, characters, businesses, places, events, and incidents are either the products of the author's imagination or used in a fictitious manner. Any resemblance to actual persons, living or dead, or actual events is purely coincidental.

Every effort was made to be factual and respectful where actual names, events, or places are used to support this work of fiction.

ISBN: 978-0-9970308-0-8

Author Photo: Corinne Martichenko & Denis Drever Photography
Publishing Consultant: Martha Bullen
Book Development Support: Marcia Jones
Professional Copy Editor: Carole Boyd
Book Design: AuthorSupport.com
Cover Photo: Larry Allan

Acknowledgements

Dedicated to my wife: My warrior of entropy

Written for my daughters: Listeners of my stories

A completed project with my friend RVK: Beaver Brother

With infinite thanks to GOW: Prospector, Mentor, Coach, and Uncle

In Memory of IBG: My childhood friend

In Memory of JLH: My father-in-law

In Memory of WTM: My father

"Sam's Poem of Poems"

THE CREMATION OF SAM MCGEE

By Robert W. Service

There are strange things done in the midnight sun
By the men who moil for gold;
The Arctic trails have their secret tales
That would make your blood run cold;
The Northern Lights have seen queer sights,
But the queerest they ever did see
Was that night on the marge of Lake Lebarge
I cremated Sam McGee.

Now Sam McGee was from Tennessee, where
the cotton blooms and blows.
Why he left his home in the South to roam
'round the Pole, God only knows.
He was always cold, but the land of gold
seemed to hold him like a spell;
Though he'd often say in his homely way
that "he'd sooner live in hell."

On a Christmas Day we were mushing
our way over the Dawson trail.
Talk of your cold! through the parka's fold
it stabbed like a driven nail.
If our eyes we'd close, then the lashes froze
till sometimes we couldn't see;
It wasn't much fun, but the only one to whimper was Sam McGee.

And that very night, as we lay packed tight
in our robes beneath the snow,
And the dogs were fed, and the stars o'er-
head were dancing heel and toe,
He turned to me, and "Cap," says he, "I'll cash in this trip, I guess;
And if I do, I'm asking that you won't refuse my last request."

Well, he seemed so low that I couldn't say no;
then he says with a sort of moan:
"It's the cursèd cold, and it's got right hold till
I'm chilled clean through to the bone.
Yet 'tain't being dead—it's my awful dread of the icy grave that pains;
So I want you to swear that, foul or fair,
you'll cremate my last remains."

A pal's last need is a thing to heed, so I swore I would not fail;
And we started on at the streak of dawn;
but God! he looked ghastly pale.
He crouched on the sleigh, and he raved all
day of his home in Tennessee;
And before nightfall a corpse was all that was left of Sam McGee.

There wasn't a breath in that land of death,
and I hurried, horror-driven,
With a corpse half hid that I couldn't get
rid, because of a promise given;
It was lashed to the sleigh, and it seemed to say:
"You may tax your brawn and brains,
But you promised true, and it's up to you
to cremate those last remains.

Now a promise made is a debt unpaid, and
the trail has its own stern code.
In the days to come, though my lips were dumb,
in my heart how I cursed that load.
In the long, long night, by the lone firelight,
while the huskies, round in a ring,
Howled out their woes to the homeless snows
– O God! how I loathed the thing.

And every day that quiet clay seemed to heavy and heavier grow;
And on I went, though the dogs were spent
and the grub was getting low;

The trail was bad, and I felt half mad, but I swore I would not give in;
And I'd often sing to the hateful thing, and it hearkened with a grin.

Till I came to the marge of Lake Lebarge, and a derelict there lay;
It was jammed in the ice, but I saw in a trice
it was called the "Alice May."
And I looked at it, and I thought a bit, and
I looked at my frozen chum;
Then "Here," said I, with a sudden cry, "is my cre-ma-tor-eum."

Some planks I tore from the cabin floor, and I lit the boiler fire;
Some coal I found that was lying around,
and I heaped the fuel higher;
The flames just soared, and the furnace
roared—such a blaze you seldom see;
And I burrowed a hole in the glowing coal,
and I stuffed in Sam McGee.

Then I made a hike, for I didn't like to hear him sizzle so;
And the heavens scowled, and the huskies
howled, and the wind began to blow.
It was icy cold, but the hot sweat rolled down
my cheeks, and I don't know why;
And the greasy smoke in an inky cloak went streaking down the sky.

I do not know how long in the snow I wrestled with grisly fear;
But the stars came out and they danced
about ere again I ventured near;
I was sick with dread, but I bravely said: "I'll just take a peep inside.
I guess he's cooked, and it's time I looked";
... then the door I opened wide.

And there sat Sam, looking cool and calm,
in the heart of the furnace roar;
And he wore a smile you could see a mile,
and he said: "Please close that door.
It's fine in here, but I greatly fear you'll let in the cold and storm—
Since I left Plumtree, down in Tennessee,
it's the first time I've been warm."

There are strange things done in the midnight sun
By the men who moil for gold;
The Arctic trails have their secret tales
That would make your blood run cold;

The Northern Lights have seen queer sights,
But the queerest they ever did see
Was that night on the marge of Lake Lebarge
I cremated Sam McGee.

Robert W. Service – Yukon, Canada (1874-1958)

DAY WELL SPENT

I'd really like to take a hike
Around a lake I've never seen
One without a person about
So I could wander while I dream
Then in time, perhaps I'd find
Some friends for company
We would talk, and go for walks
Many different lives we'd see

The Beaver Brothers, Lake Laberge, 1983

PART 1

Finding True North

RETREAT

One two three
Is really pretty easy
ABC
Isn't that tricky

But when I try to go farther
I find it starts to get harder
So I retreat back to the simple things that I know

Sam, South Carolina, 2015

DAY 0

South Carolina

I DON'T WANT TO DIE. Not like this anyway, so I need your help.

Good. I needed to get that out of the way right away.

I want to get better. That much you need to know, so please don't lose confidence in me. I need you to have faith. It's important that we keep faith because I absolutely intend to get better, and I believe I stand a pretty good chance. It will be helpful to me if you believe as well.

In the spirit of complete transparency, there is also something else you need to know up front. I'm not crazy. That much I know for sure. A few others know it as well, and I even have a doctor who will validate this for us. With that, I'll be the first to admit that I have a few things I need to work out. Yet, who doesn't have a few things to work out, right? Truth be told, I think I'm really just a person who needs a bit of a break from it all as it's been quite a ride lately, and I think a short break from everything will prove helpful. I'm sure you know how stressful things can get as nobody is immune to life's challenges these days. Nobody is immune to the ups and the downs so sometimes a person just needs a complete break from it all. That's me at this point. I'm one of those people, and the timing is perfect too, as my fiftieth birthday is right around the corner. It will be good to be rested for the next half-century.

I know I'll get better as this is just a small mid-life detour. At least that's how I'm looking at it anyway, and it's proving helpful to view the situation through this lens of improvement.

My getting through this is how my doctor views the situation, and a few friends of mine see it that way as well. They're great people, and I think you will like them. They were worried about me recently and did the whole intervention thing. That was quite the scene – talk about getting it all out there. My friends are amazing. Having close friends is an important part of life, and frankly I wouldn't be where I am today without them. But please don't let where I literally am today confuse this last comment. I'm actually in a good spot in general. In fact, I'm considered very successful by most standards. I just need a bit of a break. Life is like flying a kite, and I guess you could say I caught an unexpected gust of wind.

The good news is there's no real time constraint for my visit here. It's not as if I've been committed. I can leave whenever I want, although my doctor is suggesting I may want to rest for a few weeks at a minimum. This seems like a long time, but I'm committed to do what is right as the status quo is not practical and progress needs to be made. I'm on a break from work, no worries there. My team has everything under control, and it's very comfortable here at the hospital. So in totality, all is fine. No doubt there are a lot of people in worse shape than I am.

I'm sure you've gathered I'm in a hospital, or should I say, a hospital of sorts. It's more like a country club for people who need a rest and is a great example of premium health care services. If you need to take a break from it all, and if a hospital is a part of that break, and you have money, then this is the place to do it. In fact, right now, I'm looking at the Atlantic Ocean on the South Carolina coast. It's the beginning of July, so of course it's hot and sunny. I don't mind the heat as I know too well what the alternative is. I know about cold because I grew up in Canada. Not just Canada, but in the northern part of Canada, so it will be years before the sun of South Carolina thaws me out even though I've been here since 1984. That's over thirty years of thawing, and I'm still not done. The true north will do that to a person. Frozen is frozen, just as dead is dead.

I can see waves hitting the shoreline from my spacious room, and sometimes I watch the ocean from my private deck or through the window over my writing desk. The tide is currently coming in, and it will be a six-foot tide today, just about average for the South Carolina coast. I prefer a rising tide as I'm feeling it's more appropriate for my current situation. Falling tides are certainly a part of life as well, and we need to embrace them, but right now I prefer a rising tide. Directly in front of me is the Atlantic in all its vastness, and to my right, to the south, is one of many South Carolina rivers that flow into the ocean. The rivers are fantastic because you can see the speed of the water flowing as a result of the tidal currents. I learned a long time ago never to underestimate the force of natural currents as they are much, much stronger than you imagine.

I've had the privilege of travelling to every state in the USA, and South Carolina is by far the most beautiful in my opinion. It also happens to be where my family and I live. In fact, I'm not far from home right now. I'm Canadian by birth, but I became an American citizen a few years ago. That was quite the process, and I was honored to become a citizen. My wife Sophie and son George are both American born – they are my true red, white, and blue Americans.

My doctor and I are friends, so I just call her Doc. The informality helps create an environment for progress to be made. We have known each other for over ten years as we are both part of the local professional community. She is a board-certified psychiatrist and very good at what she does, as well as being Sophie's friend. I know she's a good doctor because I'm a trained psychologist. Considering my profession, I recognize the irony of my current state.

I haven't worked as a practicing psychologist for some time because I've been building a business. That is, I was up until I took this self-imposed time off. Apparently I'm pretty good at what I do; at least that's what my employees and customers tell me. Doc is trying to get me back to work so I'll get out of this funk. She believes getting back to work is the remedy to my ills, and others agree. My employees want me back to work so we can continue with the positive momentum we've been generating, and my customers want me back so they can continue to improve their lives. I help people improve their lives, and once again, the irony is not lost on me.

My room is perfect, spacious and comfortable – all in a simple way. I'm looking for simplicity right now as simplifying your life makes it easier to relax and find peace of mind. Simplicity creates calming energy; complexity creates chaotic energy. Energy is important to me right now, in particular, positive energy. I have a bed, a dresser, and a nice writing desk with a lamp on it. My window looks over the ocean – it's a great view. This is what I meant by this being a nice place, and while I know money isn't everything, and it won't buy happiness, it sure can help out when you need a break from it all. The ocean is a natural healer; the rivers and the ocean are my healers. The only thing I would remove from this room is the television. It's a new high-tech flat screen with a thousand channels where many of the channels are the Talking Cable Heads' shows. You know the kind – where a bunch of people aggressively spew their opinions on matters they know absolutely nothing about.

I don't do so well with these shows, so I have the television unplugged, and I fight with myself when I get the urge to turn it on.

I'm working at the desk right now. When Doc and I aren't talking, you can find me sitting on the beach or at my desk. My desk is where I write; the beach is where I think about what to write. Writing bridges the physical world and the mental world; at least it does for me. Writing allows me to synthesize all the complexity of my life into manageable pieces. Everything is more manageable when you chunk it into smaller pieces. I've always enjoyed writing, and I mostly write poetry and song lyrics. I'm the poet, and my musician friend Ray and I collaborate to bring songs to life.

I haven't been the model patient for Doc as I haven't exactly been a chatterbox. Psychology requires dialogue; it's a cognitive therapy and requires communication between doctor and patient. It's not as if I'm not talking to Doc. I'm just not talking about the right things. I know it, and she knows it, but that doesn't change what I'm doing. I am ready to talk though, so I guess I just need to get warmed up a little. Doc told me to spend some time writing down my thoughts as part of this warm up, and I think that was clever. I would never have thought of it. I guess that's why she's here as the doctor and I'm here as the patient.

The real problem is I'm out of energy, but I need energy to get better. I know that. I'm also tired of being frustrated and angry, or being frustrated and angry is making me tired. I'm not sure which way it goes. Maybe it doesn't matter what's the cause and what's the effect, because either way you end up tired. But I'm committed, and I'll give it everything I have. I'm willing to try. *Eat tree, Beaver!* That's my motto to my customers who are seeking my advice. I should try to practice what I preach, as practicing what you preach can go a long way. It's hard, though. Giving advice and actually implementing your own advice are two very different animals. The former is much easier.

I suppose I should introduce myself. This would be appropriate since I'm asking you to stay with me. You can call me Sam, the name I've gone by forever, even though Sam is not the name you'll see on my birth certificate or passport. I've never used my real name because I've always just been Sam. My friend Hats was the first to call me Sam. I'm named after *Sam McGee,* the character from the Robert Service poem *The Cremation of Sam McGee.* It's my favorite poem. I really love the poem, and Hats loves the fact that I love it. He also believes I have a bit of the Sam character in me, so he started calling me Sam when we were kids. It stuck, and everybody, including my own family, saw the congruency as well. Everybody calls me Sam. *Sam McGee* is still my favorite poem, a classic in every sense; it's simply the poem of all poems.

The master plan here is for me to get better, so I'm going to do this by talking through some issues with the Doc, and I'm also going to attempt to do some writing to organize my thoughts. I plan to share all of this with you as this is the only way any progress will be made. I'm going to do my absolute best to share everything you need to know, exactly when you need to know it, so you have all the information and background required to help me.

With that, here's what you need to know at this point. Everything you are about to read really happened. I'm not saying I might not get a few things mixed up, and I'm not saying that everybody remembers it the way I do. I'm just saying that it all really happened.

I hope Hats, RC, and Ray can tell it their way someday as well because it's really their story too.

OK then, buckle up, and let's get started.

I hope you enjoy the ride.

Canada

The True North Strong and Free

CANADIAN CONFEDERATION happened in 1867. I won't go into all the reasons why Canada finally became a country, but suffice it to say, there were many internal and external forces at play. Money and war are probably the two main categories; I guess some things never change. The word *Canada* means *settlement* or *land* when translated from its original First Nations' language, so in summary, Canada is a very young country with a lot of land.

Chinook River, Manitoba, incorporated as a town fifty years after Confederation, with the reasons and forces for the town to incorporate being largely economic. That's where my friends and I grew up. Chinook translates into a lot of things in multiple native languages, but the most common is *warm wind*. My favorite translation is *snow eater*. A Chinook is a warm wind that comes from the mountains in wintertime to warm up the surrounding mountain towns. This happens mostly in Alberta, so ironically our town does not get Chinooks. We're a river valley town, and the Rocky Mountains are two provinces to the west. We do, however, get a lot of snow, and that's why we like the snow eater translation.

Chinook River is on the Chinook River – no surprise here. The river is approximately six hundred miles long, or one thousand kilometers in the metric system. Its source is Lake Timagimi to the south, and it flows north into the Hudson Bay. Our town is almost at the halfway mark of the river, with the largest nearby city center being Winnipeg, Manitoba, a few hours to the southwest. Chinook River is a nice place to grow up because it's a good place that's filled with good people. A lot of people have done well there. I hope you get a chance to visit one day to form your own opinion.

RC, Hats, Ray, and I have been friends forever as there has never been a time we did not know each other. With varying background stories, our parents all arrived in Chinook River to support the mining and logging that takes place in our hometown, and all four families were established in town before we were born. I have no idea how we all first met, where it was or when it was, and our parents have no idea either. We've just always known each other; I guess true friendships are like that. They just are.

Chinook River is considered northern Canada. This is a differentiator because Canada is much larger than most people realize, and there are big differences among Canadian cities and towns. For example, you can't compare Toronto and Chinook River. This would be similar to comparing Mobile, Alabama, and Minneapolis, Minnesota. It can't be done.

The first and main differentiator is that Chinook River is cold. My friend RC still lives there. In fact, he's a police officer with the Royal Canadian Mounted Police, or RCMP. He's the Staff Sargent of the division – the big boss. Even though he still lives in Chinook River, he always complains about the cold, mostly because this is the Canadian way. Regardless of what the weather is, it's very important to complain about it. This is easy to do in Chinook River because normally it is just really cold. Global warming is not a term anybody in Chinook River understands or believes.

I once asked RC why he still lives in Chinook River, and he said because that's where his job and family are, and that he wants to grow old and die there. I asked him when that would be, and he responded, "Probably in about an hour, right after I freeze to death." It was forty degrees below Celsius and Fahrenheit at the time. At forty degrees below, it doesn't matter what scale you use, it's all the same. Forty below is where the scales meet. Frankly, I don't even know why we bother saying forty below. After thirty below it should just be called *really, really cold*. To me, that explains the situation better because everybody understands really, really cold.

Chinook River is not big or small population-wise. It's small enough that you can know a lot of people but big enough that you can have your space when you need it. You don't get crushed, but you don't go it solo either. It's a very cultural place, with amazing language dynamics – people speak the two official Canadian languages of French and English, and the local aboriginal First Nations people still practice the art of their native tongues. It's pretty neat when you stop to think about it – Canada is a unique country, and my friends and I are proud Canadians, even though Hats and I have spent most of our adult life in the USA. Irony is a funny thing.

The town is a lot like other northern Canadian towns. Because of our two official languages, we have both French and English schools, and I suspect it would be this way even if it weren't the law of the land, which it is. The town has a downtown core – municipal buildings, one hospital, several hockey arenas, one curling rink, a Canadian Legion, and multiple churches. The United Church of Canada is the church we attended growing up.

Another interesting point about Chinook River is that it's bigger in area – land mass measured in hectares – than New York City and Los Angeles combined. This is because the town started as a mining town. We are into everything to do with minerals – gold, copper, nickel, silver, and all things involving valuable rocks. When the town was established, the founders made the town as big as they could in case a new mine was discovered in the future, which proves that Canadians like their tax bases as much as the next country. The result of this is that when you're heading into town, you will come across the sign that says, "You are now entering Chinook River," but don't get too anxious at the wheel as you will drive another half-hour before you actually hit the town center. It can confuse first-timers who think somehow they missed the town, even though it's up ahead another fifty kilometers, or thirty miles.

Did you know that approximately eighty percent of the Canadian population lives within a two-hour drive of a border with the United States of America? In Chinook River, we are over six hours from the closest border. Did you know that over fifty percent of the population of Toronto, Canada's largest city, was not born in Canada? In Chinook River, almost everybody was born in Canada, most probably at Sacre Coeur Hospital. Those not born in Canada came to the country years ago when they decided that the land of *really cold* was better than the land of the communists or fascists. I guess really cold is better than really dead. To be sure, Eastern European cultures mixed with the French, English, and First Nations do form an interesting union. The people of Chinook River have a sense of history and are survivors and hard workers. This makes sense because northern towns are full of hard physical work and consequently, embrace hard physical workers. Hard work is a survivor's trade mark.

Canada has a few global stereotypes. People outside of Canada identify Canada with hockey, cold, snow, beer, and the saying, 'eh?' This is reasonable as Canadians love to play hockey, winters are very cold with lots of snow, and of course, the beer is the best. But the story is much deeper and richer than the puck on the ice, the mercury in the thermometer, the height of the snow bank, or the beer in the cooler. Here's the part many people don't know about, and this includes a lot of new Canadians living in southern Canadian cities. Winter nights may be cold and short on sunshine, but they are still and quiet and create an aura and feeling that meditation experts would die to replicate. Summer days and nights are nothing short of spiritual. Picture a sunset that never ends but only fades into a sunny shade of grey. It is the feeling of glory to be had and felt forever. Chinook River is where I grew up. It was a good place to grow up, and I'm happy I grew up there. Not that I always felt that way, though, as there was a time I was not thrilled with the town. Again, the irony is not lost on me.

Here's what you need to know about saying 'eh?' Canadians are officially peacekeepers from a global-affairs point of view, so Canadians want to keep the peace. As peacekeepers, we do not want to seem assuming or display characteristics of arrogance or rudeness, and the delivery system and technique to accomplish this goal is to turn statements into questions. We do this by ending sentences with 'eh?' This is the Canadian weapon that disarms people around the world, and this is why young Americans put Canadian flags on their backpacks when they travel through Europe.

Here's how it works. Suppose you are a total dumbass, and I want to call you out on it. Instead of calling you a dumbass and risking a fight, I would simply say, "You're a dumbass, eh?" The onus is now on you to verify you are in fact a dumbass, and in this situation I am not the antagonist but rather just the supplier of a relevant question for a given situation. Even after having been in the USA for over thirty years now, I still use the 'eh?' technique regularly. It's very effective.

RC, Hats, Ray, and I, friends forever, were all four born in 1965 at the Sacre Coeur Hospital, the only hospital in our town at the time. (The French Catholics got to name it, but that same year the English Protestants got to name the curling rink. It was a fair trade off.) All people born in 1965 are part of the changeover from Baby Boomers to Generation X. We don't fit into any of the generational profiles. We are the lost souls, we are unique, and we are proud of this little detail. When Hats, Ray, and RC were made God used new and unique molds, and the molds were broken after their birth. God does that between generations: a set-up year where the newborns don't fit any stereotyped category.

As RC would say, the four of us are tight as bark on a tree, and we are as close as can be in any variation of the group of four. We are tight, whether all together, in a combination of a group of three or all the variations of groups of two. It's just always been that way. We take great pride in our friendship, so we treasure and protect it at all cost. When we were young, we understood this implicitly without understanding why we felt this way, and as we got older and life started to happen, we learned the importance of our bond. Friendship is a non-renewable resource because you simply can't make new childhood friends. You either have them or you don't, and we have them. We like that, and it's recorded at the top of the ledger on the balance sheet of our lives.

Our first twelve years of friendship were filled with the simple fun of being young. We were typical Canadian boys living in the far north in that we watched hockey on television, and we played hockey on indoor rinks, outdoor rinks, ponds and roads, and in our basements. We had mini-sticks for the last. We went to school, actively participated in winter, and really enjoyed our summers. We played our music and determined who could command what instruments best. We talked, argued, dreamed, explored, and developed our visions and hopes for our futures. Everything was perfect. We were kids and the universe allowed us to be kids.

The spring of 1977 is when our story really got started, as the spring of 1977 is when we developed the plan for the Lodge. In hindsight, there is no question that this was a pivot point for us as brothers.

DAY 1

South Carolina

Colors of the Day

I CATEGORIZE MY DAYS as Red, Yellow, or Green. It's my measurement system to know whether I'm on the road to recovery, and I've told myself that seven Green days in a row means it's time to go home, and twenty Green days in a row will mean I'm probably ready to get back to work. Doc likes this approach as it's objective, visual, and easy to administer. Today is starting out as a Yellow day, which means it will probably end as a Yellow day. I've noticed my attitude in the morning has a significant net effect on my entire day. This is something I need to work on.

A Yellow day is a day that I'm feeling very anxious but able to keep my anger controlled. Yellow means anxiety *Yes*, but anger *No*. You see, I suffer from anxiety and anger issues. While Doc seems to talk about them in combination and relation to each other, I don't see them as related at all. At least they don't feel related when I am in either state of emotion. Anxiety to me is nervousness and worry. It lacks self-confidence behind it. Anxiety is the outside world coming into your world where you are scared of the world and all that's in it. Anger is different. Anger has self-confidence behind it. Anger is outward where you take your world to the outside world, where you are no longer scared of what's in the world. With anger, you just want to crush everything with your fists. That's why anger is so dangerous. Anxiety and anger together form a very strange union, and most of the time, you don't know whether you are coming or going.

Today is a Yellow day, and I'm completely exhausted because I had a dream last night that felt as if it lasted my entire lifetime. I woke up with the sheets tightly wrapped around me and I was shivering from cold and sweating from heat at the same time. I felt as if my feet were in the freezer and my head were in the oven.

In my dream, I was the lead weatherman for what I understood to be the largest global television network in existence. The essence of the situation was that I was the most important and most watched weatherman on Earth. It was my job to report on the weather from all parts of the world, and I was very important – a celebrity in my field, famous beyond measure.

I started off updating people about the weather on each <u>continent</u>. There were seven summaries in all, and each continent had blue skies and sunshine. I was very confident; I felt good about my position in life and profession; I was the *go to* man for the weather, and people trusted me. Then I received a report from my assistant that had the weather for all the <u>countries</u> in the world. There were almost two hundred summaries in all, and it took me over an hour to go through each one. Each country had severe thunderstorms, but this didn't make sense! How could all the countries have severe thunderstorms when all the continents have blue skies and sunshine? The whole did not equal the sum of the parts.

Then it really began to unravel. My assistant came over to the news desk and handed me a report that had the weather for every <u>city</u>, <u>town</u>, and <u>village</u> in the world. There were over one million places I needed to report on, and I began to panic as I recognized it would take me weeks or months to get through the list. As I started to scan the list, I noticed that every city, town, and village was experiencing hurricane force winds. My panic started with my heart rate going up; I started to feel shortness of breath and everything started to seem as if it were in slow motion. I could see people's lips moving, but I couldn't hear what they were saying. There was no sound at all, and nothing made sense. I felt as if everybody in the newsroom and all viewers in the world were staring at me and looking for answers. Although I didn't know how many people were watching me from their television sets, I sensed it was the whole world.

Then my assistant came up to me and handed me another report that was so big it would have fit into five dump trucks. It was the weather report for every single person in the world, with no fewer than seven billion names. Everybody in the studio was looking at me as if to say, "It's your responsibility to tell us what the weather is in the personal space of everyone on Earth!" I started to read the first few names, but my panic had turned to fear and I had no breath to speak. I couldn't utter a word. I wanted to run from the studio, but my legs would not work, and the only thing that would work was my eyes. I started to scan the names of people on the list, and every name had a report of category-five tornados heading directly at that person. I started to file through the pages, and the same tornado warnings were beside every name on the list. Suddenly, I felt responsible for warning everyone on Earth to take shelter. But where would they take shelter? Then I started to hear voices coming through the camera, and it was all of the people on Earth blaming me for the tornadoes that were about to hit their personal space. There were hundreds of different languages all telling me I was responsible for their impending doom, and I understood each language and responded in it. I tried to beg for their forgiveness, and I wanted them all to know that I believe intrinsically in blue skies and sunshine, just like the forecast for the continents. I was screaming for them to trust me again and to allow me to fix everything.

Then I woke up exhausted. So I went for a walk on the beach hoping the day would get better, doubting that it would.

Canada
Spring 1977

The Lodge

CANADA IN 1977 was an interesting place. Prime Minister Trudeau was still in power after a blockbuster 1974 federal election, and he was busy dealing with the economic and energy crises of the mid-1970s. The Beaver had recently been named the national symbol of Canada, barely beating out the Moose; the metric system implementation was in full swing, and we were all trying to switch from miles to kilometers, with some of us never quite making the transition. Down in Quebec, the provincial legislature passed Bill 101. This was *The Charter of the French Language,* which is a law making French the official language of Quebec. It had many broad implications and over a million unintended consequences, and the jury is still out on whether the law was a good idea.

The Toronto Blue Jays played their first Major League Baseball game, and they defeated the Chicago White Sox nine to five at Toronto's Exhibition Stadium. Most people believe the only reason Toronto won was because of the snowstorm before the game, giving Canadians a sense of pride, even though very few of the Blue Jay players were Canadian. Most were American and freezing their asses off alongside the Chicago team, not that we cared much either way as the four of us didn't find baseball very interesting. Hockey is a sport, baseball is a game, and there is a big difference.

On the music scene, the Rolling Stones Tour came to Toronto, and the RCMP greeted them by raiding Keith Richards' fancy hotel suite while he was sleeping. They seized over twenty grams of heroin, close to five grams of cocaine, and a bunch of narcotics paraphernalia needed to consume the heroin and cocaine. Nobody believed Richards was actually sleeping. Instead of sending him to jail, they made the Stones play a benefit concert for the blind in Oshawa, Ontario. This all seemed reasonable to us.

Gordon Lightfoot finished writing his hit about the Lake Superior sinking of the Great Lake vessel *The Edmund Fitzgerald*. Ray would tell you it's still the best song ever written. He would know too, because Ray is an amazing musician. In fact, even back in 1977 at the age of twelve Ray was a gifted artist. RC also has real talent, but Ray is the one with a genetic gift, and he's a great teacher as well. He taught all of us. He is the leader of the band – no question.

Other than the Beaver's being named the national symbol of Canada and the ship wreck, we didn't much care about what was going on in Canada at large, as life was far too interesting to be worried about people and events in Quebec or Ottawa. For us, the nation's capital was a million miles away, or should I say one point six million kilometers away. Instead of world events, we were focused on hockey, music, and how best to utilize our obvious overabundance of unproductive energy. We were twelve-year-olds, and we knew how to be kids. We liked being kids. Sometimes I think kids don't know how to be kids anymore, and many don't like being kids these days. Being a kid in the north was easy, as there were an infinite number of things to do – so the four of us grew up moving from one adventure to another.

We went to Ecole St-Pierre together. It was a French-speaking Catholic elementary and junior high school. I suspect our parents got together and hashed this plan out because it was an odd school choice: not one of us was French or Catholic. Not one of us is French or Catholic today. Parents make funny decisions when they want better things for the next generation, and I guess they decided bilingualism and Catholicism fit the bill. I'll never forget our first day of kindergarten when Hats showed up with a blue velvet fedora on his head. It was the real deal with a bird's feather in it and the whole bit. Hats believed that French Catholics all wore them, so he was surprised when he was the only one with one on. Hats loves his hats – that's why we call him

Hats – and he has thousands of them. You name the hat, and I'll guarantee you he's got it. He knows a lot about them too because Hats likes to understand the things he chooses to pursue. Consequently, he knows hat history, hat fashion, hat manufacturers, hat prices. You name it, he knows it when it comes to hats.

Spring had arrived in 1977, and we were only a couple of weeks from making it through Grade 7. It had been a long, cold winter, and the only thing that kept us going was the Stanley Cup playoffs. The Stanley Cup is the Cup of Cups. It is the ultimate championship in sport. In 1977 Hats was on fire and borderline unbearable because his Philadelphia Flyers beat my Toronto Maple Leafs in the quarter-finals, which made Hats believe they would win the Cup again. I have to admit, I was a bit envious of Hats because the Flyers were the real deal in the 1970s. Their star player was Bobby Clarke, a hometown boy from the neighboring town of Flin Flon, Manitoba, and we all secretly cheered for him, regardless of our official team loyalty. Unfortunately for Hats though, the Flyers were beaten in the semis by RC's Boston Bruins. Unfortunately for RC, Ray's Montreal Canadiens beat Boston for the Stanley Cup, four games to zero. It was a sweep, and Ray was on top of the world.

"Take that, ya Bruins Fuckers!" Hats yelled out at RC as Montreal skated around the ice with the Cup. As far as Hats was concerned, the team that had beaten his team was the enemy. Side note here, something you need to know about Canadians is that many of us swear a lot, and we start swearing at a young age. Something you need to know about Hats is that he swears more than most other Canadians, and he started swearing younger than most. His mother says he threw out his first *F bomb* at the nurse in the hospital when he was born. I'll admit, he's pretty good at it. Actually, he's the best I know, and he can turn swearing into a form of music. I will apologize for him up front, and I truly hope you don't find him offensive. Hats is a good man in spite of his colorful language skills.

Back to hockey. I was personally pissed at Hats because his Flyers beat out my Toronto Maple Leafs. I'm a huge Leafs fan, Ray is a Montreal Canadiens die-hard, and RC is a Boston Bruins fan. We all love Bobby Orr. Three of us are followers of the original-six teams. Hats moved over to the Flyers after cheering for the Chicago Blackhawks, which at the time meant we had four of the original-six teams covered. We were only missing New York and Detroit. Hats began to cheer for Philadelphia because he said they exemplified his style of game, which is rough and tough. Dave Shultz and the Broad Street Bullies are his heroes.

Hockey was hot in Canada in 1977. Even though five years had passed, the whole country was still vibrating from the *1972 Canada–Russia Summit* series. Many Canadians just call it the Super Series, where we played four games in Canada and four in Russia – our best against their best. We got to go to game three in Winnipeg when Coach Vince took us. Game three was the only tie game of the series and set up game eight in Moscow as the go-ahead game to win the series. Paul Henderson scored the winning goal with thirty-four seconds left on the clock in the third period, and Canada won the Super Series four games to three. Our whole school watched the game on television sets brought into the classrooms. The 20-year-old Russian goalie Vladislav Tretiak became my new hero, and Bobby Clarke remained Hats' hero when he accidently fractured the ankle of the best Russian player. It was an accident, and we still believe this to this day. The fact that it looks intentional is just a function of the angle of the cameras that filmed the slash and the fact that the lighting was bad in the old Russian arena.

Mostly because of Hats, we are also big fans of the Memorial Cup. This is the championship tournament that decides who is the best Major Junior Amateur hockey team. It was originally the Ontario Hockey Association Memorial Cup, and in 1919 the Ontario Hockey Association donated the Cup to the Canadian Amateur Hockey Association in honor of the soldiers who died fighting for Canada in the First World War. The Cup was re-dedicated in 2010 to honor fallen soldiers who died for Canada in any war. The Cup is a big deal in all of Canada, and it's also a way for Western Canada to compete against Ontario, Quebec, and Eastern Canada. These days, there are also American teams in the league. The players are all young amateurs, and many are also only one step away from playing in the National Hockey League. That's a big deal.

Unlike our NHL allegiances, the boys and I all cheer for the same major junior team. In 1977 our team was the Winnipeg Monarchs. They were our *close to home* team, but unfortunately, in that same year they moved to Calgary, Alberta, and changed their name to the Calgary Wranglers. We continued to cheer for them, but we also continued to call them the Winnipeg Monarchs. Then in 1987 they moved south and became the Lethbridge Hurricanes, and we continued to cheer for them. We also continued to call them the Winnipeg Monarchs. It's very important to stay true to your original team.

The real Winnipeg Monarchs won the Memorial Cup in 1935, 1937, and 1946. The relocated and renamed Monarchs have never won a

Memorial Cup, although we came close a couple of times. Sometimes it's hard to stay a loyal fan, but it must be done. It's principle.

In our neck of the woods our 1977 hockey year went well. Our team, the Maple Tree Hockey Team, would go on to win the Pee Wee Championship. Our coaches, Vince and the Judge, were very happy with us and the team.

The end of the 1977 NHL playoffs also meant summer was coming, and this meant we were going to have a full two months to do whatever we wanted. It was Ray that came up with the idea for the Lodge first.

"We need a clubhouse!" Ray told us one day while sitting in the basement of my house.

"All right," we all replied, knowing he was absolutely right.

Ray is an idea guy. He has more than a hundred ideas a day. We know this because we counted once. Most of them are pretty good too, and when I say I suspect Ray is the smartest guy I've ever met, I'm not talking just school smarts. Sure he's a whiz at all the math and science you want, but he's smart in different ways – world-smart without having travelled the world, street-smart without having lived on the street. He's just smart. In this particular case, he was right: we did, in fact, need a clubhouse.

Building the Lodge that summer was our first tangible accomplishment together from a teamwork point of view other than our hockey. We started that spring and poured our hearts and minds into the initiative. We ate, slept, and breathed the construction of the Lodge. To this day, I tell people there is no better feeling then being on a mission as people on a mission will overcome most obstacles that get in their way. That summer, we were on a mission in every sense of the word.

The planning was the first step, and I was given the role of overall project manager. Apparently I knew the most about lodges in the woods. Seemingly, I gained this knowledge from my studies of Robert Service's poetry. Because I could recite *The Cremation of Sam McGee,* it seemed logical that I was the most knowledgeable about lodges in the woods and snow. I didn't argue.

When the planning was complete, we had full agreement and alignment. It would be a log lodge in a place that nobody would be able to find, and it would be fully capable of keeping us warm in the winter. As well, we would call it the *Beaver Brothers Lodge.* Hats was the only one that argued against the name.

"Fuck that, guys," he said. "Let's call it the Moose Brothers Lodge! The Moose got a bum deal in Ottawa and needs a little boost!" It actually wasn't lost on us that the Beaver had won out as Canada's national symbol and that maybe the Moose did deserve a runner-up award. But we couldn't ignore the fact that the Lodge would be built of logs and that we might even use the odd logs already felled by a cooperative beaver. We were able to get Hats on board without too much coercion, and he came up with the Brothers part. We all liked it a lot and the *Beaver Brothers Lodge* was born that day. In hindsight, that was a great day. With the high-level planning complete, we began construction, with site selection the first step.

There was no shortage of possible places to build the Lodge, as our town is surrounded by bush and wilderness in all directions – serious bush and serious wilderness. RC was in charge of site selection because he was most knowledgeable about living in the bush and orienteering through the woods. I can't remember a time when he did not know how to use a compass, and orienteering through the bush was his way of training for his ultimate profession. From the age of five, he knew he would become a police officer when he finished school. More precisely, he knew he'd become a member of the Royal Canadian Mounted Police. In fact, that's why we call him RC. At first we called him RCMP, but that got too complicated, and we shortened it to RC for practical reasons.

RC did a great job with site selection, even with Hats giving him grief about every detail. When we stopped at the spot he recommended we were deeply into the heart of the bush. It was a perfect-size clearing that had every tree species known to man surrounding the plot. The clearing was beside a small creek bed that ran a quarter-mile to a beaver pond that had no fewer than three dams supporting and creating the pond. The pond was almost like having our own private mini-lake. It really was perfect. We were as remote as could be and there was no beaten path to the spot. To find the spot, you had to know the identifying trees and actual coordinates to the place. You had to orienteer. Even though it was difficult to find, we purposely changed how we would get to the Lodge each time. This was Ray's idea, and the purpose was to avoid making a path. We didn't believe in paths, and to this day, other than the four of us, only a few people know about the Lodge. This does include a few constables from the Royal Canadian Mounted Police. I haven't been there since the search, and I suspect the RCMP hasn't either as there's no reason to go now.

We loved building the Beaver Brothers Lodge. We loved hiking to it, we loved working on it, and we loved being in it. It was paradise by the northern lights.

Hats was on main log detail, and Ray had responsibility for the roof. We had ample pine trees around us so we began felling trees and using a drawknife to peel the bark off. We didn't have time to dry the logs for a year, so we just had to deal with working with green logs. We were in absolute heaven. The main tool was our *Hudson Bay Axes* with their funny-shaped axe head, and we also had a host of other tools required to raise a lodge fit for The Beaver Brothers. To this day, I can recall the smells, sounds, and feels of that summer – the smells of wood chips caused by the axe chipping away at a tree that was standing tall; the sounds of the bucksaw and hammer and chisel being used to create a notch in a tree that had offered itself up for our cause; the feel of wood chips hitting us in the face and eyes as we tried to get the logs to fit together, and the tree sap sticking to our hands, forcing us to walk to the nearby beaver pond to wash it off in the still water. It was all perfect.

We skinned the pine logs, notched them, built the structure, and then chinked in between the logs with mud and grass. The floor was made from cedar logs with plywood on top of them and was 12 inches off the ground with hay stuffed underneath the plywood for insulation. We hauled the plywood in at night so nobody would see us. That was quite the show. When the Lodge was done, it was an imperfect square of 12 feet 8 inches by 11 feet 5 inches. The final dimensions were completely random and had been determined by mistakes we made and had to correct along the way. The Lodge had two good-size windows made from *Plexiglas,* and inside we had a table for eating and playing games – mostly *Risk*. We built two sets of bunk beds with logs as the frame and using binder twine to imitate mattress springs, and we packed in a few old wooden chairs and a couple of lawn chairs for sitting. In the end, the Lodge was the real deal.

Ray was in charge of roof detail, but Hats didn't feel we had time to build proper roof trusses, and we didn't think we knew how to either. Time and skill go hand in hand for success. Ray was pissed and would have no part of not doing it properly, and he also said he could build proper trusses. He was right, and even though Hats was secretly impressed, he still gave Ray a hard time.

"This fucking thing will never hold, Ray," Hats screamed at him while we were putting the finishing touches on the roof of the Lodge.

"Sure it will, Hats," Ray replied, not even remotely taking the bait for a senseless argument.

That summer Ray taught us about rafters, rises, and runs and all things roofing. The roof was completed with logs and some steel panels we borrowed from the dump. When I say dump, I mean some site where we decided the rightful owners did not want or need the property any longer. Ray always said the roof really tied the place together, and he was right again.

Of course we needed heat due to the fact that cold is really cold where we lived and does not warm up for any creature. We also had full intentions of staying at the Lodge overnight and in all seasons, so we needed serious warmth. As luck would have it, we got what we needed when RC found us a vintage *Findlay Brothers* woodstove. It was beyond perfect. It was simply meant to be.

The stove was built in Carleton Place, Ontario, in 1898. It actually had 1898 stamped on the cast iron door. The fact that 1898 is the first official year of the Klondike Gold Rush made the stove an unbelievable find. A true Canadian classic, the stove was an upright design, which made it a space saver for the Lodge. The stove had a split door on the front with no glass on it, which meant we could simply leave the door open to enjoy the view of the flames, and when we only cared about heat, we would close the door and let the stove do its thing. There was a cooktop with a removable handle on the top of the stove, which meant we could load the stove with wood from the front or the top. We decided to call the stove *Findley*. We changed the spelling a bit, but otherwise it just made sense – Findley the Woodstove. The Findley! Sometimes the answer is right in front of your nose. Findley easily weighed two hundred fifty pounds, or close to one hundred ten kilograms, which was not a trivial point. Once we got it inside the Lodge, we cut a hole in the top of the roof and fitted a stove pipe we salvaged from the dump into the top of the Findley. We were more than in business from a heat point of view.

Hauling our materials to the Lodge, in particular Findley, was an absolute blast. We crunched through trees and branches and rock cliffs and creeks and clay, not to mention the piles of bear crap that we stepped in while dragging the stove. It took all four of us and every ounce of our strength to get Findley to the Lodge. We built a tripod of sorts and had a single wheel on the end so we could pull and push the stove through the bush. It was a symphony of sounds and smells that only a mountain man can truly understand or appreciate, and it was our first appreciation that some things in life can only be learned by doing.

We did rely significantly on RC during the transportation events. At this point, he was the biggest and strongest of the four of us, and he ended up with so many cuts and bruises hauling the stove and steel roofing into the Lodge that we decided to dedicate the stove to him. Recognition needs to go to those who suffer most, and no good deed should ever go unrecognized or unpunished. Findley worked great, and even when it was really, really cold, we would be toasty, toasty warm. Findley could get the Lodge up to ninety degrees Fahrenheit within twenty minutes of our starting a fire in its belly. That's close to thirty degrees Celsius. Good Canadian hardwood and a classic Findlay stove will do that, not to mention the odd inferno caused by dumping a gallon of kerosene through the stove pipe down into the stove. If you want to see fireworks, we had fireworks, and I will admit, we got a few burns along the way. This was life as an adolescent in the northern land of gold and cold. Kids don't do this anymore; technology has ruined the life of the kid.

Once completed, the Beaver Brothers Lodge was everything we had planned and imagined. We were ready for the upcoming school year and another cold winter. Nineteen seventy-seven had been a good year.

DAY 2
South Carolina

Warming Up

"HOW'S THE WRITING GOING, SAM?"
"Pretty good, Doc. A little slow going, but I'm enjoying it."
"Great! Want to talk about it?"
"Not really."
"Why not?"
"Just not ready, I guess."
"Or you're not interested in the exercise?"
"Look, Doc, I know what you're trying to do. You want me to write a few poems or notes so somehow I'm going to have some lightbulb go off. Some epiphany that says, 'Oh, it all makes sense now. Don't worry, Sam, you're fine! Stop being so stressed and angry and get on with your life!'"
"Maybe."
"Maybe what, Doc?"
"Maybe that's what I'm looking for you to do, Sam, and if so, is that a problem?"
"This isn't amateur hour, Doc. Freud would be embarrassed by your techniques."

"You think these are techniques, Sam? That I'm putting something over on you by asking you questions? By asking you to use your skills to try to understand your situation? We can just talk about it if you want?"

"I don't know, Doc. Why are you doing it?"

"Because this is my job, and I care about you. Sometimes a cigar is just a cigar, Sam."

"This is your job so you care about me, or you care about me because this is your job?"

"Is there a difference, Sam?"

"I think so."

"Either way, I want to help you, right?"

"I guess. Seems like a strange way to make a living, Doc."

"You studied psychology, Sam. I'm surprised by your response!"

"Yes, but I don't practice as a psychologist anymore."

"But you help people, Sam. You've done amazing things. You do amazing things. You've changed people's lives for the better, and you can continue to change people's lives for the better. The world is a better place because of you!"

Silence

"I'm not what I seem, Doc."

"What are you?"

"Frustrated. Angry. Tired."

"What does that mean, Sam? You mean you need some sleep, a rest?"

"No."

"Then what do you mean when you say you're tired?"

Silence

"It means I'm tired. Tired to the bone. I can't wake up, and I can't sleep. I'm too tired to do either one. No single thought that goes through my mind produces positive energy. Every thought I have drains me. And I have thousands of thoughts per day. It's rapid fire. The more I think, the more tired I get. It's as if my head is a gas tank that only drains and never gets refilled. Eventually you run out of gas and end up on the side of the road. That's where I am. This hospital is the side of the road for me."

"Do you want to go back to your room and rest?"

"No, I'm fine. That won't help anyway."

"You want to keep talking?"

"No...sure, fine."

"Do you want to talk about Sophie and George?"

"No."

"Why not?"

"Because I don't."

"OK, Sam, tell me about your parents."

"Really, Doc! Good lord, you really are 101, eh? My parents? Fine. Not much to tell. My mother is fine, and my father is dead."

"Tell me about your father."

"The Soup Man?"

"The what, Sam?"

Canada
Winter 1978

Risk

THE LODGE WAS EVERYTHING to us, and when we weren't in school or playing hockey or music, we were at the Lodge. Nineteen seventy-eight was a good year for us, mostly because we had successfully become teenagers. The news in Canada was uneventful. Montreal was still reeling in debt from the overspending and corruption of the 1976 Summer Olympics, Prime Minister Trudeau was trying to outlast any Prime Minister in Canadian history, and down in Sudbury the miners were threatening to strike for better working conditions. Up north of us the Soviet Satellite *Cosmos 954* had crashed onto Canadian soil. This was the only thing we found interesting in the news.

"Fucking Commie Russians," Hats would say every time the crash came on the news. "Just send Bobby Clarke in there to fix them. He'll do it 72 Summit Series Style – one stick on the ankle, and they fall like the little weak fucks that they are!" Hats didn't like the Russians much. His grandfather had immigrated to Canada in 1917 when the Bolsheviks were killing Ukrainians during the revolution that introduced communism. He never forgave them for this act, although it was not lost on him that had the revolution not happened, his grandfather would not have fled his homeland and Hats would not have been born. Herein lies the challenge of going back to the past and wishing for a change of events. It's not practical.

The NHL year proved to get us worked up pretty good. The Montreal Canadiens would go on to win the Stanley Cup for the third time in a row, defeating the Boston Bruins in six games. Two of the original-six teams! Ray and RC could barely contain themselves. Hats acted as if he didn't care after the Flyers got beaten. Bobby Orr was not playing for the Bruins due to his knee injury, and this made all of us sad, regardless of our team affiliations. In order to get to the finals, the Canadiens beat the Maple Leafs and the Detroit Red Wings. All original-six teams. It was pure joy for all us, including Vince and the Judge, who are huge Detroit Fans.

On the local front, the Maple Tree Hockey Team was having continued success. We would go on to win the Bantam Championship, which was an accomplishment since it was our first year in the Bantam league. Vince and the Judge were very, very happy with the Beaver Brothers and the rest of the team.

The music scene was also off to a thundering pace. Ray had us listening to, and attempting to play, the best music that has ever been written. *Boston, Triumph, The Guess Who, Rush, April Wine, The Eagles, Bruce Springsteen, Gordon Lightfoot, Stompin' Tom, Stan Rogers, Neil Young,* and *The Grateful Dead* were among some of the bands we were listening to and trying to cover. We were all over it, and Ray had us fully equipped with instruments as his parents were very supportive of our music. The result was we had a small band set up in Ray's basement. "We're beginning to get our sound, boys!" Ray would often say. It's a good thing we had Ray and RC because Hats and I didn't have any musical genes, although we did have the teamwork gene. We learned over the years that we can do just about anything when we put our minds and /or backs to it.

I'll never forget one particular Saturday that exemplified our ability to quickly become an effective team.

In February of 1978, we were spending our cold winter Saturday the way we often did – in the Lodge looking at *Playboy* magazines and smoking torpedoes. This is our name for *Peter Jackson* cigarettes. We named them torpedoes because they look like a torpedo and produce smoke when you light them up. The *Playboys* came from Ray's place, where his father would keep them in the sauna bath they had in their basement. Canadians are a lot like the Swedes in that we have saunas in our houses, and the Beaver Brothers knew that where there was a sauna, there was a *Playboy* magazine. Ray's father only had one joke about the *Playboys*, which was, "I read them for the articles." Like that was original in the 1970s. His only other comment to us about the magazines was not to steal them.

"Don't steal my magazines, ya bunch of perverts," he used to yell at us and laugh hysterically. We obviously didn't heed his request very well.

The cigarettes came from the Soup Man's bathroom. The Soup Man was my father, and he would always say he smoked while he went to the bathroom and had a rest from life. I don't remember a lot about the Soup Man, but I do remember his telling me the most underrated thing in life was a good bathroom break and a cigarette. We stole his cigarettes and didn't much think about what is underrated or overrated in life. As far as we were concerned, the Lodge, *Playboys*, torpedoes, music, *Risk*, hockey, and our NHL teams were life in the bag. We were living in the now, thoroughly enjoying the present – a concept that can haunt a person as life progresses.

This particular day, we were playing *Risk*, smoking torpedoes, and looking at naked women. *Risk* was our game, and over the years we must have played a thousand rounds. The game never got boring, and we never got bored with the game, which is surprising considering we never once changed our personal approach or strategy from round to round. *Risk* is a game about world domination, a goal we liked implicitly. The board looks like a geo-political map of the Earth and is divided into six continents that contain forty-two territories or countries. The main pieces in the game are called armies. The object of the game is to get your armies on all forty-two territories, and once you accomplish this you own the world. By doing this, you also eliminate all the other players by taking their armies off the board. It's a last-man-standing kind of game. The armies are simply little pieces of colored plastic, but they meant everything to us – they meant world domination, and when you're thirteen, looking at naked women, and smoking torpedoes, world domination just makes sense.

Each of us had our preferred color of armies. We never wavered from this, and it was simply a given which color we would take at the beginning of each new game. Hats always chose red because he wanted us to believe he was a communist. He called this his psychological warfare. RC chose green for the trees and forests of the north that he would one day protect. Ray chose yellow because it was the color of the sun, and I chose blue because I believed any true poet needs to know the essence of the blues.

The fundamental strategies for the game are simple. Roll the dice against your opponent and try to win the probabilities of the dice throw. By doing so, you attempt to take over one of the six continents. Once you take over an entire continent you get bonus armies, and you then use these additional armies to take over more continents. This turns into more armies and more continents. It's a self-fulfilling prophecy game and is not that far off from real global affairs.

The four of us always strived for the same continents. Hats and his Red Army always went for Asia and Europe, RC always fought for North America, and I always tried to dominate South America and Africa concurrently. Ray would hunker down and build his base of armies by owning Australia. This is known in *Risk* circles as a good move. We always went with these individual strategies, although the outcome was unique each and every time we played. *Risk* was, and still is, our favorite game. It's a complex game where the complexity resides in the dynamics of simplicity. It's also an easy game to play in any location, situation, or frame of mind. This makes it attractive.

Lodge rules are that the person who loses his armies first has to go get wood for Findley. We gathered wood during the summer and fall and stacked it between two birch trees that formed a perfect set of bookends standing proudly about fifty feet from the Lodge. This particular Saturday, Hats lost the round of *Risk* and consequently had to go for wood. We needed it too, because it was, as usual, really cold, and the fire was running low. The irony was that inside the Lodge, it was like a sauna. We were sitting in there with just jeans and t-shirts on – our parkas, mitts, hats, and scarves had been shed twenty minutes after the fire was started. A good fire will do that. Hats was hot and mad about losing, so he decided he would go get wood without putting his winter clothes on. I remember plain as day Ray's telling him that it was really cold out there.

"It's really cold out there," Ray said, really saying, *Brother, I would put some clothes on if I were you.*

"I'm hot as hell's kitchen," Hats replied.

"OK, have fun," we all said in unison as Hats headed outside the Lodge to get wood in million-degree-below-freezing temperatures.

This is how we treat these situations, as we learned early on in life that you should never question people when they're onto something and displaying passion about that something. There's an old joke in the south that *you know you are Southern if you've ever had a friend die right after saying, "Hey y'all, watch this!"* In Canada, the saying is slightly modified to *you know you are Canadian if you've ever had a friend die right after saying, "Hey, hold my beer. I've got an idea."* As I've mentioned, Canadians are peacekeepers, and as a consequence we just don't want to get in the way of an idea that is fueled by vision and passion. This was the case with Hats on the day he went for wood wearing nothing but jeans and a t-shirt.

What is important to understand is that while many people will argue this point, vision and passion can be trumped by natural forces. In other words, vision and passion may not win out over Mother Nature and the really cold. I've learned that forty below trumps passion every time. It's the simple natural laws of physics where forty-below temperatures with a fifteen-mile-per-hour wind produce frostbite on human skin within five minutes of exposure. Now, I don't want to seem as if I'm a closed-minded dogmatic, so maybe passion can trump natural laws at times in this crazy world. Maybe it can, but I can tell you, it didn't this particular day.

Hats headed out to get wood without his winter gear, and about four minutes later he returned with an armload of wood. We were quite impressed and helped him put another log into Findley. We really were quite awestruck as when he returned with the wood he seemed fine, and the only thing he said was, "It's really fucking cold out there." So we went back to our *Risk* game and naked women. War and chicks.

It took about eight minutes before his fingers, ears, toes, and nose started to burn.

"My fucking fingers, ears, toes, and nose are burning," Hats complained.

He didn't need to tell us. We could see it happening in front of us, at least the fingers, ears, and nose. And when he took off his boots, we could see the toes as well. His fingers, ears, toes, and nose were turning beet red, a red that was so red it would have made Stalin proud.

"This isn't good," Ray said.

"No it's not, Ray," Hats said.

"This isn't good," RC said.

"No it's not, RC," Hats said.

"This isn't good," I said.

"No it's not, Sam," Hats said.

"Is it cold out there?" I asked Hats.

"Yes, it's really fucking cold out there, Sam!" Hats said back.

"Told you," Ray said to Hats, really saying, *You dumbass.*

"Fuck off, Ray," was Hats' completely expected reply.

We went into problem-solving mode, and without the gift of any medical education or real knowledge about frostbite, we focused on the obvious. RC had some ideas from reading his RCMP manuals, and from that we decided we needed to warm up his fingers, toes, ears, and nose. As a team, we have always believed in a division of labor to get stuff done because dividing tasks up is the most effective way of getting multiple tasks accomplished at the same time. Ray taught us this after he read a book about automobile manufacturing. Ray reads a lot and then teaches us the stuff he likes about the book. Dividing the labor in manufacturing fashion, we each took a piece of Hats' body to focus on. RC told Hats, "It's a good thing your pecker didn't freeze or you would be on your own, man!"

I got his toes, RC got his fingers, and Ray got his ears. Hats got his nose, and we spent a few minutes brainstorming till the solution became clear.

There is an old saying that there is nothing like an idea whose time has come. Well, in this case, we witnessed a culmination of one idea being the solution for three problems. Effective collaboration will do this. RC, Ray, and I grabbed our wool toques and scarves and put them on Hats' ears, toes, and fingers. When we were done, he had a toque (wool winter hat for you non-Canadians) on each foot and each hand. We then twirled a scarf around his face and head to warm up his ears, which also solved the nose problem as the scarf covered his nose. He looked like a masked bandit going to rob a bank. Hats was pissed.

"I was supposed to come up with the idea for the nose!" he complained.

"OK," RC said and took out his jackknife and cut a hole in the scarf so Hats' nose would be exposed. Hats then took another scarf and wrapped it around his head so he had two scarfs around his face, the last one covering up his nose.

'Perfect," he said.

"Perfect," we all confirmed, proud of our work.

Hats looked warm but absolutely ridiculous. I've learned over the years that warmth and fashion do not necessarily go together. Warmth trumps fashion in the true north, but unfortunately this is not as true in the south. People in the south walk around freezing their asses off so they can still look good, the irony being they look like frozen dumbasses. No outfit can look good if the one wearing it is shivering and shaking. There are a lot of dumbasses in the world.

Feeling sorry for Hats, we allowed him back into the *Risk* game. We helped him lay out a few armies since he had hats on his hands. He really is a Hats. He was slow to play, both because of the hats on his hands and the pain of the freezing appendages, and it didn't take long for RC to get impatient. RC can be low on patience, in particular with Hats. RC butted out his torpedo, turned a page in the magazine, and yelled at Hats.

"Roll the dice, man!"

Hats let him have it right back. "Fuck you, man. You try playing with frozen fingers, toes, ears, and nose, not to mention I've got these dumbass hats on my hands, you dumb shit!"

"OK, Hats, calm down!" Ray shot back.

We all looked at each other and started laughing uncontrollably. It was absolutely hysterical. There was our best friend Hats covered in hats, and as a team we got him warm and saved him from obvious death by freezing. It was a teamwork moment for sure.

It was during these times, during these moments of adolescent immaturity, that we became true brothers. Our friendship was molded with each ridiculous event we got ourselves into. Each fit of laughter created bonds that forged our belief system. A belief and value system that ultimately gave us confidence that together we could get through anything.

Little did we know how much this belief system would be tested over time.

DAY 3
South Carolina

Talking Cable Heads

TODAY IS A RED DAY. I'm anxious and angry. I think I'll get through it if I go for a walk on the beach. For sure I have to avoid the television and the Talking Cable Heads.

When I got out of bed, I turned on the television and sure enough, the weatherman was on. As if that's what I needed after my bizarre dream yesterday. Frankly, I don't give a crap about the weather anyway. It's as if they think we are all farmers and need an hour-by-hour, play-by-play to determine whether the year's crop will be successful. It's not like the weather will dictate my day's activities. I'm no farmer, and I'm not growing anything other than frustrated and angry.

Morning is the hardest part of my day because it's when the quiet makes the most noise. The sound of the quiet is deafening in the morning. It didn't always feel this way though. Mornings used to be the best part of my day – the sounds of morning and positive energy once created a symphony of life – the background music, the smell of breakfast cooking, the voices, the activities, looking for lost car keys, wallets, and school backpacks. It was the routine, the dance of life. It was perfect. It was harmony, although I didn't know it at the time as

I was busy working. I miss it and I wish it were like that now. I wish Sophie would understand that I feel this way and maybe she could also explain it to George. I wish things could go back to the way they were. I would be much better at it this time around.

I know I need to stay away from the television, but some mornings I just can't help myself. This morning was one of those mornings so I started surfing the channels. Of course I had to plug it in first. This is the equivalent of the first drink, but I just can't help myself some days. I've promised myself, and it is part of my personal therapy plan, that I will avoid the television, and most days I wonder why I just don't have them remove the thing from my room. The Talking Cable Heads on cable drive me crazy. I wish I could just get rid of all television sets. I know it's the right thing to do, but I just can't help myself. It's as if I don't really want to get better. What does it say about me if the solution is right in front of me and I choose not to embrace it? I continue to tolerate my own condition.

Sure enough, I landed on a twenty-four-hour news channel. I secretly seek these out as they are the TV crack in the world of TV cocaine. I stopped at a classic story where some sick dumbass went into his old place of work and shot the place up. He allegedly killed his boss and the boss's secretary before it ended in a shootout with the police. One police officer wounded and the bad guy dead. He was armed with three 9MM handguns and a .223 caliber assault rifle. Great, now we get to listen to all the Talking Cable Heads on the news go on about gun control. Some will be for it, and some will be against it, and for sure it will be a waste of our time and energy. It makes me so angry, and I know I should just turn it off. What do the Talking Cable Heads know about any of this anyway? Do they have personal experiences from which they're drawing their infinite wisdom?

It really makes me angry when the Heads think they can build logic into any situation. This in itself is illogical. Like when a sick man goes on a shooting rampage, and people love to ask, "What was he thinking?" What the hell do you mean *what was he thinking*? I'll tell you what he was thinking. He was thinking that he didn't much like strangers walking around a shopping mall, or maybe he didn't much like women, or maybe he was mad at Ronald McDonald for having funny hair, or maybe he just didn't like the movie he was watching and wanted more than his money back, or maybe he didn't like the fact that his boss was an asshole and the secretary was covering up for him. We never get the background story. I wish these sick guys wouldn't always end up dead because we really need the background story before we move to judgment. Maybe the boss deserved it and had it coming to him. Really, what the hell are you talking about Talking Cable Heads when you ask, *What was he thinking?*

I know, I know; there are no circumstances where the boss would deserve to be shot dead. I'm just saying, what the hell do the Heads know about it anyway? What gives them the right to try to explain the situation away with some random statement based on logic?

I'm not saying it's OK to go shooting up the place. I'm just saying that you can't always find logic where logic does not exist. Don't get me wrong. I feel for the families of the victims and the families of the shooter, for that matter. They are all victims. I know, because I've had customers from both corners. It's a tough go when you have lost a friend or family member due to violence. It's the worst, and it's equally as tough a go when your family member was the perpetrator of the violence. You have to deal with your own loss and the loss of the victims. This is tough. I guess all I'm saying is some things should just be left alone after they happen; not everything that happens to us requires an analysis from people unqualified to analyze.

Most people aren't shooters or ever will be one. I'm no shooter, that much I know for sure. Shooters know they are shooters; non-shooters know they are non-shooters. I'm a non-shooter, even though I'm struggling with anger issues. Most shooters know they are shooters at a young age, but luckily not all shooters actually end up on a shooting rampage. Lots of shooters successfully fight the urge, but they're still shooters, and they know it. There are a lot of them out there. As RC once told me after ten years in the RCMP, "Sam, if average people knew who was out there with us, most would never leave their houses."

All I'm saying is what frustrates me and makes me so angry is when all the Talking Cable Heads go on about trying to find logic in an illogical event or situation. This is plain stupidity, and I wish I didn't watch it. As I've pointed out, though, I just can't seem to help myself. I must be addicted to watching dumbasses, and you sure don't have to go far in this world to find one – just a remote control away. What really drives me crazy is how the Heads can switch topics on a dime. One minute they're experts on workplace violence, and the next minute they're spewing their opinions on the President and happenings in Washington, DC, and the next they are all-knowing about the environment and pollution issues in Africa. Really, Heads? How did you get so smart? I wish we could go back to the days of real news where the news anchor gave the facts without an opinion on the facts. When did the Heads decide we care what they think? Every time they open their mouths, their arrogance and narcissism are right there in their opening comment: "I think." No you don't! You don't think at all!

"I think this, I think that," spew the Talking Cable Heads.

"Who gives a shit!" think I.

So now the gun-control nuts will say all the violence is because of guns. Wrong. And the gun activists will say it's got nothing to do with guns. Wrong. Everybody is just wrong, and it doesn't really matter because they aren't even trying to solve the same problem. What is the problem? Is it too many guns, gun magazines, crazy people, stress at work, failed relationships, poor education, revenge, drugs, booze, jealousy, envy, passion, not enough hugs, and bottle-fed babies?

What if it's just a simple fact that the world is broken, falling apart, and heading towards absolute malfunction and implosion? Is that not possible? Think about it, if all living things on the Earth have a finite life cycle in a certain form, then why not the Earth itself? And the end will be defined by violence and dumbasses! Or maybe this is just what people do, and it's been like this forever. Let's face it, it's not like people killing other people is something new. But who's to blame? The gun, the shooter, or whatever made the shooter act upon his urges? But he's dead, so we'll never find out.

Do you know where the first mass school shooting was? It was in Montreal, Quebec, Canada, 1989, and is commonly known as the Montreal Massacre. Indeed it was. The USA should not feel so bad. A twenty-five-year-old sick man killed fourteen women who were studying sciences at École Polytechnique in Montreal. Of course after he did the whole thing with a .22 caliber rifle and a hunting knife the sick man killed himself. Apparently he didn't like women, in particular smart women. Try to create or find logic in that. Sometimes there is no logic that can define or determine the causes of a tragedy, although the Talking Cable Heads will try hard.

Sophie and I went to Montreal for the public funeral as I needed to go, and she supported me. Many of the victims' families decided to have a service together, and they invited the country. RC and Hats met us there. We didn't know any of the victims personally, so we stood on the street where you could listen to the service on loudspeakers that had been set up on the sidewalks outside the historical Notre Dame Basilica Cathedral. There were thousands of people in the street, and the service ended with a victim's friend playing *Let It Be* by *The Beatles* on the piano. RC, Hats, and I understood the significance of the song, and Sophie had to help us pull ourselves together. I told Ray all about it that night when we connected and he understood all too well.

Apparently Hollywood wants to make a movie about the whole Montreal Massacre. The Hollywood Heads. Apparently they like the story. Apparently they feel there may be money in it.

The Hollywood Heads on cable television. Talk about who let the dogs out! Here's a Hollywood Head telling me what he thinks needs to be done to cure violence on our streets! All coming from a guy who just made another fortune with the release of the most violent movie ever made! And the movie was followed up by its own branded video game that's so realistic that young future shooters have virtual-reality training capability! The hypocrisy is enough to make you want to scream. Yet the Talking Cable Heads put the Hollywood Heads on all the time because they're pals. It's a conspiracy, and we watch because we're part of the conspiracy. We play the part of the unknowing fool consumer who pays for the advertising.

Maybe the cable news and the Talking Cable Heads are to blame for all of it. They will struggle with this, I can tell you that. For example, now they will say all the shooter wanted was his day of fame and his face on TV. Yet just by telling us that, they have given him what he wanted! I tell you what, I wonder if shootings would go down if it were illegal to report about them in the news. There's an idea. Take all the bullshit in the world and make it illegal to report on it – out of sight, out of mind, and maybe, out of action. Ignorance is bliss, right?

Don't worry; I get all the reasons why this is a stupid idea. I'm just mad as hell about all the crap that happens in this illogical world.

I need to calm down. That's what Doc says: "Calm down, and stop watching TV, Sam." I just couldn't resist this morning. I don't know why I get so angry, so frustrated at these things. I can feel my blood begin to boil. It's like pure hate towards all the dumbasses in this broken world. Do they not see how stupid they are? Is it just me or shouldn't we be able to yell out at somebody and say, "Hey, dumbass, can't you see how much of a dumbass you are?"

I know I need to work on my anger. I know it makes no sense to be this angry. To hate at all makes no sense. Hate is a snowcapped mountain of emotion. It's a self-fulfilling prophecy, and it will only grow precisely because there is so much to hate in the world. Once you start to hate, you can't stop building the hate mountain. Once you hate one thing, your eyes open up to hate, and you start to see all the other stuff you can hate. It's a mess of a process, a total mess. The hate snow grows and grows and grows on the mountain. I guess for some people the hate mountain eventually results in an avalanche. The hate mountain avalanche – that's it – the hate mountain avalanche. That's how the news should report on it: "*So and so dumbass had his avalanche today. Three are dead, including the mountaineer.*" End of story. I could accept that. No logic required other than the fact that there was a hate mountain avalanche.

I wish I had never started hating anything. That's the trick you know – don't even start building the mountain, and don't even venture to base camp. I can't even remember the first thing I decided to hate. I need to think about it and figure it out. I hate that I can't remember what it was. How's that for broken logic – hating that I can't remember the first thing I ever hated. Of all the messed up things in the world, that's probably the most messed up of all.

Canada
Winter 1979

The Soup Man

TIME STARTED ROLLING faster the minute we became teenagers and started high school. There was a lot going on, and we were all over most of it. Nineteen seventy-nine was a pivotal year for us – the end of a decade. It was also our first real experience with understanding the concept of time – the concept of saying goodbye to an era and welcoming in another. The Eighties were next.

Down in Ottawa, 1979 saw Pierre Trudeau finally get defeated when Joe Clark won the federal election and became Canada's sixteenth and youngest Prime Minister. He didn't last long though. Down south, the Sudbury Miners' Strike of 1978 finally ended after nine months, and this provided good news in Chinook River as we support miners. But back east, twelve miners were killed in Nova Scotia from an explosion underground, and this provided bad news in Chinook River as we support miners.

There was big hockey news in 1979. The World Hockey Association failed to compete with the National Hockey League, and this brought four new teams into the NHL – the Edmonton Oilers, the Winnipeg Jets, the Quebec Nordiques, and the Hartford Whalers. This was not particularly good for fans of the original-six NHL teams. Times were a-changing, but we did like the fact that Winnipeg had an official NHL team.

Our hometown hockey was going as planned, which meant we were winning. It was our second year bantam, and the Maple Tree Hockey Team had the players, the coaches, and everything else we needed to win the Championship two years in a row. All was good in Chinook River, and life was good for the Beaver Brothers.

The four of us never went to school on the first Friday of an odd month of the year. In all our years of high school, our parents, teachers, and principals never cracked the code or pattern of our ditching class. It started in our Grade 9 year and continued on till graduation. The first Friday of every odd-numbered month, we could never be found in school. It was Ray's idea, as he loves puzzles, patterns, or anything that requires solving. Some days, we would simply play sick and our parents would tell us to go back to bed. After our parents left for the day, we would congregate at one house and hang out and design our master plans for life. Sometimes we would go to the Lodge for the day and plan the upcoming weekend as well as our master plans for life.

One particular Friday stands out for me as a life pivot point. It was the first Friday of March 1979. My house was the meeting place for this day of skipping school, and Ray, RC, and Hats had all made it there by nine in the morning. We were busy setting up the *Risk* board, and the house was empty as the Soup Man was at work and my mother was out running errands. The boys had just climbed through my bedroom window from the rooftop. Even though they could have come through the front door, we always climbed through the windows of our bedrooms. This just seemed more appropriate considering the secrecy and risks taken by skipping school. We also could have just gone to the Lodge for the day, but that did not seem risky enough – sneaking into our houses through the roofline and playing *Risk* all day seemed riskier.

We were playing *Risk* when the phone rang. There were only two phones in the house, so I went to my parents' bedroom to answer the upstairs phone.

"Hi, is your mother there?" the caller asked.

"No, I'm sorry she's not home right now," I responded.

"OK, thanks. Is this Sam speaking?" the caller asked.

"Yes," I said.

"Great, Sam. This is Doctor Tremblay at the hospital. Do you remember me from hockey tournaments?"

"Yes, sir," I responded.

"How old are you now, Sam?" the Doctor asked.

"Thirteen, about to turn fourteen in September," I answered.

"Oh, OK. Well, when your mom gets home, can you please ask her to call the hospital and ask for me?"

"Sure," I said.

"Goodbye, son," he said.

"Goodbye," I responded.

We went back to our game of *Risk,* and about an hour later we heard the downstairs door open and my mother coming into the house. The boys got ready to head under the bed, which was the plan if and when the general public entered the room. Oddly enough, though, we rarely needed to do it as parenting was different back then. Parents were not consumed with their kids. We could disappear for a day or so without our parents even knowing we were missing. We know that for a fact. I'm not trying to criticize our parents. They did a great job with us. It was just a different time, a different place, and they parented differently. Back then, a helicopter was for flying, not a parenting technique.

We also knew that the best strategy to avoid your parents' entering your room is to meet them outside your bedroom door, head them off at the pass, and hide in plain view. So I stood at the top of the stairs and shouted down to my mother.

"Mum, you need to call Dr. Tremblay at the hospital."

"What, Sam?"

My mother stopped what she was doing and came to the bottom of the stairs. She stared up at me.

"Dr. Tremblay called and said you need to phone him at the hospital."

"Dr. Tremblay? Did he say why?"

"No."

"OK."

I went back to my room and closed the door behind me. We were on alert now that a parent was in the house, so we went back to the game in silent mode. *Risk* in silent mode is actually a whole new game. Hats hates *Risk* in silent mode as he likes to argue, and silence does not support direct arguing. Sometimes we go into silent mode just to get Hats going, knowing he has a bit of a temper and knowing that tempers and silence don't go together very well. RC loves silent mode because he is a strategic thinker in spite of a lack of patience. Strategic thinking and silence go together, and RC's strategic thinking trumps his lack of patience. Hats' temper trumps everything.

After ten minutes in silence mode, we heard my mother coming up the stairs. Hats, RC, and Ray all scooted from the floor to hide under the bed. I jumped on the bed, got under the covers and went into sick mode. There was a knock on the door.

"That's odd," I thought to myself, really thinking, *My mother has never knocked on the door before.*

"Hey, honey, are you in there? Can I come in?"

"Sure, mum," I said, while a new unknown emotion flowed through my body.

My mother opened the door and stood in the doorway and just stared at me. She didn't say anything, but for some reason, I got up and stood on the bed. While standing on the bed, I moved two feet backwards and retreated to the corner of the room while still standing on the bed. I was still on my bed and had pushed into the corner of the wall, seemingly trying to push right into the wall, as I watched my mother's face staring at me in a blank expression.

"Your father died today, Sam," she said.

She then turned away and closed the door behind her.

My mother shut the door behind her, leaving me crouched in the corner of my bed against the wall. I was trying to push myself farther into the wall, trying to make myself disappear when the boys crawled out from under the bed and stared up at me. Tears were streaming from their eyes. I crawled my way to the edge of the bed, sat with my feet on the floor, and put my face in my hands and my hands on my knees. I looked up at my three best friends as they stood and looked down at me. Then they all bent down, and the four of us hugged each other as tight as you can hug a person. I started to cry, and then we all started to cry.

Hats was the first to speak as this is how he confronts crisis, how he displays no fear, how he shows he is tough, and how he demonstrates he can be completely irrational.

"What the, what the, what, what the fuck just happened?"

I was stunned and could not answer, so RC finally spoke up, proving he takes things head-on as well, although with a very different approach.

"You heard her, Hats. She said Sam's father is dead!"

"Ya, RC, I got that part. I heard Sam's mum the first time too! But you know what, RC? You know what, RC? I'll tell you what, RC. This is bullshit, man. I mean how about a little fucking information, eh? Like shit, man, you don't just walk into a guy's room while he and his brothers are playing *Risk* in silent mode and drop a shit sandwich and head out without any explanation! Fuck, man. That just ain't right! Like how about a little respect here, eh? How about a little information, eh?"

RC, Ray, and I just looked at Hats in silence as we didn't know how to respond. For some reason, he was really angry with my mother over her techniques of delivering tragic news. Meanwhile, my head was spinning with part of me thinking about my father and another part of me paying attention to Hats and trying to make sense of what he was saying. Ray broke me out of my trance.

"What now?" Ray asked. He's the smartest one of the crew, and when it's time for a plan, he'll tell you it's time for a plan. And if it's time for a diversion and interruption of the current plan, he'll execute an interruption and diversion of the current plan, which is exactly what he was doing.

"What now?" Ray asked again, this time looking at Hats so Hats would feel it's his job to come up with the plan, a classic Ray diversion and interruption of Hats, executed flawlessly.

"OK, this is what we're going to do," Hats said after a few seconds of thought, really saying, *I am about to make this up as I go.*

Hats laid out the plan in great detail. All three of them would head home and sneak back into their bedrooms. Then they would immediately find their parents, wherever they were, and tell them I had just called them and informed them that my father had died. They would then say they needed to come to my house right away to be with me. If their parents said they wanted to drive them over and give condolences to my mother, they would say that my mother was not ready for that yet. They would say my mother would call them as soon as it is convenient and appropriate.

The plan seemed as sound as any plan we had ever hashed in the past. Pretty good too, considering the stress and uniqueness of the situation. So my pals got their coats and hats and gloves from under the bed and headed out my second-story bedroom window. They went out on the roof, where they would jump from the roof into the deep snow beside the house. RC jumped first and Ray second, but when Hats stepped onto the roof, he was still swearing under his breath about my mother and the inadequacies of her bad-news delivery. As a consequence, he was not paying attention. He stepped on a small patch of ice on the roof and flipped right up and landed on his back and started to slide down the roof towards the driveway where my mother's car was parked. He managed to get himself on his butt with his legs straight out in front of him as he was gaining speed and heading right off the roof. When he hit the end of the roof, his boot heels caught the eavestrough rain gutters and that slowed him down a bit, but not completely. When the momentum of the slide stopped, he was perched with his legs dangling over the roofline and his butt on the eavestrough, which was now trying to separate from the roof under his weight. Hats started to scream as quietly as he could, knowing my mother was still inside the house. He was attempting a library scream.

"Guys, guys, get me off this eavestrough, guys! I really need to get off this roof quickly, guys!"

I was standing in my bedroom looking at his back from the window. There was nothing I could do, and Hats did not expect help from me anyway. He assumed RC and Ray were his saviors because they were at the side of the house, having jumped off the roof and into the snow banks. They were looking up at Hats from an angle, but they weren't moving at all.

Hats' voice went up a notch. It was an up-notch of desperation.

"Guys, guys, get me off this eavestrough, guys! Really, guys, really, I'm hanging by my fucking crown jewels here, guys!"

RC and Ray went around the corner of the house and onto the driveway and stood below Hats. They looked up at him in silence, and it became clear to Hats and me that they had no plan, which is ironic, because Ray always has a plan. I'm pretty convinced Hats decided that Ray was not thinking about a plan. Meanwhile, I was watching the whole thing from my bedroom window with my head spinning out of control. What the hell had just happened in the last fifteen minutes? I had this flash that I was standing in the Chinook River United Church. At the front of the church were two caskets – one was a normal-size casket and the other the size of a shoe box. They were beautiful oak and identical other than the size. I walked up to the caskets and looked inside them. In the big casket was my father, the Soup Man, and in the little casket lying on a pink silk cushion, were Hats' two nuts. There was a brass plate with an inscription. It read, *Rest in Pieces*.

I came back to reality with the sound of Hats' voice.

"OK, guys, this is not working," Hats yelled down to RC and Ray, who were still looking up at him in awe. "I'm fucking dying here, guys," Hats continued. "I'm hanging by my damn gonads and you guys aren't doing shit!"

RC and Ray just stood in the driveway and continued to look up at

Hats. It was as if they were as amazed by the situation as Hats, who oddly enough at this point had realized that he was on his own. Finally he took matters into his own hands. He decided not to wait around for other people. He decided to take care of business. He decided to control his own destiny. *Good boy, Hats.*

"OK, guys," he said calmly to Ray and RC. "Come and stand right below the roofline, right below me."

RC and Ray looked at each other and dutifully moved a couple of feet until they were right below Hats. He was about six feet above them, and the second they were in place, Hats gave his butt an upward thrust and released himself from the eavestrough. It looked as if he were trying to make love to the sky, and on the second thrust, he released his *boys* and sent himself hurtling straight down, whereupon he landed right on top of RC and Ray – all by plan of course. The three of them collapsed and splattered hard onto the ground like a snowball hitting a pane of glass. I couldn't believe what I was watching.

"Holy shit, Hats! How about a little warning, man?" RC complained as the three of them got up and assessed themselves for damages.

"Warning? Warning, RC? I'll give you a little warning," Hats yelled back. "The next time any of us is hanging from a roof by his balls, you better swift up to action or you'll be hanging by your goolies too! How's that for a fucking warning, you dumbass? Like shit, man, we're talking about my future generation here, man! Fuck!"

Hats was lit up, I mean really lit up. His temper was flared in bright red.

RC didn't like the way Hats was talking to him so he tackled him into the snow bank on the side of the driveway and they started wrestling in the snow. Ray went in to help RC, but RC didn't need any help as he was, and still is, the biggest and strongest of the four of us. But Ray joined in anyway. Teamwork is like that. You help the team even if the sub-team is fine on its own. They wrestled like Eskimos until they gave each other a suitable snow bath, then came up for air, laughing out loud through their cold lungs. RC went to give Hats a high five for a fight well fought, and Hats pulled his hand away at the last minute and tried to kick RC in the groin. RC stepped out of the way at the right moment and Hats ended up on his back again.

"Fuck!" Hats yelled in frustration. "This is bullshit, man!"

"Sometimes you just can't catch a break," RC laughed.

RC helped Hats up, and both RC and Ray brushed the snow off of him, and the three of them then did a three-way high five – acorn-kicking to high fives in an instant.

An hour later when the doorbell rang, I ran from my room to beat my mother to the door, although I didn't need to rush as nobody was competing with me to get there first. The house seemed empty. I didn't know where my mother was and suspected she had left to pick my older brother and sister up from school.

I answered the door, and Hats, RC, and Ray were staring at me. RC walked through the doorway and took my right hand into his left hand.

"We'll get through this, Sam," he said to me.

"We'll get through this," he then said to Hats and Ray, looking for confirmation as he assumed the position of group protector.

Hats stopped rubbing his knackers for a minute and said, "Yes, we will."

"Yes, we will," Ray said.

"Yes, we will," I said.

"Yes, we will, Sam. We'll get through this and some," RC said in closing.

No more was needed to be said as RC has a way of knowing how to put an end to a thought or conversation. He has emotional intelligence. He knows how to end a conversation when nothing more needs to be said. It's easy actually; just stop talking when talking is no longer required, or stop talking when talking is no longer adding value to move the conversation forward. RC got that at a young age.

We carried on, and the afternoon became surreal in many ways. At some point, my mother, brother, and sister ended up at the house, although I don't remember really having a "moment" with the four of us. It may have happened, but I don't remember it. Mostly I just remember hanging out in the basement with the boys playing mini-stick hockey, and as the hours progressed people started to congregate at our house. It began with friends and neighbors at first, and then there were people whom I had never seen in our house before. Small towns are like that. People come together when they need to and leave each other alone otherwise. Small towns show their grit and worth in tragedy, and for our small town, this was a tragedy. The Soup Man was well liked in Chinook River. He was a professional, and he helped people, so this was a tragedy in relative terms for a small town. It was certainly a tragedy in our house, and there was nothing relative about that other than all the relatives heading toward town to come see us.

At some point, a friend and neighbor came downstairs looking for me and the boys.

"Don't you boys have a hockey game tonight?" he asked.

We all looked at each other, and Ray responded.

"Yes, sir, at seven o'clock tonight, but we thought..."

"It might be good for you to play," our neighbor said, sincerely giving us the option. "Well, do you want me to take you?"

Ray, RC, and Hats all looked at me to let me know it was my call.

I thought about it and said, "Sure. Vince and the Judge are expecting us, so we should show up and give it a shot!"

"OK, then," our neighbor said. "Sam, get your equipment, and we'll all hop in the truck and go collect the rest of your gear." So we left my basement and headed off to play hockey. On the way out of the house, right in the same driveway where the marble-breaking altercation had happened a few hours before, RC slapped Hats on the back and said, "Don't forget your jock, dumbass!"

Hats tackled RC into the snow bank and managed to shove snow down his pants. Ray didn't help RC because RC deserved it. It was uncalled for, and Ray always looked at all fights from all angles. RC was on his own, and I wasn't exactly firing on all cylinders, so I just watched and laughed nervously. "Come on, boys, save it for the rink," our neighbor said as he headed to warm up his truck.

"There's an idea," RC said as he slapped Hats across the head, knocking his hat into the snow. "Save it for the rink."

DAY 4
South Carolina

Setting the Bar

"HI, SAM."

"Hi, Doc."

"How are you today, Sam?"

"Not bad, maybe a bright Yellow."

"Good, Sam. We'll take that."

Silence

"Sam, I have a question for you."

"OK."

"Do you think the fact that your father died has anything to do with our challenges?"

"Our challenges, Doc?"

"We're in this together. I care about you, remember?"

"Fine, Doc, thank you. I care about you as well."

"I know you do, Sam. Caring is who you are and what you do, and you are very good at it."

Silence

"So do you think the fact that your father died when you were a young boy has anything to do with our challenges?"

"Can you call him the Soup Man?"

"Sure."

"No."

"No? No what, Sam?"

"No, I don't think the Soup Man's dying has anything do with my current situation."

"Why is that, Sam?"

"Why would it, Doc?"

"Well, maybe you miss him. Maybe you feel you were cheated of something most people have? Maybe you feel things might have turned out differently had he not died?"

"I don't feel any of that, Doc."

"You don't? Why not?"

"Because of a lot of things. First, at this point in my life, I barely remember the Soup Man. He's been gone a lot longer than he was ever here. Second, I was very happy with my life until recently, and none of that would have happened had the Soup Man not died. His death was an event along my path that was simply part of my path. I like where my path ended up. Third, and I can't stress this enough, I don't believe in 'ifs'."

"You don't believe in 'ifs'?"

"No."

"What do you mean?"

"What do I mean? It's not that complicated, Doc. I don't believe in 'ifs'. What's the point? All you'll do is 'if' yourself to death with no end. All you'll do all day is say, 'If this had happened, if this hadn't happened.' When I play that game, I always say, 'If my Aunt had balls, she would be my Uncle!'"

"What?"

"Never mind, Doc, it's a Canadian uncle thing."

Silence

"Can I tell you something, Doc?"

"Of course, Sam."

"Do you know that there is a statistical relationship between successful men and the fact that those men lost their fathers at a young age?"

"Really? Like who?"

"The list is endless, but the group includes Churchill and Washington."

"Wow, what do you think the connection is?"

"Between their losing their fathers at a young age and their becoming successful?"

"Yes."

"It's not complicated. It's about the bar."

"The bar?"

"The bar. The bar that tells a person how well he is doing. Parents set the bar to communicate with their children regarding how well they're doing relative to reaching the bar. This is the essence of parental feedback as the bar represents the goal. Fathers in particular set the bar for their sons, and in the absence of a father you have an absence of the bar. The result is the son never knows how high is high, he never knows when he has done well, and he never knows if his father is proud of him. Therefore, he never knows when to stop trying to do better. Subsequently, the fatherless son works and works to achieve a status that will never be achieved because the achievement bar does not exist, and the son continues to seek affirmation from a father who will never affirm. This has made men in history do amazing things, Doc. In fact, world history, both good and evil, is riddled with examples of the absent bar."

"Interesting. Did you set the bar for George?"

"I don't want to talk about George, Doc. I'm not the father I wanted to be, I'm not the father I know I can be."

"OK, do you have any memories of your...of the Soup Man?"

"Sure I do, but they're just still snapshots now."

"Snapshots?"

"Yes, like old Polaroids – no moving pictures, no memories of actual events – just snapshots of images, which truth be told, I'm not even sure are accurate anymore. Pictures can fade over time."

"What are some of the snapshots?"

Silence

"Well, there's one of us shoveling snow in the driveway, another of him building a fence in our backyard, maybe another of us skating together, but that is an actual picture we have at my mother's house. I'm not sure I remember the actual event."

"That's it?"

"Well, not quite. There's one of him lying on the couch the morning we were supposed to leave for a family trip."

"What do you mean?"

"My brother and sister and I were supposed to leave on a trip to meet our mother who was already at the destination."

"And?"

"The Soup Man didn't quite get us to the airport. When we woke up, he was on the couch in the living room. He was sick."

"What happened?"

"My brother made a phone call, and a neighbor came over and drove us to the airport."

"Your...the Soup Man must have been really sick."

Silence

"That depends on your definition of sick, Doc. The right question is, 'Was he sick that morning or sick the day and night before?'"

"I don't follow, Sam."

"I have another image from that morning, Doc. This might help complete the picture."

"What's the image?"

"Early that morning, around four o'clock, I heard a loud thump in the kitchen. So I woke up my older brother and forced him to go with me to investigate. I was eight years old; my brother was thirteen. We went down the stairs and into the kitchen."

Silence

"Yes, Sam. Then what?"

"We saw my...the Soup Man lying on the floor of the kitchen with a kitchen chair collapsed over him. There was a bottle of wine in his hand that he didn't lose on the way down. That's the Soup Man for ya. He had excellent coordination. Wine was all over the floor imitating blood at that point. Fortunately, though, there was no real blood other than in his eyes. The eyes tell all, Doc. Anyway, the sound I had heard was his hitting the ground when the chair did not cooperate in the party any longer. Chairs are like that."

"Your father drank, Sam?"

"He did that night, that's for sure. Please call him the Soup Man."

"Was he an alcoholic? Was he an addict?"

Silence

"That depends, Doc."

"On what, Sam?"

"What's your definition of an addict?"

Canada
Winter 1979

Hockey Game

ALL CANADIANS PLAY HOCKEY, at least that's what the rest of the world thinks. I don't think it's true, but I can tell you that up north a lot of people do play hockey, and for sure, RC, Ray, Hats, and I played. We like the game, and we're pretty good at it too. Ray and Hats are forwards, RC is on defense, and I am the goalie, the last point of defense. We are like a mini-hockey team and are very successful with four-on-four pond hockey.

Nineteen seventy-nine was a decent hockey year on the national hockey front. Montreal beat the New York Rangers in the Stanley Cup finals four games to one. It was another final with two original-six teams and was also Montreal's fourth Stanley Cup in a row. Ray was happy with his team and let us all know about it any chance he could. We were a little disappointed that nobody in our circle was cheering for the Rangers. Philadelphia and Toronto made it to the quarterfinals but did not progress, making Hats threaten he was going to stop watching NHL hockey. The fact that the Peterborough Petes won the Memorial Cup did not help his mood. The Boston Bruins lost to Montreal in the semifinals allowing RC to feel that his team had shown up and done their best. What we didn't know though was that it would be another twenty-five years before the finals would be played by two original-six teams. The NHL was changing faster than we could ever have imagined.

Closer to home, the Soup Man had just died, and we collected our equipment and accepted a ride to one of the Chinook River arenas. Even though it is a small town, we had three rinks at the time – there was more square footage of ice per capita than in any other town in the province. It is a claim to fame for Chinook River, and it's on a sign outside of town that you see on your way in. As a town, we had our priorities – ice rinks and bars. I never thought about it before, but there may be a connection between the two.

That particular day we were playing at the St-Joseph Ice Palace. It's pronounced with a French accent. The French Catholics got to name the rink because some of the money came from a local French Catholic hockey player who had made it into the National Hockey League. His name was Joseph, although I don't think he was a Saint. The Montreal police didn't think so anyway. The place wasn't much of a palace either. A big steel barn would be a better descriptor, although we all liked the palace a lot. Small northern towns are proud of their rinks, as they should be. They are also proud of their bars, where in some cases they shouldn't be.

The Beaver Brothers played for the same team our entire career. We played for the Maple Tree Hockey Team. Vince Charlabois owned the Maple Tree Hotel and was our sponsor and head coach. The Maple Tree Hotel was the most popular bar in town. Vince had money, and he liked hockey. He was our sponsor and coach the entire time we played, and he actually moved his team up in the leagues as we grew older. To be sure, we were in it together.

Vince was always good to us. In fact, he was a lot better to us than he was to himself. The life of a third-generation bar owner took its toll on Vince, and as a result he did not have a wife for long or kids of his own. He was our coach and our friend, and he was generous with his time – in particular when it came to hockey. Vince was a good man. He was also a huge Detroit Red Wings fan, although our Maple Tree Hockey Team colors were Toronto blue. He told us the blue was a holdover from his father and that he did not have the energy to change the team to red. His love for the Red Wings was based on a respect of Gordie Howe, who he believed in large part and rightly so was the best hockey player that has ever played the game. You don't get the name *Mr. Hockey* easily. Vince's favorite story that he retold given any opportunity was how Gordie Howe ended up wearing number nine.

"Do you know how Gordie ended up with nine on his jersey?" Vince would ask us frequently.

"No," we would lie, really saying, *Come on, Vince, great story. Tell it again, good buddy.*

"Well," Vince would begin, "his rookie year with the Red Wings was in 1946, and he wore number seventeen. Then a player named Roy Conacher moved to play in Chicago and this freed up number nine. It also freed up a better sleeping bunk on the train they rode from town to town, so Gordie took number nine so he could get the better pullman berth! Number nine to get a better night's sleep! Is that cool or what?"

"Very cool!" we would always answer, immediately looking forward to the next time Vince would tell the story.

The Judge was our assistant coach. He helped Vince in every way and never missed a game. The Judge was our County Judge. He was a man of the town and exemplified our community in all respects. He was also a huge Detroit Red Wings fan and supported Vince's belief in the intrinsic value of Gordie Howe. When Hats wanted to get the Judge going, he would remind him that Gordie Howe never won a Memorial Cup as a young amateur Western Canadian hockey player. The Judge would respond that four Stanley Cups are better than one Memorial Cup, although Hats was never satisfied with this answer.

We played Chesley Lumber the day the Soup Man died, which was fitting as there could not be a team that is more opposite of the Maple Tree Hockey Team. These guys were bushwhackers and bootleggers, and even though we were all between thirteen and fifteen years old, you could tell many of their players would end up in the prison league before their hockey careers were over. These guys were a piece of work, and they hated us, partially because we had nice uniforms, new skates, and extra sticks. But most of all, they hated us because we had navy blue team jackets. In the north, having a team jacket is everything, and Chesley Lumber didn't have jackets or much of anything else. Their team jerseys looked like oversized red and black lumberjack shirts, although Ray always thought they looked cool. Ray – always the optimist.

The mood in the dressing room was somber as bad news travels fast in a small town, and it was clear that everyone knew my father had died. Vince and the Judge were being especially nice to me. "Can I get you anything?" Vince would say a few too many times. It actually bugged me, and Hats saw my reaction, so he told our coach to leave me "the fuck alone." Vince just smiled at Hats and went back to coaching.

I put my goalie equipment on in silence. I had RC on my right, Ray and Hats on my left, and I felt as if they were my protectors. Vince gave us the lineup from his clipboard, and we waited until it was time to go onto the ice. Meanwhile, all I could think about was the fact that the Soup Man was dead, and I had no idea how he had died. My head was swirling like a whirlpool at the bottom of a mountain stream, and I couldn't see straight. "*What the hell am I doing getting ready to play hockey, and how the hell am I going to play?*" was what I was thinking.

There are a few things in life that stay with you no matter where you go or what you do. The smell of a hockey rink is one of those things, and stepping onto a freshly cleaned sheet of ice is another. I actually forgot about my present situation when I stepped onto the ice and headed towards the net to scrape my crease with my skates prior to the start of the game. Getting the crease ready is an important job for the goalie, and I took my job seriously, regardless of the situation.

Watching bantam hockey players is quite the scene. At an average age of fourteen, we were all over the place from a physical point of view. Players' heights can range from four feet ten inches to well over six feet on skates. Weight can range from seventy pounds to one hundred seventy-five pounds. I was a goalie, and on skates I was about five feet eight inches tall and weighed one hundred thirty pounds. I was somewhere between a smart player and a grinder player. I had good flexibility, kept my stick on the ice, worked hard, and had some hockey smarts.

Ray was not much bigger than me. He played center and was as fast as lightning. He was also the smartest player in the league, as he understood the game and didn't grind it out at all. "Play smart, not hard" was his motto, and he did just that and scored goals as a result.

Hats was bigger than Ray and me. At five feet eleven inches on skates with lots of muscle on his body, he was strong like a body builder. Not surprisingly, he was also a total grind-it-out forward, and for a guy who is pretty smart, it appeared as if he had no hockey sense at all. What he may have lacked in sense though, he made up in grind. If two players went into the corner and Hats was one of them, then ten bucks says Hats came out with the puck and the other guy was still in the corner on his ass. That's the way Hats played. "Grind it out, tough it out, fuck you, motherfucker, take that!" was Hats' motto – vintage Philadelphia.

RC was the biggest guy on our team, and maybe in the whole league. On skates, he was almost six feet four inches and weighed one hundred seventy pounds. Tall and strong, RC was a huge fourteen-year-old defenseman who also knew the game hands down. It was a rare thing for somebody to outwit RC as his strength, long stride, and long reach proved too much for most players. "Get the puck outta here!" was his motto, and he knew how to do it.

As you can imagine, the game did not go so well for me that night, and to be honest, the game did not go so well for anybody in the end. Let me try to paint the picture. The puck was dropped at center ice, and as I watched the black rubber drop, I envisioned the puck being the Soup Man's heart. I knew right away this was not a good thing. His heart dropped from the ceiling of the rink as if from a table-top hockey-puck-launching scoreboard, and it landed with a thump on the ice. Immediately after the puck dropped, a player from Chelsey Lumber retrieved the puck and shot it from their side of center ice right down the ice at my net. My head was spinning. I could not see straight, and the puck went right between my legs and into the net. I guess in this case I did not have my stick on the ice, and the result was that it only took six seconds for them to score their first goal.

RC was playing defense, and he came up to me and asked if I was OK. I told him, "Yes," and I saw him nod to Vince, the Judge, Hats, and Ray, who were on the bench. They looked concerned, which made me feel as if everybody in the rink was looking at me, and I started to imagine what they were thinking, "*There's the young kid who just lost his father! Poor thing. I hope he has a good game. He deserves to make a few good saves. Too bad that last lame shot from the red line went in on him. I'm sure that didn't help make him feel better!*" After the goal, the coach put Ray on the ice playing center. The puck went back to center ice to be dropped again, and not surprisingly, the Soup Man's heart dropped again, and my head spun around again. This time Ray got the puck and skated right through their entire team and scored a beautiful goal with a wrist shot to the upstairs right corner of their net. Their goalie looked as stunned as I did previously, and he hadn't even had a parent die as far as I knew. The puck went back to center ice, and the same image came back to me of the Soup Man's heart dropping from the ceiling. I really needed this to stop – talk about distracting for a goalie.

The puck fell to the ice, and one of the McMullen twins got the puck for the other team and maneuvered past Ray and our forwards and one of our defensemen. It was just me and RC, and Timmy McMullen headed towards us with the puck. Timmy was almost as big as RC, and almost as tough. The McMullen twins are part of a no-good clan of criminals and misfits. Brains are scarce in the family, but with what little brains Timmy did have, he rightfully decided he could not get around RC. He wound up and let a slap shot go from inside my blue line. My head was still spinning, and my eyes were blurred as the Soup Man's heart came twirling towards me. From somewhere a thought entered my mind that if I could catch the heart, he would be saved and would be alive when I got home after the game. All I had to do was just catch his heart with my trapper.

The puck flew by RC and right over my right shoulder and into the net. I didn't even move or attempt to catch it. My body was paralyzed, and I had just let in two goals in forty seconds. Most importantly, though, I didn't save the Soup Man, so I was now responsible for my father's continuing to be dead.

RC turned around and skated towards me to console me and tell me that all was OK. He used his stick to give me an "atta boy" tap on my pads when at the same time Timmy McMullan skated by us and said, "Nice save, Sam. Good thing your old man ain't able to watch you!"

RC was stunned. I was stunned.

"What did you just say?" RC yelled at Timmy.

"You heard me the first time, RC," Timmy shot back with pure stupid in his tone and his eyes.

"His father died today, Timmy!" RC yelled back as he started skating toward Timmy.

"That's right, RC," Timmy shot back as he stopped to allow RC to approach him. "And right now, Sam's playing like a dead fucking siv goalie. Good thing his old man isn't here to see it. He'd be so sick from watching, he'd be glad he's dead. What a fucking siv family disgrace!"

In hockey, when a fight is about to happen, there is always a minute of foreplay to allow both players to get ready for the fight. You skate around slowly in a small circle and allow each other to size up the respective opponent, and without talking, you make the commitment that a fight will be the final outcome. It's in the eyes and body language, and in many ways it's completely primal. It's a stare down, a confirmation and agreement session all at the same time. This is protocol. It's an unspoken rule that you must allow it to happen, and while it's not written down anywhere, it's a fundamental principle of hockey. It's virtually constitutional. It did not happen in this case.

Without any, and I mean any, warning, RC dropped his right glove and punched Timmy McMullen right square in the face as hard as he could. It was as violent a punch as any punch in the history of hockey punches. In those days, many dumbass players still did not wear full face masks, so Timmy took the punch right to the nose. It was full and absolute contact. It was impact galore, and I clearly saw Timmy's nose shatter as he dropped out cold, face full of blood, onto the ice. RC stood tall over him, begging him loudly to stand up and be a man. RC hadn't even dropped his left glove as he hadn't needed to.

At this point, Timmy's twin brother Joey, who had been on the ice at the time, started skating toward RC with his stick up in the air as if to use it as a swinging club. Now, one thing you need to know is, there is another rule in hockey that is taken very seriously. In fact, this one is so serious it is actually written down. The rule is that under no circumstance are you allowed to leave your bench to join any fight or altercation that may be happening on the ice at the time. If you are not lucky enough to be on the ice when the fight breaks out, you have to enjoy the show as a spectator. This is sacrosanct. Hats is not so good with rules – written, sacrosanct, or otherwise.

I was watching Joey coming at RC, and I was trying to warn him but he was in a fixed mad-dog trance staring at Timmy. He was waiting for Timmy just to flinch an inch so he could finish what was already finished. From the corner of my eye, I saw Hats leave our bench without a stick in his hand. He started skating to head Joey off at the pass – his diagonal extremely precise and deliberate. RC was still just staring down at Timmy, and when Joey was about ten feet from RC with his stick up like an axe, the collision of collisions happened. Joey was hit by Hats in a way that could only be described as a freight train hitting a full truckload of watermelons. Hats was going so fast and hit Joey so hard and with such skate leverage that Joey's helmet came flying off, his stick flew twenty feet in the air, and when he finally landed after what seemed like ten seconds of hang time, it was on his back with a wind-breaking thud. The McMullen twins were both out cold; that much was certain. At this point, the referee called the game over. I'm not even sure that's allowed, but he did it, and I suspect he was mostly wondering whether an ambulance was needed for the twins. Or maybe even worse – perhaps just call the coroner.

The rest of the McMullen clan, dumbass cousins and fathers and uncles, started to make gestures as if they were going to go onto the ice to deal with RC and Hats themselves. They started yelling at the rest of their players to clear the bench and get into it, but there was not one player on their bench who would even remotely think about skating over to Hats and RC. Instead, their bench was ready to stare at their skates while RC and Hats were ready for war. Sensing trouble, a couple of off-duty uniformed RCMP officers headed over to the stands area where the older McMullen clan was congregating. RC took his eyes off Timmy at this point and watched the RCMP officers take care of that part of the show. Once the dumbass clan patriarchs saw the police officers, they left the stands area and headed for their dressing room. At this point, the twins started moving a bit, and they were slowly helped up and supported to get off the ice by their coach and stick boy. They both looked like shit. We also left the ice and headed for our dressing room. The game was over. I guess we lost two to one, but I'm not sure the game was ever recorded in the league records.

"Now that's fucking hockey night in Canada!" Hats screamed with joy as we rambled into the dressing room and threw our sticks in the middle of the floor.

"You bet your ass that's hockey night in Canada!" RC screamed back.

"You guys are regular Philadelphia Flyers...I mean regular Broad Street Bullies, man!" Ray joined in.

I was in a daze. I mean a complete bafflement. *What the hell had just happened?*

Ray looked at me and decided to come over and stay close to me. He put his arm around me while RC was at the back of the dressing room explaining to Coach Vince and the Judge what had happened. I watched them while my spinning head started to slow down, and when RC finished talking Coach Vince paused for a moment, and I saw him give RC a high five and a big smile of approval. The Judge nodded and took a drag of approval on his pipe.

What did I tell ya? The Coach and the Judge are good people. They are the real deal.

Ray was still beside me, and RC came over and sat on the other side of me. Hats was finally calming down, and he sat beside RC.

"Thanks," I said to RC.

"No problem, Sam," RC said back with a smile, really saying, *any time, any place, any reason, Sam.*

There was a slight pause, and in almost perfect unison, RC, Hats, and Ray all spoke at the same time.

"We'll get through this, Sam," my best friends said to me.

"OK," I said.

And indeed, we did get through it – this and some.

DAY 5
South Carolina

The Hitchhiker

I AM APPROACHING THE END of my first week since the intervention. Today is a Green day – no anger and an acceptable level of anxiety. This is excellent news. This is progress, although I will need to work hard to stay in the Green. I managed to keep the television unplugged and decided to go out for a run. This is a big deal as getting dressed, getting outside, and getting some exercise can be a monumental task. Talk about a triple crown. It reminds me of back when I was working. I would always tell my customers they need to have balance in all aspects of their lives.

"Exercise is one of the spokes in the wheel of life," I would tell them.

Getting dressed and getting outside is a prerequisite to getting exercise, but everything seems like work right now. Why does everything have to seem so hard and so complicated? It's exhausting, totally exhausting. Something is very wrong if putting your socks on is a laborious chore.

I've never enjoyed running, yet for something I don't enjoy, I've done a lot of it. I've run all kinds of races including a marathon – one marathon – done, check, over, never again. I wasn't prepared for it, so I grinded through it and paid the price, as my knees have never been the same since. It's just another case of physical reality trumping hope and passion. You can hope all you want for 26.2 miles, but if you did not prepare properly you'd better be ready for bone-on-bone pain. I wasn't prepared for my marathon or ready for bone-on-bone pain.

People seem quite impressed when I tell them I've run a marathon, and I always respond by telling them, "I've run a marathon, yes, but I'm not a marathon runner." There is a big difference in my mind as just because you have done something, this does not mean you are a doer of that thing. I envy people that go deep on a sport or hobby because they really "do" the thing. That's why I respect people who make it to the Olympics. They've gone deep on the sport, and I can really look up to that. Sometimes it's envy bordering on jealousy because they have accomplished an amazing thing, and sometimes I wish it were me. What's interesting is many successful people regret their accomplishments later in life. I know this because I've had customers in this situation. To go deep on a sport, hobby, or profession has an opportunity cost of having missed doing other things. Such is life. You can't have everything. It's designed that way; I'm sure of it.

I believe most of my life has been wide and shallow in that I've done a lot of things but don't really *do* anything. My customers tell me I'm the best at what I do, which is nice of them, so maybe I have gone deep on my subject matter, but it doesn't feel that way to me. Perhaps it's all relative. To a person who has never run a race I may, in fact, look like a runner, but I can't help feeling that to a real runner I'm a fake, a fraud, an imposter, a pretending wannabe marathon runner. Part of me wishes I had never run a marathon since I hate feeling like a fraud.

I think a lot of people feel like frauds. For sure, I have customers who feel that way. I suspect that if we had our true feelings tattooed on our foreheads, most of us would be walking around with *imposter* engraved on our skin for the world to see. I hate this feeling, but I don't think I'm alone. I wish I were because I wouldn't wish this feeling on anybody.

Back when I was working, people would come to see me and be in awe of my ability to present and communicate to the group. I was a big draw and will continue to be a big draw if I get back to it. People come to me to develop self-confidence precisely because they believe in my own self-confidence. Confidence is contagious; this is a fact. But little do they know that I'm terrified and filled with anxiety and fear! Fear of failure, fear of success, fear of something in between, fear of everything, fear of nothing. It's as if I'm convinced that at some point in my presentation, some knowledgeable person will see through my soul and stand up and point at me and yell, "Fake! Imposter! You don't know what the hell you are talking about!" Fortunately, this has never happened, and mostly people tell me that my presentation was excellent, that my workshop changed their life. I don't like that much, though, as that's a lot of pressure to bear. To change somebody's life is serious business and should not be taken lightly.

I'm not sure why I feel like an imposter considering I've worked hard to get to where I am. I've paid my dues, completed the education, and have spent thousands of hours training, thinking, writing, speaking, and working in and on my field of study. It's not like being a professional athlete or famous Hollywood actor; at least I don't think it's equal to those accomplishments. Some days I wonder why I can't just give myself a break and tell myself, *Great job, you succeeded, you help people, be proud of yourself!* Hell, I probably made more money than most professional athletes last year, but I did it with a team. I was not an individual contributor. I could not have done it alone. Perhaps most athletes and actors are in the same boat.

Even when I debate and argue with myself, I'm never cheering for the home team. I never give myself a break, and I really wish I could figure out who the other guy inside my head is – that guy who keeps arguing with me and doesn't allow me to understand my positive traits and what I've accomplished.

It's as if I picked up a hitchhiker at some point in my life and now I can't kick him out of the car. Yes, that's it! It's as if I have a hitchhiker in my head, and he goes everywhere with me, and his only job is to continuously put me down and tell me how badly I've done in life. A mental hitchhiker – how's that for a load of luck! What mile marker did I pick him up at? I need to go back to that spot and toss him out of the car, and as far as I'm concerned, the ditch is too good for him.

The hitchhiker only lives in one time zone, which is the past. He's sitting in the car, and every time you try to go ahead on a new road or go around a corner he pushes the rearview mirror into your face. That's what he does. It's his favorite and only move – he pushes the rearview mirror right into your face so all you can see is what's behind you. The road up ahead is not visible; where you are at that exact moment is not visible. The rearview mirror is small, and the windshield is huge, but only what's in the past is within your sight. Meanwhile, while he's holding the rearview mirror in your face, he's jamming you with insults. That's right. You're trying to make the corner, get down the road a bit, and he's jamming you with criticism and abuses.

His voice is piercing and dissonant; it hurts to hear it. It's a rude ringing in your ears that won't go away: "*You're no good, man. Look at all the mistakes you've made, buddy. Look at all the people you've disappointed, brother. Look at what you let happen, Sam. Look at what you let happen, Sam!*"

I've concluded that strength of soul and peace of mind are simply a function of your ability to deal with the hitchhiker. New plan for the day – the plan to stay in the Green: get rid of the hitchhiker.

Canada
Winter 1979

The Wake

WE HEADED TO THE LODGE right from the United Church after the Soup Man's funeral. Nobody came up with the idea specifically, and it wasn't planned. I guess we all just assumed that's what we would do. It was a chilly day in March, and while most days in March are still frosty, this day was particularly cold.

"It's colder than a witch's tit!" Hats would say every two minutes as we punched through the snow on the way to the Lodge, snowshoes strapped to our feet, feeling as if it had been snowing since New Year's Day. We were forced to use snowshoes, which Ray didn't like because we would leave a more defined trail. RC loved using snowshoes as he is a bushman at heart. Fortunately for Ray, more snow would be coming soon, allowing all tracks to be hidden in a fresh dump of white powder. Ray knew this but still was not happy. He only looks to the future, and he hates leaving signs of the past.

"It's colder than a witch's tit!" Hats said again, syncing his comment up on a two-minute cycle as if supported by a piano metronome.

RC started getting irritated with Hats repeating himself and asked Hats to please stop talking, and of course Hats did not abide, finally forcing RC to engage him.

"It's colder than a witch's tit!" Hats yelled out on his two-minute queue and stable sequence.

"Hats!" RC yelled back over his shoulder, "How the hell do you know whether a witch's tit is cold or not?"

"It's gotta be cold!" Hats answered as he placed his snowshoe down in the once soft snow now made hard from the rest of us having forged the path before him.

"Really, Hats?" RC asked back. "Are you an authority on tits? And witches? Question for you, Hats – when's the last time you did a temperature check on a witch's tit? In fact, Hats, when's the last time you touched a real tit of any kind, witch or otherwise?"

"Fuck off!" Hats yelled back, continuing his march through the path made by RC, Ray, and me.

That's how Hats ends conversations. He loves to argue but as soon as he is done, he will end the argument with a simple *fuck off*. There's no point in continuing on after that. He's done at that point. It's the end of conversation, and in this case RC was fine with concluding the dialogue. It's hard to debate the temperature of breasts in the freezing cold while breaking a new trail of soft snow. Breaking a new trail is hard work. I've learned this lesson many times over.

RC was at the front of the pack doing the pioneering trail breaking. It's the hardest place to be as the snow is fresh, and you sink the farthest. It's real work, and luckily RC excels at this work as he's a hard physical worker, maybe the hardest I know. I was in second position assuming the responsibility of punching into RC's steps to firm up the trail, Ray was behind me to do the same in triplicate, and Hats was pulling up the caboose. The caboose is the stress-free place to be as the trail at that point is packed down and easy to step into. This key point was not lost on RC as Hats was bellowing about how cold a witch's tit is.

It was the slowest trek to the Lodge we had ever made, taking what felt like a frozen eternity. One reason was because of the snow, but the second reason was the weight of our backpacks. All four of us had our *Joe Muffraw Trapper* backpacks strapped to our backs, and we all had plenty of heavy or bulky cargo. We loved our backpacks. They were made with a hardwood frame and army-type canvas body and were the most durable packs ever made in the history of backpack manufacturing. They were, and still are, the real deal. Normally, we would load the packs with varying degrees of weight in them, and the lightest pack would be worn by the person in front and the heaviest pack by the caboose. The logic is the lead position is breaking trail, so therefore should have less weight. The caboose position, of course, has a trail made for him and should be able to handle more cargo. On this particular trek, we were all loaded down.

We couldn't help but notice fresh bear shit on the way to the Lodge. In fact, steam was coming off some piles as if a bear had just left the scene. We were approaching the time of year when the black bears start to wake up, and we were all too aware that the odd early riser might come out of its den early. The idea of bears being awake, hungry, and close by has its negative implications that are self-evident, but it also has the positive impact of shutting Hats up. Hats is terrified of bears, so the last part of the hike to the Lodge was completed in absolute silence. We were four explorers with nothing but the natural sounds of winter in the north, the crunching and engineering of our path building, and the irrational, yet rational, fear of being eaten by a bear.

We finally got to the Lodge and went straight into *let's get warm* mode. It's a team effort, and we work well together when survival is at risk. Hats and I went for wood and kindling while RC and Ray cleared the Findley of the snow that had found its way from the outside into the stove pipe. Some snow had also found its way into the Lodge itself. We used birch bark and pine twigs as kindling along with some kerosene to get Findley fired up. Kerosene is very effective, and before long we had the stove roaring, and the Lodge was becoming toasty warm. It's amazing how a lodge transforms in smell, sound, and feeling when it goes from really, really cold to toasty warm in less than thirty minutes. It's an amazing feeling that I miss and hope I feel again one day. It really was our paradise in spite of being absent all traditional descriptors of paradise.

We began to unpack our backpacks, and it became obvious we all had the same idea in mind. While it had not been discussed specifically, it was clear we weren't going anywhere anytime soon and that we were going to spend a couple of nights at the Lodge. Even though there was no preplanning in what we would pack, it could not have been better planned. Sometimes failing to plan does not result in planning to fail, and that day we had excellent results with absolutely no plan. The goods inside our packs represented the good, the really good, and the super good.

The theme of Hats' pack was food. He packed in Hostess dill pickle chips, popcorn, hot dogs, buns, and all sorts of food products. The highlights were a huge can of baked beans and an equally huge jar of real dill pickles.

My pack was about additional comfort and warmth. I packed in a few new blankets, sleeping bags, and an old coal oil lantern I grabbed from the mantel piece above our fireplace at home. My backpack smelled like coal oil by the time we reached the Lodge. We already had blankets, pillows, and sleeping bags from previous overnight trips, but now we were better equipped for the cold at hand. The last of my stash was three packs of torpedoes. These three packs of cigarettes represented the last of the Soup Man's stash in my parents' bathroom. I figured the Soup Man didn't need them any longer, and I assumed he would not want them to go to waste.

RC's pack was about entertainment. He brought a new cassette deck he had received for Christmas. It was the latest technology, all driven by a thousand big D-Cell batteries. He also brought some blank cassettes that he had recorded music onto from his vinyl records. It was the first time we had had music at the Lodge other than listening to Ray and RC on their acoustic guitars. This was a sign of the changing times.

"Paradise is fucking redefined!" Hats yelled out when RC put *Freebird* on while we were building the fire in Findley. Ray sat down and soaked in the sounds of the most amazing guitar solo known to man. All four of us were still mourning the deaths of several *Lynyrd Skynyrd* members due to a 1977 plane crash. Ray in particular would always maintain absolute respect for Ronnie Van Zant, Steve Gaines, and Gaines' sister Cassie. To this day, we believe Lynyrd Skynyrd is the best band that has ever lived, even though some of the original members did not live that long. There is a *whole thing* there, and we thank the sun for the contribution the surviving musicians continue to provide for their fans. RC finished unloading his pack when he pulled out new *Playboy* magazines, a new *Risk* game fresh in the box, and two packs of *White Owl* cigars. What a guy.

Ray's pack is what brought the best surprise. When he emptied his backpack, we had thirty-six bottles of *Old Vienna* beer and a purple velvet bag with a precious bottle in it. We all knew what was in the purple velvet bag – *Crown Royal Canadian Whiskey*. La crème de la crème. Our eyes lit up in an instant. A precedent was set that night, and our beer of choice became *Old Vienna*. We called her *OV*. Our whiskey of choice became *Crown Royal*, and we called her *The King*. The transgender naming was not lost on us. Our new whiskey of choice was clearly a delicate fiber of femininity, but she also packed a King's royal punch when consumption got a little excessive. Canadian whiskey will do that. In fact, most whiskeys will do that.

"Where did you get that?" RC asked Ray, really saying, *Where did you get that and how did you carry all that weight to the Lodge?*

"You don't need to know where I got it, and pure willpower helped me pack it in!" Ray shouted back with a huge smile on his face, knowing what RC was thinking. "Just enjoy, lads," he said to end his answer.

Ray always pulls a twist out of a flip. You never know what Ray will bring to the party, and if you ask him about it, he'll always just tell you, "You don't need to know. Just enjoy, lads!" Ray does not require credit or affirmation in any way. He gets his energy from being the mysterious one, not from explaining the deed or the result of his actions. There is no pretense with Ray – like him, don't like him – he could care less. The good news is we all like him a lot.

"Paradise is fucking redefined again!" Hats yelled out as he cracked an OV beer open with the double edged can opener presumably brought for the can of baked beans.

At that point, the party started, and the Soup Man's wake began in earnest. The Irish would have been proud.

Hats and I started with cigars and OVs, RC started with the King and Cola, and Ray just had straight King. Ray and RC also had torpedoes lit up.

"Now this is what I'm fuckin' talking about!" Hats yelled out as he drank his beer. "I tell ya what, boys," he continued, "while you boys tune up your guitars, I'll tune up myself!"

"10-4, Tune-Up Man!" RC confirmed and clinked his glass of the King to Hats' bottle of OV. This represented our first trip to Tuneupville. A trip we would make a few times over the years.

"Hey, Hats." Ray yelled from three feet away, our voices becoming louder because of accelerated hearing loss brought on by the alcohol.

"What, Numb Nuts?" Hats yelled back, cigar smoke circling around his head, OV in hand, looking like a cross between John Labatt and Winston Churchill.

At this point, Ray held up a centerfold from one of the new *Playboy* magazines. He pointed to the woman's breast. "I'm just wondering, Hats," Ray said. "How cold do you think this chick's tit is?"

The whiskey and cigar smoke left RC's mouth all at the same time. He spit it everywhere, and within seconds, he was on his back on the plywood floor of the Lodge laughing his head off. Ray and I followed in the hysteria, and all three of us eventually had aching bellies from laughing so hard. Hats did not even crack a smile. He just sat back in his chair, took a sip of his OV, and puffed on his cigar, blowing the cigar smoke up into the air with an air of aristocracy as if pondering the deep and intellectual implications of the question.

"You want to know how cold that chick's tit is?" he said to Ray in a serious and somber voice.

We all went quiet and got our composure and looked at Hats. We didn't know if he was serious or joking. Hats can have a quick temper so we tend to err on the side of his being serious. We were having fun and did not want to ruin the moment by unintentionally making him feel as if he were being ridiculed.

"Yes," Ray said back, really saying, *Are you serious or are you joking?*

"That tit is really fucking cold!" Hats said without breaking a smile.

Within three seconds, all four of us were on the floor laughing.

The Soup Man's funeral seemed as if it had been a lifetime ago; or perhaps it had never happened.

We stoked Findley, brought out the new *Risk* board, and started playing while drinking the King and our OVs and smoking our cigars and torpedoes. We were in heaven, paradise redefined in Hats' words. I wish I could recreate that. I would give anything to be back there right now, even if just for a brief moment in time.

"Sam?" RC said after gulping some of the King's whiskey from his tin camper's cup.

"Yes?" I said.

"We have to close the book on how your father died. We need closure," he stated.

I knew exactly what he was talking about. It was a mess, and we needed to deal with it in order to move forward.

"He choked to death," I said.

"I know," RC said, "but how did he choke?"

Hats spoke up next.

"He choked on his lunch, and no one was around to help him. All these people around and not one person to see a guy choking and make himself available for an easy Heimlich maneuver. What a joke, man. Like who was there for the guy?"

"What was he eating?" RC asked, really saying, *I need to understand the details of what happened so we can get this behind us.*

"Chicken," Hats said. "I overheard one of Sam's relatives say so at the funeral."

"I overheard someone say it was a ham or meatball sandwich," RC said, really saying, *There is a lot of confusion here about the facts.*

"What are you guys talking about?" I said to all of them as I grabbed another OV. "He was eating Borscht!"

"Borscht?" RC asked, really saying, *I have real and sincere interest, but what are you talking about, Sam?*

"Borscht," I repeated. "Good ole Ukrainian heritage soup made from beets, carrots, and cabbage. It was the cabbage that he choked on!"

"OK," RC said in a retreating tone.

Ray spoke next. "Sam," he said, "I overheard some of your family from out of town talking at the funeral."

"What did they say?" I asked Ray.

"They said that your father was in his office. They said that he may have been drinking and that the drinking may have contributed in some way to his death."

At this point there was a silence that lasted several minutes. It was not an uncomfortable silence as the four of us would never feel uncomfortable together; it was more like a respectful and required silence, an unplanned and unrehearsed moment of multiple moments of silence. In my heart, I knew Ray had it right. The whole situation had made no sense to me since the day my father had died. How does a person go from being so alive to being so dead in one morning? If only I could remember the last time I actually spoke to him. What did we say to each other? What was he wearing? How was he feeling? Was he drinking that morning? Did we even interact that morning?

RC broke the silence when the time was right.

"What do you think, Sam?"

I thought hard for a moment. A million scenarios went through my mind.

"I think I like the soup story best," I replied.

There was another thirty seconds of silence and Hats got up and raised his OV.

"To the Soup Man!" he cheered out.

I held up my glass and said, "To the Soup Man!"

"To the Soup Man!" my three best friends said back in total unison.

We clinked our drinks to show our brotherhood. We clinked our drinks to honor the tradition of making sound in an effort to ward off evil spirits. We clinked our drinks to the Soup Man – to my father.

DAY 6
South Carolina

The Addict

TODAY IS A YELLOW DAY. Not a Green day, but I'm feeling I will
make good progress nonetheless. Perhaps tomorrow will be a Green day.
    I went for a calming walk on the beach, knowing that the beach
and the ocean work for me. I understand I'm not the first person in
the world to realize this, but I'm realizing it for me alone. I need more
of it. I need more stimuli that are only about me. It's not about being
selfish; it's the realization that if you don't take care of yourself, you
cannot do well for others. It starts from within. This is the journey.
The journey that's being played out in the external world but cannot
be realized until the path is hoed from within the internal world – the
internal path. I know Ray will be appalled by my thoughts. He hates
paths. Ray will never walk the same path twice, but right now I need
to walk paths that are familiar and helpful as opposed to unknown
and possibly unhelpful. The beach and ocean are familiar and helpful.
    I'm worried about me right now so I need to focus on what I need.
It's actually very freeing when you simplify and only have one thing
to worry about, especially when that one item is you. Part of me feels
guilty for thinking this way as I don't want to seem selfish; however,

the beach and the ocean are working, so I'm going to embrace it. The feel and smell of the air, the touch of the sand and water, the sounds of it all coming together. It must have been amazing to have been an explorer when all the world's geographical secrets were still mysteries. If, in fact, I have lived a past life, I hope I was an explorer. I suspect I was, and I'm pretty sure I would have been a good one. A life of taking nothing for granted and always wondering what lay ahead, dealing with the challenges as they surfaced and taking nothing but learning from the day's experience. What a life it would be. Live, experience, learn, and then move on to discover new lands, armed with the new knowledge gained from the day before, forever leaving the old land behind to see what is around the next corner, worrying about nothing, feeling only excited and optimistic about what is coming next. This would be a good life.

I'm worried that I have made a mistake by coming here. Doc is just doing her job, and I know she cares about me, but I'm not a good patient. Sure, I know what she is trying to accomplish. I've had her training, yet I'm not helping her, and therefore I'm not helping myself. It's hard for professionals to help other professionals. Our egos don't allow us to be helped at times. As the saying goes, *you can't bullshit a bullshitter.* I'm not sure I believe this statement, though, as I frequently manage to bullshit myself with ease.

Truly to have an impact on your life, you have to venture to a new land where you challenge the mental models that rule that land. To make a difference, you have to have a fresh set of eyes – eyes that have no legacy beliefs or pre-conditions on what is happening. You have to be emotionally detached, yet open to re-attach at the same time. You need to be the ambulance driver who shows up at the accident scene for no other reason but to help: no emotional attachment to the situation. But what if the ambulance driver shows up and sees that the people in the accident are, in fact, acquaintances? How can you be subjective and impartial when this is happening? One minute you are supposed to take control of the situation, and the next minute you are part of the situation. This is how I feel about my own therapy.

The beach and ocean help. I feel bad for people who have not experienced all the goodness that comes from being at sea level. Mountains are spiritual and majestic, but there is something primitive and soothing about being at sea level. Sophie loves the sea. She is the reason we are here.

I continue to be troubled by my decision to come to the hospital. Doc knows me, and she knows Sophie and George. She knows some things about my story, but she is not forcing me to talk. Yet! What will I do if and when she forces me to address the things I need to address? I'm sure now that I've made a mistake by coming here. I'm smart enough about these things. I'm trained in these situations and I should be able to deal with this on my own. I'm not sure another person can really help me at this point anyway.

I'll take a break from Doc today. She'll understand as she knows that I know the process we're working through, so she'll give me some space. After all, I'm here because I decided to be here; I can stay or I can go, it's my choice – choice, choices, making the right choices. I've been teaching this to my customers for years. Life is about choices. Fine, fine; maybe it is, but so what? So what? What do I do with this information so it produces some tangible, practical, positive result?

It's interesting that Doc is not asking more about Sophie and George. If it were me, I would home in and get me talking, but she's staying away from it for now. The move towards the Soup Man is interesting, but it's so far in the past I personally would not find it relevant. Yet she wants to explore it. I'm not sure I follow her strategy. Maybe she has no strategy; maybe she's lost for where to go next. I'm in control of my thoughts and, therefore, our conversations. I will go where I want to go. I'm in control.

The Soup Man. Sitting on the beach, I wondered whether the Soup Man had ever sat beside the ocean and contemplated his life. These many years later, I realize I know so little about who he really was. What did he feel? What did he think? What would he do if he were me under these circumstances? Or, if possible, what advice would he give me? At this point, I'm six years older than he was when he died. Perhaps this makes me the wise one. Perhaps if he were here right now, he would be asking me for advice.

Doc does not understand. She's all theory. Granted, I don't know what her personal experiences are, but for sure they're not my experiences. Our experiences are unique. Only I know what I have experienced and how it makes me think and feel. Sure, you can generalize and stereotype to draw out commonalities and examples of who has been here before. Misery certainly loves company, but no experience is the same as your experience, and consequently only I know how I feel and think. Please don't tell me you understand, because you don't, because you can't. This is the fundamental problem with people helping other people. You will never know what I think and feel at my core as only I know, and even if I do try to explain I will not communicate effectively. You simply can't articulate exactly how you feel; even if you attempt to, receivers of the message will only process the information relative to their own experiences, to how it makes them feel relative to themselves. It's impossible to be impartial. It's impossible to be a true ambulance driver.

Doc is going to press the point about the Soup Man even though it makes no difference to anything. Dead is dead. Move on. Too much time has elapsed. Some father-son relationships should just be put out to pasture; some trees have fallen so long ago that they are nothing but compost in the ground

Addict? She wants to talk about what an addict is? She has no idea unless she is an addict herself, and I doubt that is the case. I know her well enough to know she is no addict, but then again, you never know. I've been surprised before.

I have no idea whether the Soup Man was an alcoholic. My guess is he was, although there will be nothing gained in determining whether he was or wasn't. Dead is dead. Move on. Sometimes you just have to let the fallen trees turn to compost.

There is so much misinformation out there. Is an addict somebody who missed work because of not being able to get out of bed? Is an addict somebody who got in trouble with the police because of a particular vice? Is an addict somebody who failed in a loving relationship because of making bad choices?

I do know what an addict is. I know a few things about it from personal experience, not that I will tell Doc, though, as it won't help us in any way. Nonetheless, I know what an addict is and what it isn't. It's not about the basics of missing work, not meeting commitments, or not being the person you should be. It's much deeper than that as those basics are only the outward manifestations of an addiction. What the average person observes and decides is addiction is actually only the effect of the addiction; it's not the addiction itself. Addiction is much, much deeper than the behaviors the addict shows the external world. Addiction is internal and emotional. It's not a story of hate and torment as everyone believes, but rather is a love story. It's a love story that can grow tragic in the end unless the relationship and the love are managed.

The addict is in love with his vice. The vice is also in love with the addict. This love affair is stronger than any other relationship in the addict's life. He will do anything for the vice. True love defined, but the intensity of the love can overtake the relationship. The love can become a cancer in that it wants to grow, and by doing so kills the body it lives within. This is the dysfunctional addict. This is the person who cannot show up to work or fails in relationships or does not like what he sees when he looks in the mirror. This is the addict who may kill himself in the end.

The vice holds the power in the relationship with a dysfunctional addict. The vice is the quintessential controlling spouse, completely selfish for the love of the addict and not wanting to share the addict in any way. The vice requires the love of the addict to be single minded and focused only on itself. The vice tells the addict that it loves him so much that everything will always be OK. That together they can get through anything. The vice tells the addict that nobody else loves him or understands him the way it does. The addict takes comfort knowing he is truly loved by someone or something that understands him completely. However, the vice's selfishness will turn tragic in the end.

The vice will never be satisfied with the amount of love coming back from the dysfunctional addict. The vice will grow jealous and become paranoid that the addict is thinking about something else. It will become angry that the addict is actually contemplating whether the love affair is in his best interest. The vice will turn up the pressure on the addict to show his commitment of love. This will make it almost impossible for the addict to continue the love affair, but he will try hard as he is not in control of the relationship. In the end, though, the addict will either have to end the relationship or die. If he decides to end the relationship, he will have a broken heart forever. The addict knows this – that he may find love again in other ways, but the lost love of his vice will forever be a part of his past, present, and future thoughts. This will be too painful to contemplate, so the addict tries harder to please the vice, and when he does not break off the relationship, the dysfunctional addict dies and so does the vice. The love is given to the ages, just another love affair gone tragic – *Romeo and Juliet* – in our modern age.

The functional addict is very different. The functional addict has found a way to take control of the love affair with the vice. The relationship has no doubt brought hardship in the past, and that hardship may have been addressed, but the addict is mad at the vice and seriously wonders whether the vice's love is sincere. He tells the vice that the relationship is no longer working, that something must change, or the relationship will need to come to an end. The vice believes the addict, so the addict and the vice work out agreements and compromises. The vice is not happy, and in many respects, the addict is not happy, but the addict knows it is necessary. He understands that compromise is required for the love affair to continue, and even though he is making demands on the vice that the vice doesn't like, the vice will weakly comply for the sake of the relationship. The addict does not want the relationship to end; nor does the vice. The addict has alternatives for other love, but the vice does not, and the vice knows this. The addict is truly sincere about his love for the vice, and the vice sees and believes this sincerity and agrees to support the compromises as best it can. But the vice is lying. The vice continuously waits for opportunities to strengthen the bond of love and to reassert itself as alpha in the relationship, so it plays along and behaves as long as the addict is strong to the convictions of the compromise. However, the vice will be there ready to pounce the instant the addict has doubts about the modifications to the relationship. And the pounce will be swift and powerful when it happens. It is up to the addict to be ready for the pounce. It is up to the addict to manage the destructive power of the vice's love.

"Yes, Doc. I know what an addict is. I have a best friend who is an addict."

Canada
Winter 1979

Can of Beans

THE WAKE RAGED ON. All that was needed to be said about the Soup Man had been said. It was in the past, and we had no control over life events. We knew that. We were also starting to get pretty tuned up as our brains were on overtime and our emotions were overloaded. We were not making much sense at all, although at the time it all seemed like perfect sense to the four of us. Everybody was talking, and nobody was listening, which is a good thing I suspect as it's hard to be a listener around a bunch of drinkers. In this case, we didn't need to worry as nobody was listening, and everybody was drinking. The Lodge was warm, the drinks were flowing, and the cassette deck was busting out the best Rock and Roll music ever made.

We were sitting around the game table, the Findley was roaring, and the *Risk* board was getting to the point where big moves would need to be made soon. There was not a worry in the world that could have penetrated the Lodge that night. It was just all good, proving that goodness exists – the warmth of the Findley, the warmth of friendship, and the warmth that only tragedy can create.

"You…you know what?" RC said, a little slow, clearly influenced by the fine King whiskey he had been drinking for two hours at this point.

"What?" we all said at exactly the same time.

"I...I know what I'm, what I'm going to do for a career," he said, slurring a little bit as he talked.

This was interesting to us because RC had never talked about being anything other than an RCMP officer. Hell, his name was based on this one single fact.

"W...What ?" we all said back, exaggerating his slow speech, although it didn't take much for us to get our words a bit stretched out.

"I'm...I'm gonna be a cop, man. I'm gonna be a Police Officer. I'm gonna be a member of the RPCM," RC said, quite confident in his proud declaration.

Hats perked up in an instant, like a vulture. He wouldn't miss this opportunity for anything.

"Really?" Hats said back. "A member of the RPCM, you say?"

"Yes," RC responded, really saying, *Yes, I think so, but your tone of voice has me wondering if I'm wrong about something.*

"And exactly what the fuck is the RPCM, you dumbshit!" Hats threw out at him.

RC looked at Hats, and in his fog he worked through the problem. Ray and I were trying not to burst out in laughter as we could tell this was important to RC and we did not want to ruin his moment. Hats, on the other hand, is not so empathetic. He does not sign up for compassion. "It's a cruel and unfair world, so fuck you!" is one of his favorite mottos.

"Listen, you dumbass," Hats went after RC. "If you are going to be one, you better know what the hell it is, man. It's the Royal Canadian Mounted Police. RCMP, RCMP, not RPCM, you dumbshit!"

"Ahhh," RC said back with absolute wonderment as if Hats had solved the puzzle of where Tom Thomson and Jimmy Hoffa are buried.

"So let me get this straight, Hats," RC said. "It's not RPCM, its RCMP, not RP, RC... RC, RC. Just like my name?"

"Yes," Hats said, almost sounding as if he wished he hadn't started the conversation. We couldn't decide who was screwing with whom at this point.

"RCMP, not RPCM," RC said. "Wow, Hats, you are a regular Rhodes Scholar, man. A regular combination of John A. MacDonald, Louis Riel, George Washington, Yogi Bear, and Booboo, man. I'll tell ya what, Hats, you are one smart cookie!"

Ray and I took the opportunity to seize the moment. We both stood up and I made a toast.

"To a future police officer. A future member of the Royal Canadian Mounted Police. The RCMP. Not RPCM. The RCMP...to the future RC...to RC!"

We all looked at each other, and once again, it just made sense, and we clinked glasses for the twentieth time that night. We toasted our best friend. "To RC!" we said in total unison.

RC was happy. His grin could no doubt be seen from the moon if you were standing on it looking down at the Lodge.

We sat back down, and Ray changed the topic by saying, "Well, if RC is actually going to be a police officer, I better get rid of this stuff before he does!" With that, Ray went into his backpack and pulled out a little baggie that had three joints in it.

"One for two bucks, three for five, that's my motto," Ray said with a grin as he held up the pre-rolled reefers.

"Where did you get those?" I asked Ray.

"Don't ask, Sam. Just enjoy, lads!" was his not unexpected response.

"Paradise redefined!" Hats yelled out.

Ray lit up one of the spliffs. We stopped everything we were doing, and the doobies became the center of our universe. The smell instantly filled the Lodge, and the sound of the cigarette paper burning around the weed was added to the sound of the fire burning in Findley. Ray took a hit off the reefer and passed it to me. He then lit a second one and took a quick hit on it and passed it to RC. He did the same with the third rolled cannon and passed it to Hats. I took a big long haul on the lefty and sucked it hard into my lungs, whereupon it instantly shot right back out, and I started coughing and hacking as if I had just been attacked by tear gas. I was certain that my organs were going to end up on the *Risk* board.

Ray looked at me the way a teacher would look at a star student and said, "Not so hard, Sam. Small tokes, pal."

"Thanks, Ray," was my response through excruciating hacks.

RC and Hats had watched my rookie performance and they learned quickly. They hit the doobie gently as if they were regular Rastafarians straight from Jamaica. Winter Rastas! It didn't take long for the three jays to be going in all directions. There were four people and three fatties, but it felt as if you always had a puff in your hand. Eventually, we finished the bud and began waiting for the anticipated effects of the marijuana. Several minutes went by.

If alcohol can take voices up ten notches in volume, weed can bring absolute silence to the same crowd of rowdies. Within ten minutes, not one of us was paying attention to the game board, the Lodge was as quiet as could be, and the only sound was that of the fire in the woodstove. The only sight an onlooker would have witnessed was four Beaver Brothers staring at absolutely nothing inside their Lodge. RC was the first to talk.

"Did you hear that?" RC said in a quiet voice, really saying, *I have absolutely no idea what is going on right now.*

"What?" I asked back in an insecure whisper, fearing I might have missed an all-important noise.

"A noise," RC said. "I think I heard a noise coming from outside."

"A noise?" Hats inquired, really saying, *I have absolutely no idea what is going on right now.*

"Ya, a noise. Like something moving around out there," RC said quietly, almost as if the new game was to talk in a voice that nobody could hear.

Ray said nothing, really thinking to himself, *I have absolutely no idea what is going on right now.*

We all went silent. We did nothing but listen for what seemed like hours, but was no doubt only a couple of minutes. There was no sound other than the crackle from the fire in Findley.

"Oh, man, did you hear that?" I said in a whisper, breaking the silence.

"I did," RC said.

"I did too," Hats said.

"What do you think it is?" Ray asked. "Do you think it's a bear?" he added, his question actually being based in some partial reality of the real world.

Then there was another eternity of silence as we were all busy contemplating Ray's question.

"Do you think it's a bear?" RC asked the three of us, repeating and building upon Ray's initial question.

Nobody answered RC. We spent another micro-perpetuity of silence contemplating the possibility of a bear outside the Lodge.

Hats was the one to answer the question.

"I fucking hope not, man!" was his well thought out and intellectually based answer.

All four of us broke out into a complete and utter hysterical laughter. We were laughing so hard that you could feel the Lodge roof shaking. We laughed for what seemed like centuries, and then the paranoia set in for a second round. We went completely silent, allowing the sound of Findley to become the rhythm of our world.

After a millennium of paranoia-based bear-fearing silence, Ray spoke in a very quiet and serious voice.

"Hark, hark," he said, using a voice that would remind you of a wise old owl. "I hear a snowflake falling!"

Well, that was all it took to set us into a fit of more extreme laughter. We were consumed with nothing but pure happy hysteria. We were living in the present, and the present was excellent – paranoia and bears notwithstanding.

"I'm hungry," Hats said when the laughter had died down.

"Me too," the rest of us said in unison, allowing the idea of food to supersede snowflakes, bears, or anything else happening outside of our castle walls.

Hats got busy getting the food organized. We stoked up Findley and set the popcorn on the top of the stove. It started popping in no time. I'll never forget the sound and smell of the popping popcorn in the Lodge. Ray and RC moved the *Risk* board off the table so no armies were accidently moved off their rightful countries, and Hats got the hot dogs out, and I found some sticks we had whittled during the summer. We used them to cook the hot dogs right in Findley's flame coming from the open front door of the stove. Hats took the huge can of baked beans and threw it into the fire in the stove as well.

"What'd ya do that for?" I asked Hats.

"They'll warm up in there and then I'll pull the can out and open it up for us," he answered.

"That's a great idea, Hats," Ray said in passing as he went for the popcorn.

"I'm not sure that's such a great idea, Hats," RC said in passing as he went for the popcorn.

We went about our feast, and a munchie feast it was. We were plenty tuned up, and we were equally as hungry. An outsider would have thought we were four bears who had just woken up from our hibernation and needed to get a hundred pounds back on in a day.

"These are some fantastic pickles, Hats!" RC said, absolutely sincere is his compliment.

"Thanks, RC. My mum bought them at the grocery store," Hats said back.

"Wow, that's cool, man," Ray said, admiring the dill pickle with a smile of admiration as he took a bite out of it.

And thus the conversation went on for some time with the main topic the food itself. We settled into our absolute amazing munch until RC asked us all a question.

"What do you guys want to do for a living?"

We all paused for a minute to think. Hats was the first to speak.

"Well, RC, if you're going to be a cop, I'd better become a lawyer. Somebody's going to have to defend all the bad asses you bust! I'll be their man – your fucking pain-in-the-ass, getting-criminals-off, son-of-a-bitch lawyer."

This did not surprise any of us. Hats' mother was a lawyer – the only woman lawyer in town, in fact. She cleaned up with divorce cases as women love being represented by a woman when the goal is to win over the man. Hats is very proud of his mother's accomplishments, as we all are. His father was an engineer working for the mines. Hats is no engineer, not even close. His wiring is all lawyer. He loves to argue, loves to win arguments, and does, in fact, win all of the arguments he gets involved in, even the ones he loses.

We all looked at Hats and it made perfect sense. If anybody should be the lawyer that everybody hates, it's Hats. Perfect. Just absolutely perfect.

"What about you, Sam?" RC asked me.

"I think I want to be a writer, a poet, maybe even a song writer," I said without much hesitation.

"Wow, that's cool, man," Ray said, looking at me with a look of understanding and complete approval.

I could sense what Ray was thinking, and oddly enough, I was thinking the same thing – the singer/song writer combo. Ray as the musician, the singer, the front man, and me, Sam McGee as the lyricist, the poet, the storyteller – a dynamic duo. Add some rhythm guitar, bass, and drums, and the Beaver Brothers Band will go down the road to fame and fortune.

"I like it," RC said, and we clinked our dill pickles in a cheer of agreement.

"I like it too," Hats said. "A cop and a poet and a lawyer – now that's a trio!"

Then we all looked at Ray as he looked back at us. We were waiting for him to answer.

"What about you, Ray? Has anything changed?" Hats asked.

Ray answered without missing a beat. "The answer hasn't changed since we were five-year-old boys," he said. "When I'm ready, and only when I'm ready, I want to be one of the sun's rays."

Not one of us was surprised or shocked by his answer, knowing he had always told us the same thing. Ray is different, and we're proud that he is ours. Only Ray would want to grow up and be a ray of the sun. When we were five, Ray told us that he wanted to be the sun itself, and of course we told him he was crazy, that he could never be the sun. Believing us, his answer was, "Well, if I can't be the sun, then I want to be one of the sun's rays." That was how Ray got his name. To this day, I don't know why he allowed us to deter him from his original goal. Perhaps he compromised just for ease of conversation.

I got up and said, "Well, if that's not the Aurora Borealis combined with all things good and bright in the universe. My friend is still going to be a ray of the sun, forever casting his light of warmth and coolness upon us all."

RC got up and held his glass up and said, "To the rays of the sun!"

Hats stood and built upon the cheer, "To Ray, one fucked up bright motherfucker if ever there was one!"

We had just participated in an incredible journey of determining and verifying our futures. We were saying goodbye to the Soup Man and inventing ourselves all at the same time. It was a moment to be marked in time forever. We were in a moment of real peace of mind. Unfortunately, it did not last long.

The enormous can of baked beans that Hats had tossed into the fire exploded in such a way that it could only be compared to D-Day or Pearl Harbor-type events. When I shook off the initial blast and realized I was still alive, I looked around the Lodge for carnage, assuming Ray and RC and Hats would be dead. The sound had been so loud I was temporarily deaf and devoid of all senses.

Ahhh, the lessons of life. Little did Hats know that you can't put a sealed can of baked beans into a fire! Let alone a *Findlay Brothers* woodstove that is roaring at a million degrees Celsius or Fahrenheit. We had the front door of the stove open at the time, so fortunately we did not blow up Findley or the Lodge. Instead, we blew baked beans and red hot coals all over the inside of the Lodge. The direct hit came straight from the stove's front door. It blew out in a shotgun spread that was about three feet in diameter. Hats took a direct hit, which in hindsight seems appropriate. What a dumbass.

RC, Ray, and I did not get any substantial red hot coals shot our way. Hats was not so lucky. Even though most of his face was spared, his chest and arms were covered in beans, tomato sauce, and fire-laced coals. The coals were trying desperately to stay alive on his body, competing with and fighting against the juices of the tomato sauce and the beans that were acting as a natural fire retardant. However, Hats was not registering any of the chemistry of the situation, and he began to scream like a four-year-old who had just stepped on a snake. RC knew exactly what needed to be done, and he rushed up and opened the door to the Lodge. Hats did not require any coaching, and he immediately sprung up and threw himself out the door and into the winter, whereupon he rolled and trundled in the snow until he was sure he was flamed out. When he was done, the snow was a mix of charcoal and tomato sauce garnished with the odd baked bean.

The three of us were still inside the Lodge watching the spectacle outside. We did not really know whether we were directly involved or innocent bystanders waiting for help to arrive. While we were wondering about Hats, he was not remotely wondering about us. Once he realized he was going to live and that any burns suffered were minor, he got up from the snow and stood up straight to brush the snow and canned food off his clothes. But right away, we knew something wasn't right. It was his own expression that alerted us to his concern as he started looking down at himself, his chest, his arms, his legs. He started sniffing himself and then looked up at us, and we knew exactly what had happened. Hats had rolled in a fresh and steamy pile of bear shit.

"Well, I guess it was a bear, you fucking morons!" was all he said, and then he started to look around in a three-hundred-sixty-degree circle. After that, he quickly took off his sweatshirt and jeans and threw them on the roof of the Lodge. He headed back towards us with nothing but long underwear and socks on, and just before he stepped back into the Lodge, he looked at the three of us and said, "The beans are ready, boys!"

We got back to the party. Hats played the rest of the *Risk* game in a pair of one-piece red flannel long underwear. This was perfect for his Red Army persona. He had five burns that left small scars on his body – one on each arm, two on his chest and one on his forehead. He was most proud of the one on his forehead. Still today, his marketing tagline for his law practice is, *"I've been burned; you've been burned; let's burn somebody else together!"*

The irony was, there were still more burns to be had at the Lodge.

What a night that was. We finished off all our tuning supplies, the *Risk* board was decided upon, and Ray and RC played on their guitars. Eventually we got our sleeping bags ready for a sleep that could only be described as a dream state. Findley kept us warm, and the energy of our friendship kept us content.

We were in our bunks, and sleep was coming soon. All four of us were thinking our own thoughts and happy to be together. Right before the night ended, RC posed a question to the three of us. "Life can be short, eh, guys?" he asked, really saying, *What a week, a week like no other we have ever had.*

"Very short," I replied, thinking about the Soup Man and the day's events.

"Too damn short!" Hats said.

"Certainly a lot shorter than death," Ray added.

There was a calm silence as we all thought about what Ray had said. Even Ray was thinking about what he had said.

"How long do you think you're dead for?" RC asked the three of us.

"Long fucking time!" Hats answered right away.

That was the end of the conversation and our night. I wrote a short poem while we were all falling asleep. I memorized it while staring at the ceiling of the Lodge from my top bunk. I was thinking about what Ray had said, and I was thinking about the last six days of my life. I said a final goodbye to the Soup Man and recited my poem over and over until sleep came.

Life is short and getting shorter
That's what the wise man said
Once death comes, it lasts forever
A person is a long time dead

From this day forward, life's a mystery
I have no idea how things will be
Stoke the fire and take my childhood
And put it in a can of beans

DAY 7 — Morning

South Carolina

Start

"**I'VE BEEN DOING SOME** thinking, Sam."

"What have you been thinking about, Doc?"

"I don't think we need to talk about your father."

"Can you please call him the Soup Man?"

"Sure, Sam, but I don't think it matters anyway."

"Why is that, Doc?"

"I just don't see how it will add value."

"Freud will be upset."

"That's funny, Sam. Yes, I suspect Freud would want me to dig deep into the story of your father-son relationship. I just don't see how it will help."

"I couldn't agree more. Let's move on, Doc."

"What should we talk about?"

Silence

"Sam, what about talking about Sophie and George?"

"I could see that coming, Doc."

"I'm sure you could, Sam."

"Good, so we can talk about them?"

"What's to talk about, Doc? They left me, end of story."

"That's how you see it, Sam? They left you?"

"Sure, how else is there to look at it?"

"A few ways, I suspect. Why do you think they left you, Sam?"

"Because of my work. Because of my decisions relative to my priorities."

"You think your work caused Sophie and George to leave you?"

"Yes."

"I don't see it that way, Sam. Why do you see it that way?

Silence

"Doc, I don't want to talk about this anymore."

"We need to talk about this, Sam."

"Fine, but not now."

"Then when?"

"Later. Soon. I need to go now, Doc."

"That's fine, Sam. We'll talk later. We'll talk soon."

DAY 7 — Afternoon
South Carolina

Prospector

DOC FINALLY DID IT – a classic technique of pulling the old bait and switch on me. Bait me with the Soup Man and switch me out to Sophie and George. One thing for sure, there's no need to talk about the Soup Man again. Dead is dead. Move on.

Great bait and switch though. I'll have to commend her when we talk next.

I'm really trying to stay focused and not be mad at Doc right now. I'm trying to keep today a Green day as I need a Green day today. I know Doc is just doing her job. I get that. I respect that. I need to give her the benefit of the doubt that her approach will be helpful in the end. Oddly enough, I knew she was going to approach Sophie and George next. I was anticipating it. I was actually ready for it, or at least I thought I was. It's just hard once you actually get to game time. You always think you're ready for something until game time, but at game time, everything can change. Everything is just an optimistic plan until you actually step out onto the ice.

What is Doc expecting from me anyway? What does she want to know about Sophie and George anyway? Sophie and I met in South

Carolina – we fell in love, we went to school together, we got married, we had George, I started a business, I screwed up, and they left me. Now Sophie won't talk to me. Story over.

So that leaves me being analyzed by the analyst. The analyst versus the analyst in a game of one on one, full rink with no goalies in the net.

I left psychology and started my own business trying to help people in a broader sense. My work became my life, my work got in the way, now Sophie and George are gone. It's not like this is some unique story. Hell, show me a prospector and I'll show you the same story.

A prospector is a person who gets things done. A prospector is as tough as they come, is an explorer with a purpose, a worker on a mission. *What does it take to be a prospector?* This is a question I always ask my customers at our conventions. *What does it take to be a prospector? Everything! It takes everything!*

Doc doesn't understand what Sophie and I have been through together. We are completely in love. This has not changed. We love George with every ounce of energy our bodies can produce, and this will never change. The problem is I continued to make decisions based on my need to be a prospector, on my need to build my business. Sophie often asked if my drive for success was becoming all consuming, and I tried to explain that it wasn't a drive for success, but rather it was a fear of failure – a twenty-four-hour, seven-days-per-week, all-consuming, all-intense fear of failure. Doc needs to understand this fear can take a toll on a person!

Sophie would continuously ask me why I would want to do something that creates so much fear and anxiety in my life. It's a good question, and I don't have a good answer. It's the mystery of *Gold Fever*. You get started with a vision and you believe in yourself, so others believe in you because you believe in yourself. You convince yourself you can accomplish what few people are able to accomplish. You convince yourself that you can build something from the bottom up. It's the ultimate challenge for the prospector, so people get behind you, people invest in you, you invest in yourself, and you go for it. It's the golden recipe and true beauty of prospecting. Creativity drives vision, vision drives mission, and mission creates the energy required to get initial results. Then you have some small successes because hard work works like that.

With small success comes momentum; momentum rationalizes more investment, which results in more success for the ones who are lucky, or unlucky, depending on your perspective. With more success comes more fear. The prospector is never without fear, but the fear can actually produce positive results as fear drives performance when directed effectively. With fear and performance comes more success. The prospector gets juiced by the fear and the success, and the fear turns into excitement, the excitement turns into thrill, and then the kite ride begins. Once on the ride, it's very hard to get off.

It all seems wonderful, but the prospector has no idea what he is getting himself into. The prospector is too busy to deal with complications or negativism. Only optimism is allowed, and the prospector is blind to the unintended consequences of the decision to mine for gold. At some point, this catches up to the prospector. At some point, the prospector has to stop and deal with the opportunity cost of his decisions.

Sophie and I are at this point.

We are still in love, we've always been in love, and we always will be in love. That much I know for certain. Sophie knows as well. Sophie is the only woman I ever want in my life. She's perfect in every way. Her physical beauty is stunning, her approach to life is calming and soothing, she's funny and caring, and she loves all the creatures on the Earth. She loves herself, she loves me, and she loves George.

She brought George into our lives fifteen years ago even though the doctors had told us that we would never have children. She didn't believe them, I didn't believe them, and so we never gave up. We did everything a couple could do; we spared no expense and we were open to all ideas. It was hard on Sophie physically and emotionally, and it was hard on me because I wanted a child, but mostly because it was hard on Sophie. And then it worked, and one day the odds went in our favor. George is the greatest gift either of us has ever been given. Sophie had to undergo serious surgery when George was born, and the doctors made it very clear we would never have another child. This time we believed them, but it didn't matter, because George is all we needed. George is everything to us. George is a great kid.

It just doesn't make any sense that we're not together. If only I could talk to her, I would tell her that everything will be OK. I would tell her that we will work through all of our challenges. I would tell her that nothing is more important than our being together as a family. I would tell her that we can get through this.

If only she would talk to me.

I need to figure out how to get through to her.

DAY 8
South Carolina

Stupidity Prevails

IT'S A RED DAY. A really bad Red day, so I will apologize up front.

I didn't want you to see me like this, as I don't want you to get the wrong impression. I'm actually making progress. I really am, but I'm just so pissed off thinking about my conversation with Doc yesterday. What exactly is she trying to do? I can only assume she knows what she's doing, and if so, why would she do this? Why would she purposely do what she did?

I am so mad right now that my blood is boiling and I think I'm ready to snap, even though I told myself I wouldn't get this way, even though I told myself I wouldn't let you see me like this. I'm here. That's me, transparent to a fault. Sorry.

After my visit with Doc, I told myself not to turn on the television, but I didn't listen. To listen to oneself requires discipline I don't have, so I plugged in the set and cranked it on. The Talking Cable Heads were all there. The Talking Cable Heads were everywhere. They must be following me. Great, I'll add paranoia to my list of mental assets. Anyway, it didn't matter which Head was on, because it was the same story on every channel. Did you see it?

Young men in big cities are randomly walking up to people in the street and punching them in the head. It's a game. They call it *Punch Out* – ten dead and counting in the last two days. The attacks are all on video as that's part of the rules. It has to be captured on video to count. If not captured by public video, then the sick dumbasses video it on their own smart phones and put it up on the net. *Smart phones.* Right.

The punch recipient today was a school teacher walking home from a hard day's work. Thirty years old, with a wife and two young kids. The average age of the sick boy punchers is sixteen. As the unsuspecting teacher passed the gang, one of them jumped out and punched the teacher in the head. The teacher fell over, out cold from the punch, and hit his head on the curb. Dead on arrival at the hospital. The video gets uploaded for all to see, and the cable stations get first dibs. This is like heroin to them. They shoot it into their veins as quickly as possible.

Good God, I am so mad right now. One Talking Cable Head is screaming racism, another is preaching that parents aren't doing their job anymore, another says that schools are to blame, and another says it's because the kids aren't getting a proper breakfast! Really? Breakfast? Breakfast? I haven't eaten breakfast in ten years, but you don't see me randomly sucker-punching kindergarten teachers! Really, Talking Cable Heads? Breakfast?

The story gets better, it really does. You just can't make this stuff up. According to the Heads, the police caught one of the sick boys who killed a young lady in another incident a few weeks ago. It's all on video, and you can see the sick dumbass punching her. This time it was a twenty-year-old woman. Guess what? She was pregnant. Only she and her husband knew because she was only two months along, and they had not told their families yet. The video shows the whole thing. She was walking up a subway exit staircase and was heading for the bus stop on the corner of the street. She required two modes of transportation to get her home from work; she had a ninety-minute commute every day. She was a social worker, and she was out there helping young people try to have a better life. I'm sure you saw it too. It's all over the cable news. You just can't make this stuff up. It's too broken to be fiction. Nobody can make this up. It's so bad; it's so bad I'm ready to scream. Only sick human beings are capable of this.

That's right, a twenty-year-old pregnant social worker who needed ninety minutes to get home on a subway and a bus was randomly punched in the head, fell and hit her head on a garbage can. She went into shock, and then she and her two-month old unborn baby died on the way to the hospital. Nobody on the street helped her, although countless people had time to video her lying on the ground. It took twenty minutes for the ambulance to arrive. People walked right by her, not wanting to get involved. Most stared down and looked, maybe took a picture or two, and kept walking. Finally somebody called 911. It's all on video. The puncher sick boy is on video smiling at the camera. He knows it's there and he looks up at the camera and smiles and does a little dance and shows off his tattoos. He then held up to the camera a driver's license that was not his, but belonged to some guy who was mugged and viciously attacked three weeks ago. The story went on. The sick boy got arrested. End of story, right? Wrong! Wrong! Wrong, wrong, wrong!

The sick boy's lawyer, a pretentious media junky working for ego air time, said that his client wasn't even there at the time, and he said that all the public video footage gathered was a violation of his client's civil rights. Then he said that his sick boy client has filed a ten-million-dollar law suit against the city transit system and the retail store whose cameras caught the footage of the attack. He said they had no right to be filming the incident. The video violated his client's civil rights and freedom of expression!

The delusional lawyer went on, looking for any air play he could get with the Talking Cable Heads. He loved every minute of it. His new cheap suit and butt-ugly haircut showed he had recently groomed himself for the show. He told us that even if the sick boy were found guilty, he'd get no more than three years in some juvenile detention center. He was only sixteen you see. Only a sick kid, not a sick person. Six feet tall and one hundred ninety pounds, a man. But no, he would go to some place for three years and be out before we knew it. You just can't make this up.

And then the bleeding heart Talking Cable Heads said it's all because his father left his mother. A Talking Cable Heads doctor said the sick kid's mother didn't hug him enough. He added that the school system failed him. He ended with the fact that the sick kid didn't get enough breakfast. Like we haven't heard that one before!

I can't deal with it, and I really need to turn it off. I know I can't stop the sick-boy stuff from happening, so I can only stop myself from being the victim of it. The Heads who make a fortune reporting on the world's deviants love this stuff, they love me for watching it, and they can't wait until the next sick boy makes some more great news. They can't wait until I glue myself to the tube to watch it, and when it happens they'll be the first to report it. Hell, they will report it before the social worker even knows she's dead. They are that good at what they do. Speed is everything, and facts are nothing. The goal of the Talking Cable Heads is to get the story first, regardless of whether the facts being spewed are accurate.

I'll bet you anything that the husband found out about his wife and unborn daughter through cable television. I can just picture his sitting in front of the television, bending down towards the screen asking himself, "Is that my wife lying beside that garbage can? Thanks, Talking Cable Heads, it's good to know where my family is! I guess it's only one for dinner tonight!"

Punch Out. I simply can't believe it. When did being a good person stop being important? When did accountability stop? When did our fear of liability and litigation start and any sense of respect for humanity stop? The police have their hands tied, the courts have their hands tied, the public have their hands tied, the victims have their hands tied, and the stupid sick people doing the punching are punching because they have their hands tied! Everybody in the whole chain, in the whole ecosystem, has his hands tied. This equals no respect for humanity. You see – hands tied equals no values, no values equals no principles, no principles equals no responsibility, no responsibility equals no accountability, no accountability equals no standards for behavior, no standards for behaviors equals no respect, and no respect equals do whatever the hell you want to do whenever you want to do it to whomever you want to do it to. Don't love your wife anymore? Kill her! Don't like your job anymore? Burn the place down! Don't have the car you want? Steal one and murder the bastard who had the nerve to work hard and earn the thing!

Why? Because we have lost all respect. Why? Because having respect starts from within. First, you have to respect yourself, and then you have to respect the person beside you. Then you have to respect the small group around you, then the larger group, then the town, then the city, then the state, then the country, then the continent and ultimately the world. Respect starts from within and then cascades out, but this cascading collapses and implodes the minute you don't respect yourself. The whole world and all its weight implodes on you. At that point you are done, and so is anybody around you.

It all starts with internal self-respect. You don't need anybody to teach you this because it should be innate. It should be natural. Self-respect is not a noun, it's not a place, and it's not a point in time.

Self-respect is a verb. It's something you do, and you do it for yourself and with yourself. It is yourself. It is you.

Is this so hard to understand? I can't imagine I'm the only one who sees what's going on! What is happening to this world? I am so mad right now. I'm turning the TV off. I really have to turn it off. I need to go back out to the beach. A walk is about the only thing that will calm my mind. Maybe I'll connect with Ray. Maybe we can write a poem or song together. That will help as well.

Maybe he can also help convince Sophie to talk to me. I need her more than ever. I feel as if my head is twirling out of control.

In Ray's Voice

SAM WENT FOR A WALK today and reached out to me. He's reaching out more and more these days, and I'm getting progressively more worried about him. He thinks that he's making progress, but he's not; he's got a long way to go. His problem is he thinks he's invincible. He thinks he can just rebound from anything life throws his way because he doesn't realize he's as human as the rest of us. Nobody is invincible. My experience is there is an inverse relationship between how tough a person acts on the outside and how tough he actually is on the inside. The bigger they are, the harder they fall.

He reached out after getting himself all worked up with the television. I just don't know why he does that to himself. The enemy within us is extremely powerful. Sam keeps wondering if I can connect him to Sophie, and I keep telling him that he cannot communicate with her in his current state. His anger needs to subside for communication channels to open up. She can't talk to him when he's so full of rage. He says he understands, but I don't buy it. Only time will tell the tale.

Sam suggested we write a song to calm his mind. I think it worked, and I really like the lyrics. Maybe RC will put it to guitar, it's written perfectly for a country feel and acoustic sound. Sam wrote it all, although he loves to give me credit. He's always done that. He's been my biggest fan our entire lives. Next time he reaches out, I'll work on his anger. I'm sure Sophie will be able to talk to him if we can significantly reduce the anger.

Anyway, here's the song.

TWIRLING

Looking back now
I guess I can see
How you worked so hard
To make something out of me
But I wasn't looking
At what I could be
I've been too busy twirling around

Chorus

Life is crazy
Crazy as a hound
Howling at the moon
To try to bring it down
Never knowing which way
We all go round
Life is crazy
Crazy when you're twirling around

I got a friend
Haven't seen him in a while
When I do think of him
It always makes me smile
He's as crazy as they come
Never changed from a child
He's been too busy twirling around

Went for a walk
Up a trail the other day
I kept on going
Until I lost my way
Took a nap against a tree
Dreaming of what may
Come from all this twirling around

Think I'm gonna go
And find me a place
Where I can hang my hat
And make me a case
For slowing it all down
Can't take this pace
I think I'm dizzy from twirling around

Now I'm thinking
Thinking I just might
Ask you to join me
Along for a ride
I think you might like it
At least for a while
Grab my arm while I'm twirling around

Well I guess I'm outta here
And yes I understand
It's not what you want
All this twirling in a man
Not thinking I can change me
We've played out our hand
See ya next time when I'm twirling around

Canada
Spring 1982

Politics

NINETEEN EIGHTY-TWO was an interesting year in Canadian politics. Down in Ottawa, our nation's capital, Prime Minister Trudeau was keeping busy. He managed to get a proclamation from England's Queen Elizabeth to re-patriate Canada's constitution. This gave Canada full political independence from the United Kingdom, and it also gave Canadians our very own thorough bill of rights. It didn't mean much for the average Canadian, though, as most of us assumed we already had all of these things.

On the NHL front, the spring of 1982 was a year of interest but with a lack of excitement for our teams. The New York Islanders would win their third straight Stanley Cup by crushing the Vancouver Canucks in four straight games. Of all of our teams, only the Boston Bruins made it through to the quarterfinals, but they went no farther. Of interest though, the hockey world was watching the rise of *The Great One*. The Edmonton Oilers hot superstar Wayne Gretzky began to shatter records, including the record of fifty goals in fifty games. He did it in thirty-nine games. Even though the city of Edmonton was closer to us than many of our teams, not one of the Beaver Brothers considered switching our long-held allegiances. Another cool thing that happened in 1982 was that the Philadelphia Flyers became the first pro team to wear long hockey pants on the ice. The idea was to create a more efficient uniform with lighter padding. The concept was it would make the players faster, but an unintended consequence was that the players hit the boards faster when sliding on the ice after being body checked. Hats loved it and he got himself a pair the minute they hit the local sports store in Chinook River. He tried to convince Vince to buy them for the whole team, but luckily Vince decided to wait and see if the pants would stay around as the new norm.

On the music front, the bands and sounds of the 1980s were going strong. The synthesizer was making it easy for any goofy-looking dumbass to become famous. For the most part, we didn't participate in the sound of the eighties as we had our bands, many of whom were still producing good old classic rock. It was all we needed. At the time, we were particularly grooving to *The Grateful Dead,* so this did not leave much time to explore other bands.

In the spring of 1982, the Beaver Brothers were all hovering around 17 years old and finishing Grade 11. This meant we were one year away from graduating high school, and therefore had begun to talk more seriously about plans for our futures. Hats and I were committed to university, although where we would go was still undecided. RC would attempt to get into the RCMP right out of Grade 12, but his research was suggesting it was not probable this would happen, and a two-year college degree would most likely be required. Ray was non-committal as he had not sorted out the best approach to becoming a ray of the sun.

Overall, we were doing well as we progressed through high school. We continued to play hockey, the Lodge was our place to go, and we had managed to arrange ourselves musically to the point you could almost consider us a band. Of course, we believed *The Beaver Brothers Band* would be on the world's stage one day. Some things just are what they are, and sometimes it's important to believe what you want to believe. Life really can be a self-fulfilling prophecy in all directions.

Two new very cool things had also happened along the way to 1982. The first was that Ray's mother had brought a dog home to Ray. She became our dog, and we named her Ozark. She was quite the dog, and I am certain you will enjoy getting to know her.

The second thing was that RC had us learning *Krav Maga.* This is the self-defense technique developed for the military in Israel. RC believed we all needed to know how to take care of ourselves physically, and in his mind Krav Maga was the best discipline to learn. RC didn't want us caught up in the so-called "spiritual" aspects of karate and other Japanese martial arts. He did not believe in bowing down to a Sensei. He just wanted us to know how to deal with real-world situations and to be extremely efficient and effective if required. I have to admit, the four of us really enjoyed the craft, and it was a good workout. We all got pretty good at it as well, and before long we were proficient in self-defense techniques. "Prospectors need to be tough, Sam," RC would tell me. He was right.

So in summary, by 1982 we were hockey players, full-time Lodge dwellers, dog owners, part-time musicians, and part-time self-defense fighters. This defined the Beaver Brothers as we became young adults. We were comfortable in our own skin, confident in our abilities, and our friendship cemented and sustained this confidence. There was no reason to feel anything but optimistic about the future, because in the end, we had each other. Everything would always be fine because we were certain we had the capabilities to get through anything.

The school year went along as it should. School was not a problem for any of us, and we did well, but not for the same reasons. Ray is just smart and everything comes easy to him. School bored him, as the curriculum and course topics seemed basic to his interests. Ray has many gifts – one being he can memorize anything the night before it needs to be transferred onto a test paper. People will say this is a sign of intelligence, but Ray will tell you this is a sign of an outdated and infinitely broken school system. Ray does not consider learning through memorization to be actual learning. He was uninterested in most subjects at school and did not even remotely struggle to get good grades. Most importantly, though, Ray did excel at music. He was quickly becoming an incredible musician with the ability to play virtually any instrument and play it well. In particular, he mastered the guitar, both electric and acoustic, and his piano playing is also incredible. To this day, I find it very interesting that he did not pursue a path to become a professional musician. He could have made it easily. I guess there are things about him I'll never understand. He had God-given gifts, good looks, and all the charm required to be famous. I guess it's just not what he wanted. Ray could be anything he wanted to be, yet he never talked about what he might do after high school. If we asked, he would just say that he is sticking to his plan of becoming a sun ray.

RC did well but worked for every grade. He knew he was going to join the RCMP so he was already working towards that track. And even though he did not need to, RC still took the advanced classes that Hats and I took in preparation for university. Ray took them in the hope of being challenged. We took all our classes together. RC had to work hard at it, but he always did well. Ray would help him in English and history as RC was stronger in math and sciences but struggled with languages. RC was good with numbers. He was also very good at phys-ed and music. He was very strong and an amazing athlete – tall and muscular. In Grade 11, he was well over six feet tall and on his way to his final adult height of six feet six inches. The RCMP loved him. He also played the guitar very well and had a great voice. Ray was an excellent teacher, and RC was an excellent student, so together, RC and Ray made a great duo. RC's work ethic is what really has allowed him to succeed in everything he has done. Nothing in life has ever been handed to RC, and his personal value system reflects this. He works hard and achieves the goals he sets out for himself, which makes him a classic role model for young and old people everywhere.

Hats and I were similar students. We knew we were headed to university and so we worked as hard as we needed to in order to get the grades we needed to be accepted to a program. Hats can do well in anything he puts his mind to, although he doesn't always put his mind to things. Hats is less about books and more about the street. He did what he had to do to finish law school, but once he was done, he was on the street scrapping it out. He doesn't have one law book in his office. He is a grinder, a roll-up-your-shirt-sleeves-and-simply-pound-through-the-problem guy. He's good at everything he does, although he often leaves a wake of destruction behind him. Musically, Ray taught Hats how to play the drums. It just made sense, as all he had to do was pound the hell out of the drums and hope there was some semblance of a beat. He actually did pretty well. Physically, Hats was turning into a strong man. He always had an athletic build and complemented that with lifting weights for hockey. You can't be a scrappy, hard-grinding hockey player without being strong. Hats knew this.

I personally focused on English. I knew early on that I enjoyed writing, and this seemed appropriate considering I was going to become a poet and prospector for a living. I had no idea how a person would do that, but that was the plan at the time, and I was sticking to it. On the music front, I played the bass, more by default than anything. Ray and RC taught me the basics as I do not have any true musical talent. I did, however, get to write some lyrics for Ray, and our combined talents were proving that we could produce original songs that we felt were pretty damn good. I fully recognize the bias here. Physically, Ray and I were trending in similar fashion. We were average height and average weight. I lifted weights with Hats so I was a little stronger, although Ray was much better looking with a *pretty-boy* look to him. The Krav Maga helped Ray stay fit, and at the end of the day, we were all just healthy northern boys.

So we tolerated school and did what we needed to do. It was a necessity, and we conformed as best we could. School did not define us or drive our activities. We stayed below the radar and avoided being a high or a low for the teachers and administrators. At least until our Grade 12 year. What a tragic train-wreck school year that was.

We did have one exciting event happen in the spring of Grade 11. Hats decided he was going to run for President of the Student Council as he was convinced this would help his application for entrance into a political science program at a good Canadian university. At the time, an undergraduate degree in political science was the road to law school. We all agreed with his decision, but it was also a stretch for us because none of us had ever participated in the Student Council up to that point in our high school career. And we were the English kids in a French high school.

"That's fucking why it's perfect!" Hats replied when we expressed our concern. "I'll be the new fresh guy, the smart guy from left field, the guy with the new ideas – it will be Hats Mania!" finishing up his comment by drawing a parallel between his running for Student Council and the mania of Pierre Trudeau, the long-running Canadian Prime Minister.

We thought about it briefly and agreed he could pull it off. Truthfully, there is no point arguing with Hats when he sets his mind to something. He tried to get us to run for office in supporting roles, and we all declined. We did, however, become his campaign team and helped him with the election. We had twenty days after our March Break to solicit the votes of the student body. We did our best to put Hats' best foot forward, and I have to admit that Hats worked hard at it. He really wanted it. He even tried to curtail his language a little in an effort not to offend the religious right of the electorate, which was almost every French Catholic, which was almost the whole school.

We each had our roles, responsibilities, and accountabilities. I was responsible for slogan development and writing the campaign speech. RC was responsible for getting buttons made up and putting up posters around the school. Ray was responsible for making sure we were connecting with and translating effectively for the Francophone population of the school. Hats would, after all, need to complete his campaign speech in French. At this point, the four of us were pretty much bilingual, but Ray really sounded bi-cultural. When Ray spoke French, you had no idea that English was his first language. With the rest of us, you could tell right away. Hats needed Ray's help as speaking French is one thing, but making a speech in French is a whole new ball game for an Anglophone. Our informal polls taken in the smoking area and the lunch room of the high school suggested we had the English vote in the bag and only about forty percent of the French vote. The school was eighty-five percent French. The French vote we had was primarily from the female population. They loved Hats. The French male population did not like Hats so much though, primarily because the female population did. That and his hockey tactics, of which they had no doubt been on the losing end a time or two.

We started with posters and buttons. RC bought a button-making machine through mail order, and it proved to be an absolute blast. If we could think it and draw it on a piece of paper, then we could make a button. That button machine came in handy over the years. We put campaign buttons out in French and English, as this was the law in our province and school. We decided on two official slogans and one unofficial one for people who knew Hats personally. The two official slogans were *Keep Yourself Covered with Hats* and *Vote Hats on Top*. We thought the latter was very creative. Complexity is always best dressed in simplicity. The unofficial slogan that we had on selected buttons was *Stop the Chats and %#$& Vote Hats*. Hats loved this one and made up a two-minute curse rant that he would recite on the spot if somebody asked what the icons on the button stood for. It was perfect, and he would recite the rant at least ten times a day in the smoking area while students would smoke their torpedoes and try to stay warm in the early spring air.

I'm not sure how it works in other schools, but in our school in 1982 the campaign speech was what determined the winner and loser of the election for President of Student Council – that and who was good looking and popular. Hats was solid on the last two, so we focused on his speech. I have to hand it to Hats in that he actually took my role as writer seriously, and he tried his best to sit still and focus on the task at hand. We even did some research and talked to a few folks around town who were politically active to get some advice. The Judge was very helpful. We then used this information to devise our overall high-level strategy for the speech. In the end, we had a three-legged-stool strategy. The first was to keep the speech short and simple in order to mitigate the language issue. Second, we would make no more than three promises. These would be promises that we felt were relevant to the masses of the school. As well, as taught to us by people with experience, we would not take our ability to actually implement the strategies into consideration in any way. *Get elected and then worry about what you said!* was the motto for the campaign. The third and last strategy was to use humor to deflect the obvious lack of content and depth in Hats' and our campaign.

Speech day came and Hats was ready. He wasn't nervous at all, or if he was he sure hid it well. He was the last to speak. His competition was two very smart Francophone female students. One in particular was on her way to be valedictorian of the class the following year. Their speeches were what we expected. They talked very eloquently about their past experience on student council, the things they had accomplished along the way, and the great and very practical things they would do if elected President. I would have easily voted for either of them, and they were both cute.

Then it was Hats' turn to make his speech. By design, RC walked him up on stage as if he were his bodyguard. RC looked the part. He was in jeans and a t-shirt that showed off his height and athletic build. RC wore aviator sunglasses for effect, and when Hats got to the podium, RC stood beside him as if he were not going to leave. As choreographed, Hats gave RC a look that said, *It's OK, you can leave. I'll be fine.* On cue, RC looked out at the student body assembled in the auditorium and pretended he was examining each and every student. He then went to the podium and tilted it sideways as if to look underneath it for hidden explosives. Satisfied with his search, he put the podium back in place and left the stage. The crowd roared in laughter. Humor tactic number one was successful. Ray and I looked at each other and nodded our heads in approval. We were quickly becoming successful back benchers.

Hats was dressed in a new-vintage early 1980s suit that we all chipped in to make happen. He dressed it up with a crisp white shirt and thin brown leather tie. His hair, which was shoulder length, was combed back and parted and feathered in the middle. Ray's younger sister Rose had taken care of these details for us. She had him looking spectacular, and he looked as if he should have been running for Prime Minister of the country. When RC left him at the podium, he took his speech out of the breast pocket of his suit. He held it up in an exaggerated way for the crowd to see what was written on the back of the back page. What the student population saw on the back page in large letters was *French Version of Speech*. This got another loud roar of laughter and approval. He laid the pages out on the podium and started into his pre-rehearsed stump speech for President of the Student Council.

The speech went as planned, and Hats did a reasonable job with the tough parts relative to the translation into French. I had written the speech in English, and Ray did the translation and language coaching. As per our strategy, the entire speech lasted only three minutes. He started out by thanking everybody for considering him for President. He then laid out his three promises. The first was to build a roof over the designated smoking area of the school so smokers would not have to stand in the rain and snow depending on the season. The promise was *Dry Torpedoes*. This received resounding applause of approval. The second promise was to expand the size of the outdoor ice rink on school property to be official Olympic size, all with proper lines painted and real nets for the goalies to use. This got another round of applause, but from a different section of the room. Our strategy was working. The third promise was our effort to humanize and personalize Hats as an individual and fellow student. His third and last promise was that if elected he would try really hard to attend school regularly and do the best he could as President. This had the entire room laughing, including his two opponents. He was doing an amazing job and all of Ray's language coaching was paying off. That was until the very end of the speech.

The speech was almost done, and Hats had executed it flawlessly. At this point, he just had to complete the ending we had prepared. If he accomplished this, he would no doubt win the election.

The English version of the ending that Ray translated into French was:

Thank you again for allowing me to ask for your vote. However, when looking at and listening to my excellent competition today, it strikes me that whatever way you vote, you cannot lose."

The idea of this ending was to show Hats as a nice guy and to give a warm appreciation and compliment to the other candidates. They were, in fact, better qualified for the job. The problem was that Hats was on a roll and feeling good about how the speech was going, so he became relaxed. He became too relaxed and lost his way relative to the translation. Translated to English from his French translation, what Hats actually said to the school population was:

Thank you again for allowing me to ask for your vote. However, when looking at and listening to my competition today, it strikes me that you don't have much to lose.

The moans started right away with the teachers who were standing at the back of the auditorium. Hats immediately got a confused look on his face. He had no idea what he had actually said, so he looked over at Ray and me, and Ray gave him a *you dumbass* look. Hats realized he had messed up the translation somehow. He was pissed because he knew he was so close to a game seven overtime goal. I walked over to RC and told him to go get Hats off the stage before he did anything stupid. Unfortunately, RC was not there in time. The student body was mixed in their emotions – some were laughing because they realized he had mixed up his words, others were giving him dirty looks for criticizing the other two candidates, and others were just wondering what he was going to do next. What he did was pure Hats. He folded his speech up and calmly put it back into his breast pocket. He tapped the microphone for effect to ensure it was working and that people were listening. RC was moving fast but was still ten feet away from Hats on the stage. Hats then bent down into the microphone on the podium and speaking English yelled out, "Vote for me and we will smoke dry smokes, play open ice Olympic hockey, and get some really other fucking cool shit done!"

RC tackled him before he could say anything more. There was silence in the auditorium for ten seconds while RC hauled Hats off the stage. Then the place exploded into laughter and applause. It was a total roof-raising dismount. RC and Hats headed out of the auditorium as if he had another appointment to be at. Ray and I followed in tow, making people believe we were going to be hoisted into big black SUVs. As I left the auditorium, I saw the principal going to the podium in an effort to calm people down.

It was no surprise that Hats won in a landslide the next day when the ballots were counted. The principal called Hats into his office and expressed his disappointment with the results and asked Hats if he wanted to consider handing the title over to one of the other two more qualified candidates. You can imagine what Hats said to him in reply.

And so we began the end of Grade 11 knowing that Hats would be President of the Student Council in our last year of high school.

If only we had known how that would end.

DAY 9 — Morning
South Carolina

Man's Best Friend

TODAY IS A GREEN DAY. I connected with Ray yesterday and we worked through a cool song that helped me calm down and get a good night's sleep. Life always looks a little better after a good sleep, and it allows me to enter the new day on my terms. Mornings are an interesting event and we all have our own approach and technique to entering a new day. My most successful technique is to start by waking up rested. No surprise or high science here.

I've also unplugged the television. This is probably ten times as important as being rested.

I went for a very peaceful walk on the beach this morning, and now I'm at my desk staring out at the ocean. I can't get enough of it. I'll be meeting with Doc this afternoon and I'm feeling pretty good about it. It's a Green day and I'm up to whatever she wants to talk about.

The walk this morning is what really helped – no question. What made it special is there were several people on the beach with their dogs. Before nine o'clock, you can run your dogs on the beach without a leash. This is the best. There is nothing that compares to running your dog (or dogs) on the beach first thing in the morning. If you're really motivated, you will do it at dawn. This is spectacular. The dogs love it. I've seen dogs actually smile when they are running after a ball and chasing it into the waves of the sea. I love watching them try to jump over the wake, only to end up with a face full of salt water. To be sure though, they will not be deterred. They'll get that ball.

Dogs have always been a part of my life. I've always professed that dog people have dogs and those with dogs are dog people. It's a self-fulfilling prophecy. We had a poodle named Pierre when I was really young. *Pierre the French Poodle* seemed fitting. Pierre was as dumb as a bag of hammers. He would run away any chance he could, and eventually the Soup Man stopped looking for him. We would normally get a call from someone who had found him and had seen the phone number on the tag attached to his collar. The Soup Man would tell the caller to put him in a cab and send him to our house, and we would pay for the cab when it arrived with Pierre. I have no idea what happened to Pierre. I have no recollection of when he left us. I know we didn't put him to sleep as a family. I suspect he was given away after the Soup Man died.

Ozark was next. Ozark was Ray's dog. Actually, Ozark was the Beaver Brothers' dog. Ray's mother brought her home for Ray when we were in Grade 10. She was just an eight-week-old puppy at the time. Ozark was a liver-spotted Dalmatian who had amazing beautiful brown spots. What a gorgeous dog she was. We all participated in naming her. I wanted to call her "Spot" and argued that it's such a stereotyped name that no dog is actually named Spot! The boys liked the logic, and we seriously considered it. RC wanted to name her Pongo and argued it was cool because it was the male dog's name in the Disney classic, the play on names being that she was a female. Hats wanted to call her Stella with no reasoning behind his idea other than that he liked the name. Ray was the one that came up with Ozark, and we all loved it immediately. She's named after the mountain range and the band *The Ozark Mountain Daredevils*. We love the band. *It'll Shine When It Shines* is our favorite Ozark song. In the end, Ozark was a great dog and she had an incredible thirteen years of life.

In fact, Ozark was more than just a dog. During her life, Ozark would travel and see most of Canada and the USA, and almost made it into Mexico. While it was Ray who brought her into our lives, she lived with all four of us at some point in her life. Kind and gentle, Ozark was also the fastest dog I've ever seen. You could walk an old country dirt road with her, and she would dash out of the woods on one side, take one leap across the road, land in the opposite ditch, and then run back into the woods. One minute later, she would reappear and do it all over again. We always assumed she would have a head-on collision with a tree and die. We were actually prepared for this eventuality, and we are grateful that it never happened. God forbid she would see a deer or moose on a walk. She would be gone for days.

Ozark grew up with the Beaver Brothers. All four of us took care of her. She knew us as a team, but also as individuals. It was amazing to watch her manage us as each of us had our own way of taking care of her. Each of our homes had different rules and different standards of behavior that she learned. In this house, you can sleep on the chester-field (sofa for you Americans), in this house, you can't; in this house, you only get dog food, in this house, you can beg for food off the table. She knew the rules of each ecosystem and she could flex among them in a heartbeat. She was amazing. She loved all of us, but she really loved Ray. He was her first owner and the most sensitive of the four of us. Ray would sit and talk to Ozark for hours. They would go out to the Lodge, and Ozark would sit at his feet while he strummed his guitar. They both loved the Lodge. It was borderline clichéd, but in retrospect it was perfect. I have a picture of them sitting by a campfire somewhere – Ray playing his guitar and Ozark watching him in awe. I should find that picture. The day Ozark died was a very hard day for all of us.

We are all dog people. Ozark was the first Beaver Brothers' dog, but she sure wasn't the last. In our lives there have been Ozark, Curly, Oscar, Klondike, Molly, Ruby, Scoobie, Niki, Annie, and Bandit. All were beautiful animals. All were big dogs, mostly labs and lab mixes, although Bandit was an Australian Shepherd. He was the smartest dog I've ever met. Bandit belonged to Sophie and me. Hats in particular loved Bandit, and we were very sad when he died young of a blood clot on his spine. We did everything we could to save him. I miss Bandit.

None of us ever got another Dalmatian. Ozark was a one and only. Some dogs are just like that. There's no need to try to replicate an original, as this will only bring disappointment.

RC has four dogs right now, mixed-breed husky types that he mushes and dog sleds with his two daughters and two sons. God bless RC. He's still up there in the north, and he is getting it done winter style. He has a goal of at least one of his kids running the Iditarod Race in Alaska. I told him that if they make it I will pay for the whole trip and personally recite the *Cremation of Sam McGee* at the starting line.

I really hope he takes me up on it. That's something to look forward to, and having something to look forward to is helpful.

RC also has my two Labradors right now. Their names are Georgia and Texas. They are named after the two states. Sophie likes both of these states. The dogs are both yellow labs, and they are brother and sister from the same mother, but litters two years apart. They came from a breeder outside of Savannah. This breeder is extremely good at what she does, and they are beautiful dogs. Georgia is older. Sophie, George, and I got Georgia two weeks after Bandit died. Those were a very long two weeks. We got Texas two years after we got Georgia to hedge against ever again having a two-week period without a dog. As I said, dog people have dogs, and those with dogs are dog people. If you're one of us, you know what I'm talking about.

RC took Georgia and Texas back home after my intervention. For practical reasons, Sophie could not take them, and they are not allowed here at the hospital. RC has a big country acreage which is perfect for dogs. Hats offered to take the dogs, but he's in Philadelphia for the summer – not a great place for big dogs. Not to mention the standard would be food scraps. Hats has done well for himself, but he is also alone and on the road most of the time. Three ex-wives and counting, with law offices in Toronto, Mexico City, and Philadelphia to pay for the three exes. "One set of offices for every damn mistake," Hats will tell you. He jokes that he always marries women who are excellent housekeepers. "I marry them and then they keep the house!" he says. He loves that joke. He's built an incredibly successful law practice in criminal and environmental law. The world loves Canadians when it comes to the environment. They trust us implicitly, and with good reason, as we would never do anything that would hurt the world. Hats uses this to his advantage, but I do believe he sincerely cares about the environment. He really loves the criminal work though and is at his best when defending people and fighting on their behalf. I will admit as well that he is a good father, notwithstanding the divorces. He has a son and a daughter from his first marriage, both in college in California and both nice, smart young people. Hats is still pure character, but he's alone and busy most of the time, so Georgia and Texas will do better with RC.

Thinking about all the dogs from my life is good for my soul. Sometimes I chunk my life up into my dogs. Traditionally, people will think of their lives relative to decades or ages, or maybe elementary school, middle school, high school, university, marriage, kids, retirement, grandkids. Or maybe by their jobs and the companies they worked for. I'm sure there are other traditional ways to stratify and cascade your life.

I like to think about my life and chunk it up by the dogs in my life during that time – Pierre, Ozark, Annie, Bandit, Georgia, Texas. There's an easy fifty years right there. I just like thinking about my life in these terms. Looking at it this way is not so linear, not so predictable. Who cares what the decade was or where you worked or when you went to school. I prefer to think of it as *Those were the years that Ozark watched me make all the decisions I made. Those were the years that Annie helped us through the tough times. Those were the years that Bandit participated in our life and all the changes that happened.*

If only Ozark, Annie, and Bandit were here now. If only they could talk, what a story they would tell.

I'm looking forward to seeing Georgia and Texas. I miss them. I miss all the dogs from my life and I wish they were all here now. I would take them out to the beach and throw the ball high and far – up the beach and into the water. I would bring the hard orange balls that will go for half a mile on the hard sand. Oh, to be able to watch them all play together. To be able to see my whole life in front of me – running and playing and swimming and fetching. I would introduce them to each other and they would share stories about their time with me, the boys, and my family. They would all look up at me as if I were their hero, their one and only. They would shake, roll, jump, bark, and smile. I would be able to look at them and know all their characteristics, all their idiosyncrasies, their likes and dislikes.

It would be my whole life staring up at me and asking for one more throw. Just one more pitch of the ball. *Come on, Sam, just one more, please?* Of course I would throw the ball, and I wouldn't come in until they all quit on me. I wouldn't come in until they were all completely and utterly exhausted, which means we would never come in, because in all her years Ozark never, ever quit. Annie never quit. Bandit never quit.

I miss Ozark. I miss Annie. I miss Bandit. I miss all the dogs that are not here any longer.

I really do. I wish they were all here with me right now.

Thinking about them is really good for the soul.

Dogs just make sense.

DAY 9 — Afternoon
South Carolina

Insignificant

"HI, SAM. HOW ARE YOU?"
"Good, Doc. How are you?"
"I'm good. So are you ready to talk?"
"Sure, what would you like to talk about?"
"Well, I was thinking we could talk about your business and your work."
"Oh, OK. That's not what I was expecting, but that will work fine. Where should we start?"
"Why don't you tell me about how you got started in your business?"
"Don't you know the story? We're friends after all."
"I sort of know some parts, but I'd like to hear it from you, Sam."
"OK, Doc, so you want to talk about Iowa and tsunamis?"
"What?"
"It's an interesting tale, Doc. You sure you're up to it?"
"Try me, Sam."
"Fine, let's rewind a bit and start with university. Some of this you'll already know, but I'll go over the highlights."
"Good."

"Sophie and I both stayed in school after our undergraduate work and finished a master's degree. Mine was in psychology, and hers was in mathematics. She's a talented mathematician."

"That was the route to her becoming an actuary?"

"Yes, Doc, the ultimate sign of a gifted math student is the ability to pass all those actuarial exams. The irony is, after all that work you end up in a job that pays well but is as exciting as watching paint dry. There's an old joke that an 'actuary is somebody who didn't have the personality to be an accountant.' This is not Sophie. The fact that she's an actuary is a complete paradox in that it makes sense because of her gift with numbers, but it does not make sense relative to her personality and character. She's much more an artist than scientist. That's why I fell in love with her, and that's why I'm still in love with her."

"How did you even end up going from Canada to a university in South Carolina?"

"I applied and got accepted as an international student."

"I assumed that, Sam. Work with me here. Why did you apply to a school outside of Canada? South Carolina is a long way from home."

"I needed a change of scenery. My last year of high school was somewhat stressful. I made a very last-minute decision in late August and ended up going to South Carolina in September for the beginning of my first semester. I had to jump through some hoops, and it sure wasn't cheap, but I got it all figured out."

"Your last year of high school was stressful?"

"Yes."

"You want to tell me about that?"

"Not really."

"OK, then how did you end up in psychology? What happened to being a poet?"

"I started off in English with a psychology minor. I was very focused on my poetry but then realized poets don't exactly live with the middle class. Somewhere along the way I decided to do poetry as a hobby and psychology for a living. The plan worked pretty well."

"Are you still writing poetry?"

"Not as much as I once did. I'm still writing a little with my friend, Ray."

"Great. Did you enjoy practicing psychology when you had your practice?"

"I did and I didn't."

"How so, Sam?"

"You should know, Doc. You listen to people's problems all day, and then you go home and have to deal with your own life which, by the way, can have all of the same challenges as the people you are trying to help. It's tough. Sure it's rewarding, but it's still tough. I'm not saying it's like that for everybody. I know a lot of psychologists who seem to balance it well. I'm just saying that for me it was tough."

"But you are great at what you do, Sam!"

"Yes, I work hard, and I pour myself into my work in order to give my customers value for their time and money. I wouldn't be able to do it any other way. When I do something, I have to do it well. Yes, it can be exhausting, but I do it that way because my work is not about me, it's about the customer. It's about the person who is asking for help. My customers can't know that I'm struggling as well because if they did they'd worry about me, and if they're worried about me, they can't work on their own challenges."

"Do you think your customers expect you to be perfect?"

"Maybe, I'm not sure. I suspect not. Maybe I expect myself to be perfect."

"Maybe you do, Sam. So what does this have to do with Iowa and tsunamis?

"Great question, Doc, and we're leading up to that. So, Sophie and I both graduated in 1989. We stayed in South Carolina, and Sophie got a job with an insurance company and started completing her exams for the actuarial certification. I started working with a firm doing Employee Assistance Program counseling. The world knows that as EAP. I was doing mostly marriage and addiction counseling – love and drugs. I was seemingly pretty good at it, but for some reason the company I was working for closed up shop in our town. So I hung a shingle and started practicing on my own, and I was able to pick up a few corporate EAP contracts that had been serviced by my old company. When you consider it was a new practice, it all went very smoothly, and I had close to a full schedule in no time. Everything was humming as it should – life was good, two professionals and some money coming in. So we bought a house and we started working on having a child. That proved a challenge, but eventually we succeeded, and George was born in April of 2000. George is everything to us, so life was complete. Then the attack on the Twin Towers happened, and we made it through the emotional roller coaster that many people experienced. My practice had a huge surge in demand as people needed to talk about the attacks. I had patients who had family members die, and I had patients who simply could not get over the event even though they had no personal loss. It's a unique thing when something that severe happens, and so we carried on – the world now different, but the same in many respects. We were both working hard and raising George. We were doing well in every respect. Then in 2004 a couple of things happened."

"What happened, Sam?"

"The first thing is Iowa. I went out to Iowa for an educational conference. It had been a good conference, and I was on my way home. I was sitting in the airport waiting for my flight to Atlanta that would eventually lead to my flight home. Eastern Iowa Regional is a small airport, and once you are through security there's only one small café in the terminal. I bought a beer and sat down at one of four tables. I was alone in the café. The whole place was no bigger than a good-size kitchen, and I took out my cell phone to check for messages. Cell phones were still pretty new, but I had had one for a few years at this point. They were still novel and not quite the nuisance they are today. So I checked my voice mails and decided to return a few calls while waiting for my flight. I was totally in my own world with my back to the other table, and I didn't even notice that a man had walked in and sat at the table behind me. I guess I was too busy chatting with people on my phone, so I finished one call and I was about to dial another when I heard this voice from the table behind me.

'Do you hear me reading my newspaper out loud?' the voice said.

"I was surprised to hear a voice, as I thought I was alone in the café. I turned around and just smiled at the gentleman sitting at the table behind me. He was facing my back.

"He raised his voice a notch, 'Hey, Pal, do you hear me reading my newspaper out loud?'

"I realized he was talking to me, but I could not decipher the context. He was sitting at the table with a newspaper out; he was a little older than me, not in great shape, overweight actually, and his clothes looked one size bigger than he was. He had a scowl on his face. My first impression was 'here's a guy who is not healthy or happy, or not happy because he's not healthy.' Either way, it finally dawned on me that he had an issue with my talking on my cell phone in the public space where he was trying to read his newspaper. In other words, it became clear to me he wanted to create a situation. So I tried to think up a response to his question. I was neither clever nor quick in my response.

"All I came up with was, 'Really?' The 'Really' was just to convey that I finally realized what he was saying and that I was completely surprised by his obvious antagonistic approach. A good 'Really?' can do all that. Then it got better. He started in on me, and he was really mad.

"'First day with the new phone?' he said in a very mean-spirited tone.

"'Ya, actually just got it at the gift shop,' I said back sarcastically, immediately pissed off at myself for such a weak comeback. Not only was it not remotely clever, the airport didn't even have a gift shop. Then he verbally came at me again.

"'So, what are you expecting me to think? You want me to think you're some big business man? Doing important million-dollar deals while the rest of us sit here in awe over you? You think you're teaching us all about life and success while we listen to your one-sided conversations?'

"I was silent. I was stunned, as this type of confrontation was new to me, and all I came up with again was, 'Really?'

"Then he went into his personal Manhattan Project and he came out with the final assault – the big boy bomb. He stared directly in my eyes as if he were some Vegas trickster, and he said, 'You must be so insignificant!'"

"Really, Sam, he called you insignificant? For talking on a cell phone?"

"Yes, Doc, and that was my reaction as well. Obviously, it was more than a cell phone call though."

"So what did you do?"

"Well, first of all, I couldn't believe what I had just heard. This guy wanted to cut me down to the core, wanted me destroyed emotionally, and somewhere in his own travels, he picked up some psychology along the way. His tactics had one intention, which was to win this perceived altercation at all cost. My first instinct was to be completely childish and make fun of his weight. I could have accomplished that by saying, 'Yes, in fact I am insignificant, but you my friend, are very significant.' I decided against this approach and then wondered what my buddy Hats would do. This led to the possibility of my just saying, 'I tell ya what, you stupid fuck, why don't we just take this outside?' At the time, I was still strong and confident in my abilities to handle myself, and I was reasonably riled up. Then it struck me that fighting in an airport post-911 is probably not a brilliant idea. Then I thought about just getting up and walking out to the seats in front of my departure gate. All these ideas were going through my head at lightning speed while he was just staring at me. I began getting mad. I was mad at him for starting this whole thing, and I was mad at myself for several reasons. The first was that I should have seen him walk into the café.

Why was I so oblivious to the world around me? The second reason was I could not conjure up a really good comeback. It's as if he had thrown a dagger that can only fly one way. He was out-clevering me. Last, I was upset that what he had said actually did upset me. Was I, in fact, insignificant? What does it even mean to be insignificant...or to be significant for that matter?"

"Good lord, Sam. This is an amazing story. So what did you finally decide?"

"I finally realized that I'm a professional. So I got my heart rate calmed down and I asked him very calmly, 'Why did you just say that?'

"'What?' he replied, still looking for the hostility to escalate.

"'Why did you call me insignificant?'

"'Because I hate you.'

"'You hate me? You don't even know me.'

"'I know everything I need to,' he said back. 'I can read you like a cheap book.'

"'Do you know that I didn't even realize you were in the café while I was talking on my phone?' I said to him.

"'What does that have to do with anything?'

"'It has a lot to do with it,' I said. 'First of all, I'm a very considerate person, and had I seen you walk in I would have ended my phone conversation, or at a minimum if you had asked me politely I would have been embarrassed for talking so loud and would have apologized and ended my calls. You see, you don't know anything about me, and frankly, a person talking on a phone should not warrant your approach to the situation. In fact, I'm sitting here wondering what you are so angry at.'

"'You,' he said back.

"'Me?' I replied. 'OK, I can accept that, and I hope you can accept my apology. I'm very sorry for disturbing your reading.'"

"Wow, Sam, what happened next?"

"What happened, Doc? He started to cry like a baby. He started sobbing and asked me for forgiveness. I moved my chair over to his table and he opened up his whole life to me – family, work, friends, health, and finances. In his mind, his life was a complete mess."

"Was it?"

"Who knows, Doc? That stuff is all relative isn't it? A mess for one person is a normal situation for another. Obviously for him, it was not great. So we talked for forty-five minutes until our flights left for different cities. I gave him my business card, and two months later, I got an email telling me I had changed his life – for the better of course!"

"Wow, Sam, great story, but what does this have to do with your leaving your practice and starting your own business?"

"I'm getting to that, Doc. So, I get home and I tell Sophie and a few friends and professional colleagues the story. They all love it. Sophie loves it. George listens and smiles but is too young to really understand. Of course my old poet and storytelling skills surface, and the story becomes a larger tale, a tale that is interesting from many perspectives – the setup, the antagonism, the anger, the verbal sparring, and then the enlightenment at the end. A hurting soul converted. A happy ending. It's a story about disarming a person and listening to his fears to understand what's driving his anger. It's about not deciding on basic instincts of fight or flight, but rather about recognizing that there are more than these two options. It's more about stay and play, it's about asking good questions to seek a deep understanding about how somebody feels, to uncover the mental models and beliefs that are impacting someone's day-to-day emotions, and doing all of this without judgment and without opinion on what the person should do next. I was curious and interested in why he hated me when he didn't even know me. I recognize the irony that now I'm filled with my own hatred. I spend my days hating things I've never experienced and people I've never met! Yet that day, I helped this man."

"So what happened next, Sam?"

"Some professional colleagues asked me to tell the story for some small groups, then some small public events. I think you came and listened to the story once."

"Yes I did. I really enjoyed it."

"It became larger than life. I wrote it down on paper in story format, and it got some great responses. It was published in a few journals, then in a couple of mainstream magazines. I was asked to speak and tell my story in other cities. I added some new stories and a little pop psychology, and in time I was being paid to speak. People really liked it. I liked it. I enjoyed the speaking, and I was writing more as well. I was helping people in ways and in scale that I could never do in my private practice. The economics looked attractive as well, as a practice is constrained by the number of hours you can work in a week. I started getting more and more invites, and eventually I had to make a decision about whether I would do the writing and speaking full time or whether I would stay in private practice."

"And you decided to leave your practice?"

"Not quite. First the tsunami needed to happen."

"Ahhh, the tsunami. I was wondering how that fit in."

"I figured you might be wondering about that, Doc. I'm a little tired though. I tell you what, Doc. I'll write down some thoughts and share them with you that way. Good?"

"Sure, Sam."

"Thanks, Doc."

DAY 9 — Evening
South Carolina

Entropy

I WASN'T SURE I NEEDED to take Doc through the story of the tsunami as I don't see how it will add value to my therapy or recovery. There's no connection in my mind. I'll write it down and let her read it. I do remember it as if it were yesterday.

On December 26, 2004, there was an earthquake under the sea in the Indian Ocean. The epicenter was off the west coast of Sumatra, Indonesia, and the earthquake caused a series of devastating tsunamis along the coasts of many countries bordering the Indian Ocean. Nobody knows the true number of dead, but it is estimated that over three hundred thousand people died in no less than fourteen different countries. Some of the waves were over thirty meters high when they hit land. The Talking Cable Heads all agree it was one of the deadliest natural disasters in recorded history. Indonesia was the hardest hit, while other countries such as Sri Lanka, India, and Thailand also suffered devastating impacts. In a word, it was brutal.

At home, it hit Sophie and me very hard. We did not personally know anybody who died in the wake of the massive waves, but it was the Christmas holidays, and therefore, we were home and had time to

123

become glued to the television. Sophie could not seem to take her eyes off the destruction. The images of children were, of course, the worst, and Sophie was calling the Red Cross with a new donation every two hours. Her heart rules her emotions and therefore her life. I wasn't too far behind her though. It's hard to watch the injustice of poor countries with poor people seemingly being the ones that always get it the worst. Perhaps this is not factual, but it certainly feels that way if all you do is watch bad news on television. The poorer places in the world always seem to get hit harder and more often. I envy those who don't watch. Ignorance can, in fact, be bliss.

Make no mistake though, we were watching, and Sophie poured her energy into helping. Local outposts of all kinds in all states began gathering everything and anything to send to the impacted countries. This is America at its best. Even though the world likes to paint the USA as an overbearing world power, the truth remains that the country does far more than its share when disaster strikes. I'm always amazed how it can be the most hated country on the planet and the most popular country to immigrate to, all at the same time. The irony is that the person who hates the USA is often the same person who is trying to immigrate there. Hate and dreams make for strange and often friendly bedfellows.

While Sophie externalized her grief and put her energies to good use, I did the opposite. I internalized the situation across the world and used it to work on some unanswered questions I was dealing with. The first question I needed to answer was whether to leave my practice and be a prospector in the self-help and motivational speaking industry. The second question I was dealing with was not so practical. I was trying to make some determination relative to my spiritual belief system. What is it that I believe from a spiritual point of view? All the devastation and death of the tsunami truly affected us, and I simply could not comprehend how something like this could happen in a world created by a supposedly loving God.

I tried to write some poetry, but it did not flow. Even though there was devastation beyond measure, I could not connect to my poetic side. Normally a good tragedy would lead to the words bursting out of my mind and onto paper. I suspect in hindsight this means I was not connecting with my spiritual side. I believe the creative and spiritual sides of the brain sit alongside each other, if indeed they are not the same thing. Yet I was not able to take the devastation of the storm and put it into words as I had lost any sense of my own spirituality. I've always believed my spirituality rested in watching the world and seeing what others don't see. To watch a sunset and sunrise and be able to articulate their beauty and how they affect the human experience – I believe that poetry is spirituality.

Sophie believes the entire universe is one mysterious power and that we live in a state of some pre-planned and thoughtful chaos. That's a mathematician for you – pre-planned but chaotic at the same time. *Pre-Destined Entropy* is what she calls it. Her theory is illogical, contradictive, and perfect all at the same time. Sophie will tell you that life is pre-destined, so don't worry about anything because you are not in control. However, her theory part two is that the entire Earth and all its processes and functions are driven by the laws of entropy. So don't worry, everything is supposed to fall apart. Smile, don't worry; tomorrow will be worse! Pre-Destined Entropy. I love that. You have no control, and it's a certainty that it's all going to fall apart and turn to shit! It's perfect. It's pure Sophie.

It's interesting how upset Sophie gets when her theories appear to be true. For somebody who believes everything is destined to fall apart, she gets very intense when, in fact, everything does fall apart. The news on the tsunami was not helping her or me. On one segment the Talking Cable Heads were interviewing a person who had just lost his entire family in the wave. It was a man around thirty-five years old who had lost his wife and five children. He had a Bible in his hands. He held it up and said, "Only by the grace of God was I saved!"

Saved? By the grace of God? Really? Isn't it God who created the heavens and the Earth? Did God not begin time knowing exactly how the story would end? Did God not design the timetable knowing the tsunami would happen exactly where and when it happened? Does that not mean that ultimately God is responsible for the tsunami? So you are thanking Him for killing your family? Come on! Where does the buck stop, brother? What kind of father would do that to his children? As far as I can tell, God is either nonexistent or completely and utterly incompetent to the point of criminal mismanagement! Regardless, there is one thing for sure, buddy, and that is His absence. God simply does not show up. He is an absent father. And that's the beginning and the end of the story.

I knew I was heading into areas and thoughts that would lead nowhere and in the end prove unhelpful. I'm no religious scholar so who am I to question? Ignorance is bliss. I know many people of deep faith, and I actually envy their faith. I envy their outward happiness with life in general. It's obvious and contagious, and I like being around it, but I'm full of questions as I'm Socratic in my ways, and I have good reason to question. Yet my good questions are passed off as trivial by my friends of deep faith. Once you have faith, all paradoxical idiosyncrasies of God are no longer a problem. They no longer require rational explanation. As soon as a story or concept or belief does not make sense from an earthly point of view, we can always default to "just have faith." At times the whole racket seems like a house of cards. It's a racket, and I guess I'm staying out of it. But as I said, I'm no biblical scholar even though I've spent a considerable amount of time reading the good book. Don't worry; I know I'm going to offend some people if I voice my opinion too loudly. Some topics are simply off limits, and the people with self-interests in these topics are very happy about this fact.

Here's a neat fact for you though. More atrocities have been committed in the name of God than any other contributing cause, perhaps maybe even more than any other root cause, and this includes greed, power, money, politics, hatred, and sex. Sure, perhaps the atrocities were actually being committed for greed, power, money, politics, hatred, or sex, but the leaders driving the atrocities no doubt convinced the masses, and hence the soldiers, that it was all in the name of their God. It really makes no difference what the propaganda was masking, as the result is millions of people being killed by millions of other people in the name of their God. How do we reconcile this one simple fact of human history? It's still going on today. But don't worry; just forgive and forget. Just have faith and know that your God is the right God to be cheering for.

Faith is everything. Faith – the antidote and krypton to fear. It would be interesting to see what would happen to all the world's religions if you eliminated the emotion of fear from our list of possible human emotions. In fact, I wonder what would happen to the world's religions if we just eliminated one specific fear. The fear of death and what comes next. We could run an experiment. We could announce some news using the Talking Cable Heads: *"Good news, folks. We have determined that after we die, we all go to a great place – a really great place. And we all get in regardless of how we lived our life on Earth. Regardless of what you believed or what you did! There are no gates. No interviews. No reading of the record. In other words folks, all will be fine no matter what!"*

I wonder what the turnout at local churches would be on that subsequent Sunday. I wonder how busy our police would be. I once read that law and order would completely collapse if only three percent of the population went renegade. That would be quite the experience. Entropy for sure. The question is whether this is the pre-plan for the future.

Please don't be upset with me. I'm not talking about these things because I'm a bad person. I actually do want to feel a spirit in my life. I believe that on the great wheel of life spirituality is as important as all other dynamics of a balanced life, and I know what it feels like because I felt it once. I truly believe I felt the powerful feeling of true spirituality.

When we were ten years old, Ray and his family took us to a revival. His father loaded us up in their camper, the kind that sits in the bed of a pickup truck. Ray's mother and father sat up front in the single cab of the truck while Ray, RC, Hats, Ray's younger sister Rose, and I rode in the camper. You wouldn't ride in a camper these days, but back then it was a given as we wouldn't have been able to all fit otherwise. Back then safety decisions weren't made based on the assumption of having an accident. We're more proactive these days. Today, we always assume the worst will happen. Today we plan for the entropy even though, according to Sophie, it's preplanned. I know. It's complicated.

The camper was a fantastic place to ride. We would perch up top on the sleeping bunk that hangs over the roof of the pickup truck, inventing game upon game. Most games had us shooting all the other cars that passed us on the highway. Even Rose would join in. She had no choice as she was captive for ten hours with her brother and her brother's friends. Rose was the quintessential little sister. She was eight at the time. Ray and Rose are very close. RC, Hats, and I all cherish Rose, and we all thought of her as our little sister. Rose is a beautiful young lady in all respects, and she reminds me of Ray in so many ways. It's hard to think about one of them without thinking about the other. Sophie says they are mutually inclusive.

We were out for ten days on this particular summer trip. When you live in the north your summer trips are important as northerners need a break from the winter blues. Consequently, families go to great effort to make sure everybody gets out and sees the beauty of the sun, the water, and the country as Canada's geography is a treasure to be seen and held. Ray's family invited us on their summer trip that year as it was very common to travel with other families, and parents would take turns to ensure everybody had a chance to see the country. Canada is the second largest country in the world from a land mass point of view, second only to Russia, but ahead of the United States, which is third. From the Pacific coast in British Columbia to the Atlantic coast in Newfoundland, there is a lot to see and experience, and it takes a village to ensure we see as much as we can.

Our particular destination that summer was a Pentecostal Christian revival in the heart of the Canadian Rocky Mountains in the province of Alberta. The location was spectacular. I can't stress this enough. It was absolutely spectacular. Whoever created the earth and the heavens spent a lot of time in this location. The sky, mountains, trees, air, and lakes there have no rival in the entire stratosphere. I'm very proud to live in the USA, but believe me when I tell you the Canadian Rockies are breathtakingly spectacular from a global perspective. Take all this physical beauty and throw in the spirit of God and you have the makings for a memorable summer vacation.

I witnessed, felt, and was consumed with the spirit of God that week. It was a week like no other. I watched people have demons exorcized from their souls by spitting the devil out onto the wood floor of the makeshift church in the wilderness. I watched people hold their arms up into the air pointed to the heavens on a starry mountain night filled with northern lights, all to receive the power of the Holy Ghost. I watched families pray, walk, swim, fish, and hike together. If you looked carefully, you could literally see a physical aura around their bodies as the spirit joined them, and us, in our activities.

The pinnacle of my week was a conversation I had with a man of possibly thirty years of age. He had travelled over two thousand kilometers from Ottawa to be part of the gathering. He told me that he was a reformed drug dealer from the streets of the nation's capital. God had taken him from that life, and now he was saved, and he knew the path forward. My memory of that interaction is a snapshot of twenty seconds. I can't remember his face, but to this day I still remember his feeling of peace. He was at peace. He was telling me his story, talking to me, a ten-year-old boy, as if I were his peer. He was tranquil, and his peace and tranquility rubbed off on me. I remember that feeling, and I believe to this day that was the feeling of God, the feeling of a Great Spirit. It didn't stay with me though. I don't have it today, and now I have many doubts. But I am not doubtful that some higher power exists, and that the power is good. To feel the spirit is good. I know because I experienced it.

I started to yearn for these feelings again while watching the devastation caused by the tsunami. I was looking for an awakening. I wanted and needed a sign of some sort. I needed help to make big life decisions.

Sophie was on her mission. She was working on local tsunami relief efforts while I was internalizing these events to help me decide the next stage of my professional life. I was torn with the choices in front of me. We had a good thing going; I knew that. And we could have easily lived out our days and ridden into the sunset together. But something was telling me I needed more than that. It was too predictable, too preplanned. I wanted less preplanning and more entropy, more chaos. I wanted to be part of more chaos in this absolutely chaotic world, so I made my decision. I didn't even discuss it with Sophie, and that was a mistake.

Did the experience in Iowa affect my decision? Absolutely! It taught me that I can help people and that I can add value and make the world a better place.

Did the tsunami affect my decision? Absolutely, but maybe not in the way I was hoping.

I wanted help to make a life decision. I needed support. I wanted God's help, the help of a father. I wanted to take all the death and destruction on the television and see the light from the darkness! I wanted to find my own spirituality knowing there was somebody actually in control who was looking down and trying to help. In the end though, I really only learned one lesson from the tragedy in the Indian Ocean.

Life is short and getting much shorter. Live now while you can. There is no God.

The next day, I closed up my practice and started up my new business.

Canada

Spring 1982

Strategy Session

EVERYTHING CALMED DOWN after the high school election, and summer break was on its way. Spring and summer in the north are cherished, and spring in particular is embraced by all people and creatures that choose to live in the far north. To this day, I can close my eyes and imagine the smells and feel of snow melting and the sun warming up the Earth. Going from boots to running shoes, from heavy winter jackets to jean jackets, getting your bicycle out and riding on the streets that are now bare of snow and ice, and being able to skid off the street and ram into a snow bank that is melting fast but still sits five feet high. The change of seasons in the north is an evolution and not a revolution, and it doesn't happen in a day or week. In the north it's like you live through eight seasons – the four seasons as we know them, but also the four transitional periods that last close to a month in themselves. I miss that.

So with the spring comes planning for summer. For the Beaver Brothers, this also meant summer jobs. "We need to make some fucking money, man," Hats would tell us as we were sitting in the Lodge wondering what we would do when school ended. Both Hats and I looked to RC and Ray for ideas.

When RC puts his mind to something, it will produce something in some practical shape or form. When Ray puts his mind to something, it will produce some form nobody ever intended to shape. They are both idea people; they both push forward, but in very different ways.

Hats and I looked at RC and Ray. RC and Ray looked at each other and then began to lay out our plan for the summer. To this day, I'm convinced they had already talked about the plan prior to our first strategic planning session in the Lodge that day. I'm completely convinced of it, although they won't admit anything.

Ray took a pack of torpedoes apart and used the white cardboard from the cigarette box as a piece of paper. He found a pen that was lying around and called us to order. It was our first strategic planning session, and it was very, very exciting.

"All present?" he asked us in a very formal voice, really saying, *I'm about to act like the CEO of Bay Street.*

"Yes," RC said back, clearly positioning himself as Ray's second in command.

"Roll call, please," Ray said to RC, confirming his promotion.

"RC, Ray, Hats, Sam, and Ozark – all accounted for," RC pronounced.

Ray then gave RC a nod, and in doing so, handed him the floor. Ray was already showing excellent delegation skills, a sign of true leadership.

"OK," RC said, "this is what we're going to do. We're going to have a two-pronged strategy for this summer to meet our professional and financial needs."

Ray was smiling at RC and loving every minute of it. I looked at Hats, and Hats simply stared at me in disbelief, and I gave him a look that suggested I thought RC was doing well. I thought he might actually remain silent long enough to hear RC out, but Hats just can't help himself.

"What the fuck are you talking about, RC?" Hats shouted out. "Who do you think you are, fucking Howard Hughes? You wouldn't know a two-pronged strategy if the two prongs were sticking up your ass, you dumb shit! Sam, help me out here. Fuck that, you're as dumb as these other two. Ozark, help me out here!"

I love listening to Hats. He just tells it like it is. The world needs more people like Hats. RC shoved Hats in the chest and continued talking.

"The two-pronged strategy is," RC laid out for us with a voice of authority, "one, we are going to start a business, and two, we are going to get some paid gigs for the band."

Hats just sat there and stared at RC. "Oh fuck!" Hats said. "You finally fucking lost it. The time is here. Let's haul RC to the nuthouse, and you too, Ray, you too for being his accomplice in this." Hats then grabbed a torpedo and lit up while he kept talking. Ozark was watching Hats with full intrigue, and you could tell she had not picked an alliance yet for this particular topic.

"OK, RC," Hats went on. "I like your plan. I really do, man. It's a hell of a plan. I mean, I really like it, it's solid, firm, well thought out, visionary, yet strategic, yet also tactically available to us. Tight, buddy, really tight, as tight as a Vancouver prostitute on the first of July, man!"

I knew RC wanted to burst out laughing, but he knew he had to keep his composure. The worst thing you can do with Hats is let him get a single wedge in. Once he has a wedge in you, it's all over. Hats is the rabbit-hole expert. Hats can kick most doors wide open without effort, but RC is a big door, too big for Hats to kick down, so Hats had to get a little wedge in and then work it one inch at a time. RC knows this and works the other end better than anybody else. RC can stare at the face of death and smile a smile that would suggest he was expecting the visit. The grim reaper runs from RC.

"OK, Hats," RC said, really saying, *OK, I'll play the game with you, little brother. What's the problem?"*

"Well, RC, let's see," Hats began. "Your two-pronged strategy calls for us to, one, open up a business, and two, convince somebody to let the Beaver Brothers Band perform for actual money?"

"Correct, Hats."

"OK, good. I'm with you so far, RC. Can I ask a first question?"

"Sure."

"Question one," Hats asked. "What type of business are we going to start?"

"We don't know yet," Ray answered for RC, letting Hats know RC was not on his own. Again, showing signs of leadership.

"Brilliant," Hats replied, really saying, *Perfect. I have won round one.*

"Question two," Hats asked. "Who is going to pay us to play our music?"

"We don't know yet, but I'm thinking we can convince Vince," Ray answered for RC.

"Brilliant," Hats replied, really saying, *I think I won round two as well, but I'm not quite as confident as I was in round one.*

Hats didn't argue against the plan after he finished his interrogation. After all, neither Hats nor Ozark nor I had any alternative strategies. So with that, the strategy discussions began. We had to put some meat on the bones of the vision. By the time we finished the strategy work, we actually had a reasonably solid plan. RC and Ray led the discussions, and Hats actually allowed them to. That's how you know that Hats is interested in something. He actually participates in a non-disruptive way.

The overall plan continued along the initial two-pronged strategy.

Prong #1: The Business. We decided that we would be all things leaves, branches, and trees. This meant that we would rake leaves, clean out eavestroughs, and do basic tree trimming. The list of services lined up with both the needs of local residents and our personal skill sets and ability to deliver to the marketplace. Most importantly, though, the services would be congruent with the company name, which of course was *Beaver Brothers*. It was my job to come up with the marketing tagline. It was easy. *Beaver Brothers – No job is too dam big*. If only this had been the truth!

Prong #2: Get the Beaver Brothers Band a paid gig. We were relying more on Ray to help with this plan as he was better connected to the music scene around town. However, Ray and RC really wanted to make sure that Hats and I felt comfortable with the idea in general. We were, after all, members of the band not because of our musical talent, but rather because RC and Ray needed a drummer and bassist. RC and Ray are the true talents. I will, however, continue to take credit for writing some original lyrics.

The paid gig strategy for the Beaver Brothers Band was for Ray to go and offer our professional services to our coach and friend Vince at the Maple Tree Hotel. No longer an active hotel, the Maple Tree Hotel was the premier watering hole that had been around since the first gold miners arrived at the beginning of the twentieth century. While a stranger might say it was a complete and utter dive, which was in fact the character of the place, it also had some fame for being the spot where many Canadian musicians played prior to their becoming famous. The wooden floor was said to have been stomped on by many a rising Canadian musician, so it seemed only fitting that the Maple Tree Hotel would be a perfect spot for the Beaver Brothers Band professional debut. As Ray pointed out to us, "We only need one paid gig for us to make our goal." It seemed like the right plan, and besides, Vince was our friend.

And so with the strategy discussion complete, both Beaver Brothers the Business and the Beaver Brothers Band were ready for action. RC officially ended the meeting.

"And with those decisions made, I declare this meeting over and complete," RC said quite officially.

"Thank God," Hats replied. Ozark looked up at the four of us, tail wagging in anticipation of what adventures these decisions would bring. The next day, we got busy executing to the plan.

The Beaver Brothers Band's one paid gig proved to be much easier to set up than we had thought it would be. As planned, Ray went and talked to Vince. Ray said Vince was looking tired and very rough when he went to see him. "Vince was a little weak and nervous," Ray said after his meeting. The Maple Tree Hotel was Vince's life, but it was a tough life. Vince had inherited the hotel from his father after his father died from running the place. His father had inherited the hotel from his father after he died from running the place. The fact that Vince was born into running one of the busiest and roughest bars in town was a local joke. Vince was in his late-fifties at the time and had hard years on him. Normally by the time last call rolled around Vince had taken one shot for every one he sold or gave away, although I have to admit I don't ever recall seeing Vince intoxicated. Seeing him hung over is another story.

Ray offered Vince that we would play one night for the low price of fifty dollars for the gig. Vince told Ray that because the four of us were not eighteen and age of majority, we were not allowed in the hotel. Ray reminded Vince that on any given busy Friday night we got served in the hotel as a matter of rule, in particular if our hockey team had won that night – his hockey team. Vince tried to act surprised by this, but nobody was fooling anybody. Vince told Ray that we should be honored to play on his legendary wood floor. In fact, Vince suggested we should pay him for the privilege and the exposure. Ray was not deterred and Ray got his deal. The deal they struck was that we would play the Monday night of the Civic Day long weekend in August.

The Civic Day long weekend is normally the last weekend in July or the first weekend of August. Vince's logic, we assumed, was that there would be a small crowd left over from the long weekend, but that most party goers would be gone by Monday night. He didn't trust us as musicians the way he did as hockey players, but maybe some live music would bring in a miner or two. If we sucked, then no real harm would be done. The deal was set at fifty dollars plus twelve free bottles of OV for the band, age of majority and the fact that we were only seventeen notwithstanding. Vince did his own negotiating in the deal as well, and Ray agreed that the Beaver Brothers would clean out the eavestroughs of the Maple Tree Hotel and Vince's residence for free as opposed to the fee we would be charging other local residents.

Ray had accomplished his goal, an actual paid gig, and Ray and RC were ecstatic. I was nervous. Only Hats argued the logic of the deal and whether we were actually getting paid to play after we did the eavestroughs for free. You can imagine what he said to Ray. I won't bore you with the details, and in the end Ray did in fact get us a paid gig. It's never about the money with Ray anyway; he could care less about the money. So while Hats was going on about Vince screwing us, Ray interrupted him to remind us that we only had eight weeks to prepare for our first live show.

On the business front, Beaver Brothers Leaf Maintenance Company was coming into full swing and all major hurdles were overcome. First, we created five hundred copies of a one-page flyer to advertise our services. Hats actually has some artistic skills, and we utilized those to draw a picture of a beaver standing upright with a rake in his hand. During the process, we named the Beaver *Boomer*. Picture Boomer the Beaver on the middle of the page and above Boomer's head it says: *Ray–RC–Hats–Sam and Ozark are the Beaver Brothers.* Below Boomer's feet it says: *No job is too dam big.* We strategically placed the flyers around town and in the mailboxes of houses where we believed the owners had both money to spend and a leaf problem. This really meant understanding who had money and who would be willing to spend that money on their leaf problem, because everybody in our town had a leaf problem. It's part of living in the north.

After we dealt with the marketing plan, we focused our attention on operations. What would we need to execute the services we were marketing? Vision was phase one, strategy was phase two, and actual execution was phase three. Phase three is very important as phase three is where you answer the question, *OK, so how is this actually going to work?*

We all went back to our houses and rummaged through our garages for what we thought we needed or for stuff we might be able to find a purpose for. When we reassembled at my place, we put all our assets in the middle of the driveway. RC took inventory of our assets to create our first balance sheet. Ozark looked on in awe as RC yelled out the particular asset and Ray wrote the item down on our new clipboard.

1. One twenty-foot ladder when extended
2. Three garden rakes
3. Six boxes of *Big Green Garbage Bags*
4. One electric chainsaw
5. One 50-foot extension cord, presumably for the chainsaw
6. One 50-foot garden hose with power spray head
7. One clipboard (in use) and multiple pens (for doing estimates)
8. One 1961 Volkswagen Type 2 Micro Bus with roof racks
9. Two used left-handed hockey sticks, good at this point only for road hockey
10. Two used right-handed hockey sticks, good at this point only for road hockey

I'm sure you will take notice of the last three items on the list. There is no doubt that the Volkswagen van was a major score and pivotal to the success of the company. The van is, and was, a classic. RC still has it at his house and he takes great pride in it. He has the skills to keep it in great classical shape. Even in 1982 it was on its way to becoming a classic. It had belonged to the Soup Man. The story I was told is that he bought it from an American Vietnam draft dodger who had arrived in town sometime in the late sixties. The guy needed money to stake a gold mine claim outside of town, and the Soup Man helped him out. I have no idea whether this is true, but it's a great tale, and I hope it's the way it went down. I will continue to tell the story as truth. Regardless, Beaver Brothers and the van had a few things going for us. The first was that the van was in good shape as it had been stored in our garage since 1969. The second is my mother hated the van because it had been stored in the garage since 1969. The van itself was being stored, and it was also being used to store other stuff. The third thing going for us was that my brother and sister could have cared less about the van. It was a classic case of opportunity meeting preparation and necessity. My mother gladly offered the van to us under the condition that she would never again see it in her garage or driveway. She even went as far as to license and insure it for us so we would be legal. It was a classic case of new business startup seed money. She was our first supporter and investor! We took the deal. We had to clean the van out, get a new battery, and change the oil and lubes and all other fluids, but it ran great. We took it to an outdoor car wash bay and literally unleashed the pressure sprayer inside the van. We sanitized the whole thing. What a score.

Hats offered up the hockey sticks as a burst of entrepreneurial ingenuity. He grabbed them from the corner of his garage where we kept our old game sticks that are now being used for road hockey sticks. Two lefts and two rights meant one stick each.

"The perfect fucking tool for cleaning eavestroughs, boys!" Hats yelled as he threw the sticks down in the middle of all our other implements for all things leaf management.

"What?" RC said, really saying, *Hats, have you finally lost it for good?*

"Think about it," Hats replied. "The blade of a hockey stick is exactly like the contour of the inside of an eavestroughs gutter. From the roof or from the ladder, we use the hockey sticks to scoop up the leaves. No bending over on the roof, no leaning off the ladder. It's the perfect tool for the Beaver Brothers! Safety first, lads! And we won't call it a hockey stick. For this purpose, we'll call it a *Mik-Maq*. Gotta give credit where credit is due, right? And the Nova Scotia Mik-Maq First Nations Band invented the hockey stick after all! Am I right, or am I right?"

We all looked at Hats in silence. Our brains were working overtime while trying to visualize what he had explained. I was the first to talk.

"He may be right!" I said, really saying, *Good Lord in heaven, he may be right!*

"I think so too," Ray said with a tone of his own disbelief.

"I'm in," RC said.

"Fucking right, you're in!" Hats said, really saying, *Are you suggesting you doubted the idea?*

He was right, and with that last stroke of genius, we were ready for business. All we had to do now was finish off a couple of weeks of school and then get Beaver Brothers working, rocking and rolling.

It was the beginning of a great summer.

DAY 10 — Morning

South Carolina

Searching

TODAY STARTED OUT with unfortunate potential of being a Red day. I was feeling angry when I woke up this morning, but I'm getting smarter, and I was able to turn the day into a Yellow day – anxiety but no anger. I accomplished this by doing three things. The first and most obvious to me now is that I did not turn on the Talking Cable Heads. No news is good news I guess. The second thing I did was move my chat with Doc to later in the day. Morning chats don't seem to work, and I'm figuring out that timing is everything.

The third and smartest move I made was I reached out to Ray. This helped me immensely. I talked to him for over an hour while on the beach, and I was able to ground myself and keep my mind from racing. Ray is a good listener, and when we talk I do not change topics in rapid fashion the way I do when I'm talking to myself. This allows me to focus and not feel as if I need to solve all the world's problems in one conversation. This is a fundamental issue with people today. We don't have patience or attention spans to take a deep breath and carry on a pleasant conversation. Small talk is a thing of the past, and I don't know what the cause for this sad situation is. Perhaps it's the role of technology in our lives today, or maybe it's from listening to the overwhelming sound bites of the Talking Cable Heads. The Heads couldn't keep a thought on one track if their lives depended on it. I don't know, maybe it's just not a priority for people. Who ever said people need to be good conversationalists anyway? Regardless, Ray doesn't subscribe to the new world, and he is a good listener when I need him. He did not fail me today.

I talk to Ray as often as I can, and our conversations have become my form of spirituality. I normally chill down a notch after talking with him. Very rarely will the conversations take me towards feeling Red. Years ago, I allowed Ray to get me angry, but that doesn't happen much these days. Time has allowed me to think about and better understand his situation and his decisions. As a psychologist, it was my job never to tell anyone my opinion on how to live life. The role of the therapist is to ask questions and use inquiry skills to let the patient *snap out of it* and realize what he needs to act upon to improve his particular situation. It's the proverbial *How do you feel about that?* It's interesting, though, how we don't take this approach in our own personal lives. Why is it that people wake up in the morning and think their job is to walk around all day telling other people what to do? *Really, friend?* And what experience and facts have given you the confidence that you know what is best for me? Have you walked a single step in my shoes?

The irony is that often the advice we get is bang-on accurate. This really pisses me off. At some level all people are life consultants. We borrow each other's watches to tell each other what time it is, because we can't seem to tell time by looking at our own watch. It's the power of having a fresh set of eyes to look at an external situation. Too bad we can't be as focused on our own behaviors as we are on other people's. Seriously, what if we simply worked on improving our own situation instead of telling others around us how to fix their sorry-ass predicament?

Ray never tells me what to do. He only listens and leaves it up to me to think, to calculate, and to sort out what I need to do. I wasn't always that way with Ray. There was a time when I did tell him what I thought he should be doing with his life. He didn't listen to me at all. Interestingly though, he never stopped talking to me, never tried to avoid conversation about what he was doing in life. In fact, he would even encourage it at times. "And what does Sam the Great Prospector think I should do now?" he used to say to me and then laugh out loud as I told him how he should go to university and study music or make a record with his original songs (many of which I wrote lyrics for, by the way). I had at least twenty ideas for Ray and what he should do with his life. In many ways, I have always envied Ray. He was given artistic gifts that very few people have, and he was also blessed with an outlook on life that is unique. Some people just march to a different drumbeat, some receive stimulus and get their energy in different ways, some just don't need to live life based on a roadmap that society has drawn up for the masses. Ray is one of those people. That's not to say that I envy everything about Ray and his life. He's had a tough go and has been on the front end of tragedy. I've tried my best to talk to him about these events. He'll listen but never really take heed of the points I'm making. Ray isn't interested in learning from what other people have experienced or lived through. It just isn't important to him. "Every life and response to that life is unique, Sam," would be his response when I tried to draw parallels between his personal story and the narratives of others.

These days I'm not trying to tell Ray how to run his life. He charted his course and the big decisions have been made. I'm on the receiving end of advice these days anyway, and it will be a while, if ever, before I start giving advice. Ray is helping. When we talk, I just lay it all out there and ask him, "What would you do, Ray?" When he finally talks to me, it's normally questions that are so simple I just sit back in my chair in amazement on how he can take a landscape of dark pain and repaint it in such a way as to turn the picture into a scene of sunshine and light – the sun's rays.

Today I talked about Sophie and George. I've realized that losing them is probably the main reason I'm not coping well. There are a few other things I need to deal with for sure, but I'm trying to limit my range of issues at hand. I just don't understand how the circumstances of life resulted in their leaving me. It just does not make sense; it's not congruent with the way our path was supposed to play out. I can't help but wonder what Sophie was thinking the moment she left me. If only I could talk to her and ask her, if only I could see George and give him a hug and tell him how much I love him, to tell him how much we wanted him, and to tell him how much I miss him.

When I asked Ray what he thought, he told me that events are what they are, and life is what it is. He told me I could talk to Sophie when I release my anger. The trick, he said, is to take the good and filter out the bad. Take the good and cherish it in the moment, to pay attention to the moment, and if that doesn't work, he said, sit down and write. People should do what they do. *Do what you do, Sam. Eat tree, Beaver!*

I could probably heed Ray's comments if today were a Green day. I would try to live in the moment and appreciate what I have, but today is not a Green day, so I'll default to his default and I'll try to write. We finished up our talk, and I told him I would write some lyrics that I hope we might put to music someday. When I wrote the lyrics, I envisioned a nice acoustic rhythm to the song.

SEARCHING

I went searching for an answer
I went searching on the town
I went searching for an answer
But there's no answer to be found
Not sure that I can carry
This heavy load upon my mind
Not sure that I can carry on
For something I may never find

I just gotta feel some sunshine
Before this day is through
I gotta feel the feel of warmth
While I'm here thinkin' of you

Some days I wish I could just
Fall inside the sky
Some days I wish I could just
Find a reason why
To stop me from this fearing
This curse upon my soul
To stop me from this fearing
That stops me heading down the road

I just gotta feel some sunshine
Before this day is through
I gotta feel the feel of warmth
While I'm here thinkin' of you

Where did it all go so wrong
Where did we lose our way
Where did it all go so wrong
Why didn't you want to stay
I'm not saying it was perfect
I know there are things I can do
I'm not saying it was perfect
Why am I here missing you

DAY 10 — Afternoon
South Carolina

Gold

"I READ YOUR NOTES on how the tsunami played a part in your decision to start your own business, Sam."

"Great, Doc. What did you think?"

"I thought it was interesting that you've experienced the essence of God, but in the end you decided that there is no God."

"That's what you got out of the narrative, Doc?"

"Yes."

"Do you believe in God, Doc?"

"Of course, Sam. I grew up in the south."

"I know you're half joking, Doc, but there is an element of truth in what you're saying. Are you saying that you believe in God simply because you grew up believing in God?"

"I would need to think about that question, Sam."

"Fine, you think about it. In the meantime, what should we talk about?"

"That was a big decision. To leave your practice and start a business."

"Why do you say that, Doc?"

"Well, you had a lot to lose. It was high risk."

"I never thought of it that way, Doc. What's your definition of risk?"

"I don't know, Sam. I guess the chance of losing something you already have, or losing more than you can afford to lose?"

"You mean my practice and whatever money I had, or do you mean other things?"

"Well, I'm not sure."

"I didn't have any more to lose than anybody else who makes a decision to change jobs."

"But to start a new business, that's high risk, is it not?"

"This is the most misunderstood element of business, Doc. Everybody thinks you have a lot to lose when you start a new business. This is completely incorrect. At the beginning, you don't have anything, so you have nothing to lose. The worst case scenario is your idea doesn't work and you lose a little money and a little time and then you go get a new job! And getting a new job is easy for any prospector. Prospectors take initiative. People with initiative will always be able to find work if they want it. *There is more than enough gold in them there hills and rivers for all the prospectors.*"

"Prospectors, Sam?"

"It's a Gold Rush thing. A prospector dreams about the gold. A prospector searches for the gold, stakes a claim, and mines for the gold. It's hard work, but he is up to it. A prospector is a person who can create a vision and take initiative to work towards that vision."

"So a prospector is an entrepreneur?"

"Doesn't have to be, Doc. Many entrepreneurs are prospectors, but not all prospectors are entrepreneurs. It depends on whether the person is adding value to the world or not. Some prospectors are teachers, lawyers, doctors, police officers, janitors, or any other profession that they chose because they wanted to prospect that particular claim. A claim is the piece of land or place where you are saying *this is my spot where I will mine for my gold.* We all take pride in our claim, but prospectors can have very different definitions of what their gold is. We're not all mining the same things in life, Doc. It's not about actual money; it's much more than that. It might be helping others, building a building, raising a family, farming a field, writing a song, or developing a new medicine. The list is infinite as for every prospector on the Earth there is a unique definition of gold. It's not about dollars. The poorest person in the world is the poor soul who only chases the dollar. He is lost and adds zero value to the world in the end. He may be rich financially but he is not a prospector. He's simply a lost soul with lots of money."

"Interesting, Sam. So most people are prospectors?"

"No, they're not. Not even close. Prospectors are unique. You have to decide to be a prospector. To be a prospector is hard work. I mean really, really hard work. You have to commit to your claim, you have to work the claim every day, you have to learn from experience, you have to be willing to make mistakes, and you have to force yourself to learn from these mistakes. Becoming a prospector takes time, and only time and commitment will create true prospectors. But back to your question, prospectors don't see prospecting as high risk. They see it as a way of life; they see it as the journey to their gold."

"OK. But you closed down a successful practice to start your business?"

"Yes I did. You have to close an old door to open a new one."

"Really? Could you not just have slowed your practice down while building the new venture?"

"No."

"Why not?"

"Because I didn't want to have both things going on at the same time. Mining two claims doesn't show respect for either one. You end up screwing up both ends, and that's not the way to roll out a new chapter in life. That's not the way a great adventure begins. I believed in what I was doing. I was confident in my plan and abilities, and I was driven by vision and mission. When you're in this state of mind, you can only go forward at warp speed. Distractions are just that, distraction, and all distractions need to be eliminated. I felt alive with a clarity that is impossible to describe. Only those who have experienced it will understand. Some feelings can't be defined in words, and only those who have actually prospected, staked, and worked a claim can actually appreciate the work that goes into finding gold. It's about eating trees."

"Eating trees. What do you mean by that, Sam?"

Silence

"Nothing, Doc. It's a long story from a long time ago. Let's just say it's about knowing when to drift and hum."

"Drift and hum?"

"Oh, I guess that wasn't helpful. Anyway, that's an even longer story, Doc."

"Try me, Sam."

Silence

"Look, Doc, I'm just trying to help you understand what a prospector is. To prospect is to set out on an amazing adventure. You are lured by your gold, and you are prepared to work as hard as required in order to work your claim. Prospectors have peace of mind and clarity and security in their own abilities, even though it won't always be evident to the prospector or to the outside world. There is joy of success and agony of defeat, but the prospector will grind through the minutia of failure, self-doubt, and discouragement because he is on a mission. This is a much different life than most people live, not that there's anything wrong with the way most people live. In fact, being a prospector can possibly be a curse in the end."

"Is that an issue, Sam? That you feel you're a prospector who has had a curse cast upon him?"

"Really, Doc? That's what you perceived from my comments? That I'm somehow projecting my comments on the outside world in an effort to disguise my own internal feelings of myself?"

"Maybe."

"You're on the wrong track, Doc, and here's why. First, I've hoed my own row, and I'm very proud of my personal prospecting. Consequently, I deserve anything I have in the way of success. I am the initial prospector. I staked and worked my claim and I deserve all the gold that I panned. But believe me when I say that my gold is not money. My gold is helping people to become prospectors. My golden nugget is when I help a person get out of a rut and find the prospector inside. This is my pay dirt! And I try to live the essence of a true prospector, the code of conduct if you will, to choose humility over vanity, because no matter what your brain is selling you, you are not that good, and you did not do it alone. Second, the prospector knows life is about working hard, really hard, and we always remember that money alone does not create sustained long-term happiness."

"You don't believe having money creates a good life, Sam?"

"No, Doc, I don't. That's part of my point. For every happy rich person there's an unhappy rich person, and in most cases these unhappy rich people are not prospectors. This is my main point. Happiness doesn't come from the money itself but rather from the knowledge and pride of how it was made. That's why the prospector is always happy regardless of how financially secure he is. Pride in hard work and a job well done are much more valuable than dollars. That's why prospectors can work for years and find only small financial success and still be content. Hard work and pride are the source of contentment, not money. That's why many of the happiest people in the world are prospectors of modest means."

"I'm not following you, Sam. What point are you trying to make, and how does this help your situation?"

Silence

"I guess I'm not tracking with myself either, Doc, and I have no idea how this will help my therapy. All I'm saying is that in the end, I didn't think I was making a high-risk decision by leaving my practice. I've had success financially, and I won't be ashamed of that. I worked hard, I staked my claim, I worked my claim, and I found gold, but I'm smart enough to know that nobody accomplishes these things alone. Sophie and others helped me."

"But yet you feel your success is why Sophie and George left you?"

"Yes...I guess."

"So you regret your prospecting?"

Silence

"I don't know. Yes...No...Yes...I don't know any more, Doc."

Silence

"You mentioned you had help. You had help in your prospecting, Sam?"

"Of course, Doc! Nobody achieves anything in life without help. *No man is an island,* right? Truer words have never been spoken. Show me a famous person in Hollywood, and I'll show you someone who was given an opportunity. Show me a financially successful business person, and I'll show you a person who had support early on and later on. Show me a professional athlete and...you get it, Doc."

"But how does that fly in your definition of the prospector? Are there no people who are wholly and completely self-made?"

"Look, Doc, I don't know. Who am I to answer that question? I'm the one who's the patient here! All I can tell you is that I've spent my whole career helping people help themselves. Helping people to realize the prospector inside them, and here's the part that will surprise you. Many of the people who come to me would be considered the successful people of the world – CEOs, politicians, Hollywood actors, professional athletes, professors, and religious and community leaders. These are the people that the outside world sees as successful, but inside many of them are hurting. It's lonely at the top, Doc. Many of these people have exhausted themselves prospecting and helping other people, and the opportunity cost of their time and energy is their own happiness. There is a dangerous set of unintended consequences to being a prospector. The world looks to prospectors as the successful ones, when in truth they are the most in need of help!"

"Sam, I'm sorry. I'm struggling to follow your train of thought. I thought you said that hard work and finding the gold is the prospector's ultimate reward? Are you now saying the success is actually the downfall and not the reward? Is your success your downfall, Sam?"

"What's with you, Doc! Everything I say about the outside world does not refer to my own feelings about myself!"

"Fine, Sam, but which is it?"

"Which is what, Doc?"

"Are you saying your success was the initial reward and then became your downfall?"

Silence

"I guess that's what I'm saying. Yes."

"Why is that, Sam?"

Silence

"Well, Doc, I suspect it's because we lose sight of the bar. We never know how high is high enough. We never know when good is good enough. We never know when to take a break because we never know if people are proud of us."

"I'm sure you have a lot of people who are proud of you, Sam."

Silence

"A lot of people helped me along the way."

"Who helped you?"

"Initially, it was Sophie, Sophie's father, and an uncle of mine. Then as the business grew, I had immense help from employees who joined me and made the vision a reality. I hired a lot of young prospectors."

"You've never mentioned Sophie's father or an uncle before."

"You never asked."

"Are you getting aggravated, Sam?"

"A little."

"Do you want to take a break?"

Silence

"No, we need to grind through some of this."

"OK, tell me about Sophie's father."

"Grandpa James. Well, he was an amazing businessman, a great father and grandfather"

"Was?"

"Yes, he passed away five years ago from cancer."

"I'm sorry to hear that."

"Me too."

"What about your uncle?"

"Uncle Alec. I just call him Alec. He's my coach and mentor. He's still alive and well."

"Have you talked to him lately?"

"No, well, yes. He helped bring me here."

"Was he part of the intervention?"

"Yes, if you can call it an intervention. I see it more like a gathering of the nut. Me being the nut at the time."

"Why haven't you talked to him if he's your mentor?"

Silence

"I think I'm ready for a break, Doc."

"OK, Sam."

Canada
Summer 1982

The Judge

BEAVER BROTHERS *the business* got off to a great start. Our flyers paid off and we got our first job reasonably easily. Well, maybe the flyers didn't play a big part in our first job as the customer was the Judge, the assistant coach for our hockey team. His name is Judge Jeremiah; at least that's what we call him. His real name is Judge Johnson, so we decided to name him after *Jeremiah Johnson*, the mountain man we hold in the highest regard. Normally we just call him the Judge. It's easier. Judge Jeremiah is a great man of the community and a great judge as far as we know. He was appointed to be a provincial judge so long ago that nobody remembers when it actually was. There is a lot that people don't know about the Judge. He's a very private man and his wife Johanna is a very private woman. The rumor in town is he fought in World War II, although he never talks about it. He loves hockey, though, and joins Vince in coaching our team and in cheering for the Detroit Red Wings. He also joins Vince as a great fan of Gordie Howe. Over the years we all got to know him very well. In particular, Hats collaborated with the Judge on his way through law school, and RC did the same on his path to the RCMP. Both of these career aspirations were well suited to cozying up to the local provincial judge. He did a lot for Ray and me over the years as well. Cozying up to the Judge was easy for us as the Judge is a big fan of the Beaver Brothers, and this made it very exciting for the four of us and Ozark when he became our first customer.

School was now finished for the year. We headed out to Judge Jeremiah's to execute our first job, and we pulled up to his house looking as professional as we could. Hats had painted a brown *Boomer the Beaver* logo on both sides of the Boomer Mobile. He then painted *Beaver Brothers* in yellow in a semi-circle over the top of the beaver. It actually looked good and made the van look very commercial. On top of the Boomer Mobile we had roof racks, and on top of the roof racks we had our ten-foot ladder that would extend to almost twenty feet. Also attached to the roof racks were four hockey sticks and two rakes tied down with bungee cords. Inside the van we had the four Beaver Brothers, Ozark, and other implements of the trade. These included a rubber hose with power nozzle, green garbage bags, electric chainsaw, and a fifty-foot extension cord. For the most part, I would drive, Ray would sit shotgun, and Ozark, RC, and Hats would sit on the bench seat in the back of Boomer. When we pulled up to the Judge's house, we looked as if we were ready for business.

The Judge's house is one of the most beautiful houses in town. It's an old historical home that was built over a hundred years ago by the owner of a gold mine that does not exist today. The house is part of the town's history and culture. It's also a house with very high and steep roof lines, which means the eavestroughs are unusually high up as well.

When we pulled up to the Judge's house, he was in the driveway waiting for us. No doubt he heard us coming from four blocks away. Boomer's 1200cc, 30 horse power, rear-mounted air-cooled engine was a symphony of sounds – a symphony of consonance and dissonance meeting at some halfway tone house. There is no other sound on the Earth that compares to it.

We pulled up and parked, and exited Boomer. Our routine was that I jumped out of the driver's side, Ray jumped out of the passenger side door, while RC would swing the side doors open from the inside and Ozark would leap out first, followed by Hats and then RC. We actually made quite an entrance. The Judge's driveway was pretty big, and there was ample room for Boomer and the two new shiny *Saabs* that the Judge and his wife drove. Nobody else in town had *Saab* vehicles, and we had no idea where the Judge actually had to go to buy them. You could tell he loved his two cars by the way he admired them parked in single file in his driveway. When we pulled up behind the two cars to form a straight line, we formed a triad of three very nice-looking vehicles.

"Good morning, boys," the Judge said as he watched our impressive dismounting out of Boomer.

"Good morning, Judge," we responded in unison with absolute enthusiasm, really saying, *How cool is this? Our first paid job with our very own business!*

The Judge was a good-looking older man, maybe sixty at the time, with distinct facial features and short grey hair. He stood a little over six feet tall and looked fit in an athletic way. He was always dressed up and carried himself like a man of great confidence – he was a man of great confidence. On this late spring morning, he wore dress pants and a nice polo shirt. He was also smoking his pipe. This was not uncommon as the Judge loved his pipe and would stand up straight with an erect posture, dressed in his impeccable outfits, and smoke his pipe with great sophistication. Judge Jeremiah Johnson was the real deal.

There were two main jobs the Judge had for the Beaver Brothers that day. The first was to clean out the eavestroughs, and the second was to trim a branch on a blue spruce tree that was growing over the roof of his house. The six of us, including Ozark, headed to look at the eavestroughs first. This is when we encountered our first business challenge. Well, not really a business challenge, but rather an operational execution challenge.

We were standing in front of the Judge's house, all of us facing the house and looking up at the eavestroughs. They looked as if they were somewhere between us and the sun. The Judge's house was old and stately. It was also four stories high, and it had eavestroughs on every level on some part of the many roof lines. We stared up at the roof in wonderment while the Judge took a few puffs on his pipe.

"What do you think, boys?" the Judge asked as the smoke swirled around his face. The aroma of the pipe tobacco was sweet and nice to smell, and it made us want to light up a torpedo, but we would never smoke in front of the Judge.

"Our fucking ladder ain't going to reach!" I heard Hats mumble under his breath. The Judge heard him as well and pretended not to hear.

"Our ladder won't reach, Judge," I said. "We'll need to come up with an alternative plan to get to the eavestroughs."

"All right, boys," the Judge said, and we all went to the side of the house to look at the tree-trimming job.

The Judge's house was built on a beautiful tract of land. I suspect it was easily three acres, and it was populated with amazing trees. The north is blessed with an array of different trees – oak, birch, pine, spruce, and many others. This particular tree was a big blue spruce. One branch around twenty feet up in the air was growing out and up towards the top of the second story of the house. It was a weird situation as normally blue spruces grow out and up evenly, similar to a Christmas tree shape. For some reason, this one big branch was heading way out and up on its own. Ray said it was on a mission to the sun, and we had no reason to argue his logic. In fact, Ray was a little disappointed the Judge needed the unique and independent branch trimmed, but he understood as the branch was heading toward the windows of the house.

"I figure we can just trim about five feet off the end of the branch?" the Judge suggested to us with a question statement.

"Perfect. We'll get it all done, Judge," I replied. As the driver of the van, I had also become the lead ambassador and spokesperson for our first job.

"Great, boys," the Judge said back to all of us, and then he headed into his house with pipe smoke trailing him along the way.

When the Judge was out of sight, we had our first business huddle and problem-solving session. We learned early never to discuss problems in front of the customer. After staring up at the roofline and scratching our heads a bit, we finally came up with a plan. The plan we came up with was for RC and Hats to go borrow a longer ladder, while Ray and I would focus on the branch. RC had an uncle who was in the house-building business and believed he had a huge ladder we could borrow. So Ray and I grabbed our ladder off of Boomer and carried it over towards the blue spruce tree. We also grabbed the electric chainsaw and the extension cord. When Ray and I had everything we needed, RC, Hats, and Ozark headed out in Boomer to pick up the ladder – where Boomer went, so went Ozark. She loved that van. In many respects, it was her van.

Ray and I went to size up our job. After some discussion, we decided that we would extend the ladder and rest it on the branch a foot away from where we would cut the branch. Then I would take the electric chainsaw up the ladder and cut the branch off. Ray would stabilize the bottom of the ladder and try to keep the extension cord on the right side of my body so it would not become a bother for me while I was acting as lumberjack on top of the ladder. This all seemed like a solid plan, so we got busy executing the strategy.

The first snag came when we extended the ladder and propped it up on the branch. I climbed up the ladder, and when I got to the point I could touch the branch I was very near the end of the ladder as the vertical of the ladder only extended around four inches past the horizontal of the branch. I was not feeling that this was a stable situation.

"Can we extend the ladder some more?" I yelled down at Ray, really saying, *I don't feel like dying today!*

"No," Ray yelled back up at me. "It's out as far as it can go."

"OK," I said, and I headed back down the ladder. It wasn't a comfortable feeling being at the end of the rungs. We brainstormed, and our solution was to tie the last rung of the ladder to the branch with some rope in order to keep it from moving in the event the sawing action made me shift from left to right. We didn't have any rope, so we had to knock on the door and ask the Judge if he could lend us some rope. The Judge led us into his garage, and we rummaged around until we found some yellow nylon rope that would work well.

I climbed back up the ladder and tied the rope around the last rung of the ladder and then around the branch. I tied a secure knot and was pleased with my work. Ray then climbed part way up the ladder and handed me the electric chainsaw as I descended to meet him. I climbed back up to the top of the ladder, and by the time I got near the top, the extension cord pulled out where it was connected to the chainsaw.

"Can we let out any more extension cord?" I yelled down at Ray, really saying, *What the hell is with the electric chainsaw anyway!*

"No," Ray yelled back up at me. "That's all we have."

"OK." I yelled back and headed down the ladder again. We knocked on the Judge's door and asked him if we could borrow an extension cord. He smiled, puffed on his pipe, and headed us back to his garage to find an extension cord. While we looked around for the extension cord, RC, Hats, and Ozark pulled up to the house with the borrowed ladder on top of Boomer. It was quite a sight. I have no idea how long the ladder was, but I can only imagine it was the longest extension ladder available. When they pulled up into the Judge's driveway, the ladder easily extended ten feet from the back of the van and another ten feet in front of the van. When RC stopped Boomer, the front of the ladder was literally extended over one of the Judge's Saabs. The Judge stopped looking for the extension cord and watched Boomer come to a stop. I could tell he was looking at the ladder hanging over his fancy car. He took a puff on his pipe and blew out the smoke while RC and Hats and Ozark got out of the van and went around the back to unload the ladder.

Meanwhile, Ray and I found an extension cord, and we headed back to the blue spruce tree while RC and Hats unloaded the enormous ladder. The Judge decided to stay outside and watch the Beaver Brothers in action. Using his pipe tool, he emptied his pipe of burned tobacco and filled it back up for a fresh smoke. He lit the new bowl with his *Zippo* lighter and smoke hung around his head once again. He positioned himself right between the action of Ray and me on one side and Hats and RC on the other. This was the show of the Beaver Brothers at work, and the Judge wanted to watch and learn.

Ray connected the Judge's extension cord to ours, and I headed back up the ladder with chainsaw in hand. RC and Hats pulled the borrowed ladder from the back of Boomer and started carrying it to the front of the Judge's yard. I could see them struggling under the weight of the ladder. The Judge just stood in the middle of the action enjoying his fresh smoke.

I ascended to the top of my ladder and quickly realized I couldn't cut on the right side of the ladder because I would end up going down with the branch when it fell. This meant I had to use my left hand to cut on the left side of the ladder. It also meant I had to use my left hand to handle the electric chainsaw. Fortunately, it was not that heavy, so I could manage the weight, even though it was very awkward. I rested the chain of the saw on the branch where I intended to cut and pressed the trigger to get the saw going. The sound of saw on branch was invigorating, and I instantly felt very industrious. The Judge was looking up at our progress, and he looked pleased at the location of my cut. Ray was looking up at me, with one foot on the ladder for stabilization, and a hand on the extension cord to keep me from accidentally getting the cord caught up in the blade of the saw. He was my wingman.

Meanwhile, RC and Hats had picked out the spot where they would extend the enormous ladder to begin the sweeping of the eavestroughs with our hockey sticks. They picked up the ladder, pointed it straight up into the sky, and started pulling the ropes that would begin the mechanics of extending the ladder to its full length.

I kept working through the branch. My leverage with my left hand was not great, so it continued to be slow going through the branch, which was approximately eight inches in diameter. Ray was settled into his support role at the bottom of the ladder. The Judge continued to look on, shifting his eyes from one side of the yard to the other in order to see both operations in progress. Ozark sat by his side assuming the role of worksite director.

Hats and RC continued to extend their mammoth ladder, and they had it completely vertical as if they were joining it to the sky itself. It looked as if you could use it to climb to the sun. I couldn't help but think of *Jack and the Beanstalk.*

Meanwhile, I was working my way through the branch. Ray continued to look up and asked if I needed any help, while RC and Hats continued to extend their ladder, and the Judge continued to observe the work. Ozark continued to supervise the action while sitting beside the Judge. Then things got a little chaotic. It was a case of one planned event and two simultaneous unplanned events.

The first planned event is that I made it through the branch, and as planned, the five-foot section of the branch I was cutting fell to the ground. As per the plan, it missed Ray on the way down. The first unplanned event happened when the five-foot section released from the main part of the branch. What we hadn't anticipated was that when the cut section fell to the ground, the remaining main branch on the tree shifted up a full foot as a result of the reduced weight. The ladder shifted up with the branch as it was tied tightly to it with the Judge's rope. This meant the ladder was now hanging freely in midair at the bottom. Ray was holding the bottom of the ladder with his foot, and that helped to keep the ladder from swinging uncontrollably. My first instinct was to drop the chainsaw and hang onto the ladder with both hands. I went with this first instinct, and fortunately the chainsaw missed Ray on the way down.

Meanwhile at what seemed like exactly the same time, RC and Hats had the borrowed ladder at its full extension and at a completely vertical angle, a perfect ninety degrees to the ground. Both Hats and RC were holding onto the bottom of the ladder, but their height seemed inconsequential to the overall height of the ladder itself. I was holding on for dear life in my own situation but could also tell that Hats and RC had a look of concern on their faces. At the time, I thought the concern was for me, but I was mistaken. The big ladder started to sway somewhat at the top. I watched RC and Hats try to change their footing in order to stabilize it. This did not work, and the ladder started to sway more and more near the top, almost as if there were a wind moving its top rung. I looked on, Ray looked on, Ozark looked on, and the Judge looked on. He took a mildly nervous puff on his pipe.

RC and Hats called over for Ray. They tried to sound calm, but it sounded exactly like a frantic call for help – which it was. Ray immediately left his post at the bottom of my ladder and went to their aid. As soon as he walked away from my ladder, it began to sway from the bottom as it was then six inches off the ground. The rope at the top of the ladder was holding, and I suddenly realized what it's like to be a trapeze artist. My only instinct was to get off the ladder as quickly as possible, but as I started climbing down each descending step created more swing in my predicament. I yelled at Ray to come back to his initial post, but he was too busy with RC and Hats. It's hard to have two items that are, in fact, both number-one priorities.

The three of them were holding onto the enormous ladder but things were not improving. It was moving to and fro, and the movement was gaining momentum. RC was the first to see the situation as hopeless and in a last ditch effort for safety, he screamed out, "She's going down, boys! Let's get the hell outta here!" Reacting to RC's orders, Ray and Hats followed RC's lead, and the three of them released their grip on the ladder and ran for cover under my blue spruce tree. The Judge and Ozark watched the scrum of activity. The abandoned mountain of a ladder was finally freed, and it seemed as if it took a split second to decide what to do. And what it decided to do was to start crashing down right in the direction of the Judge's two Saabs. Watching that ladder fall to the ground could only be compared to watching a three-hundred-foot redwood come crashing down in the forest. Time was suspended, slow motion began; none of us, including Ozark, could hear or see anything unrelated to the ladder's falling. Our understanding of reality was changed for a brief few seconds as the ladder continued its free-fall towards the driveway, and we all continued to look on with absolute amazement and deep concern over what was happening.

The ladder finally hit the ground right between the Judge's two Saabs. There was a five-foot gap between the two cars, and the ladder found the exact center of the gap. It hit the ground hard and bounced up a full three feet, only to conform to the laws of gravity and hit the ground again in the same spot. The ladder then fell silent, and we all came back to reality. The Judge took a big puff on his pipe. Ozark turned her attention to me and started barking at me up at the top of my ladder. I was in full swing at this point. Ray snapped back to his original responsibility and gained a hold on the bottom of my ladder and brought it to a stop. I carefully climbed down and kissed the ground when I stepped off the last rung.

The intensity of the situation lessened like air releasing from a balloon. We all stood silent, happy to be alive. We all looked over at the Judge, and he looked back at us all while taking another haul on his pipe. He blew the smoke up in the air.

"I've always liked you, boys," he said after a moment of silence. "You boys are interesting!"

We looked at each other for confirmation of our own confidence level, and with the Judge's words of encouragement, we shrugged our shoulders and got back to work.

Five hours later, and with some reflection and learning from the first hour on the job, we successfully completed our work for the Judge. He congratulated us on a job well done, paid us cash with a tip, and told us he would recommend us around town. He even let us keep the rope and extra extension cord for our next job. You just have to love Judge Jeremiah. He's one of us. He's a prospector. He's the real deal.

And with our first job done, the Beaver Brothers began to get new customers and have a successful first summer in business.

DAY 11
South Carolina

James

TODAY IS A GREEN DAY. This is as good as I've felt since I arrived. My talk with Doc yesterday left me feeling somewhat frustrated and borderline Red, but I pulled it together today. I'm starting to crack the code. A good night's sleep, a solid breakfast (maybe the Talking Cable Heads are right), no television, and then some fresh air and exercise. Sometimes the answer is inside the box, and sometimes the box is simply a box of the basics. Mental health is probably just about living by the fundamentals. I'm convinced now that my anxiety and anger are stemming from having too many thoughts going on at the same time. I need to slow my brain down and differentiate what is real from what is imagined. I am wondering if I have blurred the two in some respects.

I'm sitting at my desk looking out at the ocean and sun. I feel as if today will stay in the Green. I'm also feeling good because I'm thinking about Sophie's father James. He was one of the good guys. He was an adventurer and a prospector. He loved Sophie, he loved George, and he loved me. James died of cancer five years ago. We miss him dearly.

He helped Sophie and me with our first house, and he helped us with our wedding. He was also there with support when I proposed my business venture, and in the end he made a generous loan for a small stake in the company. He wasn't doing it for business purposes; he was doing it for his family. Grandpa James believed in family, and he espoused family values. He was as conservative as they come. Born and raised in Texas, he was taught to work hard and be thankful for what he had. He was raised to respect his elders, say please and thank you, and say grace before each meal. He was raised properly, and he raised Sophie properly. He died while visiting us in South Carolina. We had to inform everybody and get his body back to Texas. That was a *whole thing*. I did the eulogy at his funeral. It's still on my laptop. I'll read it to you.

A TRIBUTE TO GRANDPA JAMES

Mental models of western society leave us to believe the success of a person's life is measured by diplomas on the wall, money in the bank, titles on a business card, or cars in the driveway. While James meets all these criteria for a successful life, he did not subscribe to material measures. James knew that the real measure of a person's life is not a statistic of money, but rather a statistic of character. James understood at an early age that character is everything.

Character is easy to define. To have character means to do the right things and to do them even when nobody is watching. Having character is having core principles and beliefs that guide your decisions, guide the path you choose, and ultimately guide the life you live regardless of what events the universe puts in your way. To paraphrase Ralph Waldo Emerson, "Character is higher than wisdom," as "wisdom is knowing what to do next, but character is actually doing it." James was a man of character.

There is an old saying that you can't take it with you. Yet somehow I'm not feeling this to be truth. Something is now gone. The world has lost another member of an endangered species – a man with character. In my effort to understand what this means to me and to my family, I start to think about the future. But before I can do that, I have to go back to the past.

If we rewind twenty-five years, my life was that of a typical, reasonably rebellious young Canadian. The crazy days were winding down, harsh realities of making a living were becoming evident and nature's silent signals to start a family were flowing through my veins. But to journey this next stage of life required a partner – my Sophie, my princess – the one I would rescue from the castle tower to spend life with her building a home, raising a family, and living happily ever after. What I didn't realize at the time, in fact what I didn't realize until only a few days ago, is that I was not just in search of a wife – I was in search of a package deal. You see, if we rewind thirty years, we see a story in my life that parallels the tragic events of James's childhood. Fast forward from that single event in my childhood, and we understand what package I was looking for. Not only did I want to find a smart, beautiful, and caring partner; I wanted and needed the package to include a father. While James never overtly told me so, I know he saw what I was looking for in the deal. As a businessman, James implicitly understood the dynamics of a deal.

Now we review the last twenty years in fast forward. What we see are all the good things that life has to offer – hard work resulting in modest comforts, loving relationships to navigate through life's challenges, and a beautiful son and grandson, George. Yet, when we peel the onion back a few layers, when you watch the day-to-day activities, you will see me being coached, you will see me being mentored, you will see me being taught about character, and you will see James as a primary teacher in the story.

Sophie and George and I had the privilege of spending significant time with James. He enjoyed the climate in South Carolina, and he enjoyed the company of his daughter and grandson. As a result, I received the gift of his time. Let it be known that I don't take this point lightly. Time is arguably the only true non-renewable resource on the Earth. Therefore, by definition, time is impacted by the economic theory of the "zero sum gain." That is, time spent with one person can be considered to have an opportunity cost of time spent with another person. Consequently, I have enormous respect for the time I spent with James.

James believed in the power of learning. He understood what Aristotle taught us in that the more you learn, the more you realize you don't know. It drives the definition of the wise man as the man who knows he knows nothing. James understood the cycle of learning. Fiercely conservative, James believed with his entire mind and spirit that we should get up in the morning and do what is right, and in the process we will learn. Use the potential that life has afforded you, get an education in something you enjoy, and then earn a fair day's pay for a fair day's work and continue to learn along the way. James laughed one day when I told him there are three kinds of luck in this world — blind luck, dumb luck, and get up every morning with the sun and sweat the details luck. Because of the last, James was a very lucky man.

They say that when the student is ready, the teacher will appear. In my case, however, the teacher arrived and the student became ready. I learned a lot from James. Not just about revenues and costs or the history of the family. In fact, most of James's lessons were implied and not explicit. They came through questions and not overt advice. They came from stories and not encyclopedia facts. I recall a powerful story James told me about when he was considering buying a yet undeveloped plot of land that was thought to contain oil reserves. History has proven this investment would have been an extremely successful venture as measured in dollars. In my youthful zeal of entrepreneurialism, I asked him why he didn't do it. "Didn't you have the cash?" I asked. His answer was, "Sophie's mother didn't feel her health was up to it at the time." I actually had the nerve to ask, "Do you regret that decision?" "Of course not," was his reply, and there the conversation ended. You see, men of character don't look back, men of character don't brood and whine, men of character don't feel sorry for themselves or swim in the pit of despair of woulda, coulda, shoulda. Men of character make decisions based on their guiding principles, and then they move on. Men of character live with character. That's what makes them men of character.

And that brings us to the present and the future. I enjoyed many talks with James about the state of current affairs. Never a man to be critical or over-opinionated, on many occasions he expressed concerns about our youth and the upcoming generations. While James would never over-generalize, the daily news left him feeling as if people today have a sense of entitlement, a lack of work ethic, and attitudes of pessimism as opposed to optimism. These characteristics were so far from James's genetic fabric that he simply could not relate to them. However, I feel what he was truly scared of was that my generation and the next and the next would live lives devoid of character. You see, James understood that life is different today. When James grew up shelter, food, shoes, clothes, and an education were not taken for granted. You appreciated and were thankful for what you had. You respected, and treated with respect, those who provided these basic comforts. Character formed at an early age with the realization that you shouldn't take anything for granted. But now our job as parents has changed. Because our parents and grandparents did their best, our children have all the comforts of nice homes, plenty of shoes, food in abundance, and stuff beyond need. And that's OK. That's how it is supposed to work. The next generation should live better than the last. However, if character is formed while working for the basic necessities of life, but the basics are now a given, how will our children develop character? That's where we come in. Our job now is not so much to provide the comforts of life to our children, but rather to ensure they understand and respect the history of the comforts they have.

Herein lies the next lesson from the teacher. So perhaps James did not take anything with him. As the practical man James was, I can't see his taking anything with him that he could leave here for our benefit. Perhaps James' character did not go with him, but instead sits as an invisible torch ready for us to grab.

And so the story goes. We are left with memories and lessons from the time that James gave us. I can choose to do with them what I wish. I can ignore and rationalize, or I can build and develop. I can choose to evolve with James's teachings and create the environment for his grandson to receive the torch of those teachings. Either way, this is my choice, my decision to make. Whether I do the right thing or not is solely up to me. I am responsible and accountable. And that's the ultimate lesson I learned from Grandpa James.

As I read this I'm struggling to stay in the Green Zone. James taught me to be responsible and accountable for my actions, and now Sophie and George have left me. Am I not responsible and therefore accountable for this? I am so thankful James is not here to witness what I have done; and if he were, what would he tell me? What would he advise me to do? How would I explain my careless actions that so impacted his daughter and grandson?

I really need to slow my brain down and differentiate between what is real and what is imagined. I'm now convinced I have these blurred and confused.

Canada

Summer 1982

The Band

THE SUMMER PROGRESSED as planned, and the Beaver Brothers stayed plenty busy. There were leaves everywhere and eavestroughs filled with all those leaves needed to be emptied. This fact of nature and the Judge's endorsement around town created a buzz and a lot of business for the Beaver Brothers. We were literally and quintessentially busy as a beaver. We spent some money to get a pager and printed new business cards with our pager number on them. A prospective customer could call the pager and leave a phone number or a short voice message on the device so we could return the call. RC and Ray also crafted up some buttons that we left in strategic spots around town. We didn't have much space to play with on the buttons, so all they had on them was the pager number and *Beaver Brothers – We won't leave a leaf*! When we received a page, we would head to the closest phone booth and return the call. If we happened to be on a job when the page came in, we would ask the customer if we could borrow the phone. This favor was always obliged, and most of the time it resulted in the four of us having lunch, or at a minimum, a cold drink – Ozark included. Everybody loved the Beaver Brothers. As the Judge said, we were interesting.

All of our jobs paid cash, and I was elected to be CFO and handle the money. Our cash inflow was pretty impressive, and our cash outflow was moderate. Cash out was gas for Boomer, replenishment of green garbage bags, and a few new hockey sticks to replace ones damaged by a nasty roof. We had two Boomer breakdowns that resulted in the purchase of a new alternator and a new starter. Other than that, our *not-so-business-related* expenses amounted to food for Ozark, food for us, a few packs of torpedoes, and a few cases of Old Vienna beer. Maybe there was the odd bottle of the King's whiskey. As well, we started every morning at our favorite local diner, the local greasy spoon called Frank's Diner. This was our spot. The food was fantastic, and Frank and his wife provided equally fantastic service. They would allow Ozark inside the restaurant, and Frank's wife would give her a delicious meal while we ate our equally delicious breakfast.

Truth be told, each working day that summer began with bacon and eggs and ended with a case of OV and a pack of torpedoes. In the end, our revenues still exceeded our costs, and we actually made some money – quite a bit actually. Collectively, we decided to split fifty percent of the profits among the five of us and leave the other fifty percent in a kitty for future use. To bank the kitty, we used a Crown Royal Whiskey purple velvet bag and stored it hidden at the Lodge. The split for the five of us included Ozark as she was on every job, and we felt it was just the right thing to do. We stashed her money in the back of Boomer's glove compartment. Ozark used most of it the following summer.

July's weather was outstanding. Northern Canadians pay their dues all winter and deserve warm summer days with endless nights of northern lights creating sun-grey skies covered with a million stars. The north is blessed with this combination of a display of the universe's art skills, and it's a wonder we ever slept: to go to sleep is to miss something spectacular from the skies.

Not that we did sleep that much. We appreciated the gifts of nature, but we were also focused on our first live band performance, which was coming up soon. We moved our band setup from Ray's basement to my garage, taking advantage of the space where Boomer used to be stored. The setup looked and sounded like the real deal. We were a true garage band. We had cables and stands and amplifiers and instruments and all sorts of things band oriented. The stuff would just show up via RC and Ray, and while Hats and I had no idea where the gear was coming from, we knew enough not to ask. All we knew for sure was that Ray wanted us to be prepared, and he wanted us to sound good for our first paid gig. RC agreed, and they were both working hard to make sure we earned our paycheck. Of course, Hats had a different opinion on the situation.

"We aren't even getting paid, you dumb shits!" he went off on RC and Ray one day. "That numb nuts Vince has us cleaning leaves all over fucking town, man! He's using us like his personal leaf garburator!"

Ray and RC would just ignore him. The truth is, we only did the two jobs that Ray had committed us to, but Hats would never admit it. I suspect he was just anxious about the performance and was taking it out on Ray.

We practiced hard, and Ray and RC believed we were ready. Meanwhile, Ray and Vince had discussed the plan for the show at the Maple Tree Hotel that was scheduled for Monday evening of the Civic long weekend. We intended to play two sets starting at 10:00 pm and ending at midnight. Vince didn't see the value in starting earlier as early-bird customers are a given, and he didn't see going past midnight because as Vince would always tell us, "Ain't nothing good ever happen after midnight, lads!" He also told Ray to play only songs that people would know. This really disappointed Ray, as we had some original songs of which I was proud of the lyrics and Ray and RC were proud of the music. I didn't actually hear Ray confirm to Vince that we would only play covers. Ray just smiled at Vince and nodded confirmation that he had heard the request.

Ray and RC finalized our set list, and it contained all covers except for one original song for the end of the night. Ray figured at that point in the night Vince would be so tuned up on Canadian whiskey that he wouldn't know a cover song from a cover of a magazine. Our list of covers was really the list of our favorite songs from our favorite bands, including an equal assortment of Canadian and non-Canadian bands. We have always been supporters of Canadian artists, which is easy to do because the list of amazing talent is long and varied. Our first set was planned to be forty minutes long with a ten-minute break before the second set. The songs in our first set were our favorite songs from non-Canadian bands and included songs from *The Eagles, Boston, Lynyrd Skynyrd, Bruce Springsteen, Dire Straits, The Grateful Dead, Jackson Brown, The Ozark Mountain Daredevils,* and a few others. Our second set lineup, which we planned to be seventy minutes, was all Canadian – songs from *Gordon Lightfoot, Stomping Tom Connors, Ian Tyson, Rush, Neil Young, Max Webster, Saga, April Wine, David*

Wilcox, Teenage Head, Stan Rogers, The Guess Who, Rob Knox and Compass Rose, and a few others. We planned to end the show with our one original song called *Tommy Weeks the Carpet Man.* The last set was a total eclectic arrangement of songs that fit no theme other than that all were Canadian bands. Ray and RC chose all the songs. Hats and I didn't really care, and for the most part we just played the same thing for all songs anyway. RC and Ray carried the show with their guitars, keyboards, synthesizers, and voices – a four-member band with two musicians. Hats would always joke with Ray and say, "Are my drums even fucking plugged in, man!"

The Civic long weekend arrived and all day Saturday we prepared for the gig, spending most of our time getting our instruments tuned up. Ray told us we would take Sunday off and relax to get ourselves in the right frame of mind for Monday. So we went to the Lodge and spent Sunday getting ourselves pretty well tuned up. I'm not sure that it was helpful for the next day's performance, but RC and Ray seemed to think that's how rock stars do it. Hats and I had no complaints; we were quick studies and malleable enough to comply with the rules of rock stardom.

The Monday of the Civic long weekend is a holiday for most Canadians. Not all provinces officially recognize it as a statutory holiday, but it has evolved into an official, or unofficial, holiday in most of Canada. Normally, it is the first weekend in August. The idea of a Civic holiday is to recognize a particular city or town's birthday, so instead of each city or town having a separate birthday celebration, we group them all together and take a day off. Most Canadians just call it the *August Long Weekend.* It's a very important weekend because in many places it's the last long weekend when you are somewhat guaranteed summer weather. The next long weekend is Labor Day, which is not so predictable in many parts of Canada.

The Monday of the August long weekend 1982 was upon us, and we headed to the Maple Tree Hotel to set up for the first paid live gig of the Beaver Brothers Band. It took three trips in Boomer to get all our gear into the Maple Tree Hotel. Vince watched us unload, and I could tell he was pleased with the fact that it appeared we had the right equipment. Let's face it, a good carpenter should have good tools. Hats and I did the muscle work while RC and Ray did the knowledge work of getting the equipment hooked up properly. Ozark looked on. Vince liked Ozark and allowed her into the bar as he did his own dog, a nice-looking Boxer named Curly. Ozark and Curly became lifelong friends. After all the instruments, amplifiers, cords and other stuff required to be a band were unloaded, Hats and I let RC and Ray have some space to get us organized. We sat at the bar and had a few drafts. Truth be told, Hats and I were still both feeling a little weak and nervous from the day and night before, so a small 'hair of the dog' was proving to be helpful. Vince poured us the draft while clearly forgetting to ask us for ID. The drinking age in our province was eighteen, and we were only months away. All was good.

The Maple Tree Hotel was the perfect place for our first gig due to the fact it was a town focal point and a drinking nucleus for many people. There was absolutely nothing unique or fancy about the place other than the energy and spirit that happened when people arrived and began to drink. For every day of the year that existed, the Maple Tree Hotel was a different bar. It all depended on who was there that particular day or night. A building is just a building until people bring in the mood and energy.

You would walk into the Maple Tree Hotel off of Chinook River's main street, which is called Main Street. There were two big glass doors that took you into the main entrance of the bar, and in the summertime, Vince had two old western saloon doors that he attached to the entrance, leaving the big glass doors open. It made you feel as if you were heading into a watering hole during the days of the Wild West, and some nights that was not too far off the mark.

The minute you walked in, you noticed the bar itself – a huge U-shaped wooden slab made from a combination of gorgeous maple and aged cherry wood. It was made decades ago by a local woodworker who was a friend of Vince's late father. There were no stools around the bar at all; drinking is a standup game in the north. To the right and the left of the bar were a few chairs and tables for older folks to sit down. We all knew that Vince believed the fewer movable parts in the place, the fewer things that could be thrown across the floor. There was virtually nothing on the walls – no major displays of movie stars, no neon beer signs, no chalk boards for people to write their names on saying they were there. The only items on the wall were a liquor license, a picture of Gordie Howe in a Detroit Red Wings uniform, and a set of annual pictures of the Maple Tree Hockey Team. Hats, RC, Ray, and I were in the last several years of pictures. There were easily ten years of teams prior to our joining the picture. The small piece of formal occupancy paper said the place was allowed to house a maximum capacity of 200 people, although Ray and I counted 400 one winter's Friday night when Vince had arranged an arm-wrestling tournament. The winner of the tournament was an RCMP officer who didn't seem concerned with the number of people in the bar. While devoid of typical pictures on the wall, the Maple Tree Hotel did have lots of different beers, select liquors, and a small hardwood platform for a band or some dancing if a patron got the notion. The Maple Tree Hotel was perfect for the Beaver Brothers Band debut.

Ray and RC got us all set up by seven o'clock, so we went and got some dinner at Frank's Diner. Around nine o'clock, we went back to the bar and were actually surprised that the place was filling up. It had been a nice weekend weather-wise, which meant people would attempt to keep the long-weekend feeling going as long as possible. Canadians don't take a nice summer day for granted, and they appreciate every hour of it. We stood at the bar and started in on our free OVs as per the agreement with Vince, while Ozark sat with us proud as could be with Curly snuggling by her side.

Much to our amazement and to Vince's delight the place was drawing a crowd, and people were arriving at a steady pace. There were oil guys, miners, and loggers, who were strangers to us, and there were people we did know – friends from hockey and teachers and friends from school were filing in. As usual, Vince wasn't checking anybody for age-of-majority cards. Some on-duty and off-duty RCMP officers arrived to support RC, and even Judge Jeremiah made an entrance. In hindsight, I don't know why we were surprised to see the Judge. What a guy. At some point, a small group of the McMullen clan came in, and it was clear they were already half tuned up. Timmy was one of them, but I didn't see Joey. I looked at them, and I looked over at Vince, and he gave me an *'It's cool. I'll take care of it'* look, so I turned my attention to the rest of the band. RC and Ray could not have cared less. They didn't even notice the dumbass McMullens. Hats, on the other hand, was not so distracted, and he watched the group come in and sit at the last table available at the back of the bar. I went up to Hats and grabbed his hand and squeezed it tight. He looked at me and said, "Fuck it, man. Let's jam, Sam!"

Right before ten o'clock, Ray got us together behind our equipment, and Vince joined us.

"You boys can do this!" Vince said to us in a voice of sincere encouragement, and with that he offered, and we gladly accepted, a free shot of the King's whiskey. Adding this to our pay seemed to please Hats. The five of us raised our glasses, clinked our glasses, shot the brown liquid back, and slammed our glasses down on the table behind us. The sound of the shot glasses hitting the table was the first sound of music that night. The whiskey tasted great. It hit the spot it was supposed to hit. We got our instruments strapped on. Hats sat down at the drums, and Ray gave us the *let's go* signal. Showtime had arrived. The Beaver Brothers Band was in full swing.

We started off with *Take It Easy*, probably our all-time favorite song, and it sounded pretty damn good. Ray was singing and playing lead guitar, and RC brought in the harmony while playing rhythm guitar. Beer and whiskey have a way of making music sound pretty damn good. The place was now full. I suspect we had two hundred people easy, and we figured Vince and the Judge had put the word out to show up and support their boys. People were drinking and stamping their feet while listening to the debut of the Beaver Brothers Band, and Ray and RC were completely on their game. Ray in particular was in a different world. He was in a zone that only gifted musicians get to travel to. I can't describe what or where it is, but I could tell he was there, he was all the way there, and RC wasn't too far behind him. Hats and I just did what we had been taught to do. I played the four bass riffs Ray had taught me and that I had practiced to near perfection. I just cycled through them over and over and hoped they were in the right sequence for the song we were playing. Hats just banged away on the drums and did his best to know when the song was going to come to an end. I have to admit, he did a great job banging out the beat. RC seemed really pleased with us, and I don't think Ray had to use the drum machine as often as he assumed he would. We finished off the first American set with *Freebird*, and Ray and RC totally blew the place apart. They went back and forth with a ten-minute guitar solo that would have made Ronnie proud. Even Hats and I were looking at each other as if to say, "*Where the hell did they learn to do that?*" It was a masterpiece, and every person in the Maple Tree Hotel that night thought so as well.

The music was good for the crowd, and even the McMullens were behaving themselves, relatively speaking. Timmy tried to stir things up by yelling, "You suck," in the brief silence between the first couple of songs, but each time he did this he would receive a slap on the back of his head from some big burly logger standing behind the McMullen clan table. These tough lads from the bush always stood against the wall in the Maple Tree Hotel, and it was clear Timmy was not getting any support from them in his attempt to heckle the band. Eventually he stopped yelling between songs. Fortunately for us that night, being a dumbass is not always contagious.

We stopped for the planned ten-minute break and headed to the bar to get a beer and say hi to the Judge. While we were standing at the bar, Vince gave us a two-thumbs-up, while at the same time Timmy came up and purposely bumped into Hats. "See you on the ice, motherfucker," was all I heard coming out of Timmy's dumbass trap. Hats did and said nothing. He just took a hit off his beer and lit up a torpedo, even though the Judge would see him smoking. I could see his cheeks turn a little red though.

With the break over and two quick beers in us, the Beaver Brothers Band went back to work. We started the second and all-Canadian set with *The Hockey Song – The Good Ole Hockey Game*. Well let me tell you what. You would have thought we were the *Beatles* arriving in America for the first time. The crowd in the bar downed their beer, ordered up fresh ones, and started singing the song. Even if they didn't know the words, they would sing something that sounded remotely close, because it didn't really matter anyway as the whole place was one scene of northern exposure. People started making gestures as if they were taking a slap shot, and others pretended they were the goalie saving the shot. Some folks turned their chairs around and sat on them backwards and pushed the chairs around the bar with their feet as if they were skating. On the bar, they set up two beer bottles at each end to act as goal posts and used ashtrays as pucks as they hurled the ashtray down the bar and tried to score between the beer bottles. I saw the Judge, pipe in mouth, throw an ashtray down the bar, and it hit the beer-bottle goal post. He was denied a goal. He let out a belly laugh, and even over the sound of the music, I heard him yell out, "The beer bottle, a goalie's best friend!" It was an absolute hootin', tootin', groovin' good time.

The place calmed down somewhat after *The Hockey Song*, but the positive energy remained. We had a fantastic second set of Canadian-only bands, and the crowd was very appreciative. They were also getting very tuned up. You can see it happening when you're happening with it, and it was happening. We didn't care though; we were too busy having a blast playing our songs and smoking torpedoes and trying to get more beer out of Vince. Our inhibitions were down, we were in a zone, and we played our songs hard while midnight was fast approaching. Then we ran past midnight, but Vince did not seem to mind.

"Keep playing, boys!" he yelled out when Ray looked at him and pointed to his watch.

"Great, Vince," Ray yelled back. "We're going to finish up with an original?" he said in a statement-question tone.

"Play whatever the heck you want!" a happy Vince screamed back and then poured himself, the Judge, and a few regulars a shot of Canadian whiskey.

RC and Ray huddled, and I heard RC say, "Here goes nothing," and Ray told Hats and me to get ready to play *Tommy Weeks the Carpet Man*. The crowd was ready for a last song, and I don't think they would have let us stop even if we had tried. Ray went over to the small synthesizer we had and used the machine to generate the Irish beat and rhythm of the song. I will readily admit this song is a little different. Ray and RC wrote the music, and I wrote the lyrics. Ray and RC describe the song as the Irish drinking song to end all Irish drinking songs.

We got the Irish beat going and people instantly started stamping their feet and banging their beer bottles on the bar and tables. In the first few notes, you instantly know this is a drinking song, and people were drinking appropriately. We opened up with the first verse.

> *Tommy Weeks was a carpet man*
> *Selling door to door across the land*
> *He knew his shags and he liked his swirls*
> *But mostly Tommy Weeks loved his girls*

The entire bar was loving it. Nobody had ever heard the song before, but they acted as if they knew it by heart, and the Irish beat allowed people to call the song their own. Then we went into the chorus and I swear you would have thought we had reinvented foot stomping and beer-bottle banging. We didn't need Hats anymore because the percussion was coming from the natural human gathering in the bar. Hats could have cared less anyway as when I looked over at him, he was smoking a torpedo, sucking back an OV, staring at Timmy McMullen, and banging his two drum sticks like the wild drummer *Animal* from the *Muppets*. Ray and RC were nowhere but in the music. I was all over the place. I could not decide what to focus on, so I just joined Ray and RC and screamed out the chorus.

> *Gentlemen wake up, Tommy Weeks is working today*
> *He's stepping up your walk while you're away*
> *He's rolling out his carpet, right across your floor*
> *Gentlemen heads up, he's knocking on your door*

After every verse we played the chorus, and before we were even halfway through the song, everybody in the bar knew the words to it. We carried on through each verse, with the story of Tommy Weeks becoming clearer along the way. It was obvious to me from watching faces that the story hit closer and closer to home for some of the customers as the song progressed. The chorus section became louder and louder with each verse. I suspect you could have heard us at the North Pole that night. We laid out the story of Tommy Weeks – no pun intended.

> *Tommy liked the mountain air*
> *He'd say selling carpet was easy there*
> *High in the clouds, above the sea*
> *Where floors are cold below your feet*
>
> *One day Tommy was in Grizzly Trail*
> *When he got a surprise when he rang the bell*
> *Hoping for a prospect, to lay a little rug*
> *When the door opened up, he was staring at Big Doug*
>
> *Tommy and Big Doug had met before*
> *When Tommy stretched some across Big Doug's floor*
> *And Big Doug wasn't happy with the product Tommy laid*
> *Now Big Doug's thinking he needs to get paid*
>
> *Big Doug said "Tommy, it's good to see you again*
> *I've been looking everywhere for you my friend*
> *I'd like to see your sample, your trick of the trade*
> *Pull it out right now Tommy, don't be afraid"*

We were almost done with the song, and we only had one more verse and chorus cycle to go. The place was loving every minute of it, and we had reinvented the northern drinking song. In five minutes, the chorus was firmly engrained as a new theme song for hard-working people everywhere. We belted out the last verse as loud as we could.

> *Tommy laid his sample out, not knowing what was next*
> *When Big Doug brought his pistol out that was holstered on his chest*
> *"Your product sucks" Big Doug roared*
> *"My wife said you're a bore"*

And with one shot from Big Doug's piece
Tommy Weeks don't lay rug no more

What happened next is hard to explain, as it went down lightning fast. Some big tough miner guy at the back opened up his fly and stuck his index finger through the fly hole of his jeans. He then pointed his open fly and finger at some equally big and tough miner standing close by him and yelled what I believe was, "Hey, Eddy, your wife didn't find this a bore!"

With that, the one I assume was Eddy, went over and punched the finger-penis guy right in the chest. This sent him flying backwards, and he landed in the way of some other big tough guy who pushed him back at Eddy. Eddy pushed him back again, which resulted in a few others being pushed, and the pushing momentum began. Ray and RC were still in their Irish tone zone busy cranking out the chorus of the song with the other ninety-five percent of the bar. Ozark had retreated behind the bar with Curly. Hats, on the other hand, could not give up a golden opportunity. He knew exactly what was going to happen next and decided to be a catalyst of sorts. He was banging away on his drums and then abruptly stood up, took aim, and like a master threw one of his drum sticks through the air. He then sat down as quickly as he had stood. Acting as if nothing had happened, he started banging on his drums with the remaining single drum stick. He had an OV in the other hand.

The truth is nobody did realize anything had taken place other than Hats and Timmy McMullen. Hats knew because he was the instigator, and Timmy knew because he was hit right in the forehead with the drumstick. It was a direct hit from the business end of the drum stick, such a perfect throw that the force of the stick knocked Timmy off the chair that he was leaning back on while singing the chorus of the song. Timmy was a true Irishman, and he knew a good song when he heard one. From the hit, he was thrown backwards and spilled into the guy who was behind him, the same guy who had slapped Timmy a couple of times earlier in the night. He was a monster of a man. He looked like a mountain with clothes on. His hands literally hid the glass he drank from. The north and its availability of hard work can produce very big and very tough men. This guy had clearly taken advantage of all hard work opportunities, and he was whiskey bent and hell bound. He also clearly didn't like the McMullens, so the sum of all of this resulted in the guy's literally picking Timmy up off the ground, putting him over his head, and throwing him at the rest of the McMullens, knocking them all over like a set of bowling pins.

I guess I don't need to tell you what happened next. Hollywood could not have made it more authentic. You just can't make this stuff up. It was the classic bar fight. The perfect bar brawl, and we kept playing the chorus to *Tommy Weeks* over and over while the brawl spread its tentacles. We sang our hearts out.

Gentlemen wake up, Tommy Weeks is working today
He's stepping up your walk while you're away
He's rolling out his carpet, right across your floor
Gentlemen heads up, he's knocking on your door

The uniformed RCMP officers went outside to ensure the brawl didn't spill into the street. The off-duty officers stayed in the bar to ensure the fight stayed fair. This meant fists and the odd bottle only, no knives and certainly no guns. Judge Jeremiah went behind the bar and joined Vince, the Maple Tree Hotel staff, Curly, and Ozark. He lit up a new bowl in his pipe and joined in the chorus. Half of the bar ended up on one side fighting and the other half was singing *Tommy Weeks*. Hats stayed well behaved and just pounded his drums with his one stick. It was priceless.

Eventually, Vince and the Judge decided the steam of the fight was running low, and they asked the uniformed RCMP officers to return and end the donnybrook. The Beaver Brothers Band did one last round of the *Tommy* chorus and shut the music down. The singing part of the bar booed and yelled at Vince to crank us back up. He shook his head in an exaggerated *"no"* fashion and rang the bell for last call. Their attention left the music and went to getting their last fill. Vince then went and stood by the door, and as the RCMP escorted the fighters out, they handed Vince any money they had left in their pockets. It was an expected custom that they would help pay for any damage to the bar. Many would give Vince a high five as they handed him a twenty. I heard one big-ass guy tell Vince, "Great band, Vince." Vince responded by saying, "I know, and they'll be here again Friday night!"

Vince came back to the bar and called us over after making sure his staff had everything under control. "That was one hell of a show, lads," he said to us, really saying, *Now that's what I call music that sells beer and whiskey!* Then he added, "Can you guys play every Friday until Labor Day, including Labor Day Monday?"

"Of course we can," Ray and RC said at the same time without getting agreement from Hats and me.

"Not for the same fucking deal!" Hats said to Vince, really saying, *The night for fights isn't over yet, Coach!*

"Sure," Vince said. "Come by tomorrow and we'll sort it all out, boys."

There was silence, and Vince used it to tee up six glasses for whiskey. Vince, the Judge, and the Beaver Brothers Band raised glasses and clinked to a successful debut. We drank and slammed our glasses down on the bar. The sound of the shot glasses hitting the hard wood was the last music we made that night.

"I've always liked you, boys!" Vince said as we felt the warmth in our bellies from the whiskey.

"I know," the Judge said to Vince, building on his comment. "They are very interesting."

DAY 12

South Carolina

Uncle Alec

TODAY IS A GREEN DAY – the second Green day in a row. A few more consecutive days like this and I'm going to leave this place. I think I'm ready now anyway. Yesterday's Green day was because of Sophie's dad James, and I managed to stay in the Green as I enjoyed thinking about him. He was one of the good guys, a prospector for sure. He certainly helped Sophie, George, and me at every opportunity.

People helping people is a great thing. I guess you could say I've helped a lot of people, and I've certainly had a lot of help. The Doc is smart in taking me down this path. Perhaps she knows what she's doing after all. There are still some things we need to get through. She knows that, and I know that she knows that I know that as well – all in due time. The Doc is clever to get me thinking and talking about the people who have had a positive influence in my life. Positive thoughts yield positive outcomes. This is one of the many self-fulfilling prophecies of life. Dream it, think it, do it, and then be amazed that it happened for you.

I have an uncle who has helped me a lot. His name is Alec – Uncle Alec. I call him Alec most of the time, or just Uncle. He's the Soup

Man's brother, and there's a ten-year age difference between them. I don't call my father the Soup Man in front of Alec as he would not appreciate it and would see it as very disrespectful. Then he would let me know his opinion in no uncertain terms. Alec has a lot of respect for the Soup Man, and he loved him. Their father, my grandfather, was the prospector who emigrated from Russia to Canada in 1917. Lenin and the Bolsheviks were trying to kill everybody who disagreed with them, and my grandfather was one of those people. The family folklore is that my grandfather walked west out of Russia to Italy, where he got on a boat and landed at Ellis Island in New York. From there he walked to Western Canada where he homesteaded, farmed, and started a family, with my father and Alec being two of the offspring. Unfortunately, my grandfather died in a farming accident when my father was eighteen. Alec was only eight years old, so my father took over for his father where Alec was concerned. The Soup Man may not have been around much for me, but he was around for Alec. I'm happy for Alec about this.

My father helped Alec when he was young and in need of direction and mentoring, and consequently it was very hard on Alec when the Soup Man died. But luckily for me, because Alec is a man of integrity and family values, he took over where I was concerned. There are fifteen years between Alec and me, providing a nice gap because it results in generational differences, but we also see the world for what it is. The Gen Gap makes for great debate and conversations, and seeing the world for what it is helps us come up with practical solutions to real problems. I enjoy my time with Alec. He has always been there for me, even when he was busy building his own life, and our time together increased after the Soup Man died. Then we became joined at the hip later in life, especially since I started my business. In fact, Alec is a partner in the business.

Alec is extremely successful as measured by all standards. With his father and the Soup Man gone, he has nobody setting the bar, so he continues to raise it himself. His resume includes building and selling multiple businesses, keeping company with Prime Ministers and Presidents, raising a family, and doing all of this with the ability to have several hobbies that he is really good at. One of his hobbies happens to be me. The best part of Alec though is that he's just a normal person. Money has not changed him, power has not changed him, and he's one of the good guys.

Having a mentor is truly a gift. It's a nice feeling to know you have somebody looking out for you, somebody who has your back no matter what. That's not to say mentors will accept anything from you.

In fact, an authentic mentor will be the first one to tell you when you are being a dumbass. It's tough love, but it's real love. It's different than a parent's love. Parents can be apprehensive about hurting a child's feelings, so they may hold back when they know exactly what the child needs to hear. Consequently, children don't always hear what they need to hear from their parents. A mentor has no problem telling you like it is, and they do this for your own sake, as they assume you are tough enough to take it. Too bad if they hurt your feelings a little; sometimes the end does justify the means.

Most of us have leaders in our lives – managers at work, clergy at church, and coaches in sports. These relationships are all fine but they are not mentorships. Managers want you to achieve your goals, mostly so they will achieve their goals. This cascading of goals may seem altruistic, but in the end, the manager is actually focused on achieving personal goals through you. This is not a mentorship. A mentor is not in it for himself. It's much more unselfish than that.

A mentor does not want you simply to achieve your goals; he wants you to achieve your potential in life. If he does focus on your goals, it's not about achieving them but rather for you to understand how to create and establish effective goals in the first place. A mentor sees the person you could be and tries to help you become that person. The mentor has the credentials to do this because he is accomplished in his own right. Genuine mentors have made thousands of mistakes in their own lives; they've walked the road. They want their mentees to learn from those mistakes. For us the trick is not to learn from our own mistakes, but rather to avoid mistakes in the first place by learning from mistakes made by people who have come before us! This is the real definition of wisdom – learning from other people's mistakes. Alec is wise, and I'm trying to become wise by being mentored by Alec, although it's not always easy for either of us.

I haven't talked to Alec since they dropped me off here. He was with RC and Hats during my intervention, but he has not reached out since we booked me into this *mental health spa*. Alec was called by my office. He reached out to RC and Hats, and together they decided an intervention was necessary. Alec was close by at the time as he has homes in Canada and the USA. He's done well for himself; actually, he's done *very* well for himself. He was in Florida when my office called him. Alec has his own plane with two pilots. So he flew to New Orleans, where he found me in my state. He picked up RC and Hats at the airport in New Orleans when they arrived to help.

I know he is waiting for me to reach out to him. *Mentor Rule #1: The student is only ready when he is ready, and when he is ready the teacher will appear.* Alec is waiting for me to let him know I'm ready to talk. He knows I'm safe in here so he'll wait for me. Wise people have patience because patience is a virtue of wisdom. It's a catch 22 – the chicken and the egg. You have to be patient to be wise, and to be wise you have to be patient. Lots of things in life are like this; not everything follows a linear series of cause and effect, not everything in life is predictable or is based on mathematical logic, axioms, or rules.

I have learned so much from Alec that I don't even know what thoughts are mine or what thoughts are his talking to me in the back of my mind. His stories have become my stories. He is the king of narrative leadership, examining life and leadership through stories and classic sayings. Alec can tell a story, and if you listen carefully it can change your whole day. Some days this is good, and on other days it can really piss you off. Yet when you get pissed off, it's not at Alec. Usually it's at yourself. He makes you see things from a different perspective, from a modified set of eyes, and this can piss you off even more. He can ask questions that will penetrate your soul, and his questions aren't using psychology techniques. Believe me, there is no *how do you feel about that* bullshit. I'm not sure he even considers how I feel about something because he wants me to go beyond the shell of what I'm feeling and get to the root of my understanding. It's not about how you feel about something; it's about do you understand the thing? Do you have a deep comprehension of what the hell you are talking about? Alec can really piss me off, but I love him a lot nonetheless and would not change anything about him even if it were possible.

My business helps people to live better lives. I am the self-help guru guy. I make speeches and have employees make speeches. We sell books and CDs, DVDs and electronic web-based everythings. We have over one hundred employees. The largest group I have addressed was eight thousand people. It was a giant and successful event for us, and we changed lives that night – all through dialogue. People just need to talk and listen as talking and listening are the vehicle to a calmer mind. Alec knows when to talk and when to listen, and he also knows when to tell me I need to speak up or shut up. Talking is easier than listening, even though this seems paradoxical as talking takes more energy than listening. Learning to listen is another virtue of wisdom, which once again is all built on the patience thing. Listening takes patience and Alec can listen well. Even so, he's the only person I know whose listening can piss you off. It's as if you learn from him while you watch him listen to you. His listening skills are unique; he hears and identifies incongruences in concepts. He's like a sniper who separates things that do not belong together. It's actually very weird, almost like a sixth sense or a gift of some kind. But don't get me wrong, he can also talk well when required, and when he talks, people listen. Talking and listening are his skills, and he's mastered the trick of knowing when to do each one.

His retention of sayings and stories is mind boggling. Some things he heard and remembered, and others he makes up on the fly. He has a large reservoir that he pulls from, and it doesn't matter what the topic is or what the problem is we are trying to solve. He will pull out some saying or axiom that brings the solution home more clearly than any internet search engine can. When you build a business, you need a lot of advice. Seeking advice is a daily activity, and Alec has been there for me every day.

Some of his lessons and verbal twists are engrained in my brain. Maybe I'll get a chance to teach them to George one day. I can picture and hear Alec's voice as I think back on all the conversations we've had over the years.

Sam, your job is to understand whether there is, in fact, a problem here. And even if there is, why should we actually act upon it?

Sam, sometimes you need to set the pace; sometimes you don't.

Sam, farmers can't just plant and plant. Someday we need to harvest and actually eat. There comes a time you need to sit down at the buffet and deal with what's on your plate.

Sam, there's not much difference between being middle class and being a billionaire – you can't eat more than three meals a day, you can't wear more than one pair of pants, and you can't sit in more than one room at time.

Sam, you need to work in smaller groups. Sharing and learning only works in small groups. A big group means there will only be one decision maker while the rest of the people simply get the news.

Sam, I can't and won't agree with you because if I do, we both will be wrong.

Sam, a good bird dog will retrieve the dead bird, but it can't tell you whether you should have actually shot the bird in the first place.

Sam, you can't design and document a process flow on how to be a friend.

Sam, there is a fool at every negotiation table and all of us will have our turn being that fool.

Sam, it's not about who's drinking the Kool-Aid; it's about who's making it!

Sam, win-win is always preferred, but sometimes there has to be a loser in order for there to be a winner. And sometimes there is nothing but losers.

Sam, when the bar is closing, a person's definition of ugly may need to change.

Sam, sometimes you just have to put your hands against the wall, spread your legs, and get frisked.

Sam, if, if, if – if my aunt had balls she would be my uncle.

Sam, you don't drop your line in the water unless you have some idea of where the fish are.

Sam, some actions are like marriages, easy in and not so easy out.

Sam, there's a lot of meat in that sandwich you're making.

Sam, if I were sitting at this table, I'd be inclined to throw all my chips in.

Sam, if I were sitting at this table, I'd be inclined to throw my cards away.

Sam, harsh realities first; then fix and repair.

"Harsh realities first, Sam; then fix and repair." That's what Alec said to me while we were flying to South Carolina on his jet after the intervention. That whole intervention was quite the scene. Hollywood could not have scripted it better. Let's face it, reality is much weirder than fiction. It always has been, and as I've already said a few times, some stuff you just can't make up.

I was working in New Orleans at a nice hotel downtown. It was a planned three-day conference with close to two thousand people attending, a perfect-size gathering, and I was there with about twenty-five people from our office. An event like this takes a lot of planning and actual managing during the event itself, so my staff had a few extra people there as well to support me personally. The last year in particular had been rough on me as I was dealing with the fact that Sophie and George had left me. I was working through it, and this was a good thing. At least that's what we all thought at the time.

I traditionally do opening remarks and a keynote talk at the end of the conference. We are very focused on our customers and I want to be the last one they talk to as I want to confirm that they feel they got value for their time and money. It was in the ballroom of the hotel and during this ending keynote talk that my meltdown began. In retrospect, it would have been convenient if it had ended there as well.

The interesting aspect is that nobody saw it coming, or at least I didn't see it coming, mostly because I had been doing well for the three days leading up to the ending speech.

I can't tell you exactly what I did as I don't really remember, but what I can tell you is what's been communicated to me. Let's just say that I'm not sure anybody actually received any helpful hints on improving their lives with my ending remarks. If anything, they may have realized their lives are actually in pretty good shape. The condition of your life is a relative thing. Don't worry, I didn't strip down naked, and I didn't run around the stage clucking like a chicken. Apparently what I did do was start to babble and talk about things that made no sense. According to my staff, it wasn't scary or creepy or outwardly weird but was more of a brain jumble. I was stringing thoughts and sentences together that do not belong together, all while staring up at the ceiling of the room as if my next thought was up there somewhere and I needed to coax it down.

Eventually, one of my senior lecturers came out and escorted me off the stage, and this is where it went from not-so-bad to bad. When they escorted me off the stage, they had me sit on a chair in a small corridor behind the main lecture stage, and they left me for a brief minute so they could discuss what to do with the group of customers in the room, all of whom were wondering what was going on. Apparently, I seized the moment and headed out of the hotel and got myself into a taxi.

Once in the taxi, I told the driver to take me to the airport. This part I got from RC, as he had to deal with the taxi company after the fact. He had to do this for two reasons. The first was that I gave the driver my credit card, and RC wanted to get it returned, and the second reason was so he could piece together my entire series of events. According to the taxi driver, I was a reasonably good customer until I saw his GPS. Even though he wasn't using it in order to get us to the airport, I asked him to turn it on and plug in the airport as the destination. He obliged me. The story goes that I then started arguing with the GPS about which direction it was telling us to go. According to the taxi driver, I was getting really irritated by the route the GPS was taking us, even though the entire route is just one interstate, which was what we were on. Apparently I was yelling at the GPS about spewing misinformation to the world. Taxi drivers see and hear everything, so he simply ignored me and looked forward to the trip being over. We got to the airport, and I paid with my credit card, where I also gave him a five-hundred-dollar tip. When he thanked me, I threw the credit card itself at him and told him to take as much as he wanted. I then ran from the cab, not allowing him to give me my card back, and this is when it went from bad to really bad.

The story recounted from the TSA agents at the security line is that I made it through without incident. I did have a flight booked for later that night so I was able to get a boarding pass from the kiosk. With no luggage and no coat, I was actually an easy glide past all the security measures. We know they are not capable of measuring for sane brain activity. Too bad I hadn't left my wallet in my coat back at the hotel so I wouldn't have made it past the taxi. In the sequence of events, my next stop was the VIP lounge of the airline I was flying. I travel so much I'm a member of every lounge in every airport. I made it past their check point without anybody hitting the *crazy person* buzzer and I went directly to the bar. This particular bar was self-serve, and I apparently went looking for an employee to see if they had Canadian whiskey. RC told me later that only bourbon and scotch were available to me, and so the story goes that I made a small incident about there being no Canadian whiskey. But I didn't create enough commotion that any extra security measures were required. One VIP lounge employee told the airport police that she watched me drink half a bottle of bourbon in forty-five minutes, and that's when it went from really bad to colossal.

Witnesses say I was keeping to myself in a lounge chair in one corner of the room, but I was clearly drinking heavily, as evidenced by the fact that I had removed the bottle of bourbon from the self-serve shelf and had taken it back to my chair. Near the end, I was not pouring the whiskey into my glass but instead was taking pulls directly from the bottle. At some point in my binge, two airline employees came up to the self-service bar and poured themselves two glasses of tomato juice. I still don't know what their role with the airline was. They weren't pilots. That much I know now, but for some reason I thought they were. I apparently walked up to them and asked them if they wanted some vodka for their tomato juice. According to the report, they simply smiled and tried to ignore me.

At that point, I said something like, "Don't you want some vodka in your drink so you're ready to fly? How else will you murder your next victim the way you murdered my family?"

I guess I was pretty loud, and that drew the attention of all the staff and a few fellow travelers. According to the lawyer for one of my fellow travelers, his client came up to me in a gentle fashion with open arms saying, "It's OK, brother. Everything will be OK. Let's just calm down together." I guess I wasn't ready to calm down, and when he got too close I pulled out a few Krav Maga moves that resulted in his having a broken nose and two fractured ribs. I really feel bad about that. The man was a minister with the *First Church of Christ* and was in New Orleans helping victims of *Hurricane Katrina* who were still in rough shape. Eventually I ended up making a very generous donation to his church, and he chose to call off the lawyers, producing a win-win after the initial win-lose.

Anyway, after my fighting moves I was tackled by about fifty people. This is the new post-911 world; people are really pissed off these days and can't wait to pounce on a crazy person. So in hindsight, I probably made a bunch of people's day that day. I ended up being taken to a holding cell they have at the airport, and from there they were able to use my wallet to contact my office, who contacted Alec, who contacted RC and Hats. Alec showed up in about three hours, and RC and Hats arrived late that night. Alec flew us all back to South Carolina together the next morning, and I insisted we go to my house, where I was in denial that anything was wrong and we argued for over two hours. RC was very understanding. His experience as a Police Officer allows him to be empathic. Hats wanted to kick my ass. I guess that's what experience as a lawyer does. Alec just stared at me and said, "Harsh realities first, Sam; then fix and repair."

We made a few calls that evening, and they dropped me off here. Now I need to take the first step.

Harsh realities first; then fix and repair.

"OK, Uncle Alec, I'm ready to do that."

Alec is one of the good guys.

Canada
Fall 1982

Evil Comes to Town

THE REST OF THE SUMMER was nothing but pure fun, exactly how life should be at that age. We worked hard at Beaver Brothers the business and played hard with Beaver Brothers the band. When we weren't doing those two things, we were hanging out at the Lodge being the Beaver Brothers in general.

Labor Day weekend was spent at the Maple Tree Hotel, as Vince had us play in the afternoons and every night of the weekend. We were certainly tired on the Tuesday morning that school started, although it didn't really matter: we knew what to expect on the first day, even though it was the first day of our last year of high school. Hats, on the other hand, had to be President of the Student Council, and while he had no idea what that meant in totality, he was aware that one responsibility was to say the *Lord's Prayer* over the intercom system. Every morning, it was up to Hats to recite the *Lord's Prayer* in French to the entire school population. I don't need to explain what that was like – it was priceless. As fate and entropy would have it though, he only ended up being the pseudo resident youth priest for two weeks.

Evil came to Chinook River on Friday, September 17, 1982. This

185

was the day that a fifteen-year-old girl was fatally stabbed after a failed rape attempt. She was walking home from our high school and was pulled into the woods by a young man who had violence and sexual deviancy running through his core. He attempted to assault the young girl sexually but was unable to get through the layers of clothing she had on due to the weather's having turned cold. His fit of frustration turned into rage and he stabbed the girl three times in the chest with a hunting knife he had bought at the local hardware store. He then left her to die. She was found fifteen minutes after the attack by joggers who were out for a fall run. She was dead at the scene. This, in and of itself, was tragedy for our town. What brought the tragedy closer to home, however, is the fact that the girl was Ray's younger sister Rose – our Rose. She was smart and beautiful, she was our little sister, she was our Angel Rose, and now she was dead.

Hats, RC, and I were all at Ray's house watching television when the police came to the door around six o'clock. Ray answered the door, and we listened while he led two RCMP constables into the living room. Ray then went and got his parents from whatever they were doing. We listened in from the basement without making ourselves seen or heard, and all we could hear were muffled voices. Then a sound of absolute torture came from Ray's mother.

We had no idea what was going on, and in our own panic, the three of us left out the garage door and headed to my house. We waited for Ray to join us to tell us what had happened, but Ray never showed up that evening. RC made a phone call to some friends he had at the RCMP, and all they told him was that a young girl had been found dead in our neighborhood woods. We put the pieces together. I'm not even sure what we did the rest of that evening, and I can't completely recall our emotions, the feelings we were having, or the conversations we had. I vaguely remember that we wanted to run away. Running seemed appropriate, but we had no place to run to. The three of us slept at my house that night waiting for Ray.

Ray came down to my basement around seven o'clock Saturday morning and woke us from our unsettled sleep. The four of us embraced in one hug and we stayed that way for what seemed like hours. Nothing was said; nobody knew what to say as this was new and uncharted terrain for all of us. We allowed Ray to set the path and tone for what would happen next. He asked if we could go to the garage and play some songs, so that's what we did all that Saturday. Ray played and sang and only stopped to light up a torpedo or grab a drink. Even if we weren't playing with him, he just strummed his acoustic guitar. As I watched Ray and didn't know what to say or do, I realized that our life experience to date was not quite what we believed it to be. It struck me that we were not as mature as we thought we were. We had no idea what to do for our best friend. Even our most powerful phrase of *We will get through this* did not seem to meet the needs of the moment. In many respects when I look back now, I realize that we lost a big part of Ray that evil Friday. Perhaps we did not know what to say or do because Ray was telling us to do nothing. Maybe he was busy dealing with things on his own, I don't know for sure, but I do know that things were never the same after Rose's death.

Time may aid the brain to dull and store away painful emotions, but it does not heal all wounds. That is a fallacy. Time is not a natural healer. Time is just time – invisible, odorless, tasteless, lifeless, and not engaged in existence in any way. Time is not friend and it is not foe; it is made up, fabricated as a concept throughout the evolution of man, an invention of people trying to gain power over other people. Time is a brainchild of the writers and creators of God, as exemplified by the first words in the famous book...*In the beginning*. Well, a lot of stuff has gone down since *in the beginning*, and a lot of it was not very God-like. I never understood why the writers of the Bible started it with *In the beginning*. By doing so, they ruined the whole story because all we have to ask is, "Who invented God before the beginning?" A question that has no answer, one that people of faith like to ignore because of its obvious inconvenience. If it were me, I would have started the Bible with, "Time does not exist; there is no beginning and no end." I think this would have been helpful for explaining some of the incongruences in the overall story.

The news spread around town quickly, and we were expecting the RCMP to come and talk to us as we were friends and practically all big brothers to Rose. But this never happened, although RC was our conduit into the RCMP, and he got enough facts for us to understand the story. The RCMP went to the school late on the Friday night of the murder, and they assembled the principal and all teachers and staff of the school. They asked the teachers if they had any idea who might be capable of such a crime, and the teachers were fast and very vocal about a particular student. It seemed as if it was clear and obvious to everybody that this particular boy would kill one day. The Police went to the sick boy's house and found him curled up in a ball in some sort of dysfunctional mental state. His parents were not home. Within a twenty-four hour period he admitted to killing Rose. He was hauled away from his home by the police, and by Monday morning he was gone from Chinook River. There was no arrest picture, no big fancy trial, no lawyers talking outside the court house, no twists or turns, no Hollywood of any kind. Hollywood and the Talking Cable Heads don't show the real grey dark face of true violence. The violence that happens in our world every day is cold and without story. There is no plot, no motive, and no *gotcha* at the end. There is nothing dramatic or thrilling about it. Boy gets sick, sick boy kills girl, sick boy gets caught, and sick boy is taken away. Family of dead girl is left to carry on somehow. Repeat cycle in some other town, end of story. Hollywood and the Heads should be ashamed of themselves. The people profiting from the sensationalism of violence should be ashamed of themselves.

The sick boy's family left town as well, and eventually their house was torn down as nobody wanted to live in it. That's how things work in small northern towns; people can come and go unnoticed, but stories can linger on forever. I never bothered looking up what became of the sick young man. I don't believe it was ever important to Ray or Hats either, although I suspect RC probably knows from his work, but he doesn't talk about it with us. Some things just need to be forgotten – if not forgotten, perhaps at least avoided. Sometimes management by avoidance is, in fact, a correct strategy.

The school was closed for three days following Rose's death. Judge Jeremiah worked with the RCMP, local leaders, and school officials to make sure all conversations that were required were actually happening as an event like this will turn a small town upside down. These days, a school would probably not be closed down because of this type of occurrence. These days, we just pull up our socks and move on. Today people believe in business as usual – yes, business as usual – other than two empty seats in the classroom and two *plus* broken families. Reflection is no longer seen as value, but the Judge didn't see it that way. He believed the whole community should take a few days to be with their families, to live in the moment, to hug their kids and be thankful for what they had. We spent as much time as we could with Ray, and we supported him as he got very involved with the planning of Rose's wake and funeral, which was scheduled for the Thursday and Friday of that week. Ray asked me if I would write and read a poem. I accepted. He asked all three of us to be pall bearers with him and his father and uncle. We accepted.

There was some consideration about having the funeral at the High School in order to use the auditorium. This idea was in anticipation of a large crowd, but Ray and his family decided against the idea and planned the funeral at the *Chinook River United Church,* the church we all belong to. The minister was a young-looking man in his late thirties with a wife and two young children, and he worked very hard with Ray's family during this time and the months and years that followed. We called him Preacher Pete, even though he was a minister. Canada doesn't pervasively use the term preacher. We always just thought it sounded neat: Preacher Pete. The United Church congregation made a good decision when they selected him from a pool of several candidates offered by the United Church provincial leadership. He was one of the good guys. He got up in the morning and gave life a shot. He gave life a shot all in the name of helping other people. This made him one of the good guys.

Ray's family had the wake at one of the two funeral homes in town. They had an open casket at the viewing, after which the casket would be closed for the service at the church and remain closed until Rose would be cremated. Seeing Rose lying in her casket was close to unbearable for Hats, RC, and me, but we needed to be strong for Ray. This whole situation was so wrong and so broken. Ray asked us to stay close to him during the day and evening of the wake, so we did just that.

The number of people that came to the wake was completely overwhelming. In the history of the town, there had never been an outpouring of support like the outpouring Ray and his family received. Not only did all family come in from out of town, but extended family, friends, distant friends, and strangers all descended on the funeral home to pay their respects. Fire Fighters and Police Officers and other public officials from other communities came to show support and pay their respects. Even though the fall temperatures were settling in, the line into the funeral home seemed to stream for miles. People waited patiently, some already comfortable in winter clothes, others shuffling their feet back and forth with their hands in their pockets trying to keep the chill from reaching their bones. The support was spiritual, and in the wake of the wake, some little ounce of good was created from an infinite weight of bad. RC, Hats, and I took turns standing at the front of the procession line with Ray and his mother, father, and uncle. We didn't greet people or shake hands; we simply stood one foot behind Ray and allowed his family their space. He had asked for us, and we had his back, and his family appreciated this and welcomed our presence.

The following day was cold and grey, and while Ray was hoping for blue skies and sunshine, he did not get his wish. Even though it was only September, the fall air was bitter as we were feeling the silent and subtle entrance of *Jack Frost*. Normally in the fall, the saving grace can be sunshine and the unbelievable beauty of the turning and falling of the leaves. On this day, however, the sky was grey and the air was cold, and when I thought of the leaves, all I could picture was our little Angel Rose lying in a blood-soaked pile of them. In retrospect, a spark of anger started in me that day. Perhaps that day was the beginning of the anger that is warehoused in my soul today.

Because of the wake, we were anticipating a large crowd for the funeral, and a mass of people did in fact arrive. The United Church is the second largest church in town and it did a good job of housing the vast number of mourners. People made sure every bit of each pew was used, and a lot of people stood against the walls and at the back of the church. Those that could not fit into the main church were invited to listen via intercom from one of the many rooms used for Sunday school teachings. RC, Hats, and I sat in the second row center aisle behind Ray and his family. The Judge, his wife Johanna, and Vince were sitting with us as well. Ray had asked the Judge to say a few words before my poem. Preacher Pete stood at the pulpit the entire time the church was filling up, while Rose, in her closed pre-cremation casket, was below him and level with all of us in the pews.

The United Church of Canada is the largest Protestant Christian denomination in Canada. It was founded in 1925 by way of a Western Canada-led amalgamation of the Methodist, Presbyterian, and Congregational Churches and is the second largest Christian Church in Canada, second only to the Roman Catholic Church. This is certainly the case as well in Chinook River, both in membership numbers and size of the actual church building. We were number two and very proud of it.

It's a liberal Church that ministers to the congregation, which is why the clergy of the United Church are actually called ministers. The word minister is both a noun and a verb, in that you <u>are</u> *it*, and you <u>do</u> *it*. They teach that the Bible is central to the Christian faith because it was written by people who were close to God, and they also teach that times have changed so we can't take the Bible literally in all its scripture. This little *out* is helpful and convenient for Sunday school teachers who try hard to explain away the grotesque horrors of the Old Testament. The Church is very inclusive and welcomes all people regardless of demographic or lifestyle choice as, after all, even Jesus welcomed tax collectors and prostitutes with open arms.

The two main sacraments of the United Church are Baptism and

Communion. Baptism is about receiving a new life, and Communion is about repeating a historical and symbolic meal as often as you can. Full membership in the Church comes with both of these items having been formally accomplished. Being a full member will help to provide a full and healthy life in all respects – body, mind, and spirit, and safety for the soul.

All four of the Beaver Brothers were full members of the church. So was Rose.

We grew up going to the United Church of Canada in Chinook River. Sunday school was our routine as kids, and the adult service became routine afterwards. We were comfortable in our Church, even when not comfortable with our own personal beliefs relative to God. We had our own opinions and we were taught this was healthy. *To question is to build faith; to build faith is to question.* That's what we were taught. By way of this theory, we should have built enough faith for the whole town to last a century. Ray was always the most skeptical, although he rarely vocalized his thoughts and did not bother creating constructive dialogue for the sake of understanding. Secretly he supported the beliefs of a few Canadian First Nations and American Native Tribes that churches are an invention of the white man, a place where people can go to fight about whose God actually exists. In essence, not much different from a boxing ring, although many churches are much more elaborate.

Even though we had been in the Church hundreds of times over the years, this day was different, and the Church looked and felt different. The stained glass windows looked different, the pews and altar looked different, and even though physically nothing had changed, the Church was different.

The service started and Preacher Pete did the best he could under the circumstances, as this was uncharted territory for him as well, and he was learning on the job. He read from the *Book of Matthew* and used selected verses as his theme for his talk.

At that time, the disciples came to Jesus and asked, 'Who is the greatest in the kingdom of heaven?' He called a child, whom he put among them, and said, 'Truly, I tell you, unless you change and become like children, you will never enter the kingdom of heaven. Whoever becomes humble like this child is the greatest in the kingdom of heaven. Whoever welcomes one such child in my name welcomes me.'

Preacher Pete tried his best to deal with the pain, confusion, and anger that were actively growing or had stabilized in the hundreds of people who were present. He had obviously done his homework and was prepared with the major themes – God works in mysterious ways, children are precious, God has a plan, this is all part of God's master plan, it has all been road-mapped since the beginning of time, Rose is part of that master plan, she is now in a better place, Rose is now with God, yes it may be hard to understand, and yes it's OK to be angry and confused, because as I said, God works in mysterious ways.

"*Really?*" was all that kept going through my brain. "*Rule number one…God works in mysterious ways…and when things can't quite be explained in any rational way…see rule number one. QED. Problem solved!*"

I was watching Ray from behind and at a diagonal, and I could tell he wasn't even listening. Nothing the minister was saying was registering with Ray as he was in a different place. These were the first moments that Ray was designing the new place he would spend his time. He was building a landing spot for his thoughts. I remember thinking in that moment that Ray might never be the same again, that we all might never be the same again.

While Ray looked comatose, I was sitting there wanting to stand up and scream at Preacher Pete.

Really, Pete? Really, God? Master Plan? Did Rose know about the plan when she was born? Did you ask her if she was OK with the ending before you planted the seed on the egg that resulted in Rose? Or did she miss that meeting? And what about the no good, crazy sick boy that killed her? He was another of your precious sheep? Another actor given a role in the master plan stage show? Oh, wait. He's not your problem, that's not your fault, that's the devil. But wait. You created everything, including the devil, who by the way is your fallen angel. Which I assume was part of the master plan because the plan was all scripted before it all started! Figure that one out. So, the master plan was in place with You knowing exactly how it would all unfold. You would be responsible for, and take credit for, this beautiful Angel Rose. However, the devil would be responsible for, and take credit for, sicko wannabe rapist boy. Not Your problem even though You created the master plan that included the devil getting out of the lantern. Really, God? Well, I have only one question, 'Who let the dogs out, Man!' Mysterious ways indeed. That much I'll buy for ninety cents. Do you have change for a dollar, God?

What was going on in my brain was not proving helpful. I worked really hard at that moment to slow my mind down as these rapid thoughts were not healthy, and I knew enough to know that. At my core, I don't think I believed the things I was thinking, but I was not in control of the synapses in my brain waves, and my thoughts and the speed of the thought tangents and misdirections were overwhelming. I was spinning, and I knew I had to slow my brain down. I looked over at Hats, and all I saw in his eyes was anger, which was not helpful for my situation. I looked over at RC, and what I saw helped me. He was sitting erect with perfect posture; he was listening to the minister and nodding when appropriate to show comprehension and understanding of the key teaching points. He looked confident, and in that moment, I had a mind flash and pictured him in an RCMP uniform – the distinctive red serge, the high-collared scarlet tunic, midnight blue breeches with yellow leg stripe, Sam Browne belt with white sidearm lanyard, oxblood riding boots, brown felt, and brown gloves. He looked great. He looked confident. He looked on-the-job. I pictured his majestic horse waiting for him outside the church. It struck me in that instant that although I'm sure RC was hurting immensely, he was ultimately there for Ray. He was on the job – proud, confident, and Canadian – there for his brother. In that moment, I knew my best friend RC would make an amazing officer for the Royal Canadian Mounted Police.

I came out of my reverie to see Preacher Pete sitting down and the Judge heading to the pulpit. Judge Jeremiah was exactly what the town needed – right time, right place, and right person. Sometimes the stars do align. He didn't build on Preacher Pete's words from a Christian point of view, and he did not get up and try to convince people further that a whole situation that makes no sense is somehow part of a whole situation that is based on sense. Instead, he just talked to his town. The Judge is more comfortable in his own skin than any other person I have ever met. I'm sure he has his story, but it was easy that day to believe he had no baggage that hindered him. It was easy to believe that he had thrown out the hitchhiker trying to put the evil rearview mirror in front of everything good.

He looked out at his community, and he urged people to help people. He told us that the best thing you can do when you are hurting is to help somebody else. He said it didn't matter whether you were sad, angry, confused, or scared; that all of these emotions can be cured by a simple act of kindness. He told the town that evil does exist and evil can strike you in your own backyard. But evil cannot win over kindness because one act of kindness will trump three acts of evil. He told parents to hug their children and teach them to be kind, he told the children to learn from their parents to be kind, and he told everybody to work on one human attribute – kindness. I believe our town became one degree kinder that day. Judge Jeremiah. What did I tell you? He's the real deal.

I walked past the Judge on the way to the pulpit while he was on his way down to his seat. When we were side by side he grabbed my arm and whispered in my ear, "You are a good man, Sam, and an even better friend. I'm proud of you son, and your father is proud of you today as well." While I appreciated his words of kindness, his hit-and-run statement combined with Rose in her casket in front of me was more than I had bargained for. When I got to the pulpit, I simply stared out at the funeral congregation. I was fighting back emotions I had never felt before, becoming acutely aware for the first time that certain words triggered some sentiment resting deep in my being. After what seemed like hours standing at the pulpit, I finally snapped out of it and looked at Ray. He was back from his lost place and he gave me a nod of approval. His nod told me it was my turn to be a formal part of saying goodbye to his sister – to our sister. So I recited my poem for Rose.

THE LAST WORDS OF AN ANGEL ROSE

Save me, save me, save me if you can
Hold me, hold me, hold me where I am
Hear me, hear, me, hear me when I call
Catch me, catch me, catch me when I fall

Listen to me, please just listen without reply
Think about what I'm saying, without asking why
This once, this time, the story is not you
Help me, help me, help me to get through

You can see my face, but my eyes will tell you more
Look into my eyes, as my eyes are the door
My soul is waiting, waiting for what I need
My soul is waiting, waiting to be freed

I finished my poem and sat down, and the Judge patted me on the shoulder in an *atta boy* fashion. When I looked at him I could see he had tears in his eyes. Preacher Pete went back to the pulpit. According to the agenda, and as far as Preacher Pete knew, my poem was the end of the formal part of the program. What we did not know, however, was that Ray had his own idea of how his little sister's funeral would end.

Just as Preacher Pete was about to make the final announcements, Ray stood up from his front row seat and walked a straight line to the church's pipe organ. It was not the first time he had ever played the organ in the church, but it certainly was the first time he had played unscripted and unplanned with a standing-room-only congregation. Only a handful of people knew this was impromptu, so the whole scene appeared to be normal, and Preacher Pete easily played his part and allowed Ray to sit down at the organ. In fact, being the professional that he is, Pete even said, "To end our service today, Ray would like to play a song in tribute to his sister, Rose." Vince, the Judge, RC, Hats, and I all managed to enjoy a brief smile. A simple little smile can in fact improve a difficult situation.

Hats, RC, and I looked at each other to see if one of us was in on the deal, but it was clear from our blank expressions that we were all equally clueless. Ray was now officially renegade, with no need for supporters or sympathizers to spur his actions. Whatever he was up to, he had not required our input, opinions, or approval.

Ray sat down at the organ and simply stared at the large and majestic pipes going from the organ up the wall towards the roof of the church. He straightened his posture and put his hands on the keyboard compass that sends the musical wind signals through differing timbres of the organ. He placed his feet on the pedalboard exactly where he wanted them in order to maneuver his position with the organ stops. He took a deep breath, the organ seemed to take a deep breath, and then they both began to play.

Instantly, the entire church was silent, mesmerized and watching and listening to Ray. In the end, I believe the music that Ray played that day was more spiritual than any sounds that had ever been heard in the church before.

When Ray touched the keys to the pipe organ, he began to play *Let It Be*. He played it in such a way that it has not, cannot, and will not ever be played again. With total respect to Paul, John, George, and Ringo, this was *Let It Be* by Ray for his sister Rose. Every person at the service, whether sitting or standing, was instantly grounded in the moment. The music was the only sensory feeling that existed in the universe for us.

The chords flowed through the air in a way that was unique to each individual. Some of us mouthed the words as if in silent karaoke, some of us remembered when we had first heard the song, many of us tried to connect all the thoughts, both known and unknown, that were required to know why Ray was playing what he was playing. We thought about times of trouble, we thought about wisdom, we thought about darkness and light, and we thought about today and tomorrow. We sat in our own church, in our own little town, and we thought about everything that our minds, bodies, and souls were capable of thinking about and feeling all at the same time. And when the music stopped, after a minute of self-imposed silence we all thought about Rose. Ray had clearly achieved his goal, evident by the fact that every person in the church was thinking about nothing but little Rose – our precious Angel Rose.

After Ray's hands left the keyboard for good, and after the entire population of the funeral came back to reality, Preacher Pete got back up. Continuing in perfect improvisation, he let everybody know what was next in the series of events for the day, and then he looked at us as pallbearers to accompany Rose down the church aisle. The problem, though, was Ray simply stayed seated at the organ while the rest of the huge congregation waited for the next step in the difficult process.

Ray simply continued to stare up at the pipes of the organ, looking straight up as if pondering where the pipes go when they leave the roof. His father looked at Preacher Pete in a *What do I do?* look and Preacher Pete looked at RC, Hats, and me, and we looked at Vince and the Judge and Johanna. Ray's mother was in her own world and could not help. Vince was the first to act and he walked up to Ray and put his hand on Ray's shoulder while standing by his right side. He then bent down and whispered into Ray's ear. Ray seemed to drift back to reality and stood up, and Vince and Ray walked together towards us, towards the next step in saying goodbye to Rose.

And with that, and with the magical and spiritual sounds of *Let It Be* still flowing in our minds, we led Rose out of the church.

DAY 13
South Carolina

Anger

TODAY IS A YELLOW DAY, which is pretty good considering what I've been thinking about. I actually almost stayed in the Green and could probably have rationalized giving myself Green today, but if my measurement system is going to be relevant and accurate, then I have to be honest with myself. So, in all honesty, today is a Yellow day – anxiety, yes; but anger, no.

I've been thinking all day about my anger. I ended up a little angry thinking about the many dimensions of my anger, and I actually got a little angrier thinking about how I got angrier. But don't worry; I get the irony. As Doc has pointed out, and as I've coached many people over the years, it's important for us to catch ourselves when we are trespassing close to the state of mind we are trying to avoid. So the trick initially is not to eliminate all feelings of anger, but rather to catch yourself getting angry and then work through it before it consumes you. It can be exhausting though. You have to think and feel and then think about and address what you're thinking and feeling, and then act and think and feel through it. It's no wonder some people just stay angry all the time as dealing with anxiety and anger is a lot of work. It's complicated work too.

What's interesting is my new understanding of anger and the many forms it takes. I've known about all the theory conceptually and academically, but you don't really know something until you have personally experienced it. You don't know what it's like to cut a hole in the ice of a lake and jump into the freezing water unless you have cut a hole in an ice-capped lake and jumped into the freezing water. Some things can't be described or imagined, some things can't be learned from a book, and anger is one of those things.

Anger is as common as any other emotion, and it's actually an important emotion as without anger, there would be no love or peace in the same way that without dark, there would be no light. The trick, though, is not to live in the dark all day long. Nobody can handle darkness forever, and sunlight is required for growth. The last few months for me have been like one big blackout. The electrical grids went down, and I was left in the dark – the big, black, invisible, blind land of anger. It's interesting that we associate anger with the color red. In my mind, it really should be black because anger is darkness.

We all know anger in its common everyday dress. We can recognize it easily and accept that it sometimes pops in for a visit. The stubbing of the toe that results in a punch to the door, or the low blood-sugar level that creates a cranky child or adult and a good nap afterwards. This is normal anger and it is as natural as any other emotion. Right? Well, it's not that's simple.

Anger has other outfits hanging in the closet. It has a garment for any occasion, event, person, place, or thing. It has street clothes and formal dress up clothes, it's walking around in attire that makes it unrecognizable for what it truly is, and in these disguises we fail to recognize that it's just good old anger in camouflage.

Like when you're feeling intolerant of anything that is happening around you, or feeling jealousy and envy when watching somebody have success in life. This envy can lead to anger and then downright hatred. Ahhh, anger and hatred – siblings at the core; dinner mates at any holiday feast.

Like the feeling when you are standing in front of the Talking Cable Heads while they are interviewing some member of the rich and famous, and all you want to do is scream at the screen, "I hope your career implodes." Or the feelings of malice or contempt felt when looking at a stranger in a line, concluding he is nothing but a scoundrel simply by looking at him. Road rage without understanding anything about the situation happening in the car of the perceived aggressor, or the trip into the world of stubbornness and self-pity that results in every comment out of your mouth being born from the womb of cynicism and sarcasm, or the person of financial means thinking he is somehow superior and smarter or more deserving than the lower forms of life who are servicing his every need.

Rigidity, discontent, tension, distrust, anxiety, suspicion, frustration, resentment, impatience – all of it at times developing into anger with no clothes on at all because naked is the real dress of anger – naked, cold, leaving you seeing black rage and telling you to strike out at the entire world for clearly being completely moronic. Where you just want to scream, "How did I end up being the only person who understands how jacked up you all are! Is it not clear and obvious that the whole damn world is broken! Am I the only one awake here?"

Ahhh, that felt good, and to think I can think through this and still stay in the Yellow zone and avoid Red, or should I say Black. Good for me, that's progress.

The seeds of anger and hatred are fear. Anger and hatred are the flower when the seeds of fear are germinated by sick people in the world, a flower with thorns and poisonous sap to many who touch it. Yet some of us don't just touch the flower of fear; we grow it and harvest it and eat it and take nourishment from it. Fear is our staple when we sit down to a Sunday night dinner; it's the main course.

I need to understand my fear because if I can comprehend and embrace my fear, I will conquer my anger. Tear the flower out at the roots and destroy the seed. That's what I need to do.

What exactly is it that I'm so scared of? It's not as if we're all still living in caves and fearful that a marauding group of Neanderthals are going to kill us, take our food, and kidnap our family. For most of us, there is no real threat to body and limb at all these days, so the true biological need for fear has been rendered obsolete. Basic instincts and responses for actual survival are not drawn upon very often. Physical survival is a skill we are not practicing or homing in on these days. Physical survival in the civilized world is a lost art.

So in the absence of a need for fear to be used for physical survival, the brain has developed new capabilities for fear itself. Heaven forbid the human being be without it. Fear has left the world of ensuring physical survival and has entered the new market of emotional survival, and it's a huge market with billions of potential customers. Fear has never been so busy. Those of us who are actually conscious and not in a mind-numbing narcissistic trance are actually blessed to be plagued only by fear of failure, fear of ridicule, and fear of shame.

The fear of shame is the favorite delivery system of fear. The feeling you get when you call up some distant memory and ask yourself, "What was I thinking!" That essence when you are driving down the road and the hitchhiker whacks you in the head with the rearview mirror and you close your eyes tight hoping the images will go away. "How could I have been so careless," you say to yourself over and over. You are the slave, and fear is the slave owner, and shame is the set of shackles around your ankles. You feel trapped, unable to walk or run, like the dreams where you are running but going nowhere or attempting to start a run but your legs just won't go. Your momentum has been shamed into shackles; we are helpless, and we are hopeless.

Fear loves this hopelessness, fear relies on it, and fear fears that we will someday find out its little nasty secret. The little secret that only fear, anger, hatred, and a few people know: that fear is weak. That fear is no stronger than a wet paper bag trying to hold back a monsoon. Yet fear stays strong because it knows we do not know. It knows we will not realize that we did the best we could, that all people make mistakes, that whatever decision you made, regardless of the outcome, you made the best decision you could with the knowledge, experience, and values you had at the time. Nobody is perfect; nobody is immune to the laws of entropy and chaos. To err is human, everybody messes up, get over it, get on with your life, forgive yourself, that was the past, you did not know then what you know now, you cannot hold yourself accountable for a decision made in the past just because you now have the knowledge that would change what you would have decided. Time machines do not exist. Sorry, that's just not how it works, so forgive yourself. It's not your fault; it's in the past; forgive yourself.

Fear hates this type of knowledge being spread around. Even other people hate this knowledge getting out there. In particular, evil leaders do not want this information out there. The history of mankind in large part is nothing more than an account of leaders dealing with their fears by manipulating the fears of others. Death and destruction *en masse* in the course of history, and all of it is just an account of people masking emotional fears. Very sad for us all. Want to change your world? Forgive yourself. Want to change the whole world? Forgive others. Forget fear. Come up with what Hats would say to fear and start there.

I reached out to Ray this evening to end my day. I stayed in the Yellow even with the essence of my thoughts today. We wrote a little poem together. Here it is.

COMMON GROUND

Halfway between
You and me
Is a place called common ground
It's a hard place to find
But if we take the time
Happiness just may be found

It's a place where compromise
Makes sense in each other's eyes
Where I sincerely understand how you feel
You care about what I think
We work hard to get in sync
So old injuries can begin to heal

It's a worthwhile place to go
Where we both can try to show
All the important reasons why
Before life's challenges came along
Our original love was strong
So we really should avoid saying goodbye

Canada
Fall 1982

Train Wreck

AFTER ROSE'S FUNERAL, we went back to Hats' house and got comfortable in his basement. We thought about heading to the Lodge, but it was getting late, and it was an unusually dark night, not to mention we were utterly exhausted. We sank into the basement couches, and the four of us just stared at nothing for twenty minutes – no talk, no music, no anything. It had been a week like no other week we had ever experienced, and we assumed it would be a week like no week we would ever experience again.

Eventually Hats got up and said, "Fuck this shit. I'm getting a drink."

He went upstairs and came back with a half-full bottle of the King's whiskey and a quarter-full bottle of gin, two liquors of choice of many northerners – one is the summer drink, the other the winter beverage of choice. The two are often bridged and transitioned in the fall with a few bottles of rum or vodka. RC went out into Hats' garage and found a half-case of OV as well, making us pretty well stocked to get started at least, and it all seemed reasonably appropriate, so we wasted no time in putting ourselves on an express train to Tuneupville.

The conversations stayed in the safe zones, at least at first – music, hockey, and drinking itself. We can exhaust hours talking about drinking. We know a lot about beer, wine, and liquors, and we enjoy impressing each other with our alcohol trivia acumen. It didn't take too long before we ran out of beer and torpedoes, and after we did a quick check around the house it became obvious we would need to do a run before the night was over. Logic and common sense say get the run over early while driving is not yet an issue, at least not an issue relatively speaking. Normally Ray is our best driver, but he was in no mood to do the run, and I was still in good shape, so I signed up for the job.

RC and Ozark joined me and we took Boomer to the Maple Tree Hotel to get everything we needed for the night. Our list wasn't that complicated – lots of beer and lots of smokes. We left Hats and Ray together to sip whiskey while we were gone. I drove and RC rode shotgun, and Ozark sat alert on the bench seat behind us.

It's only a five-minute drive from Hats' house to the Maple Tree Hotel. We could easily walk it, and have on many occasions, but the night was not a walking night. We also knew we would be weighed down with our grocery list. Some chores are just not made for walking and this was one of those chores.

When we arrived at the Maple Tree Hotel, it was not a typical Friday night. The place was sparsely populated, and when I looked around I could tell the patrons were all spilled over from Rose's funeral. Vince had closed the bar during the day while he attended the service, and I suspect that made people think the place was closed for the night. Vince was surprised to see RC, Ozark, and me, and he came from behind the bar and gave us all a big hug. When we finished our embrace we pulled away, and I saw tears streaming from Vince's eyes. He tried to look down and act as if he were a big tough guy as he headed back behind the bar. There is no such thing as a big tough guy – the harder they act, the softer they are.

We walked up to the bar and joined a few friends who were nursing their drinks of choice and making small town talk. There was something soothing about the atmosphere. Vince asked us what we wanted to drink, and we ordered up an OV and a shot of whiskey. The Judge looked over at us and asked me if I was driving us home. I looked at Vince and gave him a silent signal that said, "Scratch the whiskey from my order."

As we drank our respective drinks, Vince explained how he had intended to close the hotel for the entire day and night, but after the funeral a few folks congregated outside the church doors and started visiting. It seemed as if the group just needed to talk, and after a while it got a little cool to be standing outside, so the Judge suggested the small group go for a drink. Vince said he knew just the place. A few others overheard this offer as well, so Vince sincerely opened up the invitation to anybody interested, and that's how the group ended up at Vince's that night.

Nobody talked about Rose, and this did not surprise anybody as it was not the time or the place. This was the time for grief, hostility, and anger to be put on hold. This was a time for small talk and healing talk for anybody who required it. This was a time to talk about hockey, mining, and the weather – senseless small talk that can actually help in the healing process, and it wasn't just to heal about Rose. That's the interesting aspect of a gathering like this. The tragedy brings people together, and they seek calm both for the event of the tragedy and also for the stories in their own lives. A *"How are you doing, Sam?"* is no longer simply a question to ask me how I'm doing, but rather now means, *"Hi, Sam. You must be hurting. I'm hurting too, not only for Rose and her family, but for me as well. I have lost people I love, and I'm thinking about them right now, and I miss them. Rose's death has me sad for Rose and for all the other sadness in my life."*

This is just the way of good people in a good town, and Vince knew what he was doing. He was providing the place and environment for new healing to begin and past healing to continue. Our Coach Vince, one of the good guys.

We finished our beer, and we knew that another round was not wise since we had to drive the short distance home. Not to mention that RC was in conversation with a couple of RCMP constables. So I got a bunch of quarters from Vince and headed to the torpedo machine to get our smokes while RC asked Vince for three cases of OV. Thank goodness for *off sales*. In our province the bars are allowed to sell cases of beer over the counter. It's got its pros and cons for sure, but it worked for us that night. When RC went to pay for the beer Vince told him that his cash register was not working and that we could clean an eavestrough for him sometime. "Sure, Vince, and thanks," was all RC said to him as they shook hands across the bar. Armed with our beer and smokes, we headed out of the Maple Tree Hotel after saying our farewells to our friends and fellow townspeople. The last thing I remember hearing was the Judge saying, "Go easy tonight, boys."

When we arrived back at Hats' house, the place was dark other than lights coming from the basement. We went through the garage and headed downstairs with our supplies. Hats and Ray were well on their way to Tuneupville, so RC and I decided to get caught up. The quickest way to do that is to play a good old drinking game. We chose to play *caps*. This is the game where you sit on the floor five feet from each other with a beer bottle stationed at attention between your spread-out legs. You place a bottle cap upside down on your bottle and your opponent throws another cap at your bottle. If you hit the cap of your opponent's bottle, then he takes a drink from the bottle in front of him. It's a great game, and to this day I still don't know who is actually the winner or loser when your cap is hit. We decided to speed things up a bit and changed the rule to be that if you hit your opponent's cap we would all drink. Eventually, we just changed the rule to be that after every throw we would drink. Hats and Ray eventually joined us on the floor and we replaced the beer bottles with glasses of whiskey and gin. The goal now was to throw the cap into the open glass, and when this occurred we all took a shot of straight liquor. Ozark just slept beside Ray with her head on his lap, looking up every once in a while when one of us yelled a yell of success for dunking a cap. Needless to say, it got messy in no time as liquor is an accelerator – an on-ramp to the freeway heading to Tuneupville.

It started downhill when I hit Hats' glass square-on and he took his shot. He downed the drink and threw the glass hard at the couch, where it bounced back and landed on the rug without breaking.

"Motherfuckers," he said, clearly in a voice of anger.

"What?" Ray said.

"Motherfuckers," Hats said again.

"Who?" RC said, really saying, *What are you talking about, Hats?*

"Who?" Hats replied. "The fucking teachers, that's who!"

"What are you talking about?" I said to Hats. Ray was saying nothing. He was still just drinking his drink and patting Ozark, who was lying with her head on his lap. In hindsight, I'm not sure Ray was even with us that night.

"I'm talking about the motherfucking teachers who knew that sick fuck was going to kill somebody some day! They knew it. They said so themselves. They pointed him out two minutes after they found Rose. It was a no fucking brainer. 'That's the kid. It's gotta be him,' they all said. 'He's the one we all watched every day and just knew it would happen at some fucking point!'"

"You don't know all that, Hats," RC said.

"You know different, RC? You know different, Sam?" Hats shot back, looking at us with wild coyote eyes. Not only was he mad, but he was tuned up pretty good. He was whiskey bent and hell bound.

We didn't answer him. He was on a Hats tear and there is no talking to him at that point. RC looked at me and I just shrugged my shoulders as if to say, "Here we go again." Hats saw this gesture and gave it to both of us.

"Fucking cowards," he spewed at us.

RC leaned over to Ray and suggested that we take Ozark out for a walk. Ray shook his head, got up and headed toward the couch, sprawled down lengthwise, and pulled the blanket that was on the couch over his body. Ozark went to join Ray, but RC called her over and suggested to her that she should go out one more time before we stayed in for the night. He then asked Hats and me to join him, and I accepted and tried to get Hats out for some air. He just told us both to go fuck ourselves.

We went out for a good thirty-minute walk. We had packed a couple of beers each and a pack of torpedoes, so we enjoyed getting some clean fresh air. We got back to the basement, and before we could see what was happening, we could hear what was happening. Hats was in the middle of the basement floor with the phone in his hand. He had pulled the phone as far from the wall as possible and was sitting with the phone and phone book between his legs where the glass used to be for our drinking game. His glass had moved to his left hand, and his right hand had the phone receiver and a torpedo in it. The cigarette was burning close to the end and close to his first two fingers. Ray was passed out on the couch, and Ozark went over to join him.

"You're fucking responsible, man! You hear me?" was all RC and I heard Hats yelling into the phone. He then tried to say the exact same phrase, but in French. Who knows what he actually said as the only word he got right was "fucking."

I had no idea what was going on. Ray and Ozark had no idea what was going on and RC had no idea either, but he was not going to wait to find out. He immediately grabbed the phone from Hats' hand and hung it up, all in one swooping motion.

"Who was that?" RC asked Hats, really saying, *What the hell are you doing, man?*

"Who was who?" Hats said back with absolute cynicism, really saying, *Fuck you, RC, and fuck you too, Sam.*

"Who were you talking to? Who did you call?" RC said in a command and control voice.

"Oh, nobody you need to worry about, Mister RCMP. No trouble here, officer. I have not been drinking and I sure as hell don't plan on driving tonight, sir!"

"You're an asshole," RC threw back at him.

"Maybe I am," Hats replied.

Over the years as friends we had some serious moments, but this was a little more intense than normal. RC, Ozark, and I were all at full attention while Ray stayed asleep. Hats got up, lit a fresh torpedo, and headed out through his garage and into his front yard. We followed him. He went up to a big blue spruce tree they had in their yard and he started punching it as hard as he could. He started crying as he was punching, and RC and I both went up to him and restrained him by each grabbing an arm. He didn't fight us at all. He just looked down at the ground and the three of us went back inside without saying a word. When we got back into the basement we put some music on and finished every ounce of booze and every torpedo we had. We didn't talk about anything that meant anything. Ozark stayed with Ray in a deep slumber, and eventually RC, Hats, and I passed out on the floor of the basement. When we woke up, the needle of the turntable was scratching back and forth at the end of the album, and the RCMP were at the front door.

In Ray's Voice

WELL, HATS HAS GONE and done it again. What a dumbass. I feel sorry for him. I can't say that I'm surprised, though. I saw it coming by the way he was drinking and the way his thoughts were changing as the evening progressed. You can tell what track a person's brain is heading by actively listening to his conversation. The brain synapses first, which produces a thought, which will then produce words coming from the mouth. Some of us can control the gap between step two and step three, and some of us can't. Hats struggles with this. If you look back on his life to date, his every success and his every disaster were preceded by his opening his mouth. His gift of speech is his greatest asset and greatest liability. That's just how life is; everything lives by the law of balance. Good can turn to bad in an instant. It's a razor's edge, and the trick is to find the sweet spot where it all works for you.

RC and Sam went to the Maple Tree Hotel and Hats and I just sat and talked. He tried to draw me into a conversation about the teachers at school and how they should have been aware that the sick boy was going to harm somebody. I didn't take the bait, though. I wasn't interested, and this frustrated him, although he didn't challenge me. He was being gentle considering the circumstances.

Then RC and Sam took Ozark out for a walk. I was asleep on the couch, and Hats couldn't live with his own brain gears twirling any longer, so he grabbed the phone and phone book and looked up a name and dialed the number. When somebody answered, he started accusing him of being responsible for the sick boy and his actions. He

208

insinuated that this person was somehow to blame for Rose's death. He made call after call, and most of the time the person just hung up. I could tell a few dialogued with him, probably as an attempt to find out who he was. He was saying some pretty mean things to the teachers on the other end. I suspect he made as many as ten calls before RC and Sam came back and RC shut the impromptu call center down.

Hats will never learn. He's fueled by his emotions, and some days he's running on rocket fuel. Rocket fuel and whiskey don't mix well, at least not if you are trying to stay out of jail.

RC is not going to be happy about this situation. This is not who RC is and it's not congruent with his value system, but he loves Hats. We are all extremely tight, but RC has a soft spot for Hats. It's part protector and part wonder. Not that RC protects Hats from external forces as he does for Sam and me; Hats takes care of himself on the street. RC tries to protect Hats from Hats. Often, the enemy is within, and such is the case with Hats.

Sam is not doing so well. As usual, he is over-processing everything. Poets are not great with overstimulation. It's part of the DNA makeup of being an artist, and this week in particular certainly had its share of stimuli. Sam is constantly struggling with his own demons; his internal fight with God is never-ending. He really needs to give himself a break at some point. If only he would listen to me, if only he would see that the sun will lead the way. The sun and all its powers are all that you need; just follow the beams and the rays of light and warmth, and everything will be fine. I worry about Sam; I always have. I will need to stay close and watch him carefully.

As for me, thinking about Rose is very difficult. She was everything to me, everything to my mother and father, to RC, Hats, and Sam. She was a big part of what made the world a nice place to be. She was a good person. I should have been there to protect her as that was in my job description as big brother. I don't know why I wasn't there, and I don't know why the sick boy decided on Rose as his victim. Was it random, or was Rose his Angel in some absolutely delusional, sick, and twisted way? I just don't know why this happened, and there is a part of this world that I simply despise. There are times that I wish I had never been born.

Canada
Fall 1982

Weak and Nervous

HATS ANSWERED THE DOOR and invited the two RCMP constables into his home. We were the only ones at the house at the time, so RC and Ray and I followed Hats and we all sat down in the living room. All four of us were feeling very weak, nervous, and anxious; actually, we were completely hung over. We also had no idea why the Police were there, and this added to the feelings of anxiety. We knew both Constables, and we knew their formal names, but they didn't mind us calling them by their first names, which were Bert and Rob. RC started us out by having a conversation about where he was with his plans to join the force, and eventually it came time to get down to business.

"Look guys," Rob said. "We know it's been a tough week for you boys, but we need to know if by any chance you made a few ill-advised phone calls last night?"

When they asked the question, they looked over at Hats, suggesting he might be the logical culprit.

The night before hit us like a tidal wave. All four of us, in unique but similar states of fogged up minds, tried to piece together the events that had taken place a few hours before. It's a strange feeling when a recent memory is just on the perimeter of consciousness and then one spark brings the flood of reality to the forefront of the brain. It's an, *Oh, shit, right, the phone calls...uggg...*feeling.

Bert spoke next. "Look guys," he said, "we can easily get your phone records, so why don't we do this the easy way. Whatever you guys did, I'm sure you're sorry and we can get this behind us quickly. We don't want this to linger out there. People will understand. You will apologize and we can move on to more important matters."

Hats was about to say something when Ray broke in.

"I made the phone calls," Ray said in a very apologetic voice.

"Really, Ray? We wondered if it was Hats," Bert replied, really saying, *We know it was Hats. You don't have to do this, Ray.*

"It was me," Hats responded in an *OK, the jig is up* tone of voice. "Ray isn't that stupid," he added at the end.

"Actually, that's what we figured, Hats," Rob replied.

Hats looked at Rob as if saying, *Look man, I just confessed. Don't make me tell you what I really think.*

"Actually," I then said in response, "it wasn't Hats alone. I was in on it with him."

Hats glared at me as if saying, *Look, Sam, you dumb shit, I just confessed. Don't make me kick your ass!*

"Really, Sam?" Bert asked, really saying, *Come on, Sam, do you really think we believe you?*

"I was in on it as well, guys," RC then said before I could answer.

Hats didn't even look at RC. He just threw his hands up in the air and said, "Fuck, isn't this cozy."

"No, you weren't, RC," both Bert and Rob said at the same time.

"Yes, I was." RC replied, really saying, *This is the way it's going to be guys. This is just the way it's going to be.*

The two RCMP officers both stared long and hard at RC. They stared right into his eyes, and then they both smiled. At first, I thought they would warn him that *this will not be good for your future career, RC!* But instead, I believe they were proud of him because he put his brothers before himself. This is something Rob and Bert both completely understood. There was a pause and silence while the two officers looked at each other and decided what to do next. They collaborated and aligned on their decision without even speaking to each other.

"OK, Beaver Brothers," Rob said. "We'll leave this for now and give it a couple of days to settle. We suggest you make some apologies in the meantime."

In others words, they were telling us there were some pissed off people out there, but this thing might go away if we go to them and beg for forgiveness. As you can imagine, this tactic was a little hard on Hats, but in the end we thanked the constables, told them we would do exactly what they had suggested, and then went back to the basement and slept away most of the day, evening, and night. We were definitely a little weak, nervous, and anxious.

Monday morning came far too quickly, and we grudgingly found our way to school. RC, Ray, and I headed to homeroom, and Hats headed to the office to recite the *Lord's Prayer* over the intercom. When he entered the main administration office, Principal Greton was there to greet him and invited him into his private office. One of the office administration ladies said the Morning Prayer. I listened from my homeroom and was not surprised when I was summoned to the principal's office shortly after morning announcements were completed. When I was led into the office, RC, Ray, and Hats were already there waiting for me to complete the quorum.

"So," Principal Greton said in a very serious manner and in English. By speaking English he was telling us that this was a no-joke situation. "What are we going to do now boys?"

"About what?" Hats replied without a moment of hesitation.

"About what?" Principal Greton shot back to Hats and looked at him in a way that you could tell he wished he had some super laser powers to make Hats burn on the spot.

"Ya, about what?" Hats said back with an aura of cavalier nonchalance.

"I'll tell you about what, you stupid little shit," Principal Greton said with absolute aggression in his voice.

This got Hats attention, but he did his best to act as if we were still in control of the situation. The rest of us just sat there hoping to get the process over with as quickly and painlessly as possible.

Principal Greton went on. "What are we going to do about the fact that you called eleven private homes this weekend and accused them of being responsible for the murder of a student at our school?"

"Rose," Ray said quietly, but loud enough for Principal Greton to hear. The principal looked at Ray – his look a look of sympathy and not hostility.

"I know, Ray," he replied, "your sister Rose. And I am hurting too, Ray. Do you all not know how this affects the entire school, the entire community? We all loved Rose. Even those that didn't know her now love her, and she's all we are thinking about." The last comments did not come easily. Our principal choked up a little but quickly took a deep breath to try to maintain his composure.

This rendered us all into silence. RC and Ray and I had no fight to fight, and I could see that Hats was realizing there was no fight there for him either. Sometimes there really isn't a race to be run or won, so we sat silent for another several minutes until Principal Greton realized we did not want this to continue.

"OK," Principal Greton finally said to break the silence. "This is what is going to happen next. You will go to your classes until lunch. At lunch, I will assemble the appropriate group of teachers in the staff room, and you will arrive to give us a Hollywood performance of apologies. You will then go home for the week, and return next week and be the best students you can be. Hats, you are no longer President of the Student Council. Got it?"

Hats immediately went to shoot back at our Principal, and RC and I each grabbed a respective knee at the same time. We gave him a *this is a good deal* signal by simply squeezing his legs. He backed down but was flush in the face, and in his brain he was taking one for the team, somehow doing us a favor. All I could hear in my mind was his words to RC and me a couple of nights before, *fucking cowards.*

We did what we needed to do. It went as well as could be expected, and shortly after lunch we were leaving school with a whole week ahead of us. In some strange way, it felt as if we had lost the battle but won the war. It all seemed as if it was working out until we got to Boomer and saw that a page had come in on the Beaver Brothers' pager. We didn't recognize the number, and when we called it from a phone booth, we learned who it was from and were put through to the Judge.

"Come and see me right away, boys, at the RCMP detachment," was all he told us, and he hung up the phone. We all agreed we had nothing better to do with our afternoon so we headed over to see the Judge.

When we arrived at the RCMP detachment we walked up to the main reception counter. It didn't seem busy at all. There were no dumbasses to observe being dumbasses, present company excluded. Ray and I simply wished we were not there; Hats stood tall and tried to look confident, as if he belonged there and was showing up for a meeting; RC was infinitely embarrassed. He was among his friends and future peers and he was not happy about the situation. I'll hand it to the RCMP officers, though. They made RC feel as if he were one of them when we arrived. I believe Rob and Bert had told the story, and when they looked at RC they did not see a stupid kid, but rather a young man supporting one of his best friends. In the right circles, that goes a long way. We were escorted into a meeting room where the Judge was waiting for us. He was sitting at a small table with four empty chairs, the chairs clearly meant for us. He had his pipe going strong, and the room was filled with the sweet smell of his tobacco. For a brief moment I convinced myself we were there to get a job cleaning his eavestroughs. The four of us sat down in the chairs to join the Judge. Nobody talked immediately, and Hats took this as an opportunity to light up a torpedo.

"Don't do that, Hats," the Judge admonished him. "There is no smoking allowed in here, and you shouldn't be smoking anyway. It's not good for your hockey." Hats looked at the Judge without contempt for the obvious double standard, and he put his smoke back in the pack and the pack back into the left breast pocket of his jean jacket. *Good boy, Hats.* I was proud that he did not act like a punk. We respect the Judge, and even Hats can understand when true respect trumps emotion.

"We have a problem, boys," the Judge told us. "You did well at school today but one of the teachers is not satisfied with your apology. He is demanding that the police press charges and that you stand before the court to be held accountable."

"For what?" Hats said. "Speaking the truth?"

The Judge did not respond to Hats, as he is far too smart to be baited, especially by a fisherman as inexperienced as Hats.

"We have a problem, boys," he reiterated, "and we need to fix it. So this is what's going to happen next."

"Why does everybody keep telling me what the fuck is going to happen next?" Hats said in a matter-of-fact tone.

The Judge stayed calm again and took a couple of draws on his pipe. The smoke swirled around his head in that familiar way.

"Hats," the Judge said in a firm but coaching voice, "if you can learn to listen more than you talk, you will be unstoppable in this world. Do you know that? You have two ears and one mouth, Hats, so what should you be doing more of? If you can learn this one trick, Hats, you will succeed at anything you put your mind to. Do you understand that, son?"

"Pardon?" Hats said back, but in a way that told the Judge he had heard every word. We all had a nervous but good laugh, which helped to bring us back to a less complicated time when the five of us shared less complicated situations.

The Judge started laying out the next steps. "OK, you will leave this room and a constable – you know Rob I believe – will write you a citation that is, in fact, a charge of offense. You will accept this citation."

"What's the charge, Judge?" RC asked very politely.

"Indecent phone calls with the intent to harass. It is a summary conviction charge."

"Fuuuck," Hats said under his breath sarcastically in an *Oh no, my life is over now* tone. The Judge gave him a stare that said *Don't push me, Hats, or you will see a side of me you do not know yet!* Hats read the stare and reacted appropriately. *Good boy, Hats.*

"You will accept the charge and you will come back here Friday morning and stand in front of me and the court. You will plead guilty to the charges and you will apologize again to anybody and everybody in the court room. The court will accept your apology, and you will be sentenced to some community service. You will complete your community service with pride, and this whole thing will go away. You will not have a record, and you will get on with the rest of your life in a positive and law-abiding fashion. Do you understand, boys?"

RC did not allow Hats to respond for the group. "Yes, sir, and thank you, sir," was all RC said. Ray and I followed closely behind, and Hats came into line as well. *Good boy, Hats,* we all thought to ourselves silently.

"Good," the Judge said. "See you, Friday. Now, RC, Sam, Hats, please go see Rob, and let Ray and me have a talk."

Hats and RC and I left to get our summons. We left Ray behind with the Judge.

In Ray's Voice

THE BOYS WENT OUT to get our citation and court appearance information and the Judge had a talk with me. He asked me how I was doing. He asked me how I was holding up. I told him I was doing OK. He asked me why I was even back at school and not taking some time off. I told him I didn't know why but that Principal Greton had taken care of that for me that morning. He confirmed he knew about the suspension. He asked me if I was ready for the hockey season and I told him I thought so. He asked me how my music was coming along, and I told him it was coming along pretty well. He asked me what I was thinking about doing after my last year of high school, and I told him I didn't know yet. He asked me again how I was doing. He asked me again how I was holding up, and I told him again I was doing OK. Then he took a draw on his pipe, and stared past me for a minute.

The Judge then told me that he doesn't know why this happened. That all he can think about is Rose and that his heart is crushing under the weight of her death. He explained to me that he knew who the sick boy was and that the boy had been in front of him and his court. That the boy was troubled, that the Police knew the boy was troubled, that they did everything they could to help the boy and even to try to keep him off the streets. But there are laws, and the laws protect the sick boys more than they protect the Roses. He told me that he wished he could turn back the clock, that he would change some of the decisions he had made, that he would defy the rule of law and do what was right for the Roses. He then put his pipe on the table, put his face in his

216

hands and his hands on his knees, and he buried himself into his body. I moved my chair so I was in front of him. I put my arms around his shoulders and told him it was not his fault. I told him that he couldn't protect all the Roses in the world, that he was a good judge, that he was a good man. I told him even Hats said he was one of the good guys. This brought a small laugh, and the Judge came back.

The Judge wiped his eyes and lit his pipe and took a long draw, the smoke swirling around his head as if to ward off evil spirits. After he had completely regained his composure he told me that he wanted to help me with my education; and he told me I was exceptionally talented in many things – music, hockey, or anything else I would set my mind to. He told me I was one of the lucky ones, that I had God-given gifts, and that I shouldn't waste them. He told me that if it was acceptable to my parents he would like to invest in me, that he would like to help pay for my education after high school. I told him that he was a very generous man and that I would let him know what I decided to do, and we made a deal to talk again.

He then told me to get Hats in line for Friday, that everything would be fine if we simply pled guilty to the phone calls and apologized. He then told me he respected that the four of us stuck together and that it was very unorthodox that he was talking to us and managing the case the way he was. He asked that we not share anything about what he was doing. I said, "Share what?" He smiled, and there was another moment of silence.

He looked at me and told me he was very sorry. I told him I was sorry too. I told him he was a good man. He told me I was a good man as well. I told him I missed Rose. He told me he missed Rose too.

And with that, I went out and joined RC, Hats, and Sam.

Canada
Fall 1982

Sam's Cremation

WE DECIDED TO SPEND our week off at the Lodge. It was actually opportune because we had a lot of work to do to get the Lodge ready for winter. Ray believed some roof work was required, and we needed to gather and cut wood to be used in Findley. In the true wilderness, food and heat are all that matters come winter. In our case, food was a non-issue. We were not reliant on shooting a moose each year, although RC once suggested that the only food that should be allowed at the Lodge should be food donated from the forest itself. This was a little optimistic and far-reaching even for the Beaver Brothers, although RC did snare a rabbit once, and we skinned it and cooked it on the stove. We ate it and it was OK, but it seemed like a lot of work for the calories it produced. Some work benefit ratios don't add up. Hats did keep one of the rabbit's feet for good luck. "Not so lucky for the fucking rabbit," he said as he dried the rabbit foot out over Findley.

While we still allowed the modern conveniences of the world to help with our food supply, our heat source was certainly not as readily available to us. It was readily available, just not readily available to us in ready-to-go form. We had to work hard for that. The good news is we enjoyed the work as there is a pride that comes from building your own stash of wood for winter, and as you burn each log you appreciate the warmth because of the work that went into making the log a part of your life. This is something that is missing from people's lives today. There's not enough hard work going on and therefore not enough pride of hard work. It's the pride of hard work that is most important. In fact, hard work and feeling proud of the work afterwards is one of the few spices of life.

Another benefit of burning wood is that it warms you five times over. First you fell the tree, cut it, chop it, stack it, and burn it. On occasion, you actually feel bad for burning a particular log, as you remember the work that went into splitting it in the fall of the year. Not all logs are cooperative. Some will split nicely and evenly with an axe as if they believe their destiny is waiting for them. Others are not so willing; they have other ideas about their destiny. These logs need to be opened up and split with a wedge and sledge hammer. We would insert a two inch steel wedge into the middle of the log and smash down on it with the sledge hammer. Occasionally, the wedge would be pounded right into the log, and the log would still be in one piece. The log would be in that sweet spot between dry and still somewhat green, and another wedge would be required. I don't remember any log ever requiring more than three wedges, and any log needing more than one wedge was commonly referred to as a *log from hell*. The good news is that logs from hell would usually burn long and hot. I'm not joking here, and had we kept data I'm sure they would show that logs from hell burned hotter and longer. Sometimes there are benefits from being linked to hell.

We left Ray to work on the roof. He was very quiet and clearly wanted to be on his own, and this was understandable. For the rest of us, our main job for the week was to get our winter woodpile ready. We normally would have had it done by late August, but we had had a busy summer. So to help make up some time, RC borrowed a small gas-powered chainsaw that we used to cut the long logs into Findley-size pieces that could be split with an axe or wedge. After some discussion, and in an effort to improve the Lodge each year, we decided to build a small enclosure to house our firewood. It was a simple roof that hung between the two birch trees that formed the book ends of our woodpile. The goal was to protect the split firewood from rain and snow, and we worked hard for two days and made excellent progress. By the time Thursday rolled around, we had the woodpile looking proud and ready for winter under its new little canopy built from logs and branches from cedar trees. We were busy Beavers indeed.

We finished working around supper time on Thursday, and the plan was to head to our respective homes Thursday night in order to check in with our parents, clean up, and be ready for court on Friday. Before leaving, we decided to have an OV and a little smoke in order to admire the fruits of our labor. One OV led to another. We had quite a few tune-up supplies available to us because we had brought enough for the week but had not stayed up excessively late each night. This was a result of having been so tired from the hard work and fresh air. The beer was now going down a little too smoothly. One thing I've learned is that not all drinking sessions are the same – some just feel right, some just make sense. You might say we were *down a quart and needed to top off the oil.* For some reason, we seemed to lose track of time, and before long we had Findley going strong – the Lodge was toasty warm and we were well on our way to Tuneupville. To this day, I'm not sure what got into us that night. Some decisions just defy logic and common sense. We had a big morning ahead of us the following day, yet we seemed oblivious. We were prospectors enjoying the spoils that are the rewards for hard work.

At some point in the night, Ray commented on how beautiful the sky was looking. He had been out to grab some wood, and typical of Ray, he spent some time embracing Mother Nature. It was a clear and cool night, and the stars were out with full production value. Building on his observation, I suggested that we build a fire outside and spend a few hours under the moonlight to enjoy the scenery. Everybody thought this was a grand idea, and my next brilliant idea was that instead of using our outside fire pit we should burn the pile of brush that had been created when building the woodpile. It was the remnants of the logs, largely consisting of branches trimmed from the trees, and everybody thought this was a grand idea.

The brush pile was a good size brush pile. It was probably ten feet high at the center and ten feet in diameter. It formed a pyramid or round mound as opposed to a cube. Always conscious of forest fires, we rationalized that the ground and bush were wet enough for a safe outdoor fire, and this hypothesis proved true as we did not start a forest fire that night. Not for lack of trying, I might add. In fact, we struggled to get the pile of brush burning. The problem was the cold and wet ground and the fact that many branches in the pile were still reasonably green. It was my job to get the pile burning, and instead of helping me my three friends just watched and barked out orders of what I should do. Everybody is an NHL player when not on the ice. Ozark was the only one not barking that night, and she stayed close to me and provided me with camaraderie, at least at the beginning.

My first effort was to get the fire started from the bottom and center of the pile. Fires burn up, this is Brush Pile Pyromania 101, so I used some birch bark and paper products salvaged from the Lodge to help start the fire. This did not work, and my second attempt was to put a few dry sticks of kindling into the center of the pile. Essentially I attempted to build a small campfire in the middle of the big pile of green wood. This did not work either, although I did manage to cover my face in scrapes. Luckily my body was protected as I was wearing my hockey jacket, which had a wool Melton main body and leather sleeves. The boys were getting quite a charge from watching my failed endeavors, and they turned up the peer pressure, so I turned up my response. They say the third time is a charm, and I was ready to achieve success. Unfortunately, I was also well on my way to Tuneupville, as were my fellow Beaver Brothers.

I told the guys I had an idea and to hang on to their socks. I went behind the Lodge and came back with the small one gallon red plastic can of gasoline we had brought to fuel the chainsaw. The boys looked at me with a combined look of curiosity, surprise, and concern.

"What's the plan, Sam?" RC asked me, really saying, *I'm not sure about this, Sam.*

"Well," I said, "the plan is to climb on top of the pile and pour the gas carefully over the pile, thereby soaking as much of the wood as I can. I will then climb down and we'll light the fire from a distance. Seem logical?"

My friends looked at each other and then back at me and gave me a nod of approval, upholding our principle of never stopping a man on a mission, even if the mission might appear to be ill fated. I asked Ray to hold my OV, and I headed up the brush pile with my can as if I were climbing the Chilkoot Pass on my way to the land of Klondike gold. I started reciting my favorite poem as I clawed and clamored my way to the top, and the boys started cheering and giving me confidence. Ozark had assessed the situation and had smartly taken a position far from the brush pile. I made it to the top of the stack and continued reciting the poem of poems. The boys could not contain themselves, and they were literally on their asses laughing at me. I continued my oration of the poem of all poems.

Some planks I tore from the cabin floor, and I lit the boiler fire;
Some coal I found that was lying around, and I heaped the fuel higher;
The flames just soared, and the furnace roared—such a blaze you
seldom see; And I burrowed a hole in the glowing coal, and I stuffed
in Sam McGee.

On that line of the poem, I opened my can of fire fuel and started pouring it down in the middle of the brush pile, being very careful not to get gas on myself.

RC's voice was the first to warn me to jump, and in that instant it became clear to me that I had missed a vital point in my planning. There were still some lingering embers at the bottom of the pile that were sitting as potential energy. They were the stragglers of my first two attempts to make fire, and had I not intervened with my gas accelerator they were on their way to the land of being extinguished, which ironically enough was the opposite of where I was headed.

It all happened in milliseconds. The first few ounces of gasoline hit the hot embers and the fuel came up the Sam-made gas ladder in an instant. I heard RC's yell, and I instinctively released the can from my hand. Still within this one micro-second of time, there was a sound like a mournful *swoosh*. It's hard to describe the sound. It was like a sucking and blowing noise all at the same time, and it had direction, and that direction happened to be bound toward me. The red dawn wave that hit me was a combination of wind and heat, and I went flying off the pile and landed not far from the boys. Sam was down. *Man down!*

I vaguely remember hitting the ground, and for the first second the boys just looked at me in disbelief. Then Ray started yelling, "Put him out! Sam, roll! Put him out! Sam, roll!" I started to roll, and RC ran over to me and started to pat me all over my body. Ray joined RC, Hats continued his gaze of disbelief, and Ozark came over and tried to lick my face at every time she could hit skin during my rolls.

The good news is I was not on fire, as my hockey jacket and jeans protected me, and it was an amazing relief when RC finally picked me up and we all realized I was still alive and not suffering from any major burns. My right wrist was sore, presumably from landing on it, and my face and head were feeling flush, so the boys led me into the Lodge to look me over. Behind us, the brush pile fire started to gain life.

Once in the Lodge, the boys had me sit down at the table and surrounded me. They brought the coal oil lantern close, and all stared at my face. Hats was the first to speak.

"Holy fuck!" he said, "Where the hell is all your hair, Sam?"

"What?" I replied, really saying, *Please tell me what has happened. Please give me information about my own personal situation!*

Ray came in for a closer look and said, "Oh my God, Sam!" He then tried to stifle his laughter.

RC duplicated Ray's actions and before I knew it, all three of them were once again on their asses laughing at me. Meanwhile, I could hear my fire roaring outside. I guess the third time is the charm.

Ray grabbed a mirror that he had for doing experiments with the sun, and he showed me my image. My cheeks and ears were flush red, but not burnt, which was encouraging and not surprising, as I was not experiencing any pain other than my wrist. The real surprise came when I realized that the hair on my head was completely singed. I had about three inches of hair remaining on my head, shaped like a classic bowl cut with the ends of each follicle having a grey burnt twinge. This explained the smell I remember on the way down the fire mountain. The next realization was that I was completely and utterly devoid of eyelashes and eyebrows. I have to admit that at that point I joined in the laughter. Even Ozark was laughing.

Fully assured I was going to survive, we refreshed our tune-up supplies and headed back to the fire to enjoy the gains of our effort. Some work benefit ratios do work out.

We sat by the roaring green-branch fire and threw a bunch of dry logs on it to keep it going. Proud of our accomplishment, we sat in silence and reflected on the last two weeks. Hats broke the silence when he exclaimed, "Now that's a fuckin' FIER!" To be sure, he did not say fire. He said FIER in a way that only a Canadian Redneck Hillbilly with a fake French accent could say fier. Indeed it was a great fier, and to this day, that is the best fier I have ever been blown off of or sat around. Nevertheless, the night was getting late, or should I say morning was approaching, and we had things to do.

There are times when you go to Tuneupville and you don't get a hotel for the night. Instead, you arrive late and it just doesn't make sense to go to bed, as a couple hours of sleep can be worse than no sleep at all. At least that is what you rationalize, which is exactly what we rationalized that night. So we carried on until the last possible moment and then began the long hike back to town. We were very thankful for the walk as this provided much needed sobering relief, and in the process we enjoyed the walk back to civilization and our anticipated court date. We walked single file with Ozark leading the way, and I must admit I was reminded of the seven dwarfs coming back from a hard day's work.

We got back to my house and grabbed Boomer. Ray said he was fine to drive, and we all knew that Ray never pushed the envelope about these things, so we went with his lead. Even when we drank hard, he would be thinking about our next step, and it wasn't unusual for him to be ready when called upon. No doubt he slowed down at some point in the early morning. There wasn't enough time for us to get cleaned up, so we used what little time we had to go to Frank's Diner and get some breakfast. Needless to say, we were starving, and a little grease in the belly was helpful as well. We weren't quite weak, nervous, and anxious yet, but the feeling was getting nearer with every minute.

After leaving Frank's Diner, we headed to the court house and walked in not knowing what to expect. We did not anticipate anybody to be waiting for our arrival: we had no lawyer, and we had not told anybody about our court date. This all worked to our advantage as we walked into the court in day-old clothes, looking and smelling as if we had been on an ice fishing adventure for a week. We sat down at the back of the court house, and after a few minutes the court became alive and the lawyers and Judge Jeremiah got busy doing what they do.

We were called up after about an hour of watching the show. This hour of watching gave us a good idea of how the court worked, and we got to see some of the dumbasses that live in our town. It was interesting how the four of us did not think of ourselves as dumbasses; instead, we thought we were somehow above all the folks in the parade of stupid, that we didn't belong there, that we were simply at the wrong place at the wrong time. After all, the only crime we really committed was getting caught.

We heard our names called, but with no lawyer to guide us we really didn't know what to do. The protocol was outside our wheelhouse. So we stood up and walked to the front of the courtroom and stood to the Judge's left. The town prosecutor stood to our left, so the three teams in the game formed a triangle. The Judge looked at us, and I could tell he had a rehearsed plan to act as if he did not know us, or at least that he was surprised to see us. He played the part and looked up from his papers to give us a glancing look. It was supposed to be a look of indifference. Then he looked up again, but this time he kept his gaze on us. And there we were – dirty, smelly, now feeling very weak, very nervous and very anxious. And on top of all that, I had no eyebrows or eyelashes, and my hair was burnt short and grey. The good news is my appearance made the other three look marginally and relatively respectable. The Judge abandoned his plan to be a known stranger.

"Are you OK, Sam?" he asked me from his perch, really saying, *Do you need medical assistance, Sam?*

"Yes, sir. I'm fine," I answered, really saying, *Please don't ask, Judge.*

Then there was a moment of silence while he sized us up, and then he shook his head and decided to get the proceedings over with. A bunch of formalities were executed, we met our end of the bargain, and after no more than four minutes the whole thing was over. We were excused and free to leave, and I swear I saw the Judge mumbling to himself as he watched us leave the court. If I were a gambling man, I would bet he was saying, *Those Beaver Bothers; they really are interesting.*

On the way out, I scanned the room for spectators and did not identify one teacher. We got back to Boomer and headed to Hats' basement where we slept the rest of the day and woke up around suppertime. We decided to take a short trip to Tuneupville that night, then rested Saturday and Sunday in Hats' basement, which became the place of the start and ending point of our criminal activities.

In the end, it all worked out. We completed, and actually enjoyed, our community service which was to teach kids to skate. And to this day, Hats is our high school's only President of the Student Council who was ever impeached and criminally charged – a marker he is very proud of, and we all agree with him that it is quite the accomplishment.

DAY 14

South Carolina

Marriage

"GOOD MORNING, SAM."

"Good morning, Doc."

"How is the writing coming?"

"Good. I think I'm making great progress and I believe it's helping me."

"Are you going to share at some point?"

"Yes. Give me a bit, though. I need to shake a few things out first."

"Fine. You say it's helping though. How so?

Silence

"Well, a few reasons I suspect. The first is obvious. I like to write so I'm enjoying the fact that I'm writing again. People are happier when they are doing those things they enjoy. As they say, once you can make your work your play, then it's not work any longer. Second, while I'm writing, I'm not watching the Talking Cable Heads. It's my substitution strategy. Substitute a positive alternative for the vice. This reduces the stress by a factor of a million. Third, I am seeing my story progress in a linear fashion. This helps me to connect some dots, to connect some disconnects, and I'm thinking this is a good thing."

"Great, Sam. I'm looking forward to reading some of it one day soon."

"Noted, Doc."

"OK, well, I'm thinking we could talk about Sophie today."

"I'm not surprised. You want me to explain my feelings surrounding why she and George left me. Correct?"

"No."

"No?"

"No, I'm not interested in that right now."

"You're not?"

"No."

"OK, Doc, sounds good. You're the boss. So what are you interested in?"

"Let's talk about the early years. You met in college in South Carolina?"

"Yes, well, no. We developed our relationship at college in South Carolina. We actually met during the summer before we both started college."

"Really? How did you end up meeting her?"

"We don't have enough time, Doc. It's a long and complicated story."

"OK, so you met and then you both went through college together?"

"Yes, and grad school."

"Right, and then you got married?"

"More or less. We were very in love, we are very in love, and we got engaged during grad school and married the summer after we graduated."

"Where did you propose to her?"

"On Seabrook Island."

"Wow! That sounds romantic."

"It was. It's a nice memory. I talked to her dad first and got his permission. That was a nice conversation. Some traditions should be upheld. James was a good man, and he appreciated my acting like a good ole Texas boy. He respected people that treat other people with respect."

"And you got married in Canada?"

"No. We got married in South Carolina. It was our home. I was from Canada, and Sophie was from Texas, so we decided our home should be the nucleus of the new cell. Nobody had issues with this as everybody loves South Carolina. It's one of the most adored states in the country."

"Indeed it is. This sounds wonderful. Where did you get married?

"In Charleston."

"Wow. There are beautiful churches there. Which church did you marry in?"

"We didn't get married in a church."

"Oh, why not?"

"I was done...*Silence*...I am done with churches, and Sophie was fine with that. I would have given her a church wedding if she had wanted it, but she knew how I felt and it just wasn't that important to her. She wanted me to be happy on our big day, and it wasn't like we belonged to a church in Charleston. If we had really wanted a church wedding, we would have gone to Texas or Canada."

"So where did you get married?"

"In a hotel. In a very, very nice hotel. It was a small wedding, maybe twenty-five people. It was intimate and we wanted it to be five stars right across the board. Plus James said he would pay for the whole thing. He was a very generous man, and while Sophie and I are far from pretentious, we tried our best to make the wedding luxurious. Sophie enjoyed planning it."

"Sounds wonderful. How did it go?"

Laugh

"It was an absolute disaster. Not one thing went right other than our showing up and having our friends and family with us, which we learned in the end is all you need."

"Really? A disaster?"

"Our disaster. At the time, Sophie was not so happy, but now we laugh about it. What we learned is that there can be an inverse relationship between the wedding and the marriage. Fantastic weddings can produce disaster marriages, and disaster weddings can produce fantastic marriages. You see, Doc, the disaster wedding sends the couple out into the land of marriage with very low expectations. The lessons of entropy hit the couple on day one of their marriage. That way the couple just assumes marriage is about everything falling apart."

"You're funny, Sam!"

"Thanks, Doc. Nobody has accused me of being funny for quite some time."

"OK, Sam, you've got my curiosity up. What made the wedding so disastrous?"

Silent Contemplation

"Oh, man. Where do you want to start? Well, first, the hotel we chose was one of the nicest hotels in the city. We went through the hotel six months before the wedding and had dinner, and they sold us the farm. It was everything Sophie wanted, and their sales people made used car salesmen look like amateurs. We bought every upgrade possible."

"Sounds nice."

"Ya, until we arrived at the hotel on the Friday before the wedding. We walked into the hotel entrance, and the whole hotel lobby was under renovation. Instead of nicely dressed hotel staff, we were greeted by tile layers and drywall hangers – plumber's butt galore. Sophie gasped and ran outside with her dress on the hanger so it wouldn't get covered in construction dust."

"Oh my gosh, Sam. What did you do?"

"What can you do? The wedding was set and in motion. Our friends and family were arriving from all over North America, and they were all staying at the hotel. The whole event was planned and choreographed to happen at that hotel. We were stuck, so I went outside to find Sophie and gave her a hug and told her how much I love her. I told her the good news is it couldn't get any worse. She said, *Oh ya, it can*, and she was right. We had a good laugh, and we both decided to suck it up, go with the flow, and just smile our way through the whole ordeal, no matter what happened. Sophie is like that. She can take a deep breath and get on with life. I love that about her."

"Good for you guys. So that was the big disaster?"

"I guess it was more of a series of small disasters. You could say multiple failure modes all resulting in a consolidated disaster. It was disaster synergy in that the disaster *whole* was greater than the *sum* of the failure mode parts."

"How did the disaster start ... after the hotel's being torn apart, of course?"

"Well, first, Sophie spent Friday night with the ladies, and I spent it with my friends."

"Your friends?"

"Yes, Hats and RC. Ray was not able to be with us."

"Oh no. You didn't !"

"Didn't what, Doc?"

"Go out on the town and look like a wreck the next day."

"Oh, oddly enough, we didn't. I guess there are still small wonders in the world. Actually, we spent Friday night getting a traditional Southern shave and haircut – the traditional straight blade shave and a *red and white pole* barber haircut."

"Sounds like fun?"

"Yes, it was, but I broke rule number one which is never get your haircut the day before a formal event. When I arrived at the room for the wedding ceremony, half of each side of my head was tanned and the other half was white where the hair used to be. The sides of my head made me look like a zebra."

"That's hilarious, Sam!"

"That's exactly what Sophie said, Doc!"

"So, there's more?"

"Oh ya. Universal entropy was just getting warmed up. Next we lost the corsage intended for Sophie's mother, so we had to race around and problem solve in order to improvise. Then the battery in the video player crashed right before the ceremony, and we never did get it working. Next, the fire alarm went off right in the middle of our very classy five-course dinner."

"No!"

"Yes!"

"What did you do?"

"I got up and went to the microphone at the podium we had set up for after dinner speeches. I told, or should I say ordered, people to stay where they were and enjoy their dinner. My buddy RC went downstairs to check out the situation. We all continued to eat the marriage feast with the fire alarm blasting in our ears until RC came back and said it was a false alarm. The dry wall dust had set off a smoke detector in the lobby, and the alarm was turned off soon after. That was a nice sound of silence."

"Too funny, Sam. How did the speeches go?"

"Ahhh, the story continues, Doc."

"The speeches went well until James got up to welcome me into his family."

"Oh no, he decided he didn't like you after all?"

"I wish, Doc. That would have been easy to take. It's not that simple, and you need a little background for this part of the story. You see, Sophie's mother, an amazing lady whom I loved dearly, was in the early to mid-stages of Alzheimer's at the time of our wedding."

"I'm sorry to hear that, Sam."

"Me too, Doc. Alzheimer's is brutal, a curse worse than death itself, which, by the way, will come eventually after the disease has sucked the life out of the victim and all friends and family. Just another example proving that if, in fact, there is a divine creator, He missed a few engineering classes during His studies."

"Pardon, Sam?"

"Never mind, Doc. Anyway, back to the wedding. Sophie's father got up and began a very nice speech about Sophie growing up and how proud he is of her and how much he likes me. It was all very pleasant, as James was a confident and articulate speaker. He then went into a story about some summer trip that James and Sophie and her mom had taken when Sophie was a little girl, trying to mention some nice things about Sophie's mom."

"Sounds nice, Sam."

"Yes it was, right up until Sophie's mother called James a liar!"

"NO!"

"YES! She yelled it from our table loud enough for the entire intimate gathering of people to hear as plain as a Yukon summer day is long."

"Oh my...oh my, Sam. What did you do?"

"I didn't do anything. I acted as if I hadn't heard her."

"What did Sophie do?"

"She took a huge drink of her wine, grabbed the bottle, and filled her glass up well past the water mark."

"What did James do?"

"This is the best part. God bless, James. He smiled and looked across the podium at his wife. The room was dead silent – I mean numb silent – and he looked at his wife and gave her a big smile. It was a sincere smile, one that showed that he loved her so much. He then said, 'Yes, Dear,' and he got on with his speech. It was priceless."

"Oh my, Sam, what a night. Did you speak as well?"

"I did. I wrote a poem for Sophie and read that."

"Wow, I would love to read it one day."

"Sure, I'll find it for you."

"Well, it sounds like the ceremony went off OK?"

"Yes, thank goodness. We wrote our own vows, and we had a close friend perform the ceremony."

"Nice, who was that?"

"Judge Jeremiah Johnson, a gentleman from my home town who has been in my life a long time. He performed the ceremony and we had a Justice of the Peace in the background who made it all legal for South Carolina. The Judge knew the Justice from being in the business, and they worked out the details."

"Neat. And you wrote your own vows?"

"Yes."

"I would love to read those as well."

"Noted again, Doc."

"Very nice, Sam. It sounds as if your wedding was quite the experience to say the least."

"It was memorable for sure, Doc."

"Did you have attendants? People standing up with you?"

"Yes, Sophie had two of her girlfriends and I had two of my childhood friends."

"You mentioned one friend didn't make it?"

"Yes, Ray didn't make it"

"Why is that?"

Silence

"That's an even longer story, Doc, and I'm feeling a little tired now."

"OK, let's call it a day."

"Perfect."

In Sophie's Voice

MY SAM. My Sam, the romantic. Of all of his amazing qualities, I most love the fact that he is a romantic. There are not enough romantics in the world today. Men try to be cool and calm and act as if they believe that laws of economics will win a girl's heart. They believe that scarcity drives demand: just make the lady think you don't want her, and the lady will want you more. That may be what some girls like, but that's not me, and that's not my Sam. Sam's a true romantic. Love is not a game. Love is not about being clever.

Sam told me that he loved me the first night we met. We were on the beach sitting around a gorgeous bonfire, and the warmth and light from the fire set the mood. He whispered in my ear, "I love you." I laughed at him and punched him in the shoulder. He asked me if he had screwed up by saying that. He had an *Oh no* look on his face. I told him no. I wanted to tell him I loved him too, but I didn't have the courage. I didn't want to scare him off. Interesting logic when I think about it now. I guess I believed in scarcity.

We spent two weeks apart after our first meeting, and then Sam came back to me for good. He moved here to go to school, but really he moved here for me. In two weeks' time, he changed his entire life plan, as one minute he was going to university in Canada and the next he was enrolled in South Carolina. I could never do that. Sam can face these upheavals easily, and come to think about it, I think he needs this type of drastic change-of-life course in order to be happy. Sam gets bored, although we never got bored with each other. We were always in it together, and we were a team even when Sam was consistently and fundamentally changing our life and livelihood.

We met on the beach. He went back to Canada, came back, and never left my side again. That is, until I had to leave. My Sam, my romantic. We were so in love when we were young. It was exactly how true love should be and feel. The first love is the most powerful, and I treasure that we kept our first love alive. The first love is all consuming. It is a journey into a new world. As Sam would say, we were prospectors, and the gold we panned for was our love for each other. With every draw of the pan from the love creek, we came up with solid gold nuggets. It was primal, it was emotional, and it was real. We ached when we were apart; we held hands and pressed our bodies close when together. Our individual energies combined to accentuate and exemplify the concept of synergy. It was true love; it still is true love. I love Sam. I love my romantic, and I miss him deeply.

Our wedding was quite a spectacle. It fell apart right from the very beginning. I walked into the hotel and walked right out after seeing the state of the lobby. Sam followed me out, and while I was crying by the valet parking sign, he walked up to me and just held me. He didn't say anything. He just held me, and then, when the moment was perfect, he said, "I'm going to sick Hats on these sons of bitches!" My tears turned into laughter. He took my face into the palms of his hands, and he told me he loved me and that whatever happened, we were destined to have the perfect marriage. He told me we would live happily ever after no matter what. The fairy tale ending. That's my romantic. That's my Sam.

My father loved Sam. One of the reasons is because Sam talked to my father before proposing to me. This was important to my *Poppa*, although it was also important to Sam. He wouldn't have had it any other way, and it shouldn't be any other way, and my Poppa loved Sam until the day he died. I remember when my Poppa was in the hospital, the cancer had won, and we knew he was going to leave us. That last hour when my Poppa was slipping away, he took Sam's hand and said, "I love you, Son." This sent Sam over the emotional cliff. Sam does not deal well with father-son relationships, but he loved my father, and my father sure loved him. This was very hard on Sam.

My poor Poppa had his hands full at our wedding. My mom was not well, and she had not been well for a few years. Alzheimer's is a horrible disease. Not that I would wish any disease on anybody, but Alzheimer's would appear to be one of the worst. Perhaps diseases are relative, relative as to how unfair they are. The problem with Alzheimer's, though, is you lose your loved one without their dying, consequently defying and denying the proper path of life's circle. It's simply cruel and unusual punishment for everybody involved, and watching my mother die from Alzheimer's really made me question any sense of divine goodness in this world. Don't even get me going on Sam's thoughts.

My mom and her sickness sure got my Poppa good. Right in front of my whole wedding congregation, and right while he was making a very heartfelt speech, she called him a liar loud enough for everybody to hear. Sam acted as if he hadn't heard it, and I ignored her and started drinking. My Poppa just smiled at my mom and said, "Yes, Dear." It was almost as if he was proud of her, proud that she was alive and living, proud that she cared enough to call him a liar. He really did love her. I know that to be true.

After the *liar* yell out, Sam got up to say thank you to our guests. I was worried about Sam. He's not so great with emotional situations. He can break down easily, and I knew he was missing a lot of people that evening. In particular, I knew he was very sad that his best friend Ray was not at the wedding. Events just did not allow it to happen, and while RC and Hats did their best to fill the void, Sam was certainly missing Ray. I was sad for Sam, but I was happy as well. It was my wedding day. Sam did say that Ray helped him write a poem for me. They write a lot together, and in hindsight, I think this writing is Sam's only spiritual outlet.

Sam got up to the podium and stood over our small group and took a deep breath. He looked at me and smiled. I smiled back, and my gaze told him that I loved him. He looked at RC and Hats, and he nodded to them. I watched them nod back. He made direct eye contact with my father, and they communicated man to man without saying a word. Then he asked the small group of close friends and family if he could read a poem he had written. The room nodded a *Please do,* and then he read his poem.

I BELIEVE IN LOVE

I believe in Love
I believe in its power to change my world
To steer me in positive directions, toward my potential
To build a home where my dreams come true
Where I maintain the innocence of youth
To truly make a difference

That my footsteps may carve deeply into the ground
Leaving a sign of my presence
And memories in others forged forever

I believe that love does not conquer all
And love is not instant at first sight
I believe love is not based solely on romance
But that it grows through respect and commitment
To raise a family and grow old together
As the ultimate challenge and accomplishment we face
Far surpassing any material world
Love does not rely on where we have been
It tells us where we are going

I believe in family
I believe in the depth of our heritage
That our traditions must be carried on
Continuously bringing generations together
Allowing our relationships to grow
Within the soul of unconditional love

I believe I am not myself without family
And my family is not complete without me
I believe in memories of childhood
In my lessons of adolescence
And in my challenges of adulthood
I believe we are each other's greatest gift
Where we did not choose our friendships
But have chosen to treasure them

I believe in friendship
I believe in stories and laughter when we celebrate
In listening and supporting in times of need
I believe that within each of us
Is an extension of each other
In which we appreciate our varied strengths
And overlook our weaknesses

I believe that we are friends
Because we are kind and understanding
That we are sincerely happy for each other
And want nothing but happiness in all our lives
I believe we cannot replace the friendships of youth

And as we change with age, we watch each other
Proud of the directions we choose
For we are not all the same
But we are friends

And I believe in you
I believe in your love for me
And my love for you

So when the future brings us struggles
We will not run from each other
But stand to face the challenge

And I know from the bottom of my heart
That we will live happily ever after
Because, I believe in Love

There was not a dry eye in the room when Sam finished his poem. Even my mother seemed to come back to us for a brief moment, and I watched her smile as my father put his arm around her. I was so proud of Sam in so many ways as his poem told me things about him that he could not show in his actions. I always knew that he believed that love, in and of itself, can conquer all. He's my romantic. But that's not what he was saying in his words. You see, it's not that easy, and Sam was telling us this – love is powerful, yes, but work is required. Nothing of value happens without work, and working to build love is the essence of the human experience. Love is not a noun, love is a verb. Sam did not want just to love me, he wanted to be in love with me, he wanted to be actively loving me, as to love is to exemplify the act of loving. Sam knew this and he told us that on my wedding day.

In hindsight now, I realize the poem was not just for me. It was also for Ray, as Sam was telling Ray that he understood his absence. Sam had told me that he had talked to Ray the morning of our wedding and that they were both at peace with the fact that Ray was not there. All was OK.

My wedding was the best wedding a bride could ask for. It was a disaster, but also perfect in every respect. The marriage was a disaster and perfect as well. Things happen, circumstances are powerful beyond our understanding, and mathematics and fate do play a role in the greater scheme of things. Universal entropy is alive and absolutely in control, or at least that's how it would appear.

I know I had to leave Sam and I know George had to leave with me, but I take solace in knowing we will be together again. It's not over. Sam just needs some time and he needs to get control of his anger. Something has happened to him that will be short-term pain, but in the end it will all work out. In the end, we will be together and live happily ever after for all eternity.

I will have it no other way, and Sam will have it no other way because he's my romantic.

Canada
Spring 1983

Enter Barth

NINETEEN EIGHTY-THREE was an interesting year in Canada. Politically, *Brian Mulroney* won the leadership position for the federal Progressive Conservative Party of Canada. He would go on to win the next federal election and become Canada's Prime Minister for the next ten years. One of his most publicized accomplishments would be the introduction of the Canada – USA Free Trade Agreement which formalized the largest partnership between any two countries in the world. The Canadian – USA relationship is still recognized as the most successful neighborly nation friendship in existence.

The hockey season was filled with high highs and low lows. The first high was that all Canadian teams made it into the playoffs. This meant we got to watch Montreal, Toronto, Vancouver, Edmonton, Quebec, Winnipeg, and Calgary all fight for the Cup. The first low was that none of the Beaver Brothers or Vince and the Judge's teams won the Cup. Instead, the New York Islanders won their fourth Stanley Cup in a row by beating the Edmonton Oilers four games to none. It was another sweep. What the world didn't know was that Wayne Gretzky and his Oilers would soon be on a winning streak. Wayne

Gretsky–Number 99–The Great One. While we did not cheer for the Oilers, we were all proud of Wayne, as being proud of Wayne was simply principle.

Another low in the year was the last remaining players from the Original-Six Time Era retired. Carol Vadnais, Serge Savard, and Wayne Cashman left the ice for the last time, ending a legacy of NHL Original-Six Teams hockey. It was a sad time for a lot of people. We did, however, get over our grief with the high news that the long pants worn by the Philadelphia Flyers were banned due to safety concerns. Hats was beside himself while Vince was happy he had forecasted the future and saved a lot of money. Locally, the Maple Tree Hockey Team did not do so well, marking the first year we did not win our league championship since the four of us started playing hockey for Vince and the Judge ten years earlier.

The music front brought sad news as one of our favorite Canadian folk singers died in an airplane crash. *Stan Rogers* passed away with twenty-two other souls when their plane made an emergency landing at the Cincinnati – Northern Kentucky airport. They were trying to get from Dallas to Toronto, and the flight did not go so well. After the investigation, it was determined that a series of mistakes were made by a series of people over a series of time frames. Another hand won by entropy, and it seemed to us that the world and airplanes had something against our favorite musicians. Over the course of that summer, Ray and RC perfected their version of *The Northwest Passage*. Later on, we read that Stan's ashes were scattered in the Atlantic Ocean off the coast of Nova Scotia. Ray really liked that.

The year progressed slowly and quickly all at the same time for the Beaver Brothers and our families. All four of us simply coasted through the months. School went fine once Hats got over the sting of being impeached, but Christmas was brutal and depressing for everybody, in particular, Ray's parents. They were not dealing with Rose's death very well, not that anybody expected them to be doing well. We played hard on the ice, but did not take as much joy from the game. We won a few games but did so without spirit, although neither Vince nor the Judge kicked our ass for our attitudes, as I think they were feeling the same way. Ray was beginning to withdraw, although he tried hard to stay his usual self. Pretending to be what people expect you to be is hard and draining. It takes a lot of energy, and the drain was showing on his face. A good day was when we simply hung out at the Lodge, playing guitar, reading, writing songs and taking small trips to Tuneupville. Ray was also enjoying his smoke with more frequency. The town itself was getting back to normal from the previous year's events, which was to be expected as human survival depends on the ability to get up and give it another shot after you have been knocked down. It's part of the human DNA. It's an essence of the human experience. Get up and give it another shot. *Eat tree, Beaver,* because that's what Beavers do.

The end of the school year was closing in, and for the most part, our plans for the next September had been decided upon. Hats was accepted, and he accepted the acceptance, to the University of Toronto. He was headed to the big city where he would complete an undergraduate degree in political science and then go directly into law school. RC learned that he could not go directly into the RCMP as the rules were changing and entrance was getting tougher, so he decided to do a two-year Police Foundations diploma prior to applying to the RCMP. He was accepted at a local college to get this done. Ray said he was going to take a year off and stay at home and focus on his music, which seemed reasonable to us, and I think we were pleased that it actually was a plan of sorts. I was accepted to and was planning to attend the University of Manitoba in Winnipeg. I had convinced myself I wanted to stay close to Ray, although I knew I was somewhat lost myself. My planned major was English with a focus on Poetry.

With September reasonably lined up, what was not clear was the plan for the summer, and in hindsight, I suspect we all assumed we would run Beaver Brothers Leaf Company and help people clean out their eavestroughs. This was until Ray called us over to his house on a Friday evening in early April. He was as excited as we had seen him since Rose's death, and it seemed as if a part of our old friend was back, and it was the good part – the positive energy that Ray always exuded, allowing us to see that the sun was trying hard to shine into his soul to bring him back to our world.

When we arrived at Ray's house, he took us into the backyard where his father kept his new 1982 Barth motorhome, a machine that was pure house on wheels. Ray's father always upgraded for their summer vacations each year and he had bought this unit the previous summer. It was virtually brand new, with only a couple of short trips represented on the odometer as it had not moved since Rose's death. I don't think Ray's parents had any plans to use it anytime soon, if ever.

Ray invited the four of us to climb aboard the Barth. We sat at the kitchen table, a table that could fold out and double for a bed when required. We all looked over at Ray to hear the news that had him feeling so much better.

"Well," Ray started, "as you can imagine, my parents do not intend on travelling this summer. They are simply not up to it, which is understandable. However, I, on the other hand, need to get the hell out of this place for a while. So, I asked my dad if we could use the Barth for a bit this summer."

The three of us just sat in silence looking at Ray, and within milliseconds, we were imagining all the scenarios of what he was suggesting.

"And?" RC asked, really saying, *Are you saying what I think you are saying? What did your dad say, Ray?*

"And his exact words were," Ray responded, "'Ray, my son, if it will make you feel better, you and the boys can borrow the Barth for as long as you like. Go. Go do whatever you need to do, son.'"

"No fucking way!" Hats shrieked out.

"Yes fucking way!" Ray replied.

"What does this mean?" I asked the group, really saying, *What are the boundaries and bookends for our thinking here, boys?*

"It means," Ray replied, "the day after school ends, we are on the road and we aren't coming back until mid-August. That's what it means!"

The three of us and Ozark let Ray's words sink in for a solid two minutes. RC broke the silence.

"Right," he said, trying to sound very mature, "that's exactly what it means, Ray. That's exactly what it means, Sam. That's exactly what it means, Hats. And yes, Ozark, that's exactly what it means!"

"Damn right!" I built on RC's comment, really saying, *Of course that's what it means!*

"Fucking eh right that's what it means!" Hats said to end the string.

We all took another minute to soak in the news, the atmosphere, and also to look around and admire the Barth in a way we had never admired the motorhome before. The new Barth, the Barth that was now ours.

The Barth sat on a one-ton General Motors chassis and was ten wheels of solid North American engineering. Pulled by a General Motors 455 big block gas engine, it also had a homemade blower for some extra power. The frame was unique from other motorhomes as it was an all-steel frame with an aircraft aluminum skin made from anodized aluminum. But that wasn't the best part. The inside was pure luxury. We had solid wooden cabinets making up the kitchen with all known amenities, including a built-in blender with ten different speeds.

In addition, we had a full bathroom with shower, the beds could sleep the four of us and Ozark easily, and we had five big captain chairs for driving and hanging out in – one for each of us. Ozark loved it. Each chair swiveled completely around and hovered on top of a full lay of shag carpeting. There were no doors on the driver's side or passenger-side seats, and the one entrance and exit door was in the middle of the Barth on the passenger side. Other features included two furnaces, an air conditioning unit, as well as a dashboard heater and air unit. All appliances ran off of propane, and we had a diesel backup generator in case we ran off grid. We had a double battery backup with power inverter that charges as you drive and a spot light on top that ran by a joy stick on the inside dash and that could light up Winnipeg. Best of all, we had air ride suspension, so it rode like a living room chesterfield going down the road. There was a trailer hitch on the back with three hitches – one for towing a car and the other two for a motorcycle rack. And last, but certainly not least, we had a roof rack for the canoes. Wait, we also had a built-in eight track and cassette stereo hi/fi system that cranked tunes out of speakers that were littered throughout the whole vehicle. This was Barth – a luxury tank on ten wheels of pure tour machine. We loved Barth and now it was ours for the summer. All ours.

With our summer plans established, we began planning our trip, and from that day forward, we either slept in Barth (obvious name for the motorhome) or at the Lodge. These were our two homes that provided us with everything we needed for survival. At last, we were in the best shape we could be in for the shape we were in, and it appeared as if The Beaver Brothers were back in stride with our energy coming back because of the significant work to get ready for the summer's journey. So we got busy with the planning and the work that came from the planning. We were once again busy Beavers, and we validated that busy Beavers would seem to be happier Beavers.

The first two decisions to be made were: one, where to go, and two, how we would fund the expedition. We felt like Lewis and Clark, sitting at the kitchen table in Barth for the first planning session, and I pulled out one of two books I had bought to contribute to the road trip. This first book was a Rand McNally Road Atlas – 1983 Version. It was brand new, it was perfect, it was a book of maps, it was a book of roads that could take us anywhere. It was a book of paths for the Beaver Brothers, so we instantly renamed it the Book of Paths, which we quickly shortened to the BOP. We opened the BOP and began the route-planning process, starting on page three of the atlas that shows all of the USA, Canada, and Northern Mexico. It was the bird's eye view of all things possible for our adventure. A journey that began with Ray handing me a marker, after which he asked me to put a dot on the map where I wanted to go.

"You go first, Sam," he said, really saying, *I know exactly where this dot will be.* RC and Hats had similar expressions. They knew exactly where I would be headed.

"No problem there, Ray, my man," I said back with a smile and immediately put a dot on *Dawson City, Yukon*, home of the Klondike Gold Rush of 1898, home of the *Robert Service* cabin where the poem of all poems originated. My three friends all punched me in the shoulder and gave me a look that said, *I guess we could have figured that one out, eh?* Having completed my duty, I handed the marker to Ray.

Ray did not hesitate for a minute either and he put a marker dot right on *Key West, Florida*. We all looked at him with a *tell us why* look on our faces.

"Sunsets and sunrises," he said. "Energy and spirituality at its finest," Ray said as he handed the marker to Hats.

Hats looked over the page of the BOP and saw the first two dots and then started waving the marker over the map. He started chanting, "Where to go, where to fucking go, where...." and then he came down hard on the map and left a dot on *Tijuana, Mexico*. We looked at him for an explanation and his explanation was, "If you don't know, boys, then you will find out when we get there." We weren't convinced that he knew either, but Tijuana, Mexico, sounded pretty good to the three of us, so we went with it. Hats handed the marker to RC.

RC looked at the map for a few seconds and then did what any reasonable Canadian planning a road trip would do. He planted the marker on *St-Johns, Newfoundland*, completing the square, and what a square it was. The four of us sat back, lit up a torpedo, and looked at the BOP in front of us with the four dots on it. We looked at it in silence; all of us having the same feeling overcome us at the same time. It was a feeling of *holy shit, what the hell is gonna happen this summer!*

RC grabbed a piece of string that was in the kitchen drawer of Barth and he took the string and ran it from each point on our outlined square on the BOP. He framed up our route with the string and then tied a knot where the length would represent the total length of the trip as measured by the string drawn on the page in the road atlas. He then compared the total length of the string to the legend scale on the map that shows one inch being two hundred fifty miles. He was very careful to hold it up against the scale and then count how many times he slid the string over the scale. Each slide was two hundred fifty miles of Beaver Brothers Road trip, so it was important to get it right. He finished his count and looked up at us.

"Well, boys, if we assume we go to Dawson first and then to Mexico, then east to Florida and then north to Newfoundland and then home… as the crow flies, we are looking at…" he paused for a minute and then said, "we are looking at sixty inches times two hundred fifty miles, which is a grand total of…maybe fifteen thousand miles, or about twenty-five thousand kilometers!"

At that point, we all just took a haul off our torpedo and looked at each other; it was clearly evident that we had no idea what the hell fifteen thousand miles meant, but it sounded doable, as optimism reigned the day.

"Can we do that?" I said to RC, sounding like I thought RC was suddenly a travel agent.

"I don't know!" he said back, really saying, *How the hell should I know, Sam. I ain't no travel agent!*

"Yes we can," Ray said with absolute confidence. "We will have ten weeks. That's fifteen hundred miles per week; at an average speed of forty-five miles an hour, we need to drive thirty-four hours per week, so even allowing for a few unknowns, that's only three twelve-hour days of driving and four days in the week left for doing whatever we are going to. We can do this with our eyes closed, boys!"

We listened to Ray with full concentration, and we all did the math over in our head, confirming that Ray was bang-on correct, and we quickly fell into line in full agreement that we could get the job done.

"OK, good," Hats said. "That was the easy part. The real question is how are we going to pay for this *Lewis and Clark* meets *Beaver Brothers* expedition?"

"Don't know," RC answered for all of us, really saying, *I don't know.*

"I guess we need a budget," Ray offered.

With that suggestion, I pulled out the second book I would contribute to our summer. It was a hardcover book with two hundred blank pages in it.

"What's that?" RC asked.

"It's our journal for the trip," I said. "We will be taking some notes along the way."

"Perfect," Ray said.

So, we opened up the journal and we built our road-trip budget on page one. It took us about an hour, and then I read it out to the budget committee.

BEAVER BROTHERS ROAD TRIP BUDGET – DRAFT 1

1. Torpedoes: $420.00
2. Beer : $1,750.00
3. Whiskey: $430.00
4. Ice: $550.00
5. Food. $1,400.00
6. Gas : Not sure
7. Other : Not sure

Total: $4,550.00 + Gas and other things we are not sure about

I looked at RC, Ray, and Hats for confirmation of a job well done. RC was polite in his response.

"Maybe we should consider a few other costs?" he said, really saying, *We might have missed a thing or two here.*

Hats agreed and said, "Ya, I think maybe we need a little more ice, eh? You dumb fucks! Why don't we just haul a ten-ton ice cube from the Chinook River on top of Barth? Maybe we can sell a bit on the way across the country?"

"Ya, maybe," I said. "I guess we could figure out the gas part now that we know the mileage? And I like Hats' idea about more ice!"

And with that, we argued and rationalized and calculated and debated and finally landed on our best forecast for the travel budget. I held firm on the ice.

BEAVER BROTHERS ROAD TRIP BUDGET – DRAFT 2

1. Torpedoes: $400.00
2. Beer : $1,850.00
3. Whiskey: $350.00
4. Ice: $550.00
5. Food: $2,400.00
6. Gas : $2,500.00
7. Other: Unknowns – but we think we know: $2,000.00
8. Other: Unknowns that we don't know: NA

Total: $10,050.00 + unknown unknowns

We sat back in our captain chairs and allowed reality to set in. This was a lot of money, much more than we had anticipated and much more than we had. Even Ozark looked a little discouraged, but we were not allowing ourselves to be defeated. We tallied what we did have and we estimated what Ozark had stashed at the Lodge from the previous summer's work. In sum, and with eight weeks before our departure date, we had gross startup capital of $4,235.00 among us. We were actually pretty impressed, as all five of us had saved some money, mostly because we had continued to pick up a few odd jobs cleaning leaves, and Vince was paying us a little to play at the Hotel when he needed a band on short notice. We clearly had done well for ourselves, and we were proud of our current state even though we were still a long way from our capital requirements.

"That's almost halfway there," RC said, really saying, *Man oh man, we can do this!*

"Damn right!" Ray replied with complete optimism.

And with the budget meeting complete, we started a *how we gonna get cash* session. By the time we went to sleep that night in Barth, we had a plan. We called it Plan A. The plan, to be executed first thing in the morning, was to talk to Vince.

We had no plan B.

In Vince's Voice

THE BOYS CAME OVER to the hotel Saturday morning. I was beat from the night before. I don't know why they always seem to catch me at my worst. Weak, nervous and anxious can also result in gullible and malleable. I guess the boys know this, and that's why they showed up in the morning. They wanted me hung over.

I knew they wanted something the minute they walked in. It was obvious when they started helping me clean the place up. RC and Ray and Sam would do this as a matter of course, but the fact that Hats was helping clued me into the situation, so I let them clean the bar up. May as well get something for what I was about to give. Not that I knew what that was yet.

With the bar ready for the day, I asked the boys to sit down and talk to me before I opened up. I poured us five *Red Eyes*, the wonderful concoction of beer and tomato juice. It's a beautiful thing. We sat down and I asked the boys what was on their minds. Ray assumed spokesperson role and he told me about their plans for the adventure of a lifetime. I was supportive from the get go for a couple of reasons. The first is that Ray needed to get out of town. I had been coaching Ray since he was kid. I knew Ray. I had been watching him all year and he was headed in the wrong direction. Something was going on inside him, although he was working very hard not to let it show. He needed an interruption, a change of scenery. He needed to get out of town.

The second reason I was very supportive was because I was envious. When I was young, I wanted to go on an adventure like they were

248

planning, but I never did. I never left this town. Instead, I just worked the family business – my Dad's business, my Grandfather's business, this business – the gift from my Dad when he finally died from working and drinking. The day he died, I inherited the hotel and the drinking gene. Thanks, Dad.

The drinking gene is powerful beyond measure. It's passed down from generations like musical talent or athletic abilities. I can spot the gene the minute a person walks into my bar. It's in the way they walk up to the bar, the way they stare at the bottles, the way they hold their glass to take a drink, and the look when they get their first drink in them. Their entire physiology changes with that first drink – the look of joy, then the look of absolute sadness when the drink is empty, only to be rebounded with another look of pure joy when it is refilled, even though they know the next hundred drinks that night will not satiate them. Yes, I know the gene well because I have the gene. My entire life has been about living with and living within the atmosphere of the gene. I love the bar and I hate the bar. This is a hard life, but when I am surrounded by the bottles, I am surrounded by my friends. I know ultimately this life and the gene will kill me; this is a necessary eventuality, it's my fate, it shows in my face and my body, and I accept that. A person can't live forever, so he may as well accept his inherited destiny. I have no place to go anyway. I have no skills other than running the Hotel, and I have no intimate personal relationship other than with the gene. The hockey team is my one escape, and the boys are the interesting subset of that escape. It does me good when I am doing good for others. In the few hours per week while the gene is sleeping, I try to do good for others.

I told the boys I would help in any way I could, and to be sure they weren't looking for a handout, nor would I give them one anyway as nothing of value comes without work attached to it. They were, however, looking for ideas, and ironically, I was looking for something at the time as well. The stars were aligning. There is a season-ending hockey tournament every year on the May Two-Four weekend, and this is the first year that my team is old enough to participate. We started the most recent crew of the Maple Tree Hockey Team when the boys and my other team members were in Atom, and we've been progressing to the next level every two years, and now they are big and strong enough to play in the May Two-Four tournament. I really wanted to be in the tournament and actually try to win, but we had a problem. The boys had played well during the year, but their heart was not in it. With the current rate of passion, we would not be competitive in the tournament, so I was skeptical to even enter the team. And any time I mentioned it to the boys, they seemed lackluster about the idea. It's important to me, though, as it's an important tournament weekend that draws a large crowd from out of town, and I do a lot of business – a lot of business, but I would do even more if my team were to win the tournament. Plus it's fun just to win for winning's sake. Winning is not everything, but it feels pretty good every once in a while. The Judge thinks we could win if the boys played up to their potential. The Judge knows his hockey, and I agree with him.

With all of this running through my mind, I put an offer out on the table to the boys. The Maple Tree Hockey Team plays in the tournament and we play hard. If we win the tournament, I will have the Beaver Brothers Band play at the Hotel the Monday night of the long weekend. For a tournament win and the band performance, I would pay them two thousand dollars. If the night was busy, that would be a modest chunk of my profit for the night. They were floored. Ray actually choked up a bit while Hats banged his hand on the table and yelled for *more fucking Red Eyes*. I'm not sure who he was yelling at, but eventually he got up and went and fetched the drinks himself. The profit-sharing deal was agreed upon and we *Red Eye* cheered the arrangement.

Tournament weekend came and they played as if they were trying out for the NHL. I've never seen Ray play harder or smarter, and Sam only let three goals in over six games. Three shut outs and one goal per game for the other three games. One shut out was the final game. RC played so hard and physical that opponents stopped skating near him. The best part was Hats. The son of a bitch figured out how to stay out of the penalty box – no fights, no cheap shots, no temper flare ups. It was as if he was a different player, still tough, but focused on playing hockey to win by scoring more goals than the other team as opposed to hospitalizing the other team.

We won the tournament due to grit, hard work, and pure will. The boys had the fever but their teammates came to the table as well. Six straight games spread over three days. The scores were 3-1, 2-0, 4-0, 2-1, 3-1, and the final game was 1-0. Ray scored the winning goal of the final game in the middle of the third period. The game was a fast and furious and tough match up, and after Ray scored the goal, Sam put up an invisible steel wall in his net. Every person in the arena could feel the energy that my team was exuding, and I swear to God that every person in that rink was cheering for the boys. Little did I know why!

I had chatted confidentially to the Judge about my deal with the boys. The Judge was not so discreet with the confidential information and he had spread the details of the negotiation around the rink. The stakes were high and the hometown crowd was now involved emotionally. The game was pure suspense, and every shift of the puck was met with oohs and ahhs from the crowd. The players on both benches were on their feet for the entire third period.

With two minutes left in the final game, the other team had a two-on-one and they managed to get a huge slap shot off from the hash marks inside our blue line. We all watched the puck fly through the air. It seemed as if it were moving in slow motion, and Sam ended the slow motion by making the most incredible save ever seen in the arena. It was a spread eagle trapper save, where his whole body was stretched out protecting the net, yet he managed to get his trapper up to the left corner of the net where the puck was headed. He caught the puck and fell backwards, holding the puck up in the trapper as if he were protecting a beer after a fall down the stairs. My guts were torn out watching it, the crowd went wild, and I thought I might die from my eventual heart attack right then and there. It was better than game eight of the '72 Summit Series. It was off the charts and the rink went ballistic as we were presented the trophy. Ray accepted it for the team.

The boys cleaned up and got right to the bar to play that Monday night. The whole rink, all out-of-towners, and half of our town headed to the bar. It was as if the whole town just needed to blow off steam. And it was all good – no fights, no issues, and no McMullens showed up. I think the Judge had something to do with that. The night was peaceful, true brotherhood at its best, the way people should be. That was my favorite night of any night in my God-forsaken place. That night, it was a temple. That night, I was proud of the Maple Tree Hotel.

The boys played their music and rocked the place. I was busy at the bar, but I saw the Judge going around the bar talking to people, pipe in his mouth, drink in hand, making his rounds. He would bend over and say a few words to my customers and then I would notice the customer going into his pocket and coming out with a few bills. The Judge would pat him on the back and stuff the bills in his sport jacket pocket. He did this all night. What a guy. What a night. I wish I could relive it all over again. These were the moments of joy that make the days of suffering bearable.

By the time we got the last person out and locked the doors, it was three o'clock in the morning. The boys were cranked up, I mean really cranked up, but I managed to get them to stand somewhat still at the bar. The Judge was with us. I poured six whiskeys and put the drinks in front of us. Curly and Ozark were at my feet. I told the boys to wait before doing the shot. I then pulled an envelope out that I had carefully prepared after the final game and before the bar got crazy. I gave the envelope to Ray, and he choked up again. He tried hard to hide it, but I could see it in his eyes. I know that feeling, so I can see it in others. Ray put the envelope in his front pocket without opening it. Hats made some dumbass comment about counting it and then he smiled and tapped me on the shoulder in a *thank you so much, Vince* gesture. We went for our whiskey, but before we could drink, the Judge interrupted us.

He told the boys that the rest of the folks in the bar had something for us as well, and the boys looked around trying to see who he was talking about. The place was empty other than the six of us and Ozark and Curly. Then the Judge pulled out a *Crown Royal* purple velvet bag. He told the boys this was a little donation from the patrons of the bar that night – a little token of their appreciation for a great tournament and equally great rock and roll show. Unlike my envelope, the bills in the bag were not organized and were haphazardly thrown in a bunch. The Judge handed the bag to Ray, and this time he did count it. In all, the ones and twos and fives and tens and twenties, the Judge had collected $1,267.00 for the boys' trip. Ray muscled a "thank you" to the Judge and excused himself, claiming he needed to go to the washroom. Sometimes a man just needs to stop fighting his emotions. Ray was dealing with a lot and not dealing with that lot so well. Sam went into the washroom to help and after a couple of minutes they both returned. We formed around the bar.

We raised our glasses. We raised them as high as we could and we tried to reach the sky. We clinked our whiskey glasses at the top of the hand pyramid we created. We did not make a toast to anything in particular, no one voiced anything, and the only sound made was from the clinking of the glasses. We drank our shot and the next sounds heard were the empty shot glasses being slammed to the hardwood bar – six fast and consecutive bangs, separate sounds, yet somehow forming a whole. That sound says it all. Certain sounds in this world can spell out a soliloquy of literature, narrative, and symphony in a fraction of a second. Certain sounds should not try to be described in words. The sound of shot glasses hitting the hardwood bar is one of those sounds. I love that sound. It's perfect.

We concluded the night and we all went home happy. What the boys don't know is that was the best night of my life. That night gave my life meaning. That night allowed me to understand my contribution, and that night allowed me to recognize that I did some good in this God-forsaken world.

On some tiny, small and micro scale, I was able to make the world a better place. That's a nice feeling. I'll keep that feeling with me always.

Those boys have no idea what they mean to me.

I look forward to telling them one day.

DAY 15

South Carolina

Sunrises

TODAY IS A YELLOW DAY – one step above Red, one step below Green – anxious, yes; angry, no. I'll take it. Subjects and thoughts that used to send me into Red are not impacting me as harshly as they used to. I am enjoying talking to Doc and I respect that she is giving me space when I need it, and I am also happy with myself that I am taking the space when I need it, as there is no point being my own worst enemy. I'm getting my walks in and I'm working hard to get my butt out of bed in the morning to watch the sunrise. Mornings have never been my thing. I have never jumped out of bed and charged the day, mostly because mornings are an evolution for me and not a revolution. Sophie is a morning person, my morning revolutionist. I envy that in her. Her eyes just open at some fixed time her brain has programmed as an alarm, and she simply wants to get up. That sure isn't me, and lately I've been able to stay in bed for days. No doubt it's simply depression, as this is not really who I am. Even though I have never been a morning person, I can go strong all day and night. I'm a hard-working night person. There is a whole world at night that exists beyond the morning revolution. It's like an underground – a world that average people living average lives have no idea is even out there. It's an ecosystem that survives on darkness as opposed to sunlight. I do my best work after ten in the evening. I sleep best between two and eight in the morning, and I don't think I'm alone in this schedule.

Even though I struggle getting up with the sun, when I do I really like it. So that's why I wish I were a morning person. Every time I do hear the rooster crow, I tell myself I should do it again the next day. It makes sense, as seeing the sun rise is much better than seeing the sun set. The irony is sunsets are more popular. It must be because you don't have to get your ass out of bed, and a sunset normally involves an ice-cold frozen margarita. Never underestimate the power and impact of a good blender drink. That's a *Vince-ism.*

A sunrise says welcome to a new day. It asks, "I wonder what will happen today? Think about all the possibilities!" A sunrise says hello, whereas a sunset, on the other hand, says the day is over – you survived, good for you, if you're lucky, maybe you will wake up again tomorrow. A sunset says goodbye, yet it seems that many people like goodbye more than hello. I am a believer in long hellos and short goodbyes. This just makes sense to me, and the sun is like that too. The rise is much longer then the set. The sun knows what it's doing, and this is a good thing, as without a smart sun, the Earth and all its glory would be totally screwed.

Ray taught me everything I know about the sun and it's still a frequent topic of conversation when we talk. Ray has worshipped the sun since the day he was born. He wanted to be the Sun-for-a-Living and then tempered his aspiration and lowered it to being a Ray-of-the-Sun. To Ray, the sun is God, and in his mind there is no other God. I have to admit he has affected me over the years, mostly because his arguments seem much more reasonable than the man-made stories supporting all the other theories.

As Ray would say, according to man, the sun is a star that formed a little less than five billion years ago. It is close to perfectly spherical and consists of really hot plasma and a bunch of magnetic fields. It has a diameter of close to eight hundred thousand miles, which is almost one hundred ten times the size of the Earth. In other words, it's really big. The sun's mass is some huge meaningless number that is almost three hundred fifty thousand times the mass of the Earth. The sun is essentially our entire solar system, which is why we call it a solar system. According to man, about three quarters of the sun's mass consists of hydrogen, and the rest is mainly helium. According to man, the surface temperature of the sun is over five thousand degrees Celsius. In other words, it's really hot. A complete orbit of the Earth around the sun occurs every three hundred sixty-five and a quarter days. That's our year and the whole leap year thing. It takes approximately twenty-four hours for the Earth to complete a full rotation about its axis relative to the sun; hence, sunrises and sunsets. The sun is considered to be the center of the universe, although Ray does not believe this because he believes the universe is infinite in all directions, and therefore, no matter where you are standing, you are, in fact, in the center. I like this theory. It's good to be at the center of the universe no matter where you are.

Here's where it gets good. Sun worshipping, or a Solar Deity, is the oldest known religion to mankind. However, it is not popular today because modern religions successfully conspired to dilute the sun's importance as our God. For example, December 25 was chosen to be the date of Christ's birth by the Roman Empire, and they chose this date because it was the long standing date that sun worshippers celebrated the feast of the Sun God. It was considered the winter solstice, and hence was celebrated as the day of the sun's birthday by many, many people. But the powers of the Roman Empire could not control sun worshippers through fear of hell so they changed the date to be that of the birthday of Jesus Christ. They got rid of the sun worshipper's big day by giving it to another growing religion. They just happened to pick a religion where the masses were being well managed through fear of eternal life in some red hot furnace. It's interesting that the characteristics of a traditional hell are somewhat similar to the characteristics of the sun. I suspect this was another way to eliminate the Solar Deity – simply make their God look like the devil's hell itself.

What's neat about Ray is he would tell me these facts, but he could care less about them. They are all man-made facts and, therefore, he does not trust them. Ray does not believe anything that he does not witness or understand with his own eyes, and even then, he is skeptical. The reasons why Ray believes the sun is God is not based on human narratives or fabricated statistics, but rather on what he calls *self-evident observation*. I can picture him, many years ago, with feet in the water on the beach in South Carolina, both of us enjoying the waves hitting our legs and watching the sun come up.

"Sam," he would say, "our entire universe depends on the sun. You see, there is life on Earth because of water and oxygen, but the Earth has water and oxygen because of the sun. The sun gives life to everything, Sam, absolutely everything. No sun, no life. Think about it, Sam, if the human being disappeared in an instant, the Earth would do nothing but flourish. It would come alive like never before. The Earth and the health of the environment do not depend on man for one thing; in fact, every single thing humans do on the Earth is bad for it. We use everything and give nothing. Nothing, Sam. So if man contributes nothing, how could God have anything to do with man? It simply does not add up. The sun, on the other hand, gives everything. I mean everything, Sam. It works all day, every day, and works as hard as it can because there is only one sun, so it has to show up for work. If it doesn't show up for work, then we are in a bad way – a real bad way, Sam. Think about it, Sam. The sun is the only thing in the entire universe that we are completely dependent on. Remember, Sam, we orbit around the sun, not the other way around. Leave it to the dumbass human to say the sun goes up and down. Hardly, Sam, we pass by the sun. We pass by it in the morning and it stays with us while we revolve around it. Nothing is going up or down. Nothing is rising or setting. You see, Sam, the First Nations people have it right. They know that the sun is the Father and the Earth is the Mother. Together they create life. You see, Sam, the sun creates the condition for all elements of life, it is superior to everything, Sam, and here's the best part. The sun wants nothing but happiness and health for the Earth. It does not punish the Earth or put fear into the Earth. The sun is just pure love, warmth and joy. It is the one and true God, Sam."

I love these conversations with Ray. They are totally abstract but he makes so much sense. I would ask him about his theories of who created the sun and all the other questions that no religion can answer for their own theories. He would simply dismiss me with a hand in the air.

"Sam, Sam, Sam," he would say, "It doesn't matter, Sam. That's the Great Mystery, and who gives a shit what I would say anyway? Anything I say would just be my opinion, my subjective story that is pure shit. Here's all you need to know, Sam. Without the sun, we are screwed. Get it? So it must be God. What else is a God if it's not something that you are totally screwed if you don't have it? Think about it, Sam. The Earth was around well before Jesus Christ or Muhammad or Buddha or any other person who arrived and created a lasting splash. Right? So then clearly the Earth survived prior to these people. Right? And these people are not here now and we are surviving. Right? So the Earth survived before their arrivals and the Earth has survived since their departures. So the Earth has, can, and will survive without them.

Given that, how can they be considered to be God? The sun on the other hand, Sam, has been here since day one. The sun's formation is the axiom and fundamental definition of day one! And the day the sun stops showing up for work will be the end of the show, end of the story, yip, when the sun leaves the stage, the fat lady will be singing, and shivering! But it won't leave for a while, Sam, because the sun shows up. You see, the sun is not hiding and asking for our faith and prayers to confirm its existence, but rather the sun is pure transparency. "I'm here," it says. "I'm God and I can see you!" The other stories ask for our faith and prayers. Come on! How about a little show of respect! Sam, if you were God and the whole place was falling apart, would you not show up on the jobsite every once in a while? Who in the hell starts a major project and then walks away from it and never shows up again? Are we really supposed to believe that a perfect God created such an imperfect place and then didn't work on a little continuous improvement? Talk about management by avoidance!"

I love these conversations. Ray gets so passionate about it. Once he was going on about all the other Gods being no shows and I asked him why the sun would allow the world to get so messed up if it was, in fact, God. His answer was priceless.

"Sam," he said to me, "that is the best question you have ever asked, and in a different time, a question like that would get you executed, because ancient rulers didn't tend to like people who questioned their hold on the masses. The problem with the question, though, is that it assumes that people are the focus and centricity of the world and God. This is the flaw of human beings' thinking and all religions. We believe the Earth is about us. This is the ultimate result of our complete and utter narcissism and addiction of self. You see, Sam, when you read the stories from modern religions, you are reading stories about people written by people. They are people-centric stories where it's all about good and evil and love and hate. They are stories written by people to help people understand and get through their day in a messed up place littered with suffering. They are stories written by people to keep people in line in this messed up place. You gotta keep people in line, Sam, and the story is everything. Yet these stories are not stories about the Earth itself, they are only about people, and a result of this is that religions have convinced us that God is focused on people, that God created people and that the whole story is about the fate of the person. Just think about the Ten Commandments, Sam. The story is Ten Commandments were handed down on a rock by

God himself. But not one of them is about the Earth – don't steal, don't murder, and don't do a bunch of bad stuff to other people. Not one request from God about making the Earth better. Do you really think God would create this amazing planet and then not ask the moron people on the planet to be kind to the planet itself? Not one Commandment about leaving the rain forest alone, or not digging through the middle of the Earth's crust, or not putting toxins into the air? You see, Sam, all the mainstream stories are just people stories written by people about people in order to put fear into people so masses of people can be controlled by a few other people. Do you get it, Sam? But what if this people-centric view is completely false? What if the sun is the one true God and the power of the sun allows the Earth to exist for the Earth and not for people? In other words, what if the focus of God, the sun, is not people but the Earth itself? If this is the case, then the whole story changes. You live, you die, and your energy goes somewhere, maybe straight into the ground, maybe you are reborn. I don't really care where the energy goes, and why does it matter anyway? But for sure, we are not floating on clouds playing the harp or burning in the furnaces of hell. I like to think the sun absorbs our energy back into itself. That's how it keeps burning, we are its fuel, it gives us life and it takes back what energy is left when we perish. You see, Sam, the story is not about people, but rather it's about the Earth – the water, the trees, the mountains, the animals and all the ecosystems. The worst thing that happened for the Earth was for the human to evolve. I mean, just look at the path we are now on. It's screwed, Sam, and if I were the sun, I might consider shutting the whole thing down. I might just say, 'Screw it. You people are so stupid. I just can't watch this show any longer. See ya, bye. Have a nice trip!' You know what I mean, Sam?

"Sam, you are the poet, so here, add this one to your list of important poems. In fact, this should be at the top of the list as it defines the reality of things on this earth."

THE SUN – BY RAY

I believe the Sun
Is our one true God
And if we could all align on this
We would begin to get along

To me it just makes perfect sense
Some things are simply clear
For example, if the Sun goes out
There won't be anybody here

In thinking back on these conversations, I realize how Ray is such a different thinker. I know other people have debated all these theories before, and I'm not saying that Ray is unique in all his thoughts, but he has the ability to break complexity up into its simple elements. Sure, some things are complicated because they are complicated, but all things are built from simple elements. All complexity has simple origins, and this all connects to my situation. I need to better understand my anger. It's all connected in some way and I need to isolate my patterns of thought. I need to break them down into the pieces that form the whole, because I'm living with the whole splashing inside my head like waves on the beach. I need to break up the whole and synthesize it down into its elements, the essential elements of my anger. I need to design the periodic table of anger.

My talks with Ray are giving me more questions than answers at this point, but I feel the questions are helpful, although I'm not sure why I think they are helpful or how I can measure the helpfulness. It's just a sixth sense I am getting, and I need to keep this train of thought going. It's time to understand the anger from the ground up.

There's another reason I struggle to get up with the sun – my dreams. I continue to live another life in my dream world, and some of these dreams leave me exhausted beyond relief. I had one last night. I suspect that's why I'm not in the Green today. I can't get the dream out of my mind, and I can't figure out what the hell I'm supposed to take away from the dream. This feeling is proving less than helpful.

In my dream, I am walking down a dirt road. It is completely deserted. It's a Saskatchewan prairie dirt road, one where you can see for miles in all directions. Completely flat, the road is endless behind me and endless in front of me. The road has feelings and emotions – it is mournful and sad. There are no other roads connecting to it. It is a road from nowhere that goes to nowhere. It is surrounded by prairie fields whose soil has lost all richness for growth, and the soil will never support a successful crop again. The soil has feelings and emotions as well. The soil is mournful and sad as its only useful purpose – to grow life – has been taken away. As I learn about the road and the soil, the prairie wind is blowing softly against my face.

My understanding in the dream is I have walked the entire stretch of dirt road behind me. I started from its origin that does not exist and I feel tired from the walking. Then I see a small dot far up ahead in the distance. I have no idea what it is, but as I continue to walk forward, it starts to get closer to me. It seems to be moving as well, and I get the sense the dot is coming from the destination of the road, a destination that does not exist. The dot and I are working together to close the gap between us, and eventually, I can tell it is a person. Then I can tell it is a man. Then I can tell it is a tall man. And then I can tell the tall man is carrying something in his right hand. I am on the left side of the road and he is on my right; we are both hugging our respective ditches, and I still can't make out who he is or what he is carrying. We continue to get closer to each other, we continue to close the gap, and it becomes clear we will continue to walk until we meet. The road's sadness is increasing as we approach each other. The soil of the prairie begins to cry.

We close the gap more and I finally make out who the person is. It's the Soup Man. It's my father and he is waving a white flag. He is carrying and waving the flag at his side using his right hand. It's an old ragged rectangle of white material tied to a piece of a branch from a tree. The stick is maybe two feet long and has several natural wood knots in it. The Soup Man's right hand fits between the knots and I get the sense the flag staff is made from cherry wood. This is significant for some reason, but I don't know why and sense I will never learn why. We continue to get closer and I anticipate stopping. My heart begins to race as I anticipate stopping and talking to my father. I finally see him clearly and he looks exactly as I remember him.

I am still on my side of the road. He is still on his and neither of us changes course to a diagonal in order to meet in the middle. We progress at the same pace we have been walking since the beginning of the dream, and as soon as it's possible, we make eye contact. We do not release our gaze from each other's eyes. Our facial expressions are neutral – no smiles, no frowns, pure neutrality as if we are perfect strangers and want to keep it that way. I see my own image in his eyes. I am Sam. I am Sam as a thirteen-year-old boy. We continue to walk towards each other with our eyes fixed together in a trance.

After what seems like an eternity, we are side by side, but on opposite sides of the road. I assume we will stop to talk, but we don't. He does not stop. I do not stop. We do not stop. Instead, the Soup Man raises his flag at me ever so subtly and mouths a word to me without making a noise. I read his lips and I see him say, "Surrender." He says it as he is waving his white flag and walking past me. I don't look back, I can't look back. I keep walking straight ahead, and I assume he is walking behind me towards the origin of the road, an origin that does not exist. I continue walking towards the destination of the road; a destination that does not exist. The road and the soil of the Saskatchewan prairie become one entity, and the sadness of this one entity is beyond any sadness ever felt in the history of sadness.

Then I wake up.

What a dream – me and the Soup Man. This is unusual as I don't dream about my father that often anymore. As I get older, his short time in my life becomes less significant in the overall scheme of things; therefore it competes with other options for my mind's time. When I do think about him, it is involuntary, more like images or feelings of him just entering my mind in an instant and then they leave just as quickly. This was certainly the case with this dream – involuntary. He pushed his way into my world.

To tell me to Surrender! Surrender to what? Surrender from what? Surrender?

It exhausts me.

This is not helpful.

PART 2

The Road Trip

LAST THOUGHTS

What memories will go through your mind
In the last breath that you take

We should do more of those things now
While we're healthy and awake

Sam, somewhere on the road, 1983

Canada

Summer 1983

Rules of the Pond

WE HEADED OUT in Barth the first morning after school ended in mid-June. We blew off our graduation. It was simply not a priority. With the help of Vince, the Judge and a little hard work on the ice, we raised enough money to send us off. We didn't have the full amount we planned for, but we were close enough. Hats said we could still work on the amount budgeted for ice. Vince had a sendoff for us at the hotel the night before we left, and the next morning we headed north towards Dawson City, Yukon. We would have left that night but only Ozark was in a condition to drive. The adventure of a lifetime had begun, and quite an adventure it turned out to be.

Heading out of town was a feeling like no feeling we had ever felt – a true sense of freedom. The entire world was at our door, and we drove right through that door, or should I say, we 'Barthed' through it. We were a combination of *Easy Rider, Christopher Columbus, Francis Drake,* and *Burt Reynolds* from *Smokey and the Bandit.* It was fantastic. Ray drove the first few hours, Ozark sat up in the passenger side seat and RC and Hats and I sat behind them in our co-captain chairs. The first conversation we had was to establish a set of guiding principles for

265

the summer. These would be the rules that we would adhere to along the way. The idea was to have some set of values that we would live by in order to keep ourselves out of trouble, so we spent the whole day brainstorming the guiding principles, and eventually made a list on a piece of paper that we stuck on the refrigerator with a magnet.

BEAVER BROTHERS ROAD TRIP – RULES OF THE POND

1. Beaver Buddy System: At least two Beaver Brothers together at all times.
2. No Big Beaver Trails: Drive only on scenic highways and see the countryside.
3. No Buzzing Beavers Driving: He who drives will be sober and straight.
4. Busy Beaver but See the Pond: Keep a steady pace, but stop and look around.
5. Beaver Brothers Back Safely: Make it home in one piece.

We started living the guiding principles immediately: we were driving fools, stopping only for gas and Ozark breaks, and it wasn't until the end of the second day that we finally stopped for a true rest. We were in Dawson Creek, British Columbia. Not one of us wanted to stop, though. It was as if we would just keep changing drivers and do the perimeter of North America without stopping for anything other than gas, food, Ozark, and a few tuning supplies. But we did finally stop, and in total, we had blown right through Manitoba, Saskatchewan, and Alberta. Interestingly as well, this was the last time we had any sense of what day it was or how long we had been out on the road since leaving home.

Ironically, Dawson Creek, British Columbia, was clearly the place to stop. It was perfect. First, Dawson Creek is in the Peace River Valley, and in the 18th century, the valley was occupied by bands of the *Beaver First Nation*. We were among the aboriginals of the Beaver Brothers! The second reason why Dawson Creek, BC, is an amazing city is that it is officially Mile 0 of the Alaskan Highway. I was at the beginning of the most amazing highway ever built in the history of road building. I was at mile 0 and a short 1200 miles away was Dawson City, Yukon, the epicenter of the Klondike Gold Rush. Dawson Creek to Dawson City was my goal. Yes, I was heading to the roots and foundational place of all things I held dear in my life. I was on fire. The boys could all sense it, and even Ozark seemed to join in my excitement.

"Look at Sam," Hats would say to RC and Ray and Ozark. "He looks like his fucking head is going to blow up! Sam, Sam, is your head going to blow up, man? If so, tell me so I can pull Barth over. We don't want your brains all over Barth! Sam, Sam, talk to us, man!" Weeks of constant Hats harassment began that first week.

We woke up late in the morning in the parking lot of a strip mall in Dawson Creek. This began our routine of trying to avoid paying for parking or camping. We ate in Barth and immediately headed out towards the Mile 1 marker on the Alaskan Highway towards the Yukon Territory. We were totally self-contained in Barth; a complete Beaver Lodge on wheels, and Hats was correct, I felt as if my mind was going to blow up. What a great feeling.

We absolutely loved the Mile Marker system on the Alaskan Highway. Knowing that we started at mile 0, we always knew how far up the road we had gone. The highway itself is a combination of paved road and dirt sections. The World War II history of the highway just adds to the mystique of the ride. The highway, considered one the world's most impressive engineering feats, was built to connect the forty-eight continental states with Fairbanks, Alaska. The road was needed in order to supply Alaska with materiel in case the Japanese invaded from the Bering Strait. The bombing of Pearl Harbor in 1941 had everybody on alert in 1942. The history of the building of the highway and all the blood, sweat, and tears is an adventure all unto itself, and now it was my adventure. Every year in elementary school, my speech for the public speaking contest was on the building of the highway. And while I never won the contest, I never changed my topic. Not that any of us ever changed our topic. Every year RC would talk about the RCMP and Ray would talk about the sun. Hats would stand up and recite *Convoy* by *C. W. McCall*. Even though it was not original writing, the teachers would let it slide because we loved the ending. It was hilarious. Every year we all did the same speech, and every year we would listen and comment on how much better we were from the previous year. So now I was telling the boys the history of the highway once again as we started travelling the highway itself. I was the quintessential true fanatic, as I wouldn't change my mind and I wouldn't change the topic. This was my highway.

We stopped again at historical mile marker 496, which is the hot springs at *Liard River Provincial Park*. We splurged on a campsite for the night, and in the morning we enjoyed a soak in the natural hot spring swamps surrounded by the Boreal Forest which is a vast and diverse array of plant life and trees and animals of all kinds. As we soaked, Ray gave the three of us a lesson on why the sun is the one and only true God. Sitting in the natural and unique hot water bath with the sun shining on us made it hard to argue with him. Even Hats listened to Ray with interest and marvel.

We got Barth back on the road and did not stop until we hit Whitehorse, the capital of the Yukon Territory. We were at mile marker 887. We were also only a few miles away from mile marker 894 which is the junction of the Alaskan Highway and the Klondike Highway #2, more commonly known as the *Klondike Loop* route to Dawson City. We parked in a deserted parking lot that night and walked around downtown Whitehorse until we found a bar that reminded us of the Maple Tree Hotel. We drank and listened to live music until the place shut down, and on the way out we bought a tourist postcard of the bar to send to Vince and the Judge, and made a deal to hit the bar again on our way southbound. The Beaver Brothers and their Dalmatian dog Ozark were as happy as could be.

The next morning, we started on the Klondike Loop towards Dawson City. The trip is a little over three hundred miles but it proved to be a slow go. In fact, we almost didn't make it to Dawson City. We had only been in Barth for about forty-five minutes when we came to a road block in the highway. The RCMP had two cruisers with lights flashing as they stopped northbound traffic, not that there was a lot of traffic. RC was driving at the time which seemed serendipitous considering the circumstances, so RC pulled Barth over to the shoulder and got out to talk to the constables. He came back after ten minutes and reported to us. The highway was closed for northbound traffic because of a forest fire that was not yet contained, and the RCMP, along with professional and volunteer firefighters, were concerned the fire might jump the highway. They told RC we would probably be good to go by the next morning but would need to camp for the night.

"Can we help fight the fire?" Ray asked RC, clearly saying *I really want to help fight the fire.*

"No," RC said in a disappointed voice that told us he had already offered that up to the RCMP officers.

"So where the fuck are we going to stay?" Hats said, really saying, *We can't stop now. We gotta get some miles on Barth, boys. Let's go!*

At the same time, I was reviewing our position on the Rand McNally Road Atlas, our trusted BOP. Actually, I knew exactly where we were, but for some reason I was still surprised when I confirmed our geographical position on the Earth. I tried to keep it together, but eventually I couldn't hold in my excitement any longer as this was fate acting upon the universe to make my day, month, year, and life. Or maybe it was the beautiful grey pink haze of the Yukon's morning sun that acted upon the universe to change our course. The sun – maybe Ray was right – the one true God.

"I'll tell you where we are going to stay," I shot back at Hats. "We are going to spend the night on the shore of Lake Laberge! That's where we are going to stay, Hats!"

There was silence for a brief minute while my three best friends computed what I had said. Ozark got it right away, and RC was the first to speak. "You mean, Lake Laberge as in *The Northern Lights have seen queer sights, but the queerest they ever did see, was that night on the marge of Lake Lebarge, I cremated Sam McGee?*"

"That's right, RC," I said back in a fake, cool, calm, and collected voice. I lit up a torpedo nonchalantly as if I were Marlon Brando and this were just another regular morning in the daily routine of a routine life.

"No fucking way. Really, really, Sam? Really?" Hats said back with loud and sincere excitement. He really was excited.

"Yes, way," I said back, really saying, *Can you believe it. I mean, can you believe it!*

"Look at Sam, boys," Hats said. "Look at him fast before his fucking head blows up! Sam, Sam, is your head gonna blow up, man?"

"Nope," I replied, in my cool and calm voice as I took a 1940s haul off my smoke.

"Perfect," Ray said in a tone that sounded as if it was all part of a master plan that was out of our control – the sun clearly at work in the Yukon in the summer where God is banking overtime hours. Ya just gotta love the sun. It shows up ready for work making summer in the North spectacular. It is without comparison or equal.

Lake Laberge is not so much a standalone lake but rather a widening of the Yukon River just north of Whitehorse. It is thirty miles long and ranges from one to three miles wide and has an average depth of about one hundred sixty feet. The lake was formed by glacial activity during the last Ice Age, and the one thing you can be certain about is the water is freezing cold all the time. Most importantly though, Lake Laberge was either friend or foe to the prospectors during the Klondike Gold Rush of 1898. If you made it over the Chilkoot Pass, you would need to navigate Lake Laberge on your way down the Yukon River as you headed to the gold in Dawson City. If you did not make the lake before it froze for the winter, then you were stranded on the south side of the lake. This happened to a lot of wannabe prospectors and many turned around and went back home empty handed. The lake is famous in multiple writings, the most famous being *Jack London's The Call of the Wild* and, of course, *Robert W. Service's* poem, *"The Cremation of Sam McGee,"* the best poem ever written, the poem to end all poems. Interestingly, in the poem of poems the lake is spelled *Lebarge*. Someday I may learn why that is. I suppose I could look it up on the internet, but I don't really want to know why. Life should not be about getting an answer to every question. Life should contain elements of mystery, and Lake Laberge has an element of mystery. I like this, and in the end, the lake is just pure cool, making this my lake in so many ways. I had planned for us to stop at the lake when we were heading southbound from Dawson City, but here we were, at my lake. I guess some good can come from fires, and perhaps not all fires are about hell.

We did a ten-point U-turn while still learning how to drive Barth, and we went south for a couple of miles and turned east onto a back-road that took us into some remote campsites established for wilderness travelers. These sites are unmanned by park rangers and you are asked to respect the land and leave four dollars in an envelope in a mail box they have attached to a post. *Take nothing but memories and leave nothing but footprints...and four bucks.* We got Barth parked and then went outside to take in the environment. We were on the shore of Lake Laberge in the Yukon Territory. We were at the site of the *Cremation of Sam McGee*. I was home.

That night, the five of us had a great meal and we sat outside in the light grey night expecting dark that never actually comes. The RCMP told us not to have a campfire, and we respected the rule, not really needing to have a fire anyway as we could smell a healthy dose of burning from the nearby forest fires. Already having the smell was half of the joy of having an actual campfire, so we sat at an old picnic table that was at the campsite and we talked and laughed and took a trip without leaving the farm. At some point in the evening, I went into Barth and came out with the journal that I had brought for the trip.

"Looks good, Sam," RC said to me as I sat back down at the table and prepared myself to start writing. Then, for some unknown reason, I stood up and held the gold colored hard cover journal into the air and declared an announcement.

"This, my fellow Beaver Brothers and Beaver Brother Dog, is our journal. And in this journal, I plan to capture our journey in wrote."

"In what?" Hats said, really saying, *Talk English, you dumb fuck.*

"In wrote, Hats, as in the English language. I plan to write and capture what I can about our trip. In fact, my plan is that we all write in the journal, including people we meet along the way. I plan to call it *The Book,* or maybe some other title that we determine along the way."

"Perfect," Ray said in such a way that left no argument that this was nothing but a brilliant idea.

From that day forward, I tried my best to make entries into the journal every day. The boys all made their own contributions as well and we even had people we met along the trip add their own messages. In the end, the journal chronicled the entire adventure. I did my best to write in it in all circumstances, and I tried to cover all topics and viewpoints. I would write my own thoughts and would also just capture the random conversations the boys would have. I was capturing what we knew and how we felt about life and the world at the time. It was a chronicle of our state of consciousness at that stage of our maturity, and in many respects, the conversations showed how immature we still were, but also how far we had come.

At some point in the night, the boys asked me to recite *The Cremation of Sam McGee.* I did it willingly, and with every single ounce of my spirit I nailed the verses and performed the best rendition of the poem ever heard on the shore of Lake Laberge. When I finished, we all just sat in silence and listened to our hearts, in addition to all the sounds around us made by nature and all its creatures. The sound of our silence was overshadowed by the natural sounds of the shoreline by a million decibels. Nature was alive and healthy on Lake Laberge.

"Let's write our own poem!" Ray said, breaking our silence.

We all thought about this for a minute.

"OK," I said, and with that, we all grabbed a fresh OV and sat back down at the table.

We worked for hours that night with me writing in the journal and trying my best to coordinate the effort of group-based poetry. It was poetry writing at its best and its worst, and at one point I envisioned what a poem would be like if it was completed collaboratively by *Robert Frost, Robert Service,* and *Dr. Seuss.* Ray actually brought out his guitar to help with some rhythm when we could not make a word rhyme. As early morning arrived, we believed we were finished with our masterpiece.

"Read it from the beginning, Sam," RC said.

And so I did.

A DAY WELL SPENT

I'd really like to take a hike
around a lake I've never seen
one without a person about
so I could wander while I dream
then in time, perhaps I'd find
some friends for company we
would talk, and go for walks
many different lives we'd see

I can imagine, meeting a badger
together we'd burrow through her home
to hear the sound of life underground
to feel happiness that she's known
a little warm den, which the family defends against
any unfriendly passerby
buried in winter, by branches that splinter
until spring, when her young open their eyes

Then I'd stop, sit on a rock
to grab a little snack
out of the woods would come the masked hoods
raccoons on their gentle attack
sharing my lunch, to learn a bunch
about a bandit's unlawful ways
they'd want me to hang with the roving gang
an outlaw the rest of my days

That afternoon I'd swim with a loon
she'd introduce me to her mate
surrounding the eggs, she secretly laid
we'd worry about their fate
with no problem at all, I'd master the call
to sing thru the day's last light
nature would listen, as soft ripples glistened
across the lake as the two took flight

As the Sun went down, I'd look around
for a soft place to spend the night
the dusk would smile, with the music of the wild
entire worlds just beyond my sight
sitting by the fire, enjoying feeling tired

the crackling at my feet
to think again, I could meet a new friend
and offer him a seat

In from the dark, with a high-pitched hark
would be the oldest, wisest owl
we'd talk of the world, the problems incurred
offer solutions with a quiet growl
I'd feel like a fool, and ask where he schooled
a question he'd say he'll "have to ponder"
And the moment he'd leave, it would be easy to see
There were many things left to wonder

After saying goodbye, to the stars in the sky
I'd fall into a well needed sleep
dreaming of places, with rosy glowing faces
around me, busy little beavers would eat
the moon sending its glare, within the fresh air
my skin soaking it in for hours
the forest internal, to life that's nocturnal
breezes showing off their powers

Just before dawn, I'd awake to a fawn
her mother, and dad the buck
in search for fresh leaves, we'd skip through the trees
ever grateful for our luck
then in the sky, majestically flying by
an optimistic and peaceful bird
my heart would feel love, with the sight of the dove
and the message heard in its word

Yes, I think I'd like to take a hike
around the lake I've never seen
one without a person about
so I could wander while I dream
maybe then, after meeting new friends
I would start to understand
that the world belongs to everyone
and no one owns the land

I finished reading our poem and the boys all signaled their approval. RC was very happy in particular, as he believed the poem had excellent representation of the Canadian wilderness. With our work complete, we got up from our table and went into Barth to sleep for a few hours.

As we were falling asleep, I think I heard Hats say, "Are there even any fucking badgers in Canada?"

Canada

Summer 1983

The River

THE YUKON RIVER runs north and then west from British Columbia through the Yukon and into Alaska where it drains into the Bering Sea. At close to two thousand miles long, it's argued to be the third largest river in North America, just behind the Missouri and Mississippi, respectively. Most people say the source of the Yukon River is the Llewellyn Glacier at the southern end of Atlin Lake in British Columbia. However, there are prospectors, and I'm one of them, who believe the source is Lake Lindeman at the northern end of the Chilkoot Trail. During the Klondike Gold Rush, the Yukon River was the principal highway system to Dawson City, and throughout the crazy days around 1898, you would have witnessed paddle-wheel riverboats filled with prospectors chugging down the river toward the gold. On the way, they would have to survive the *Five Finger Rapids* which are located on the Yukon River close to Dawson City. At this point, the river is divided by four small islands into five narrow channels, and of all the five channels, only the most eastern channel will allow a boat to survive. A lot of prospectors learned this the hard way. Yukon means "Great River" in the First Nations language and so the Yukon River means *Great River – River*.

275

I like that. That's poetic. I also liked the fact that we were back in Barth and headed to Dawson City while running parallel with the Great River. Life was never so grand as our spirits and optimism and excitement flowed as fiercely as the great river.

Turning off our dirt road, we headed north on pavement towards Dawson City. The RCMP roadblock was gone when we hit the Klondike Highway towards Dawson. At this point, we had absolutely lost all track of time. Not one of us was wearing a watch, nor did we care what time it was, and in retrospect, we would not gain awareness of the time or date until we returned home several weeks later. In addition, we had the dynamic that it never got fully dark outside, which was acting as an enabler to our new routine of sleeping very little. I'm sure it was unhealthy, but it was working for us.

The drive to Dawson City was as interesting as a drive can be. There were very few cars on the road because of the forest fires, and the smoke from the fires held in the air almost forming cloud-like structures. We continuously drove by sections of forest that were freshly burned and still smoldering. We would also drive by a section of land that appeared to have burned in some past year, where all growth in the field would be dead other than beautiful purple Rosebay Willowherb. Also known as Fireweed, the gorgeous flower is the floral emblem of the Yukon. This sure makes sense, as it is everywhere, in particular in areas that had been burned. It's the first flower to grow in sites of devastation, and you could not ask for a more beautiful sea of purple representing the light after the dark. Ray loved hearing about the name of the flower as we read about it in some travel magazines we had picked up along the way. We had a nice conversation while driving up the road with fields of Fireweed in burned out forests on either side of us.

"Rosebay Willowherb?" Ray asked me, really saying, *I love the name Rose.*

"Yip," I said, really saying, *I know. Isn't it amazing and isn't it beautiful? Just like Rose.*

"And it's the first flower to grow after everything else has burned?" Ray asked.

"Yip again," I said.

"I like that," he said back to me.

"Me too," I said back to him.

A few minutes went by and then Ray continued our conversation.

"Told ya, Sam," Ray said.

"Told me what?" I asked.

"It's the sun, Sam. It's all about the sun with a little help from rain and fire – a triad of friends of the Earth."

With that, all five of us continued our trip up to Dawson City beholding the scenery and thinking our own private thoughts. We stopped and had a short hike through the woods to overlook the Five Finger Rapids. Ozark loved the hike, and not surprisingly, RC wanted to get the canoes off the roof of Barth and run the rapids, but Ray and I decided he would be breaking *Beaver Brothers Road Trip Guiding Principle #5–Make it home alive.* We were convinced he would not make it down alive. RC was convinced he wanted to try. Hats was non-committal, and I assumed he would have paddled in the bow for RC if RC had pressed the issue, which would be required for *Beaver Brothers Road Trip Guiding Principle #1–Beaver Buddy System.* But RC did not press the issue. Truth is, RC was already showing signs of being mature, as evidenced by making thoughtful and rational decisions when challenged. RC became a man at an early age, although I'm not sure we can say the same for the rest of us. The two canoes stayed on top of Barth for now.

A short time later, we entered the small town of Dawson City, Yukon Territory, Canada. I was now officially in my unofficial childhood home.

Dawson City, founded in 1897, was the Yukon's capital until 1952 when the capital status was moved to Whitehorse for practical purposes of weather and roads. Dawson City – historically the homeland and rich fishing and moose hunting camps of the Tr'ochëk First Nations. Dawson City – the Klondike Gold Rush town site at the confluence of the Klondike River and Yukon River. Dawson City – the town that went from one hundred people in 1896 to forty thousand people in 1898 and back down to five thousand when the New Year's bell rang in 1903 because the gold miners had moved onto golder pastures. Dawson City – the metropolis that held all the world's fascination for a short time a long time ago. Dawson City – the place where dreams and nightmares alike became reality. Dawson City – the most amazing small town on the face of the Earth. Dawson City, Yukon – my kind of town.

We found a great four-dollar campsite outside of town and we spent what I believe was several days exploring Dawson. To be sure, we stayed busy as Beavers. The first stop was Bonanza Creek, where George Carmack, his Tagish wife Kate Carmack, her brother Skookum Jim, and their nephew Dawson Charlie found the first big golden nugget that started the Klondike Gold Rush. The four Beaver Brothers and Ozark all panned for gold in the exact spot that has been famed as *the spot*. With every empty pan we raised from the creek, we felt rich. I felt as if the ghosts of prospectors before me were there watching and feeding me energy. There is just something about gold that is connected to the human spirit in such a way that words cannot describe. Gold Fever is a diagnosis devoid of prescription; there is no medication for the fever, and we had the fever. We panned for gold for hours. Ozark, in particular, was hilarious, as not normally a water dog, she would wade into a foot of water and stick her head down in the river and come up after several seconds of being submerged face first. We assumed, at some point, she would come up with a huge nugget in her mouth.

We played golf at what I believe was sometime between midnight and sunrise. We found every ball that sliced and hooked. We canoed the Klondike River halfway to *Fortymile* and fought the current back. I read the poem of poems on the porch of *Robert Service's* very own cabin, although I did not recite it by heart, but rather read it from my book of *Robert Service's* collection of poems. It felt much more professorial that way. The boys and some other tourists listened to my recitation, and Hats went on about my head going to blow up at any moment.

We joined Ozark for a nap on the lawn at the *Jack London Centre* and we watched her twitch and shake as she was dreaming about running with *Buck*. I tried to write real literature in the journal while sitting in front of the *Pierre Berton House*. We drank beer at every saloon within the town perimeter and toasted Vince and the Judge with a shot of whiskey at every saloon we drank beer in. We were every bit the historical and modern day prospector in that we did Dawson City and Dawson City did us. I was infinitely sad when we rightfully decided it was time to leave; *Guiding Principle # 4* had to be respected, we had to keep the pace. We said a mournful goodbye to my town and headed southbound back towards Whitehorse; one road in and the same road out. It was a short drive, relatively speaking, back to Whitehorse and back to the pseudo Maple Tree Hotel we had adopted a few days before. After a night of hanging at the bar, we would begin the southbound journey to Mexico. I suspect we were about seven days into the trip. One week down, and nine to go, so far so good, and all the guiding principles and rules of the road were proving to deliver excellent results.

When we arrived back in Whitehorse, we parked in the same parking lot we had camped in the first time through and we headed to our new Maple Tree Hotel and treated ourselves to a dinner of hot hamburger sandwiches with fries and awesome Canadian gravy. There just ain't nothing like it, and our timing was perfect as we were a little early and the band was setting up. Ray took the opportunity to talk to the band members and he helped them set up their gear. They seemed like the mirror image of the Beaver Brothers Band and their set list from the first night seemed to echo our own. We knew every song they played. I guess good taste in music simply transcends time, space, and talent.

It was a fantastic night. The bar was full, and having arrived early, we had the best table in the house right in front of the band. They were cranking out Canadian classics and all was good until the rhythm guitar player suddenly swerved a couple of times and passed out cold right on the stage. The place roared in approval – it was a vintage *Steve Tyler* move. The band stopped playing to check on their buddy, and Ray also went up on stage to help them check on their buddy. They poured a glass of water on the green face of the budding musician and he came to life, and I saw the leader of the band ask him a few questions. The guitar guy shook his head as if saying *Whatever I took ain't very good shit, man.* The bar patrons were still having fun with the circumstances, but were also starting to get a little restless. The bar owner, the Vince equivalent, came up on the small stage and talked to the leader of the band. They exchanged a few words, and then I saw the band leader say something to Ray. The next thing I saw was Ray strapping on the green-faced guy's guitar. Green-faced guy got up and retreated to the bar, confirming and formalizing Ray as a new member of the *Whitehorse Pretend Maple Tree Hotel Band.*

"Get the fuck outa here!" Hats said immediately.

"Holy shit," RC built on Hats' words.

"Giddy up, prospector," I said to end the string, really saying, *Oh I wish Vince and the Judge were here to see this*. I snapped a picture on the 35 millimeter camera Ray had brought along for the trip.

Ray did great. He knew their songs and he was able to jam alongside with ease which did not surprise us as this is the true sign of a gifted musician. All went well, and we sat at our table and watched Ray do what he does best. The bar loved it, and anybody that had witnessed the whole guitar player exchange appreciated the music that much more. They finished their last song and the crowd yelled for more. They wanted one last tune, so the band huddled to discuss what tune they would play as the last call swan song. I saw Ray chatting up the leader and the leader's head was nodding up and down and he was smiling a big smile. At that point, the leader of the band stripped off his guitar and put it on a guitar stand that was on the stage. The crowd was being patient in an impatient way. The leader then went behind the drums and came out with a suitcase that he opened and brought out an accordion from the case. The crowd cheered in delight at the sight of something new to the stage. At that point, Ray came over and whispered something to RC, which prompted RC to down his beer and walk up on the stage and pick up the rhythm guitar that had been perched on the guitar stand.

"What the fuck is going on?" Hats yelled right in my face, really yelling, *What the fuck is going on?* My guess is Hats had about twenty OVs in him at that point.

"I have no idea, brother!" I replied, really saying, *I have no idea, brother!*

Well, it didn't take long to find out. Once the newly assembled band made some eye contact and talked the silent musicians talk, they hit the first few chords and I knew the tune in an instant.

For last call, the residents of Whitehorse, both locals and temporaries, heard an impromptu version of *Tommy Weeks the Carpet Man.* Ray and RC ran the show. The bassist and the drummer easily held their own as they were clearly much more talented than Hats and I, and the leader of the band started playing his accordion as if he had just landed in Whitehorse from Belfast or Dublin.

"I don't fucking believe it," Hats said to no one in particular.

"I do," I said. "Some things you just can't make up, Hats!"

And with that, Hats and I both got up from the safe center table we had occupied all night and went and stood against the west wall of the bar. This wasn't our first rodeo. Yes, we were born at night, but not last night, so we found the new safest ground within the four walls of the bar. We had seen this movie a few times, and we knew the ending.

Ray and RC and the band cranked it out.

Tommy Weeks was a carpet man
Selling door to door across the land
He knew his shags and he liked his swirls
But mostly Tommy Weeks loved his girls

Then Ray belted out the chorus.

Gentlemen wake up, Tommy Weeks is working today
He's stepping up your walk, while you're away
He's rolling out his carpet, right across your floor
Gentlemen heads up, he's knocking on your door

Well, as you can imagine, the crowd loved it, and just like back home, the feet started stomping and the beer bottles were swaying and all the Irish and wannabe Irish gave it their all to sing along and make the song their own. I overheard people saying *I know this one man*, even though there was no way they could have known it unless they had been to the Maple Tree Hotel in Chinook River on a night the Beaver Brothers Band played.

Unlike back home, though, the bar didn't wait until the end of the song to throw the first punch. Nobody even got the chance to do a finger penis. I guess this is an unintended consequence of the sun never going down. A little too much tuneup in the tune and not enough sleep can make a northerner a cranky boy. Equally, unlike back home, the RCMP did not seem so eager to let the lads have their fun. The Vince equivalent opened his door wide to let the RCMP storm the bar and round up the boxers, wrestlers, and future mixed martial artists. At least twenty uniformed RCMP constables swatted on the scene and led all instigators into a paddy wagon parked outside waiting to head to the Whitehorse prison stalls. Unfortunately, this sorry lot of dumbasses included Hats. I can't say that I'm totally surprised that Hats decided to have a little fun. I suspect he was thinking that Timmy McMullen was in the bar somewhere and he just had to physically move a few guys around to find him. Equally unfortunate was that I now had to join Hats on the ride to jail. *Rules of the Pond Guiding Principle # 1* had to be respected. Beaver Buddy System was in play.

The disappointing irony was that the jail was not a jail. I'm not sure where the other dumbasses ended up, but Hats and I were put into what I would consider to be an office or interview room of some kind. It was about ten by ten feet and was completely empty with no chairs and no tables, and we had no ability to scrape the bars with our tin cups. A few other bar goers were in similar rooms adjacent to our room. We sat on the floor and lit up a torpedo.

"This is bullshit, man!" Hats said.

"I know!" I said back. "No iron bars, no cots, no big burly guy calling you bitch!"

"I know!" Hats said. "This is bullshit, man."

To this day, I have no idea why we did not end up in general population. RC suspects we just didn't look the part of the locals, or they ran out of space that night at the main jail. About an hour after we arrived, Ray and RC arrived at the RCMP detachment. They walked into the main room where the constables were sitting. Hats and I could see them and hear everything they were saying, as could the other inmates in the rooms around us.

"Can we just pay a fine, sir, and get these two dumbasses out?" RC was imploring one of the RCMP constables.

"Who you calling dumbass, you dumbass?" Hats yelled at RC through the door.

"Sorry, guys," the constable said. "Your friends will need to wait till late morning and see the Judge." I watched Ray's brain go into motion and within three seconds he had a plan.

"But, sir, we are here for a hockey tournament and we have to play first thing in the morning," Ray said, really saying, *Come on, man. Do we have a common denominator here?* I could see RC getting a little uncomfortable as he didn't like the idea of lying to the RCMP, but guiding principles are guiding principles, and we needed to keep the *pace of the trip* going. He got in line on the ruse.

The constable hesitated for a moment and then decided against whatever he was thinking and said, "Sorry guys, you will just have to play without them," and then he started walking away.

Ray hesitated for a brief moment and then yelled towards the constable's back, "But they're our goalies!"

The constable stopped and turned around and stared at Ray and RC. He used eye contact as a tool to flush out honesty versus deception. RC and Ray starred back with complete conviction of a non-convict. The constable then looked at another fellow RCMP officer who had been listening to the dialogue. The other constable shrugged his shoulders as if saying, Y*a can't play without your goalies.* RCMP are the good guys, and with that, the constable came over to the room we were incarcerated in and let us out and told us to make sure we played hard and stayed away from the bars after the tournament. No fine, no Judge, no problem. I guess everybody has his own set of guiding principles. Hockey is a powerful force in the north, and no decent man would deny his team its goalies. As I said, RCMP are the good guys.

We couldn't believe what was happening, and in that instant I believed that some higher power was watching over us. We had a protector, but even so, we didn't wait around, and with a huge thank you to the RCMP, we made our way out of the detachment. As we were leaving, I could hear other guys from the locked rooms yelling, "Hey constable, I'm a goalie too, eh!"

The RCMP constable responded with, "No you're not, you dumbasses!"

We walked out of the detachment and into the grey daylight of the middle-of-the-summer night in Whitehorse, Yukon. Ray looked up to the sky and then at me and he smiled.

"Told ya, Sam," he said.

After a big happy hello from Ozark and a short walk, we were on our way out of Whitehorse and back onto the Alaskan Highway in order to backtrack our path south. "One way in and one way out," I said to the group, very proud of my highway, although Ray was not as impressed. He preferred to make a new trail every time. A few hours later we stopped at Watson Lake, Yukon, mile marker 635, population close to fifteen hundred inhabitants. But most importantly, *Watson Lake* is home to the *Sign Post Forest* and was a stop for us to come clean on a *promise made and a debt unpaid.*

The Sign Post Forest is a tourist attraction that was started in 1942 by a homesick U.S. Army G.I. working on the Alaskan Highway. His name was Carl K. Lindley and he was a U. S. Army Engineer with 341 Company "D." While building signs as part of the highway construction, he improvised and added to a sign post a sign that stated, "Danville, Illinois, 2835 miles." This caught on like wildfire, and now there are over seventy thousand signs of various types, colors, and messages. When walking through the Sign Post Forest, you realize that many a small town Mayor woke up one morning only to find the town sign missing from its post. While the main theme is town signs and mileages to the respective hometown, many other signs represent other important themes for people. The Sign Post Forest is an array of *people and place* stories, and what an amazing book of chapters it would be if only each sign could talk.

Not only did we want to see the Sign Post Forest, we also had to stop there to fulfill a promise made to Vince. The night before we left home he took as into the backroom and handed us a sign and asked if we would hang it at the Sign Post Forest in Watson Lake, Yukon. He told us the sign was an original family heirloom and was over eighty years old, so of course we said we would get the job done. We walked the whole forest looking at signs from all over the world, and then RC and Ray found the spot for our sign. We went center and high on the section we chose. RC became the master carpenter and led the hanging, and when we were done we stood back and gazed at the sign we were leaving behind. It was a beautiful sign made of brass, about a 12 x 24-inch rectangle, with lettering grooved inside the brass. The letters looked to be painted or stained black, and although some of the coloring had faded it was still very easy to read the letters. In fact, even from a distance the sign stood out from many of the other signs as the brass would catch the sun and send a glare towards the onlookers. We finished hanging the sign and stood back to look at our work. And there it was, our sign that said *The Maple Tree Hotel: Est 1900.*

"Perfect," Ray said.

We all nodded our approval and stood back and admired the sign. Ozark looked up at the sign and let out a loud bark, and we all looked at Ozark with marvel, but nobody said a word. Ray gave Ozark a pat on the head. We were taking in the moment and we were all thinking the same thing. The sign said *The Maple Tree Hotel: Est 1900* in a literal sense, but what it really said was *Vince was here. Vince's father was here. Vince's grandfather was here. The Judge was here. Ozark and Curly were here. The Beaver Brothers were here. Chinook River was here.*

We had met the one promise we made to Vince – one down and one to go. The second and last promise made was to the Judge, but that would not happen for a few weeks. We got into Barth and headed out of Watson Lake, which was a tollgate and pivot point in our trip as it signified leg number one of the trip done. Sam's dot on the BOP was now a checkmark.

Southbound to Mexico was now the theme of the day.

In Ray's Voice

SAM HAD AN ABSOLUTE blast in the Yukon. Actually, we all did, but Sam was leading the charge. He was like a puppy dog with two tails, and he had an absolute overabundance of unproductive enthusiasm. It was amazing to watch him in all his glory in the land of gold. It was perfect.

In hindsight, I wish we had taken Sam over to climb the Chilkoot Pass, but for some reason it just didn't seem to fit on our path. Sam educated us about the Pass and he talked about it a lot, but he also seemed fine with missing it, so I guess this was just meant to be. Perhaps he was not ready to climb the Pass, or maybe the Chilkoot is not the pass he is meant to climb.

I personally find the Chilkoot Pass very interesting. The Chilkoot Pass is one of the most important milestones prospectors had to conquer in order to reach the gold in the Klondike. The Pass is a high mountain obstacle that was the pinnacle of the Chilkoot Trail, a treacherous thirty-five-mile trek that led from Dyea, Alaska, to Bennett Lake in British Columbia. The pass was one of only three practical ways to Dawson City and the gold in 1898.

The excited prospectors following the Chilkoot Trail to Dawson City would arrive at the base of the Chilkoot Pass and meet their first real test. As Sam taught us, this basecamp was known as the Scales. Pictures of prospectors at the Scales and pictures of prospectors climbing the Chilkoot Pass are the most famous images of the Klondike Gold Rush. Sam had a poster of the Pass hanging in Barth, and Hats penciled drawings of the Pass in the journal.

The Scales was where prospectors would store their provisions and supplies while going up the Pass or back down to sea level to gather more goods for the journey. The Canadian North West Mounted Police, a precursor force to the RCMP, were ever present at the Scales and would not allow any prospectors to attempt the Pass without proper provisions. They were trying to save gold rushers from themselves which makes sense as forty below and no food will win over gold fever and optimism every time. From the Scales, the ground rose almost six hundred feet over a distance of approximately a half-mile. The trail was nothing but sharp slabs of rock, which made traversing the Pass nearly impossible. The essence of the human spirit, both success and defeat, is littered along the Pass.

Winter proved a hardship on the Pass, so the prospectors cut the ice into fifteen hundred ice steps. This became known as *The Golden Stairs*, and the steps were so narrow that only one person could climb the staircase at a time. In 1898, the Golden Staircase was a pure solid line of people heading to the land of Gold. If they made it over the Chilkoot Pass they would then hike down to Lake Bennett and build or procure a boat, and from there they would hope to enter the winter flow of the Yukon River or dog sled over the frozen water highway to Dawson City.

The Klondike Gold Rush – The Last Great Gold Rush – The Last Great Adventure – Sam's Gold Rush. It is estimated that between 1896 and 1899, more than one hundred thousand people ascended onto the Klondike region, and historical estimates suggest that no more than four thousand people ever found an ounce of gold. There is something about this statistic that makes me feel an emotion that is hard to describe. How many of us live our whole lives looking for, yet never find, our gold? Why are we even so focused on the gold in the first place? The Klondike Gold Rush – Sam's Gold Rush – Sam's Great Adventure.

And now I worry about Sam.

Sam's Chilkoot Pass is not the Chilkoot Pass, and now I know that's why the sun did not steer us that way. Sam's mountain pass is within himself. Sam needs to build the Golden Staircase from his soul to his heart and then to his mind. His adventure is internal, not external, although the same obstacles exist – the storms rage, the rocks are jagged, and you need proper equipment and supplies to be successful. At times, you even need a police presence to stop you from going any further in your present state of unpreparedness. This is life. This is

Sam's life today. Everybody has his own Chilkoot Pass, but not everybody has what it takes to get over the Pass.

Not everybody wants his gold that badly. For some of us, the gold is not the ultimate goal, but we have our own Chilkoot Pass nonetheless.

DAY 16
South Carolina

Beaver Fever

STOP THE WORLD because I need to get off! I am somewhere between Green and I don't know what. I just cannot believe what happened today, and I am completely freaked out. I woke up this morning, and once again I could not help myself. I needed a fix so I plugged in the television set and headed straight to the Talking Cable Heads. There he was, yes, there he was on the show. Hats! He was one of the Talking Cable Heads, and guess what they were talking about? *Beaver Fever!* Yip, I turned on the Talking Cable Heads, and Hats was a Talking Cable Head talking about Beaver Fever! At first I figured I had totally lost it, but it was real. Some stuff you just can't make up even in your imagination. I phoned him immediately after the show to give him royal shit and then congratulate him. Then I told him he was a traitor, and then I told him he got the job done. He told me he had to do it. He told me he had to protect the beaver. My buddy, Hats – one of the good guys.

Here's the deal.

A small town in upper New York had an outbreak of sickness spread through the entire town. All the sick people had common symptoms

– loss of appetite, exhaustion, diarrhea, body cramps, upset stomachs, gas in general, projectile vomiting, and all other nastiness related to being really sick. But it gets serious as three people died, including a ten-year-old boy. This is not good, not good at all, so the town Mayor called in some consultant scientists and they determined it was Beaver Fever. The real name of the disease is Giardiasis. It's a waterborne disease where people get sick from drinking contaminated water. Some people believe beavers contaminate the water and carry the disease. In fact, it got its name Beaver Fever several years ago after an outbreak left a bunch of people sick in Banff National Park in Alberta. Just hearing the word Banff made me laugh, especially when watching Hats on television.

The scientists determined that the culprit beavers were all on a certain farm that was just outside the town, and consequently close to twenty beavers, five conical lodges, and ten dams were being singled out for removal. According to the consultant-scientist CEO, the beavers would be shot, the dams and lodges blown up, and the farm owner sued and possibly criminally charged. However, the farmer who owned the land was not convinced of the beavers' guilt, so he fought back. Actually, he fought back hard. This was criminal and environmental law, right in Hats' wheelhouse, and the farmer in overalls was a land baron and worth millions. Never judge a book by its cover. The farmer loved his beavers as they provided ponds and wet lands for his other animals and farming activities. They were part of his master plan, and he was not going to let some ignorant, greedy, snotty-nosed scientists get into his business. So he hired the right law firm, and Hats took on the case personally, because to Hats this was personal. As far as Hats is concerned, *Ya don't fuck with the Beaver.*

And now I was watching Hats debate the CEO of the firm that provided the scientists. Right there on cable news, there were three people on the screen. Three boxes – Hats, the CEO scientist, and the moderating Talking Head – all men. Hats later told me the producers of the news show did not want a woman discussing Beaver Fever. It was priceless.

"So what is Beaver Fever?" the moderating Talking Head asked the CEO scientist. He answered the question by using terms like protein, enzymes, nuclei and chromosomes. He was very confident and loved the sound of his own voice. He was obviously convinced of his own brilliance. He then threw the beavers and the farmer under the proverbial bus and told the audience the beavers and the farmer would need to be held accountable for the death of the ten-year-old boy. Nobody understood a single word that he said, but we got the point. The moderator then asked Hats what he thought Beaver Fever was, but Hats did not answer the question. Instead he posed a question to the CEO scientist. He was ready to practice law *Philadelphia Flyer Style*. I could see it in his eyes, and even though I had no idea what he was going to say I felt sorry for the CEO scientist.

"Do you know," Hats asked the CEO, "that tomorrow the county sheriff will be issuing an indictment against the Town Mayor and Town Water Supply Foreman?" Hats' tone let us viewers know that Hats already knew the answer to the question.

"No," the CEO said quietly but not unexpectedly. The moderator Talking Head got a smile on his face, as the showdown was looking good – he could smell blood. Meanwhile, the CEO was now wondering if he was being baited, which he was. But Hats didn't do the Rabbit Hole Bait trick; instead, he decided just to throw the facts out there to see what the CEO would do with them. Sometimes you don't need to be the hangman as most people are very capable of hanging themselves when given enough rope.

"Indeed they are," Hats went on with the facts. "It seems the Water Foreman has a bit of a drinking problem and maybe a problem writing and filing accurate reports about the quality of the water in town. It also seems the Mayor and the Water Foreman are brothers, and facts would suggest the Mayor may have overlooked his brother's incompetence!"

"Really?" was all the CEO said, really saying, *Ugg, I hope this ends soon and my staff should have prepared me better for this session, and now I'm wondering if we will still get millions from this work, and I may need to fire somebody over this!*

"Really," Hats replied sarcastically, and then he went on. "And the other thing you may want to know is that the three deaths were caused by *E-coli* and not the *protozoan Giardia Lamblia!* And it also seems the Water Foreman was engaged in a bunch of improper operating practices, like not using proper quantities of chlorine in the town's water supply, failing to monitor chlorine levels on a daily basis, and making all sorts of false entries about water quality in general. Not to mention the bribes from chemical manufacturers and the beer fridge in the Water Foreman and Mayor's offices!"

"Oh," was all the CEO could come up with. He was twenty leagues out of his element; he did not want to fight Hats. He simply wanted the interview to come to an end, so Hats got the beginning of the end started. He left the deflated CEO box and talked to the moderator box.

"Ask me again what I think Beaver Fever is?" he asked the moderator to ask him.

"What do you think Beaver Fever is?" the moderator complied with Hats' request, really liking how his show had developed.

"Great question," Hats answered. "I think Beaver Fever is a very serious illness, and the epidemic is growing in our world, particularly on this show!"

"Pardon?" the moderator asked, now confused and wondering what Hats was up to. Actually, we all were.

"You see," Hats continued, now fully in charge of the interview, "the contributing causes of Beaver Fever are pretentiousness, narcissism, ignorance, and egocentrism, but the true root cause of Beaver Fever is *Plenus Excrementum.*"

"Plenus Excrementum?" the moderator asked back in a voice that suggested he was losing control of the interview, while the CEO just looked as if he wanted to disappear.

"Yes, Plenus Excrementum," Hats went on, "the state of being completely and utterly full of shit!"

And with that, the moderator said there was breaking news elsewhere in the world, and Hats and the CEO disappeared from the screen. I guess the CEO got what he wanted after all.

Hats made my day. Finally, somebody called it for what it is. Beaver Fever – Plenus Excrementum. The disease you have when you are completely and utterly full of shit.

After talking to Hats on the phone, I went for a walk on the beach and connected with Ray. We wrote a poem together. Here it is.

BEAVER FEVER?

Beaver Fever? are the perfect words
For living in a dumbass world
Where everybody thinks he is so smart
It's a question I like to ask
To take somebody to task
While he's busy trying to tear someone apart

It's for the people who talk all day
With absolutely nothing good to say
That makes any rational common sense
Their egos drive their brains

While they drive their listeners all insane
With narratives that are completely bent

Like when a politician says
He knows the struggles that lie ahead
And he will fix it all if we vote him in
Or the guy on cable news
Forever spewing off his views
While telling us his opinion isn't spin

I ask, Beaver Fever?

The evangelist on his perch
Using television as his church
To tell me that my lifestyle is obscene
He preaches life without sin
That he can help me win
While the "please send money" banner scrolls the screen

I ask, Beaver Fever?

A movie star breaks the law
While driving out of the spa
The judge lets her off because he is a fan
An admitted murderer wins his case
Cause the best lawyer in the place
Gets all the evidence forever banned

I ask, Beaver Fever?

A rich athlete cheats on his wife
He's been a scoundrel his whole life
So his publicist says he has a sex disease
A doctor testifies that it's true
He has a sickness that makes him screw
So his wife should just relax and be at ease

I ask, Beaver Fever?

A famous music award show plays
And a dumbass storms the stage
He's mad at who the voters picked to win
Five million viewers let it slide
Assuming the producers have some pride
But the next year the dumbass gets on stage again

I ask, Beaver Fever?

A commercial about a pill made just for you
Doesn't even tell you what the pill can do
You're left thinking it might be what you need
The commercial is two hundred seconds long
About all the things that will go wrong
Please call the doctor when you start to bleed

I ask, Beaver Fever?

A country singing dude
His videos always filled with boobs
He sure wants us to believe he loves the chicks
The cowboy fans won't understand
When they find out he loves a man
And wants to replace the boobs with a dick

I ask, Beaver Fever?

Or all the people that want to say
How I should get up and live my day
Without ever walking one step in my shoes
All the advice they want me to take
Cause they see all the mistakes I make
While their life clearly needs a full review

I ask, Beaver Fever?

Canada

Summer 1983

The Chicken

FROM WATSON LAKE we went south and west and then south and a little east and several hours later we stopped for gas in Prince George, British Columbia. The drive and the scenery can only be described as spectacular, simply spectacular. There are very few areas in the world that have everything. Normally God gives a place the ocean or some mountains or some river valleys or plains, but not all of them. Just like our own personalities, very few of us get the whole package, but British Columbia has the whole package.

Notwithstanding the scenery, we were driving fools, and while we were still early in our trip, we were clearly forming the habits and routines that would define our travelling character. As a great philosopher once said, *you are what you habitually do,* and if this is true, and I believe it is, then we were binge drivers. Our fifteen-thousand-mile trek was not going to happen at some average miles per day with some steady daily rhythm of road being put behind us, but rather it was going to happen in driving binges. When we got into driving mode we drove for hours upon hours. We traded drivers without even stopping as the captain's seats allowed us just to slide in for each other when

294

the time was right. The only thing that made us stop was the need for Ozark to stretch her legs and the need for Barth to fuel up. The latter happened about every six hundred miles, or close to a half-day of solid driving. This was a great and convenient rhythm, as we could measure a day if we wanted to by how many times we stopped for fuel. I suspect we missed a few points of interest along the way, but we just felt the need to keep on trucking once we were trucking. When we did stop, we took time to enjoy our surroundings. We took time to appreciate the pond, as guiding principles needed to be adhered to.

We had to make a directional decision at Prince George, BC. One, we could head west to Vancouver and go south down the coast, or two, go east and south inland and then west to California and Mexico. RC really wanted to see Montana so we chose east and inland, and before we knew it we were through Jasper and Lake Louise and found ourselves parked in an empty parking lot in Banff, Alberta – absolute God's country.

Banff is arguably one of the prettiest cities in the world, sitting at almost five thousand feet above sea level, and going east to west it is the beginning of the majestic Canadian Rockies. The town is protected environmentally as it sits within the Banff National Park, and the town has absolutely everything to offer – hiking, skiing, hot springs, gondolas, sightseeing, rock climbing, and every other thing that you can do after eating trail mix and granola. Banff is a land of opportunity for any and all things healthy and outdoorsy, yet ironically we did not participate in any of these activities.

We stopped and parked Barth and got out to stretch our legs. We were right in the heart of the little resort town, but it was not busy at all, so we assumed it was Monday or Tuesday, although it was also pretty late. We had left the land of the midnight sun, and while the days were still at their longest, we did have to deal with a darker darkness coming upon us.

All five of us needed a good walk so we started exploring, and within a short time we came to and walked along the Bow River, an amazing little river that flows through town. The Bow Falls are a fast and furious short set of rapids, and we had to temper RC once again about getting the canoes off the roof racks. Along this walking path, we came to a small park that had a really grand large gazebo. The gazebo must have been at least thirty feet in diameter and was octagonal in shape. It looked like the type of platform that would be perfect for a gorgeous mountain wedding. At the time, the park was dark and empty other than four guys cooking some hamburgers on a small hibachi they had set up. Ozark ran over to them and their hibachi, and we followed and started chatting with the four lads. They offered us a beer and a hamburger, which we happily accepted, although Ozark went only with a hamburger. Eventually, RC went back to Barth to get some other supplies so we could contribute to the fair. It didn't take long for us to get things going.

These four guys were very interesting to say the least. They were from Nova Scotia and were making their way out to the Queen Charlotte Islands on the west coast of Canada. They were agricultural enthusiasts and had picking mushrooms on their agenda as the crop of choice. The Queen Charlottes are known globally as a place for mushroom enthusiasts and the laws restricting these special mushrooms had relaxed considerably since 1980. This was their second year making the trip (no pun intended), as they had been there the previous fall. The fall is the right time to pick, so they were taking their time and seeing Canada one day at time. They also still had some of the mushrooms from the previous year's pick, and when they asked if we would like to have some on our hamburgers, we were delighted to support their hobby and instantly became enthusiasts. Only Ozark abstained. *Good Girl, Ozark.*

About forty minutes after our wonderful dinner, we were well on our way to Tuneupville, or perhaps I should say Veggieville. It was simply spectacular – the area around the gazebo was deserted, and the stars, sky, and mountains were magnificent. The eight of us, and Ozark, just hung out on the gazebo and talked and laughed, although at one point it was clear that everybody was talking and no one was listening. Our vocal cords just seemed to create sound from the vibration of our lips moving. It was as if the vibrations from each of us then created waves that collided to make noise, and the conversations continued and flowed as if we were debating the future of the world at the United Nations. The mysteries of the world became clear. All major questions that philosophers have asked over the years suddenly had reasonable, practical, and obvious self-evident answers. We had become philosophers. We were intelligent beyond measure. We had most of the answers to most of life's questions, and it was an intellectual affair where almost everything in the universe made sense.

That was up until Hats decided to do the *Chicken*. After that, everything just made even more sense, and at that point we had <u>all</u> of the answers to <u>all</u> of life's questions. To this day, I don't know what triggered Hats to do the *Chicken*, and to this day I'm not sure I want to know. Regardless, it was a memorable and unique moment in the lives of the Beaver Brothers.

The eight of us, and Ozark, were having a great time hanging out on the gazebo when all of a sudden Hats started walking around the outer perimeter of the inside of the gazebo, forcing us to get out of his way because we were holding onto the railing as our makeshift bar. Hats didn't care about any of that, and he just plowed through us on his way around the octagonal stage.

On his third time around he crouched down with a deep bend in his knees and he puffed out his chest and rounded his back slightly. His shoulders were pinched back and he looked as if he had perfectly straight posture with a hint of chest creating a small semi-circle with his torso. His total height while in his crouched position was no more than four feet; his left hand was at his side trailing behind the momentum of his run, while his right hand was up at his face. His right hand was completely open, and he tucked his thumb underneath his chin. This left his four fingers dancing freely in front of his nose, and what the thumb and four fingers produced was instantly recognizable as a chicken's wattle. Adding to all of that, he was wearing one of his Fedora hats that had a feather in it.

So there was Hats, crouched with straight and curved posture, waddling around the gazebo at what seemed like ninety miles an hour. He was on an absolute mission, and you never stop a man who's on a mission. The rest of us, Ozark included, watched him make his rounds on the stage. We would take a sip of OV and toast him as he passed us by.

Then one of our new friends from Nova Scotia finally asked, "What the frig is he doing, man?"

The three of us, and Ozark, looked at each other, and RC decided to answer.

"I think he's doing the Chicken!"

Well that was the right answer, because right on cue, Hats came around the gazebo and added to his routine by making bwaking and clucking sounds. It was a patterned bwak, cluck, cluck, bwak, cluck, cluck, bwak, cluck, cluck. The rhythm and pitch were perfect. It was priceless, I mean totally priceless. In life there is nothing like an idea whose time has come, and this was one of those momentous original moments when an idea had intersected with its own fate.

Ray was the first to go, then RC and I joined simultaneously, and three of our new friends were right behind us with Ozark also in tow. Only one of our new friends did not join in, so we had one chick missing from our brood, and he was watching us with a painful look on his face. He lacked confidence. Meanwhile, we were circling and circling and bwaking and clucking and enjoying every part of the free range. We were all doing the Chicken in our own personal way but also trying to emulate the critical-to-quality aspects of the dance that Hats had invented. He was, after all, the original artist. These critical components included the crouch, the chest, the sounds, but most importantly, the wattle. The thumb under the chin and the fingers flowing in front of your face was what separated us from other human fowl. It was our differentiator.

Our one lost friend would attempt to jump in every time the chicken train rounded past, but then he would retreat right at the last minute and stamp his foot in a fit of frustration and yell, "I can't do it, man. I can't do it. I can't do the Chicken!" He had Alektorophobia, or if not fear of chickens themselves, he had a fear of *doing* the Chicken. We would circle around him again and offer encouragement, "You can do it, man. You can do the Chicken. We know you can!" All of us would chant on our way by, and he would crouch and then stand back up. He would puff his chest out and then allow it to deflate; he would put his thumb under his chin and wattle his fingers and then jam his hands into his jean pockets as if trying to discard the wattle. He was really struggling. We continued to offer encouragement each time we came around, and finally, he jumped in at the back of the line and did the Chicken, and we all cheered while Hats picked up the pace. The original seven of us, and Ozark, went fast enough that we came up behind our newest chicken so he was now in the lead. He immediately had a look of fear on his face. He was not confident that he was ready to lead the procession, so we encouraged him. He picked up the pace, did a great job, and excelled as Chicken leader.

After what seemed like forever, we chickens came to a halt and got a cold drink. One of the Scotia Boys suggested we play Frisbee, even though it was too dark to reasonably see a flying disk. We didn't argue as all seemed possible, and what we didn't know was that the Scotia Boys had a Frisbee that glowed in the dark with the help of a green neon glow stick. They were prepared for nighttime sport. All eight of us found a spot in the park and formed our own octagon. Ozark ran in all directions with the UFO spaceship flying among us at a steady speed of Mach 1. Watching the saucer fly was as fun as catching it, and every time it soared through the air you could imagine yourself as an explorer of the galaxy. All of our Douglas Adams reading was helping to create our space odyssey narrative, and we threw the illogical disc all night until the sun started to brighten up the eastern horizon.

With the sun acting as our master guide, we said goodbye to our four new pals and headed back to Barth. I often think about the Scotia Boys. They were a team just like the Beaver Brothers. I wonder how they're doing now.

We got back to Barth but sleep was improbable and downright impossible, so we sat up and talked. I couldn't look directly at Hats because every time I did all I would see was a chicken. A few hours later, Ray said he was ready to drive and we headed out of Banff. What a night it had been.

Ray and I had gone over our route in the BOP, and we decided to take a small highway south towards the next tollgate in the trip. A few hours later Ray pulled Barth over at a gas station in Cardston, Alberta, where we were only a few miles from the Piegan/Carway Canada–USA Border Crossing. The rest of us were sound asleep, so Ray shut all the blinds to Barth and put his head down as well for some well earned rest. When we all woke up it was late evening, and we went into the truck stop and treated ourselves to dinner. Nobody had a hamburger or mushrooms. While talking to the waitress, we found out that the border crossing actually closes at 11pm and does not reopen until 7am. We were too rushed to make the 11pm cut off, and this was fine as we needed to make sure Barth was ready for the trip over the border. RC helped with this analysis, and we had some fun getting rid of anything the border patrol might find offensive. We were pretty excited, and we made sure we were the first vehicle in line at 7am to travel into the United States of America.

Canada / USA

Summer 1983

Math Test

THE CANADA–UNITED STATES border is officially known as the *International Boundary*. It is the longest international border in the world shared between only two countries. The International Boundary is commonly referred to as the world's longest undefended border, and it is the border that supports more economic trade and traffic between two countries than any other border in the world. From the Atlantic to the Pacific and up to Alaska, Canada and the USA share over five thousand miles of border. The two countries are good neighbors and good friends, and if you use the world as a baseline to benchmark against, the Canada – USA partnership is a role model.

While it's considered an undefended border, that does not mean it is unprotected. The border between the countries has at least one hundred different ports of entry, many of them spectacular in their own right and very photo-worthy. Many other crossings are big and busy and commercial, and are very, very busy ports where cars, trucks, traders, smugglers, police, government employees, private enterprise employees, border patrol, dogs, tourists, business people, and many other persons and things make up a twenty-four-hour hustle and bustle.

The Piegan/Carway Canada–USA Border Crossing is none of these. It has a country feel. That is not to suggest that the border patrol officers are any less serious about their responsibilities. They are protecting the border with all the vigor of any other border crossing, but the crossing still has a country feel. For example, it is only open from seven in the morning until eleven at night. After eleven o'clock, the USA–Canada border is closed for entry or exit.

We were the first vehicle in line at seven o'clock when the border opened. There is no need to talk to the Canadians when going southbound, so we drove over the international boundary and stopped to talk to the USA border patrol. In hindsight, it must have been quite a sight for the primary inspector who sat in her booth and asked the preliminary questions. RC was driving, Ozark was in the passenger seat, and the rest of us were sitting in our captain's chairs trying to look as if we crossed the border every day. We wanted to appear to be cross-border commuters simply heading to another day at the office in Montana. Even though we had absolutely nothing to hide as far as we knew, it probably looked as if we had lots to hide. So not unexpectedly, we were interesting enough that they pulled us over into secondary for further inspection. They checked our identification, asked us where we got Barth, inquired about how much money we had, asked how long we intended to stay in the States, looked in and smelled Barth's ashtrays, and asked us if we had any drugs or weapons.

"No, sir," RC replied as our spokesperson, and he was telling the truth. We would never put RC or Ozark in a tight spot. Good thing we had our Barth spring cleaning the night before.

At that point, one particular border patrol officer started talking specifically to Ray.

"What do you do?" he said.

"I'm a student, sir," Ray replied with extreme and sincere respect in his voice.

"What are your favorite courses?" the officer shot back in a serious tone.

"Ahhh, music and math," Ray said after some slight hesitation but also with confidence that he had the right answer about his own interests.

"Math?" the officer replied, with a heightened level of interest in his voice.

"Yes, sir...and music," Ray responded, really saying, *The music is first and the math is second.*

What came next was not expected and even the most intensively trained smuggler would not have been ready for the counter-intelligence techniques of the border patrol officer. He was clearly out to catch us in a lie and prevent us from entering the United States of America.

"What's the *quadratic formula?*" the border patrol officer asked Ray, now back into a very serious tone.

"Pardon?" Ray asked back, again with sincere respect but also a large hint of sincere confusion.

"What's the *quadratic formula?*" the border patrol officer said again, sounding somewhat frustrated by having to repeat himself.

Ray looked at the three of us and down at Ozark, his silent stare really saying, *Am I on candid camera or something? Is this guy serious? Are we still in Banff and this is all imagined? Oh man, I need to remember the quadratic formula to get us into the United States? And why did he pick me?*

RC, Hats, and I looked at each other, and we knew in an instant there was no way in hell any of us knew the formula. Ozark looked equally confused. If anybody was going to know the formula it was Ray. We had a twenty-five percent chance the officer would ask Ray as opposed to the other three of us, and thank the sun for our luck, but was he going to get it? We were all watching Ray, and we literally saw Ray's eyes go from confused to enlightened. I knew in that instant that he had the answer. People are like that. Confusion and enlightenment are inward emotions, but they show outwardly. They show in our body language and in our facial expressions, but mostly, they show in our eyes. The eyes are the door to the soul. Whether you know or don't know, the eyes will tell all.

"Well, sir," Ray answered, still being respectful but with a small hint of arrogance, "I believe the quadratic formula is...X equals negative B plus or minus the square root of B squared minus 4AC all over 2A!"

We cheered and high-fived each other. We were so proud of him, and while we had no idea if he was right, we had all learned the formula at some point and it sure sounded right. So even it if wasn't right, we were proud with the guess he was able to conjure up. Even Ozark was proud and she nestled up to Ray's leg as if saying, *That's my sun Ray. That's my man. What a cool formula. All over 2A, eh? Who would have ever known, 2A!*

The border patrol officer looked at Ray and gave Ray a huge smile and completely let down the physical guard formed by his body language. It turned out the officer was also a part-time math teacher at a local community college. Seems he also had a sense of humor. You just never know who you are really dealing with when you interact with strangers. It was a lesson well learned, and with the exam completed and passed, he handed us our IDs and vehicle information and said, "Have a fun time, boys. You are free to enter the United States of America."

I learned later in life that it is not your right to enter the USA, but rather your privilege. We sincerely felt privileged that day, and after what seemed to be no more than forty-five minutes, we were safely and legally inside the USA. More specifically, we were getting ready to head onto Highway 89 southbound in northern Montana. We all gave Ray another huge high-five for his work and excellent memory, and we loaded up and got on our way.

The plan we charted on the BOP was to take Highway 89 south and west and directly through the middle of the *Glacier National Park*. From there we would head south towards Kalispell, Montana. We chose this route to see the Glacier Park but we also just liked the sound of Kalispell. It has a great ring to it. And from there we would carry on southbound and find a back way into *Beavertail Hill State Park*. This just seemed like a no-brainer, and we were ready for a day or two of rest. A back way into the park was required in order to avoid having to use an interstate. Once again, guiding principles must be honored. The BOP sure came in handy that summer. I believe the GPS of today has ruined the essence of a true road trip. Technology should never guide your direction. As Ray would say, "Let the sun and our curiosity tell us where to go, boys." I guess you could argue that the BOP was the technology of the day, but for us it was a provider of alternatives and not a requirement for the destination to be reached in the most efficient manner. I have a lot of respect for the *Rand McNally Road Atlas*. It was our Book of Paths. It was our BOP.

We spent several days resting in the *Beavertail Hill State Park*. We felt at home there, and a rest was long overdue. It felt as if we had been going strong since the day we left home, and to be sure we had been running on pure adrenaline that was flowing through our entire beings, so the rest was timely and appropriate. Time would prove that we would do this several times over the course of the summer. Drive hard, play hard, rest hard. The rest sessions were our form of meditation, even though we were uneducated and uninformed on the topic of meditation. Ray and RC would play their guitars, I would write in the journal, and Hats would draw or practice his skills at painting with a small paint kit he had brought. Often the three boys would also write in the journal, although I would never read what they wrote because that was not part of the master plan with it. Once a page had been written upon, you had to move to a fresh page and leave what was written for reading at another time and another place.

We would take long walks with Ozark and use the canoes in the lakes or rivers where we camped. Time stood still, and we learned what it was like to live in the moment. These rest times were the only time we ignored one of our guiding principles, as often we would go out on our own walking or just sit by a shore trying to locate the place that the world has named *peace of mind.*

Ray in particular would often venture out on his own during our rest times. It was a funny thing, not funny as in laughter, but funny as in peculiar. When we were driving and playing, we would forget about why we were even on the road trip. Rose's death had not even met its first year anniversary, and at times we could forget about the reality and what had happened. The rest periods were when the last year would find its way back into our consciousness. This was a good thing, though, as rest and reflection are required to heal the soul. Yes, rest and refection are required to find peace of mind.

This first rest period also played an important role because we had to redesign and redefine some of our known necessities of life. *Peter Jacksons* were no longer available to us, so we chose to partner with *Marlboro Reds* as our new torpedo of choice. OV was not available to us, so we landed on *Pabst Blue Ribbon* as our beer replacement. Crown Royal took a back seat to good ole *Jack Daniels.* We rationalized that Jack is a part of royalty as well. *Reds, PBR, and Jack.* We were proud Canadians, but we were now in the USA, and we believed in assimilating into the culture. We were proud to be in the USA. It's a great country. We wanted to be true Americans while we were there, and Reds, PBR, and Jack had rightfully earned their place over time, so they deserved a spot on our bench. Tradition and hard work should always be respected.

We spent several days at Beavertail Park, and calming the soul seemed to be a place that was within our sights. We were feeling optimistic that the town we call *peace of mind* had a dot on the BOP.

I added a short poem to the journal the last night at Beavertail Park.

RIP

Rest in Peace, the Preacher exclaimed
Rest in Peace, Written under his name
Rest in Peace, Chuck him in the Grave
Rest in Peace, May your soul be saved

Why do I have to die to Rest in Peace?
Why can't I live and Rest in Peace?
Do you know the way to Live and Rest in Peace?
Show me the way to Live and Rest in Peace

USA

Summer 1983

Wi

WE HEADED OUT EARLY in the morning after a fun pre-dawn breakfast of scrambled eggs and toast made over an open campfire. Eggs never tasted so good, toast never tasted so bad. The taste averaged out to not bad, and we were happy. Ozark actually enjoyed the toast, proving it's not very hard to make her happy as she is ruled by friendship and food for her stomach, and we were happy to provide her with ample supplies of both.

We snapped a couple of pictures of ourselves beside the Beavertail State Park sign and then headed towards Billings, Montana. We took quite a few pictures that summer, and when we developed them, we recognized a theme. Almost every picture had us pointing to, sitting beside, or standing on top of something to do with beavers. You would be surprised how many signs, rivers, parks, mountains, small towns, and many other things on the road have to do with beavers. The beaver is big. I suspect this should not come as a surprise when you consider that Canada and a significant part of the USA have historical origins based on trying to trap the furry little rodent. Beavers historically made warm coats and hats, and still today they help in the manufacturer of perfume. We don't like this much. It's yet another example of people as dumbasses. We were friends of the beaver and therefore liked to get our pictures taken where the beaver is being promoted in a positive way.

A consequence of avoiding interstates is that you tend to avoid big cities. We did pretty well that summer, and when we did end up in a city it was fully intentional and part of the plan. Billings, Montana, does not meet the definition of a big city anyway. We stopped in Billings to load up Barth with both fuel and supplies, and we found a nice little mall that had a grocery store and a few other shops. By the time we left after a couple of hours, we had a full tank of gas, food and drink, and one personal item each. This stop was also our first realization that RC had to buy our tuning supplies as he was the only one that easily passed for twenty-one years old. It was interesting for us to be part of a much stricter and more conservative culture when dealing with alcohol. It seemed as if beer and bars had been part of our lives for a long time, which they had. The irony was that this new disciplined environment actually proved to be positive, as we did not spend much time in bars that summer and therefore saved a lot of money along the way. However, it did mean we drank out of our coolers most of the time, which meant our budget for ice was, in fact, not overstated. "Fuck you, Sam," Hats would say to me every time we were digging up a buck for another bag of ice.

While at the mall RC bought a really nice silk bandana that he rolled up tight and wore on his forehead. It looked good on his six-foot-six frame and short RCMP-ready haircut. It also complemented the characteristics of being tall, thin, lean, strong, and just in really good shape. He looked healthy. The bandana was red, white, and blue. It was pure *Easy Rider*. It was cool. RC treated Ozark to the exact same bandana, and she wore it around her neck, although Ozark's was not rolled tight but rather was open in the same way a cowboy bank robber would wear a bandana over his face to hide his appearance.

Hats did what Hats does, and he bought a hat. It was a straw cowboy hat intended for summer wear, the seasonal substitute of the traditional *Stetson* heavy felt cowboy hat that is impractical during the hot summer. He also bought a classic blue and white cloth bandana and twirled it around the outside of the crown of the hat. It was pretty cool, and I pictured Hats flying a crop-duster plane over the prairies of Kansas. Not all people can make a cowboy hat work fashionably speaking, but Hats is not the average person. It worked, and at six feet tall, athletic, and muscular, in Billings, Montana, Hats could easily have been mistaken for a rodeo cowboy. He was *The Duke* in the Duke's youth.

I bought a suede leather sleeveless vest that was covered with two rows of fringes. It had overtones of Native American dress, although it was not as elaborate as other garments you might see in Montana. It was light beige and the fringes were about five inches long. It was traditional, but in a modest way. Two pockets in the lower front proved perfect for a pack of torpedoes and a box of wooden matches – youthful priorities. Because the vest was lightweight, it was perfect for evenings and even during the day when temperatures were moderate. I wore it over a t-shirt. I wore it a lot that summer, and it became part of my look – *the fringe vest, poet, smokes and wooden matches in the two pockets on a road trip look*. It was a look I was trying to invent. The boys told me I achieved my goal, and the look was uniquely mine. They said there was no comparison to the vibe.

Ray got his ear pierced. There was a little salon for hair and nails stuff in the mall, and he found out they did ear piercing as well. I think he was searching for that service specifically because he had no intention of getting his hair cut. Other than RC, the rest of us were growing our hair even longer that summer, and Ray's was already well past his shoulders. He had already grown it long enough to put it in a ponytail. Hats and I were envious but quickly catching up.

A very smart and very pretty Native American girl, maybe seventeen years old, used a little gun-type apparatus to punch a hole in Ray's left earlobe. Her name was *Wi* which was Native American for *Sun*. Of course Ray gave us the *See, what did I tell you!* look when she told us that. There were a lot of interesting coincidences that summer, and this was one that certainly made us stop and wonder. Wi had received her traditional name from her parents when she was thirteen after her father saw the sun shine in her eyes one day. We learned that many Native Americans don't name their children with a traditional name until later in life. They wait to witness a life experience, and with Wi it was the sun shining in her eyes. Ray was mesmerized as she told us the story. I could see it in his eyes – the door to the soul. There is no question that Wi reminded each of us of Rose. The Sun and the Rose.

We watched the whole ear-piercing event, no pun intended. Wi inserted a single earring that she and Ray picked out together, although he had to buy a pair of them. It was a handmade traditional Native American Dream Catcher. The main part of the earring was a circle the size of a nickel. The circle was woven with yellow and blue and red thread, and the weaves were done in such a way as to make it look like a net – a Dream Catcher net. Hanging from the circle were four very colorful small sets of beads woven into small feathers. The colors were pink and purple and orange and red. These were about an inch long, and the whole earring was about two inches long and hung from a small piece of silver surgical steel to hook into the earlobe. It was Ray. It was totally Ray. It's amazing how something so small can represent so much narrative. It's amazing how something so small can represent so much goodness, so much uniqueness.

Wi told us a lot about the Dream Catcher and the Billings area in general. Many Native Americans believe the Dream Catcher will keep bad dreams from entering the mind. The holes in the catcher net will only allow good dreams to filter through to the feathers. The good dreams will then glide down the feathers and fall benevolently into the sleeper while the bad dreams stay trapped in the catcher net and are destroyed by the sun in the light of day, with all of this being repeated the next night. Ray loved it. We all loved it, and the earring looked great on Ray. I can't think of a person to compare him to. It was simply Ray with an earring that was pure Ray.

We all gave Wi a big hug and thanked her for her sharing and for giving us ideas on what and where we should go see next. Ray stayed back a minute, and when I turned around I watched him give Wi the earring that was the second to his set and that he did not need. She smiled at him and I watched her immediately take an earring out of her ear and replace it with the match to Ray's. I'll never forget that moment. I can't describe in words how it made me feel. I suspect you understand and can feel the essence of what I felt. I turned around and saw that Hats and RC had witnessed the moment as well. Both of them had wetness forming in their eyes – the door to the soul. The Beaver Brothers, a bunch of not-so-tough tough guys. "Good grief," I mumbled to myself as I got my emotions together and headed out to Barth.

From Billings we headed east and south towards the spot Wi recommended we visit. We weren't in Key West yet, but the stops were lining up with Ray's interests significantly. First, we drove by the park and the monuments for *The Battle of the Little Bighorn*. "We're not stopping here," Ray said in a very matter-of-fact way.

"Why not?" RC asked back.

"Because it focuses on the wrong elements of what is important," he said back to RC.

He was right. Known as Custer's Last Stand, the Battle of the Little Bighorn happened on June 25 and 26, 1876. The partnered forces of the Lakota, Northern Cheyenne, and Arapaho tribes fought the 7th Cavalry Regiment of the United States Army. The battle was fought close to the Little Bighorn River in eastern Montana Territory and was the most significant battle of the Great Sioux War of 1876. It was an overwhelming victory for the Native Americans and their leaders, which included Crazy Horse and Chief Gall. From some brochures Ray had picked up he educated us how Crazy Horse and Chief Gall were inspired to victory by the visions of Sitting Bull. When the battlefield fell silent, the U.S. Seventh Cavalry, its leader George Armstrong Custer, and his soldiers had suffered a crushing defeat. Custer himself was killed, along with two of his brothers, and over two hundred American fighters.

"Sitting Bull," Hats said. "I love that. I bet he would have made an excellent coach – Vince Sitting Bull!"

We drove right by all the tourist stuff announcing where the battle had taken place as Ray was not interested in this history. "It's too commercial, Sam," Ray said. "Even when the cavalry lost, they still got to write the story," he went on. "So much for the victor being the one who writes the history." It didn't much matter anyway because we were on our way slightly south from the Little Big Horn Battlefield to our next destination.

Following Wi's suggestion, we stopped and spent the rest of the day and most of the night at the *Rosebud Battlefield State Park*. This is the area along the Rosebud Creek that offered its soil to be used for the Battle of the Rosebud on June 17, 1876. In this battle, fifteen hundred Sioux and Northern Cheyenne soldiers forced the retreat of Brigadier General George Crook's one thousand soldiers at Rosebud Creek. It was one of the largest battles of the US Indian wars. Most significantly, though, this battle is known as the reason for the upset at the Little Big Horn due to the fact that General Crook's soldiers were not available to support Colonel Custer and his men there.

"Fucking right, man," Hats would yell out from the back of Barth. "Ya gotta love it when an underdog wins in overtime!"

Ray loved this small detail of David and Goliath, but that was not what made the battlefield so special for him and for RC, Hats, and me. While the battle is known as the Battle of the Rosebud, whose name was not lost on us, the Cheyenne called it the Battle Where the Girl Saved Her Brother. The story goes that during the battle, a Cheyenne warrior, Chief Comes in Sight, was wounded. His horse was shot from underneath him and he desperately tried to flee the battlefield on foot. His sister Buffalo Calf Woman rode into the chaos and rescued her brother by scooping him up on her horse so the two could ride to safety. The folklore is that all the Cheyenne warriors witnessed this act of bravery, which fueled their war cry and rallied them to victory.

"Nothing like a little help from the bench to get the team going! No third-man-in rules in that sport, boys!" RC yelled out as Ray was giving us the history he had learned from Wi and his brochures.

The story went on. One week later, Buffalo Calf Woman went on to fight beside her husband Black Coyote in the Battle of the Little Bighorn. She has also been credited with striking the blow that knocked Lieutenant Colonel George Armstrong Custer off his horse, leading ultimately to his death. It was a great story. We didn't care whether it was all accurate or not; we believed every part of it, knowing it was as good a story as anybody else's version of events.

"Let's face it," Ray said, "there is no real truth in this world, only the perception of the participants and then the fiction and creativity of the story teller."

"I love it, man," Hats said. "A little Buffalo Cow Pie stomping a little Custard Pie!"

The four of us had a great afternoon relaxing and doing our own thing. We were soaking in the sensation of all the irony that surrounded us, and early in the evening to our pleasant surprise, Wi drove up and parked beside Barth. She told us she was hoping to find us and that she was happy we had come to her favorite spot. We were very happy to see her, and we got busy cooking a nice dinner for the five of us, six including Ozark, who was very pleased to have another lady at the table.

We made a fancy meal of spaghetti and meat balls and set a picnic table up for us to dine at. We even put out a tablecloth, a red-and-white-checked cloth overlay from a fifties movie scene. It was RC's, and he thought it was a classic. The five of us sat at the table while Ozark stayed close to Wi. All of a sudden, we realized this was a familiar scene. We had all been there before, only Wi was in Rose's seat. The four of us had sat down to that dinner configuration hundreds of times growing up – a family and friends sitting down to have a family and friends dinner. We were all feeling it, and Wi could somehow sense our emotions. I believe she knew that she brought a feeling of peace to the table. Ray seemed to be in another world. The silence lasted for over a minute and then Wi asked if she could teach us a Native American blessing. Of course, we were all ears, not to mention all hands as time would prove.

"All right Beaver Brothers," Wi said with a smile on her face, saying Beaver Brothers out loud for the first time. Repeat after me, "May the Great Spirit make the sun rise in our hearts."

This one sentence was powerful beyond belief. RC, Hats, and I looked at Ray and he gazed back at us with a *Life is much more interesting than most people will ever know* look. To this day, I believe Ray fell in love with Wi at that moment. After another minute we all came back to reality to become Wi's students once more.

We repeated the blessing a few times and got it down pretty quickly. Even Hats tried hard to be a good student. After we memorized the verse, Wi taught us the hand gestures that were required to perform the blessing properly. It was a lot of fun, even though it took us a good half hour to finally get it right. We had a lot of laughs that evening. It was a good evening; our souls were being energized by Wi and her energy, by the sun's energy.

"OK, Beaver Brothers," Wi would encourage us. "One more time. *May*, and now clap your right hand down on your left hand in front of your belly button...*The Great Spirit*, now roll your hands over each other in and upward towards your chest...*Make*, now clap three times starting up high and move your hands downwards as you clap...*The sun*, now hold your hands out from your body on either side of you and reach for the sky asking for the sun to enter...*Rise*, now put your arms on top of each other horizontally to your chest so you look like a Chief sitting by a campfire. Then raise your left arm in a "rising" gesture and place both hands over your heart while saying ...*In our hearts*."

It was mysterious and magical all at the same time. Even Ozark was paying full attention and trying to make the gestures. Our dinner was cold by the time we all felt we had the blessing engrained in our brain. We didn't care though. Something strange was going on, and we all felt it. We ate much of the dinner in silence, all of us lost in our own thoughts. Wi seemed absolutely fine with this, as not all people require incessant chatter to feel comfortable. Stimulus can come in different forms, and our stimulus at the time was silence.

Then Wi began to educate us about the ways of her people and ancestors. In particular, she educated us about the Great Mystery, the Great Spirit, and how the secret to a spiritual life is not to try to answer the question of creation and existence, but rather to enjoy the beauty of the trees, the mountains, the rivers, the soil, the animals, all of nature, and of course, the sun. She told us how the sun is the father and the Earth is the mother and together they produce life, and that life is the essence of God, the Great Spirit. She told us about how the Native American did not understand the ways of the white man, in particular how the white man can profess to know who created the earth or where we go when we die. These are elements of knowledge that are not to be known. These are the essence of the Great Mystery and the Great Spirit, and any religion that claims to explain these things is not to be trusted. She told us that nobody finds out the answer of the Great Mystery and the Great Spirit until after we die, and that nobody has ever died and somehow leaked the secrets as these answers are between each individual and the Great Spirit. It is a private conversation, and this confidentiality is respected beyond all other things. Last, she told us how the white man did not take one second to try to understand the Native American way of life, that perhaps there may have been lessons for the white man to learn, but instead the white man chose to destroy everything in his path – land, animals, and people – all in the name of his perfect God.

As you can imagine, we were mesmerized by Wi that night, and Ray just kept looking at us, knowing that he had educated us on several of these topics in the past.

After dinner, we all did the dishes together and continued to visit with Wi. We got a campfire going and RC and Ray played their guitars. We sang songs and Wi continued to tell us about the history of her people. When listening to the story from her side, you sure don't get the warm fuzzies about the pioneers and *Marshall Dillon.* The true history of the populating of the plains is painted in shades of cruelty and ambition. It's hard to believe people can treat other people with such indifference. It's hard to believe we can change a story around in such a way as to create pride from the outcome. It's hard to believe that so much history, culture, and wisdom can be eliminated in the name of manifest destiny. We would and should feel shame if it weren't for the fact that people don't know any better. The human being has never been credited with learning anything quickly or proactively. We have progressed significantly from a science and engineering point of view, but we remain socially stunted.

While the stories Wi told might leave you feeling down, her voice would lift you right back up. At one point, Ray started strumming *Bobby McGee,* and Wi started singing the lyrics to the song. Of course she had the voice of an angel. All four of us just looked at each other with a silent stare that said, *Why am I not surprised!* Ozark lay down by the fire and put her head on Wi's foot.

Near the end of the night, Ray and Wi took Ozark for a walk, and when they returned we said our second goodbye to Wi within twenty-four hours. From that day forward, we said our new blessing every time we sat down to eat. I think Ray said it when he woke up as well. Ray and Wi kept in touch by mail regularly after that day and developed a close friendship over the next twelve months. Little did we know what role she would end up playing in our lives going forward. To this day, Wi is our sunshine.

The whole day seemed somewhat surreal. Meeting Wi in Billings, the Dream Catcher, the Battle of the Rosebud, the Battle Where the Girl Saved Her Brother, the Blessing, Wi's singing voice, and the lessons of history. I have to admit, we were all feeling very out of sorts when Wi left. It was a feeling that Hats would describe as, "What the fuck is really going on here, and what are we supposed to be learning from all this?" It's a feeling as if you are stuck in limbo somewhere between utter confusion and pure fascination. It's a feeling that makes you realize there is a lot more to life than simply going through the motions of the day. It's a feeling that reminds you that in the big scheme of things, there is so much left to understand. As a great philosopher once said, "A wise person is a person who knows he knows nothing." At that point, we felt absolutely ignorant where ignorance is defined as a gross lack of real knowledge.

We all felt emotionally exhausted after Wi left, even though she had brought amazing energy. The day just seemed surreal and therefore was draining, and so we got comfortable in Barth and got lost in our own thoughts. RC and Ray strummed away on their guitars while Hats was doodling Dream Catchers on his art pad. I retired to the journal and wrote about the day and what was on my mind. A short poem came as a result.

SO STRANGE

It strikes me as strange
The way some people are deranged
In deciding who they need to defeat
It strikes me as nuts
All the blood gore and guts
Hiding silently just below our feet

It strikes me as bizarre
Our fascination with war
The fields of stupidity are vast
It strikes me as complete
How amazing the world could be
If humans removed their head from their ass

We all fell asleep in our comfy chairs that night, and I woke up just before dawn to the feeling of Barth's engine and gears going. When my eyes got in focus I could see Ray in the driver's seat. He was taking us out of the park.

"What's up man?" I asked him in a sleepy confused voice.

"I gotta get out of here, Sam," he said back to me in a quiet and forlorn voice. "I gotta drive, buddy. We need to drive," he repeated several times over, almost as if in a panic. I got up and joined Ray at the front of Barth. Ozark joined us as well, while RC and Hats kept on sleeping.

"Let's go," I said to Ray. "Let's drive."

And drive we did. The next binge was on.

DAY 17

South Carolina

Tough Love

TODAY IS A NO-COLOR DAY. Maybe I should call it a blank day. I am without measure relative to my emotional state. I am without color. My blank state of emotion is due to some medication. I decided I should try some anti-depressants, the magic pills that are the new craze and are prescribed by anyone qualified to prescribe to anyone. I got a truckload full of them shortly after Sophie and George left me. They are prescribed for everything under the sun, and I guess my condition qualified as being under the sun, although I argued with the doctor at the time that anxiety and anger are different from depression. He argued back that the active ingredients in anti-depressants will only act upon depression, and therefore people who are not depressed will have no side effects from taking them. His logic is that if you are depressed, they will help you, and if you're not depressed, you have nothing to lose. It's all bullshit, of course. It's Beaver Fever, and while I knew better, I followed his lead anyway. It didn't prove helpful back then, but I guess I decided to give it another shot. I took the first pill four days ago and ate them for three consecutive days, and then I stopped my regimen yesterday after seeing Hats on television. I stashed the rest of the wonder capsules away. I still feel blank though. I hope that by tomorrow they will be out of my system. With any luck, by tomorrow I'll be back to normal, feeling only anxiety and anger. This seems like a modest want, low expectations for sure. Life and its emotions truly are relative.

My Uncle came to visit today. He flew up from Florida on his jet. Alec – my mentor, my coach. Also my first visitor since I arrived almost three weeks ago. Time sure flies when you're losing your mind, or trying to find it. I still hadn't reached out to him, and I guess he couldn't wait any longer. He's a quintessential prospector, and prospectors have problems controlling their impulses. It comes with the territory. Prospectors actually vibrate when they want something to happen, even though they're trying to be wise and patient. It's a paradox at best. He wanted me to call, and I didn't call, so here he is. He vibrated up here on his private jet. Ya gotta love him. I do love him, and he loves me, that much I know.

Alec was here on business, or so he said, so as part of his act he didn't ask me how I'm feeling about Sophie and George. I wonder whether Doc coached him. Even a coach needs coaching when he is out of his element. Alec knows me as well as anybody in the world, but he does not know my emotional circumstance the way a trained professional would. These are uncharted waters for both of us, so we talked about some harsh realities relative to our business. He is the right guy to talk to about the topic since he has been running things for me the last few weeks, or maybe the last few months if I were brutally honest with myself.

"All right, Sam," he said, "when are you going back to work?"

"Back to work?" I said, really saying, *Do I look as if I'm going back to work, Alec?*

"Yes, Sam, back to work. Back to your business that needs you, back to your employees who count on you, back to your customers who miss you, back to what you do best!"

"To what I do best?" I replied, really saying, *Good lord, Uncle, look at me. I'm a mess. I'm done. I'm whacked. I'm almost in a straitjacket and you want me to go give people advice on how to live a better life?*

"Yes, Sam, do what you do. *Eat tree, Beaver!* Right, Sam?"

Silence

"Uncle, why in the world would anybody want advice from me about how to navigate through this messed-up world?"

"Because you have good advice to give, Sam. Because you are navigating through more challenges than most people ever see in three lifetimes. Because you may even have better advice now from this experience! Use it all to come out stronger, Sam. Right? If it doesn't kill you, it makes you stronger. Right, Sam?"

"Really, Alec?"

"Really, Sam."

"What if it actually kills me? What then, Alec?"

"It won't Sam."

"Really?"

"Really."

Silence

"Look, Sam, do you think your customers think you're a superhero? That somehow, because you are actually a fallible human, that your advice and the value of that advice are diminished? Good lord, Sam. Look what you've accomplished and look what you've been through."

"Lots of people have been through worse, Alec."

"Maybe, but not many, and what exactly do you expect from yourself? Perfection? Nobody's perfect, Sam. Nobody, and certainly not you. We're all fragile and have a breaking point. The trick is to embrace imperfection and get up when the world knocks you down. The trick is to lace up your skates and get onto the ice when every ounce of universal entropy is trying to put you on the bench, Sam. Being knocked on your ass should not come as a surprise; that's life. The world knocks people on their asses. So what! It's what you do with the entropy that counts. It's whether the effects of entropy will be your story or your excuse! Right, Sam?"

"That's sounds vaguely familiar."

"They're your words, you dumbass. I listened to one of your podcasts on the plane ride up here."

"Good lord, Alec."

"Come on, Sam. Are you one of those people who can't follow his own advice? Is your fragile ego and misguided, mildly narcissistic need for perfection going to dismantle years of hard work?"

"Wow! Tell me what you really think, why don't you, Alec. I'm only sitting here in this hospital fighting for my sanity. Like I really need this shit right now, Alec!"

"Tough love, my nephew. I'm not here to sugar coat the message. I'm not here to kiss your ass or tell you that bad is good. That won't help anybody. It is what it is, my boy. It's all for a good cause."

"Oh ya, what cause is that?"

"You, Sam."

Silence

"So you think my problem is that I'm a perfectionist?"

"Yes, well...no. That's part of it, Sam."

"Perfectionist? By what definition, Alec? That I need to dot my i's and cross my t's? That I need to be on top of the details and have my pants pressed just right?"

"No, Sam, that's not it at all. And you're no good at details anyway. That's not what I'm talking about."

"Then what are you talking about, Alec?"

"Really, Sam? You need me to tell you? The businessman-politician telling the psychologist about the psychology of your own perfectionism?"

"Try me, Uncle."

"Fine. First, you set goals for yourself that are unrealistic. You think that somehow you are invincible in the face of events that would crush the strongest of people. By virtue of this, you set yourself up for failure, and then when you do fail, you go down hard. I've seen it, Sam. You can do ten great things in a day, but God forbid you make one mistake along the way. Ten great decisions and one not-so-great decision, and what will you brood on? The mistake. And you overstate the mistake. You take a strong wind in Florida and turn it into a typhoon that's going to hit Winnipeg! You focus on the negative and lose sight of every piece of positive around you. You become blurred by the fog of negativism. Under these circumstances, you will never win, Sam. You never value the things you do well, and consequently you don't enjoy the journey or the destination. You don't benefit from the process or the result! You just get up and work and then go to bed pissed off about what didn't work out to your expectation during the day. Is that any way to live, Sam?"

"People count on me, Alec. People look to me to get it right."

"Really, Sam? Somehow you think you can go through life and not make mistakes? Your biggest weakness is that you think that what challenges most people will be easy for you. That you are somehow immune to what life dishes out; that you are stronger than the rest of us. But what really happens, Sam? You end up living with an all-consuming, twenty-four-hour-a-day, seven-day-a-week fear of failure. Think about it, Sam. If failure itself is a crushing failure, than how the hell will you ever be happy? Failure is a certainty. Failure is a part of life, Sam. We try, we win some, and we lose some too. Is this not what you teach? That life is like flying a kite? Up and down, soaring and coasting, flying high and crashing to the ground? Are these not your words, Sam?"

Silence

"It was easier before, Alec."

"Before what, Sam?"

"Before...before now."

"Before what, Sam? ...God Damn It, say it, Son!"

Silence

"Look, Sam, I'm going to tell you what I think straight on, no bullshit. Here's the deal. Life can suck. Life can really suck, but you are either moving forward or backward. There is no standing still. You keep going unless you decide to stop, and you know what that looks like, don't you, Sam? You know what stopping looks like, don't you, Sam?"

Silence

"Sam, let me tell you a few lessons from my road. I have met a lot of people along my path to what people call success – millionaires, billionaires, Prime Ministers, Presidents, Congressmen, Congresswomen, Kings, Queens, and Popes. And do you know what the smart ones – the truly successful ones – all have in common, Sam?"

"What?"

"They are optimistic about the future while totally insecure about their own capabilities and scared to death that they won't get it right. But they are confident in their ability to work hard and learn from mistakes made along the way. They embrace every day as a learning opportunity. They get up, live the day, fall down, learn, do it again, and laugh and cry along the way. They don't believe they are better or stronger than anybody else."

"What about the not so smart ones?"

"Great question, Sam. These are the folks riding on the ego horse. They are hijacked by their own perception of their success. They read and believe their own press, Sam. They listen to their own voice while their mouth is moving and actually believe they are brilliant. I've seen great, sincere people become deranged overnight because they become successful by society's standards. I mean it. I've seen good people think their IQ increased by thirty points in a day just because they won an election or closed a business deal. Yet they haven't won anything because they lose their identity, their roots, and their peace of mind. The enemy ego spits out something into the blood and it drugs these people and they truly think they are somehow smarter and cleverer than the perceived losers below them. It's wild to watch it. I've witnessed it a hundred times, but eventually these people lose it. I see it in their eyes, and eventually they implode. It happens all the time. Life is about staying grounded, Sam. Stability and peace of mind are everything, and stability and peace of mind are about being grounded. There is nothing in this world that is uglier or more unattractive than a person who thinks he is above other people."

"So, you're saying ego is the enemy, Alec?"

"Come on, Sam. Really? Are we really going to banter like this? Are you not reading me? Hello, Sam! Anybody there? What is it that you think I just said to you?"

"I think you said that our ego is the enemy, or that I think I am better than other people, but I don't get it, Alec. Lots of very successful and important people are driven by ego."

"You didn't catch my point then, Sam, or I didn't explain it well. Every emotion or characteristic we have and display has a sweet spot – the bell curve of habits and traits. The trick to peace of mind is to find the sweet spot on the curve where the trait serves you in an optimal manner. Self-confidence is an amazing thing, that is until it goes over the curve and turns into arrogance. Then you lose. Insecurity and modesty can be powerful as well when harnessed, but if you don't climb the curve of insecurity towards confidence, you may never leave the house. Every major part of our character can be our largest asset or our largest liability depending on your path over the curve, Sam. It's about how you manage the swinging of the pendulum. You have to understand the trait and find the sweet spot where your strengths are optimized and your weaknesses are managed. You can't swing the pendulum too far in any one direction. This is the trick to obtaining peace of mind, Grasshopper. And relative to your thinking you are better than other people, nothing could be farther from the truth. You see the intrinsic value in all people, Sam. Your problem is that you don't recognize your own value. You look at yourself as below everybody else, and you don't understand your own self-worth."

Silence

"So what are we going to do, Sam?"

"About what, Alec?"

"About the business! I'm here on business, Sam, not your mental condition. It's time to separate church and state."

"I don't know, Alec. What are my options?"

"You get yourself together and get back to work or you think about selling it."

"Can't I let my people run it for a while?"

"Maybe, but that's not fair to anybody. Customers and employees deserve respect. They need to know the direction, so I think you need to be in or out. Anything else will just confuse people, and the value of the business will be diminished."

"Sell it?"

"Yes, Sam, we could sell it."

"Would it sell without me? I thought I was the business?"

"Ahh, Sam. We've learned nothing today have we? The ego sure can shoot out some powerful juice into the veins, eh?"

"What do you mean by that, Alec?"

"Nothing, Sam. I tell you what. Here's my coaching for the day. You need to make a decision – In or Out. Go or No Go. Either way, I'm good. I'll take care of things for another couple of weeks while you decide. I'll even take care of things if you decide to sell. Good?"

Silence

"You think I'll be out of here in a couple of weeks, Alec?"

"Don't know, and I'm not sure that matters. But in two weeks, we need to decide what we're going to do with your business. It's not a game, Sam. Decisions need to be made, and deciding not to decide is a bullshit excuse for a decision. That's not how I roll anyway. I don't do bullshit. No Beaver Fever here! OK, Sam?"

"You saw Hats on TV?"

"Sure did, Grasshopper. Ya just gotta love that boy! So are we on the same page?"

"Yes, Alec."

"Good. I'll come back and see you in two weeks. In the meantime, you work on yourself. I'll take care of everything else. You have one job – you! Good?"

"Good."

"All right then. I love you, Sam."

"I love you too, Alec, and thanks, I think."

"My pleasure, Son. I'm only here to help."

"Ya, I know, with friends like you..."

"Give me a hug, Sam."

Hug

You are a good man. Your dad would be proud of you. I'm proud of you."

Silence

"Thanks, Uncle."

USA

Summer 1983

Big Trees

ONCE ON A DRIVE binge, we would drive and we would drive but we still saw things along the way. Observation and taking the scenic route are not about time or velocity, but rather about attitude. The question is what are your eyes seeing, and how much can you enjoy it in that instant? Some people stay in the same place for a week and see nothing, and others catch only a glimpse and see everything. We were the latter. We would drive over a bridge going across the Snake River and enjoy it just as much as if we were canoeing the river itself. In fact, we would often argue about how we would canoe the river if we chose to stop and hit the water, but stopping was not an option while in drive mode. The Beaver Brothers were getting busy getting down the road.

RC and Hats woke up a couple of hours after Ray and I headed Barth westbound. By the time we shut down for a true rest, we had been driving and making short stops for several days. We saw multiple sunsets and sunrises, and we made a point of trying to understand where and when the sun would rise and set, or more accurately, we tried to understand where we would pass by the sun in the morning or night. It just seemed appropriate, all things considered. Themes were coming together, and Ray taught us that you just don't ignore themes. Coincidences were not considered to be random events. Everything along the road had meaning of some kind.

From Montana, we headed west and kind of south. Tijuana, Mexico, was our ultimate destination, but that's not to suggest we headed towards Tijuana in some deliberate path. It was the strangest thing that summer in that we always headed somewhat towards our next goal, but the goal did not determine our decision-making relative to where to go next. While we did need to go west and south to end up in Tijuana, our true north was wherever or whatever we felt was the right direction in the moment. Three steps forward and one step back suited us just fine, or more precisely, one hundred miles west and ten miles east was fine as long as we felt good about the roads. We knew we had to make so much distance to keep to our guiding principle, but we did not allow this to turn driving into a job. Too many people take a great thing and turn it into a job; that was not us, and while we were in general heading south and west, this was not the case at all times. RC and I used a yellow highlighter to try to keep track of our actual path in the BOP. It made quite the doodle by the time the summer was over and the BOP went into the bullet box.

The driving binge from Montana to our next resting spot took us through a few neat places where we had short and expedited expeditions. We saw *Old Faithful* do her stable and predictable geyser trick in Yellowstone National Park. We met many buffalo on our way through the park as well. We were in awe driving through the mountains and forests of Wyoming, and we argued about who would kick whose ass in a tree felling contest, Canada's Big Joe Mufferaw or the USA's Paul Bunyan. In the end, we were 3-2 for Big Joe Mufferaw. Ozark and Hats went for Paul Bunyan. I suspect they realized the fix may have been in and were simply trying to provide some balance. Hats believed in a fair fight, and so did Ozark.

"What the fuck are you talking about, man?" Hats yelled from his backseat captain's chair, really saying, *Paul Bunyan is the man, the tree-felling man, and I'm not going to let any misguided sense of Canadian patriotism sway my own judgment on this!*

"What do you mean, Hats?" RC yelled over at Hats. "Let's face it, Big Joe was bigger and stronger than little wimpy Paul B!"

"What the hell are you talking about, RC?" Hats shot back. "How the hell do you know who was bigger? What are you, a historian and expert on folklore lumberjacks now? Were you there, man? You don't know Paul, and you don't know Joe!"

"I just know," RC said back, really saying, *Hats, I absolutely love screwing with your head, and you are an absolute moron at times. And this is one of those times, brother.*

"Fuck you, RC." Hats said back to no one's surprise.

"Fine, Hats," RC replied. "Give us your monologue, give us your argument, give us your rationale for why Paul Bunyan would win a tree-felling contest over Big Joe Mufferaw."

"Thank you, RC," Hats replied while he bowed to us all as if taking the floor to perform a Shakespearian soliloquy. "First, Paul Bunyan wrote the book on tree chopping, and Big Joe M was a mere student of Paul's art. An apprentice if you will, my good man, not a true chopper and not even a chopper's son! Simply a man with an axe to grind!"

"Good grief," RC replied in an exhausted tone of voice.

"Ahhh, but that's not all, my tall friend. Paul Bunyan's training and experience exceeds Joe Mufferaw's tenfold. He simply had more practice and more trees felled, and therefore he would be stronger and more effective in a head-to-head, one-on-one competition!"

"How do you figure that, Hats, my big hat-headed friend?" RC said back, trying to match his gift for the flare.

"Well," Hats went on, "Paul walked all the way from Maine to California and cut trees all along his way. This builds muscles and skill. As well, he formed the Great Lakes and he dug the Grand Canyon and he did all of this while taking care of his great friend, Babe the Blue Ox!"

"Good grief, Hats," RC replied again, really saying, *How did I ever allow myself to be suckered into this conversation by such a goof? Or am I the goof at this point!*

"Ahhh, RC," Hats went on. "But I am not done, my fair soul. Your man on the other hand, your Big Joe Mufferaw, the one you advocate for, did nothing but fell a few trees on the Mattawa River in the regions of Ontario and Quebec. And even then, he did so only in the mild temperatures of summer. When the harsh Canadian winter came to the geographic location of Big Joe's home, he did nothing but hunker down, sleep, eat, and drink Chicoutimi-brewed moonshine! And as we all know, the Chicoutimi moonshine is the worst and best moonshine of all! And as we all know, the worst and best moonshine of all will fuck you up silly as a beaver gnawing on poison oak! And as we all know, there ain't no sillier than the fucked up silly of a beaver gnawing on poison oak! Am I right or what? RC, am I right or what?"

"Good grief," RC would reply in most of these situations, and then he would turn away from Hats and ignore him for as long as he could, but he would always go back for more eventually.

We travelled through Salt Lake City, Utah, and RC and Hats argued about what vehicle would win a race on the Salt Flats. Hats waited for RC to choose Boomer and then picked Barth. You should have heard his argument for that one. While still in Utah they argued about weak Utah beer vs. Canadian beer, and Hats proved to us mathematically and on paper that he could easily drink thirty-five cans of the Utah brew in one sitting.

When we crossed into Nevada, we stopped for a couple of hours and each dropped a roll of nickels into a slot machine so we could drink free glasses of draft. Hats tried to hit his thirty-five goal in that couple of hours, although he didn't bother checking whether Nevada beer was lightweight as well. When he puts his mind to something, he is a force of nature. Needless to say, Hats didn't drive at all that day.

Going through Nevada was an adventure and an education in geography – flat, rocky, sand and dust. We drove through the badlands of Nevada, the stretch of roads that can make you feel as if your life truly is simply dust in the wind. It can make you feel small and alone yet filled with wonderment and optimism all at the same time. At one point, we stopped on an old highway outside of *Battle Mountain, Nevada,* and we got out of Barth and just stared at the land masses in front of us. There were no people around us, no buildings and no other cars in sight. The land itself looked as if it had no order to it, no master plan from the sun. It was as if the land had been used by the Great Spirit as a place for experiments of geology, or perhaps a dropping off point of earthly assets from failed experiments from past gods. We loved every minute of it. We loved the badlands of Nevada, and Ray and RC played every acoustic song they knew that had the dark and sad spirit of the land. *Thrasher* was by far our favorite. That song tells it all. We had literally left our road for where the pavement had turned to sand. We were thrashers making our way down the fields, attempting to harvest peace of mind.

While we were stopped, Ray and Ozark went for a walk and strolled straight out into the badland abyss. We watched them walk a straight line until they were just two little dots. It was interesting to watch their images disappear ever so slowly as they created more distance between us. Then we watched them walk back and grow larger as they grew nearer. It was a peaceful moment. Peace of mind was germinating in the soil of our souls, and Ray looked at ease when he and Ozark returned. The walk had generated positive energy. It was all good, and we loaded up and headed further down the road.

We stopped in Reno, Nevada, and got more than our money's worth at a prime rib buffet. I mean more than our money's worth. We drove through Virginia City and Carson City just so we could say we drove through Virginia City and Carson City. We did grow up watching *Bonanza* on TV after all, and Lorne Green is a famous Canadian. I particularly liked Virginia City because it was originally a mining town. Silver was the claim, and Mark Twain began his writing there over one hundred fifty years ago. Mark Twain was a true prospector. Mining towns and writers have a strong correlation. I'm not sure which is the chicken or the egg. I suspect the writing passion is always in the person, and the mining town brings it out. Arguing the other way around works equally as well, and in the end, I'm proud that I come from a mining town, and I'm proud that I am a writer from a mining town.

We had a great paddle on Lake Tahoe. The water was cold and crystal clear, and the scenery was spectacular. RC and Hats found out exactly how cold the water was when Ray and I dumped them while they were nearing shore in their canoe. We literally broadsided them with our canoe and paddled away feverishly to shore while they attempted to save themselves. Hats said it took five days for his nuts to come back from the shrink zone. I couldn't help but remember the day Hats flew off my roof and hung on the eavestroughs by those same nuts. After our canoe ride at Tahoe, we stopped only for gas and Ozark breaks, and eventually we came to our next place of rest. When we finally stopped, we set up camp in a remote part of the *Humboldt Redwood State Park*. We were in California, which was in and of itself a very cool thing. But we were not just in California; we were among the California redwoods. We stayed among the amazing trees for several passes of the sun. It was amazing, simply amazing.

There are some things that just can't be described by words or a picture or a painting or video for that matter. Some things require being seen and experienced in order to be understood. I don't care how talented the narrator or how gifted the photographer or artist or movie maker, there are some things on this Earth that are only understood when you are in their physical presence, when you are surrounded by them, when you experience them by touch, smell, feel, taste, sound. This is the way of the redwood, so I will not try to do what I say cannot be

done. I will not try to describe how beautiful – how utterly out of this
world – these trees are. I will not try to describe how I felt in their presence, looking up to their peaks at over three hundred feet, my six-foot-
frame seeming like a twig. Or the four of us, and Ozark, trying to put
our arms around a Redwood that had a diameter of over twenty feet,
feeling as if the tree knew everything, and we knew nothing. Feeling
that the tree had found peace of mind after fifteen hundred years of life
while we were searching for the same without even twenty years behind
us. I won't try to explain this feeling, and all I can say is, before you die
please go and stand among the redwoods. Trust me on this. It's worth it.

While I will not try to describe the essence of the great trees, I did
pencil this in the journal.

IN AWE OF YOU

Majestic tree
Standing proud and high
Feet in the dirt
And head in the sky
What have you felt
Over so many years
What was there more of
Laughter or tears

What was it like
Over a millennium ago
When you were a sapling
With no plan but to grow
Into a beautiful redwood
The largest of your kind
The gentlest of giants
Suspended in time

How many stories
Rest in each of your rings
What would the song be
If suddenly you could sing
Would it be about the sun
Or how the wind blows
Or perhaps the feel of rain
Or a winter's soft snows

And what have you witnessed
With the evolution of man
And his unsustainable desire
To consume all the land
Do you look down upon him
With confusion and dismay
Or do you pay no attention
Simply living for the day

How lucky you are
Standing confident and tall
Many years in front of you
Before you will fall
As I lean up against you
I think how lucky I would be
If in my next life
I could come back as a tree

We spent our days in Humboldt County doing what locals of Humboldt County do. We became locals for a brief time, which was not difficult, as their way of life lined up principally and perfectly with all of our interests. We canoed the Eel River and its South Fork, we hiked, we read, we wrote, we drew, we played guitars, we climbed trees, we walked around trees, and we struggled over trees that had fallen naturally. We laughed at people hugging and chaining themselves to trees so they wouldn't fall unnaturally, and then we tried being the people hugging and chaining ourselves to trees. We met some great locals, and we enjoyed a few evening campfire trips to Tuneupville. Humboldt County is a great place filled with very nice people who in many respects have it all figured out. There is a calm and sense of peace of mind in the county that made me wonder if the trees can somehow permeate peace of mind down into the souls of the people. It's no wonder they don't want the trees to be cut down as the trees provide the natural elements that build the culture for their sanity and well being.

One particular friend we made was a very interesting guy named Clive. He was camping in the bush near where we parked Barth, and he had a very cool little brindle bull dog mix named Oscar. Ozark and Oscar instantly became friends. Oscar was a survivor, and so was Clive, quite literally, as he was a veteran of the Vietnam War and no doubt was one of the guys who had been in the thick of the fight – the real war fighter, deep in the theatre, a young man with no education and no place to go in 1969, an absolutely perfect specimen for the jungle. By looking at him, you could tell he had witnessed and experienced things that no person should ever witness or experience, and at times it made you wonder if surviving the war may have been the worst thing that ever happened to him.

Clive was also a born-again Christian. He was a self-appointed minister with a mobile ministry of one – two including Oscar. He was also trying to walk around North America with a full-size cross that he had rigged up for travel. It had a wheel on the end of the vertical stipes and a piece of shoulder foam in the corner where the horizontal patibulum meets the stipes, and when he was walking down the shoulder of the highway, the cross became a full-size crucifix. We got to know Clive pretty well while Ozark and Oscar played, and we would visit around the campfire and spend our days together. Interestingly, and somewhat surprisingly, Clive was a little down on Canadians.

"What's up with the cross, Clive?" RC asked the first evening we met Clive and Oscar.

"I'm walking around North America," he answered as if this were a common thing for people to be doing.

"Why?" Hats asked, really asking, *Why?* with no other motive but to know why. We were all proud of Hats for being so open minded.

"Because I'm waiting for Jesus to come back down to Earth and take me back to heaven with him," he said. We all thought about this, and Ray was the first to speak.

"Why walk around North America while waiting?" Ray asked, really saying, *This is very interesting and I need to understand more.*

"Because it helps me think straight," Clive responded. "And I get to meet people and share the Word of God."

And so was the way of Clive. He was waiting for the Rapture to finally arrive so he could ascend to the Kingdom of God and leave the rest of the wicked sinners on the Earth for seven years of tribulation and blood, gore and guts, or put another way Earth business as usual, minus all saved Christians of course. He was in Humboldt County having just returned from Washington State and Oregon. His vision and mission of walking around North America was temporarily paused when the Canadians would not let him into the country at a border crossing connecting Washington State and British Columbia.

"Why didn't they let you in?" RC asked, interested both from a Clive and law point of view.

"Because I don't have any formal identification," Clive answered.

"What identification did you show them?" Hats asked.

"My cross," Clive answered in a sincere and *I'm serious that should be enough to prove who I am* voice.

"Oh," Hats responded, still keeping an open mind to the whole dynamic of the story.

And so was the way of Clive. He was walking the perimeter of North America, or at least attempting to. He would eat and sleep in the bush, in churches, and in people's homes. It was amazing to hear his stories of how generous and open minded good people are. "Yes, there are still good people out there, and good people do good things," he would say. I'm sure he met his share of bad people as well, but he did not share those stories.

"How long have you been walking, Clive?" Ray asked.

"Over two years," Clive responded, without pride or discouragement in his voice. It was what it was, a simple statement that was not supposed to draw any judgment, result, conclusion, or action.

Silence

Hats threw a log on the fire, and we all watched the embers explode as we thought about, and pictured, Clive walking for two years.

"What did you do before you started walking?" RC asked.

"You mean in between Vietnam and now? You mean the last dozen or so years?"

"Yes," RC answered.

"I was a heroin addict."

"Ahhh," Hats said as sincerely as he could, but was really saying, *Isn't that a big fucking shocker!*

And so was the way of Clive. He came home from Vietnam with a heroin addiction and lived with it for a decade until he found his way out of the hole. We really enjoyed meeting Clive. Ray and Clive, in particular, had several conversations and spent some time together while RC, Hats, Ozark, Oscar, and I went for a few hikes. I got the sense Clive really liked Ray's theories about the sun, and when we left Humboldt County, Clive was proficient at the blessing that Wi had taught us. On our way out, RC gave Clive his address and phone number back home and told him he would coach him through the requirements to get into Canada should he ever want to give it another shot. RC told Clive a walk through the Canadian Rockies would be good for his soul. Clive stuffed RC's personal coordinates into a small backpack that was bungee-corded to the cross, while Ozark said goodbye to Oscar. Clive and

Oscar were definitely survivors, prospectors who hadn't yet defined their gold, certainly on a mission, and you just don't stop a man and his dog when on a mission.

And so with our work in Humboldt County complete, we put the land of tree wonder in the rear view mirror to the north. We felt good leaving the magnificent trees; somehow they gave us a sense that the summer was only beginning, and we couldn't have been more correct.

In Ray's Voice

THE REDWOODS ARE everything they need to be. They exemplify the greatness that nature itself can accomplish in spite of man's trying to destroy all that is good. When you are among the trees, it becomes self-evident that a Great Spirit does exist and that It wants the Earth to be healthy and happy – all living things on the Earth, including people.

And then there's my friend, Clive. Oh my...my friend, Clive. He is hurting in every way. His body, mind, and soul are searching for nourishment and vitamins that he can't locate on any pharmacy shelf or street corner. His country sent him to war when he may have been old enough to fight physically, but he was not even close to being ready emotionally. He was just a boy in a man's body. He witnessed events that confused his views and his belief system of mankind and the world. Then he actively participated in these same events, and then he actually led the same events. He went from observer to player to coach just like that. He lost all sense of himself, and now his guilt is a bottomless pit of absolute and all-consuming despair.

Heroin was a good friend at first, and then it turned on him, which we know all too well is very typical. Religion picked up where the heroin left off. It was a swap of sorts, cheaper and more practical as well. Then Religion turned on him. This also is typical. What is supposed to be a foundation of love turned into the fear of life eternal in a furnace of fire, fear of an infinite existence in hell, all as a result of mistakes made by a young man following orders handed down by

333

old men. War is nothing more than young men dying in the future as a result of old men living in the past, and now Clive was on his way to becoming middle aged with a dump truck full of fear on top of him. This fear of hell is nothing but more jungle time for Clive, and now he is walking around the perimeter of North America with a full-size cross. Yet no one will stop and nail him to it and put an end to his misery. He does not have a minute of the day when he is not suffering. Even when he sleeps he suffers. Poor Clive.

I had some good quality time with Clive. I learned a lot about him, and I learned a lot from him. He's very transparent both in what he shares with you about himself and what you see without his vocalizing it. Some people wear their hearts on their sleeves. Clive wears his entire being on his entire outfit, and he wants to share everything he can with you because it makes him feel good to talk and to ask questions. His questions are all related to how others see and perceive the world. It's as if he's aware he is broken and continuously tries to benchmark himself against other people. For example, it surprises him when you tell him, No, *I don't feel that way or have those dreams or have ringing in my ears or wonder if I am a bad person who needs to be punished.* When you tell him you don't feel this or that, he simply nods and looks to the ground as if he is adding a note to a mental checklist of bullet points. He is cataloging all the things he should try to stop worrying about because clearly others don't worry about those things.

I asked Clive if I could walk with his cross on my shoulder, to take it for a spin around the park, and he agreed. It was a strange sensation; it was a burden, and it was work. Even though he had attempted to rig it up for comfort and efficiency, it was neither comfortable nor efficient. His foam shoulder template and small wheel did not prove to help much at all, as a cross is simply not designed for long-distance travel. The engineering is all wrong. Form needs to follow function, and a cross has no valid or practical function so proper form is impossible to design. It sure must have been a moment of sick and cruel innovation when the Romans decided a cross was the right design for hanging people up in the air. Mostly, though, the cross reminded me of when we built the tripod to haul the Findley stove to the Lodge. Not easy, lots of work, and clearly a one-way trip.

We talked about his walk and the fact that he is waiting for God to come get him. I told him I believe the sun is God and that It does not intend to leave its perch in the sky anytime soon. I told him the sun wants to nurture him and give him warmth, that the sun does not judge people or believe in the installation of a culture of obedience based on fear of burning in some place called Hell. "Heaven up and Hell down," he said to me. I asked him where he thinks Hell is. He said he didn't know. I told him I didn't get it, that the universe is infinite in space in all directions, and that the universe has no space dimension by virtue of its infinity in all directions.

"So what is up and what is down, where is Heaven and where is Hell?" I asked him. I told him I thought his fear of Hell had landed him in Hell already – the quintessential self-fulfilling prophecy. By fearing that you will end up in Hell when you die, you end up creating Hell on Earth while you are living. He nodded and looked down at the ground and silently added this key point to his mental list of things to ponder.

I told him the sun forgives him and that he should forgive himself. He told me that he did very bad things in Vietnam. I asked him if he is still doing those bad things or whether he still wants to do those bad things. He said, "No." I asked him if he ever did those things or wanted to do those things before he went to war. He said, "No." I asked him if he enjoyed doing those things while he was doing those things. He said, "No." I told him that sometimes good people do bad things, but that does not make you a bad person – that only makes you human. I told him again that the sun forgives him and that when the sun shines warmth upon his face that it is really sending him rays of forgiveness. He looked up at the sun and closed his eyes and let the sun shine on his face, and then he opened his eyes and told me he thought he felt a little better. I told him to keep looking up and not down. He said he would. We got back from our walk and leaned the cross up against a tree.

We had a nice dinner with Clive and Oscar our last evening there. When we went into Barth for the night, Clive had set himself up on a wooden picnic table to sleep. When we drove off in the morning, he and Oscar were still sleeping on the picnic table, and the sun was on the morning pass and was shining on both of them. Clive was sleeping soundly with a smile on his face, and I noticed that during the night the cross had fallen away from the tree it was leaning against and was lying on the ground. It struck me in that moment that the cross was helpless. It was nothing but sticks, and without a narrative from man, it was absolutely devoid of any value or meaning.

Crosses are not built for leaning or standing on their own. Crosses can't get down the road without the power of people as the engine. A cross is nothing but a combination of two pieces of wood, no different than any other tool humans have engineered in their attempt to progress or to punish others.

As we left the county I took solace knowing that Clive will enjoy waking up with the sun on his face. This I am sure of.

USA

Summer 1983

Laguna Seca

SHORTLY AFTER LEAVING northern California, we found a man-made gift for the driving fool. State Route # 1, better known as the Pacific Coast Highway, or PCH, or even better the *All American Road*. We fell in love with the road the minute we got on it. It was love at first mile, and just like any true love, it was beautiful and memorable, filled with optimism, surprises, and challenges, as well as being very twisty, curvy, and very slow going at times. It was a match made in Heaven, and as the saying goes *God makes 'em and God matches 'em*. We got on the highway at its starting point in the north and drove it until it ended in the south, although we did have a few stops along the way, one of which became a central event of the summer.

The PCH All American Road turns into the Golden Gate Bridge at San Francisco. This is a good deal as the Golden Gate Bridge is pure cool. The Pacific Ocean is out to the west and San Francisco Bay is to the east. While we did avoid big cities in general, San Francisco was worth a day of adventure. We took a boat and toured *Alcatraz Island* and the prison. We debated whether Clint Eastwood actually made it to the mainland alive after he escaped, and in the end we all agreed he did

337

because he did, in fact, make more movies after that one. Ray argued the point, and we all agreed the answer was self-evident. We had a few local beers and talked to the seals on the *Fisherman's Wharf at Pier 39*. From there, we rode a cable car up and down the rolling hills of the city and talked about our favorite episodes of Mike and Karl in *The Streets of San Francisco*. We all agreed we liked the episode where they had a car chase and went flying over the concrete hills, only to fly through the air and bang the front hood of the car on the cement when they landed hard in pursuit of the bad guy, which actually was every episode.

After the cable car, we got Ozark out for a walk under the Golden Gate Bridge and then headed Barth out of the city. Ray suggested we drive through the neighborhood of Haight Ashbury just to see what the old hippy scene looked like, so we did this, and it was very cool. It was all things music and peace and love. RC and Ray loved it, while Hats and I appreciated it with a *wish we were real musicians too* envy. When we got to the middle of Haight Ashbury, we came across a small convoy of Volkswagen vans. They were all Boomer look-alikes, many the same vintage as Boomer and some from a generation newer. You can tell the generation by the tail lights. Boomer's generation is a prize to be held in Haight Ashbury – the true microbus, and RC said we should have towed Boomer behind Barth so we could have joined the convoy. The real question, though, was, W*here in the hell is the convoy going anyway?* RC drove Barth up beside the convoy of at least twenty microbuses and he yelled from the driver's window to one of the Boomer vans that had a passenger window open and a passenger in the van. The passenger was a cute little hippie chick, and we all instantly fell in love.

"Where you going?" RC yelled out to our new love.

"Laguna Seca!" the cute hippie chick passenger yelled back.

"Laguna what?" RC yelled back, really saying, *I have no idea what you're saying, but I intend to talk to you for the rest of my life so let's start with understanding what you just said.*

"Laguna Seca. The racetrack outside of Monterrey," the cute passenger yelled back.

"You're going to see car races?" RC volleyed back a yell.

"No, Dude, we're going to see the *Dead*!"

RC paused for a minute while his brain processed this, and he looked across at Ray. They had a moment of surprise mixed with absolute clarity. Then RC replied to the groovy chick, "The Grateful Dead?" really saying, *Are you kidding me, girl? Are you telling me the Dead are playing within spitting distance of where the Beaver Brothers, Ozark, and Barth are right now, girl? Tell me right now if you are kidding me, girl, because this kinda shit ain't funny if you're kidding us, girl?*

"Ya, Dude, the Grateful Dead," the cute hippie chick yelled back to RC. "You want to join in the convoy with your extra-large cool microbus and follow us into the scene, Dude?"

RC did not remotely take his eye off the passenger nor did he look across at Ray or back at Hats or Ozark or me for a meeting of the minds or even to fake an act of group consensus. "Yes, Dudess!" was all he said back, and then we let several Boomer vans go by us so we could pull up behind to be the caboose of the convoy. Hats remembered his speech from elementary school and yelled out, "Looks like we got ourselves a convoy!" Barth made a great caboose to a great convoy, and we started heading west and went through Monterey, California, and all its beauty. Then we headed towards Laguna Seca, the race track converted into a rock stage for the Dead. The Grateful Dead – one of our favorite bands and certainly a scene and experience we would no doubt embrace with all our fiber. The universe was still working in our favor.

The traffic started building as we got closer. It was stop and go for a while so we spent the time meeting new friends while hanging our heads out the windows of Barth. None of the Beaver Brothers was at *Woodstock*, but we imagined this was what it had been like. We eventually got into the grounds of the racetrack, and the gravity of our score hit us like a ton of bricks. We were in the epicenter and nucleus of all things hippy – all things peace and love and music and wild people and cool clothes and multiple colors and strange sounds and weird smells. It was the counterculture of the 1960s reborn and making a clear and pointed statement that it was not gone, but rather was alive and well – at least for a few days anyway.

We got Barth parked on what would normally be a racetrack, and we started to size up the scene. There was a stadium set up by the race track with temporary fencing used to keep people in and out. To get to the stage, you had to go through the fence and over a big grass hill and then down into the valley on the other side. This was where the Dead would eventually play three shows over three days. On the racetrack were thousands of cars parked for the day. You could not stay in these spots overnight, and this is where we were, and to be more precise, we were on racetrack curve number five. On the outside of the track close to the starting line was an area where people were parked and set up for camping for the long weekend. That was where we needed to be. The problem, though, was that it was fenced off, and when we inquired about how to get in we were told that no spaces were left and that the camping area was full and closed off. This was not good news, but we didn't let it get us down, even though it was late in the day and the sun was heading away, and we knew we would need to leave at some point. Notwithstanding all this, we just hung out and took in the vibe until luck came upon us.

We were sitting in front of Barth with our lawn chairs having a few cold beverages when a cool guy came up to us and asked about Barth. He loved Ozark too, and we chatted for a while and learned that he had a Barth as well and that he was there in his. He then told us to get in our Barth and follow him to see his Barth, so we did, and when we got there we learned that it was being used as a barricade to block off a ten-foot unfenced entrance into the campground area. He was a Barth fence. He told us to park our Barth in front of his in a configuration, so we formed a "T" with the front end of our Barth almost touching the broad side of his. He then told us to stay alert in our Barth and act quickly if we saw movement of his Barth. With those instructions, he then got behind the wheel and backed up about nine feet, making a gap in the Barth wall that he had been creating for the concert organizers. RC seized the moment and started easing our Barth through the gateway to all things hip. Just as we thought we had squeezed through the tight spot, Barth's bumper caught the fence post on our left and hooked onto it. RC had no intention of not getting into the campground area, so he just kept going and our bumper was barely hanging on in back by the time we cleared the hole. Once our new friend saw we were through, he moved his Barth forward and closed the virtual wall once again. We were in. We were totally in.

"Thanks, man!" RC yelled back at our new Barth friend.

"Groovy, Dudes!" he yelled back.

We drove around for a couple a minutes and found a great place to park in what would serve as our home base for the next few passes of the sun. We parked and got out of Barth and went to the back to assess the damage to the bumper. The minute all four of us and Ozark were lined up staring down at the bumper, it released itself from its hinges and fell to the ground with a thud. We all looked at each other and shrugged our shoulders. Ray and RC picked the bumper up and threw it on top of Barth with the canoes.

"Let's go get groovy, boys," Ray said to all of us.

"Fucking far out groovy, Dudes!" Hats yelled back, and we all did a high five.

And groovy we did. Groovy we were. It was just plain groovy, man.

USA
Summer 1983

Dancing Bears

THE DAYS AT LAGUNA SECA were an absolute trip in and of themselves, as we were transformed into neo-pseudo hippies within one minute of getting Barth behind the barricade. It's hard to explain exactly what happened, or what didn't happen, or what might have happened, or what we think might have happened. Some things just need to be experienced, or thought to have been experienced. What I can tell you with almost certainty is that I don't believe we slept the entire time we were there. It was an absolute blast, an absolute blast from the past, experienced in the present, to be taken into the future as some memorable event comprised of nothing but fuzzy yet crystal clear memories. You simply had to be there, and we were there.

Been there, done that, tie-dyed the t-shirt.

Ray looked the coolest with his long hair and ponytail and his Dream Catcher earring. It was perfect. Hats and I both had long enough hair to have a pretty cool ponytail that was around five inches long. RC was a total hoot. He took his RCMP police-officer-short haircut, found about an inch of hair at the back of his head, and had Ray put an elastic band around it to form a ponytail of sorts. It was hilarious. The

341

elastic band actually showed more than the hair sticking out. Ozark had her bandana on and she roamed the grounds freely the entire time we were there. We all roamed. I learned that not all those that roam are lost. We sure didn't feel lost anyway. Everything made complete and utter sense, and clarity took on a whole new meaning where sounds, sights, and smells had never been so pronounced. Everything else in the world seemed like complete and utter nonsense, and peace of mind seemed closer than ever in the wake of Tuneupville being transformed into Groovyville.

The days were spent either doing things or watching things being done. Even though it was hard on our cash, we spent the money and went to watch the Dead play the first afternoon. It was a great show. It's just one big long jam session where you have no idea what song will play next. There are no expectations for the hits to be played as the Dead never really made any hits. They say that if you can actually name songs written or played by the Dead, then you are not really a Dead Head. True Dead Heads couldn't name a song title if their bags of dope depended on it, and this fact is a compliment, not a criticism. The Grateful Dead's music is similar to pornography in that you cannot define it, but you know it when you hear it. The concert was great. We sat on the grass on a hillside overlooking the stage down below in the valley. Ozark didn't follow us into the concert area, but she found us on one of her trips around the grounds. She was one crazy groovy dog that weekend, a total free spirit, and when she found us at the concert she had a new bandana on. Somewhere in her travels she had made a friend and done a deal and swapped out her red, white, and blue for a very hip multi-neon-colored tie-dyed bandana. Ozark was in an element that only she understood.

For the most part, we simply parked our groovy asses in our lawn chairs and listened to the music from right outside the fence area that kept the non-ticketed people out of the main concert area. Lawn chairs and our OV cooler were all we needed during the day, and although we couldn't see the band, we could hear the beat and sounds of the music coming from the stage area. Instead of watching the band, we watched an all-inclusive and very tuned-up and tuned-out world. Shakespeare said, "All the world is a stage," and this was a stage of all the world. The actors were quite the cast, quite the cast indeed; a motley crew would be an understatement. This was worth any price of admission, and the price for us was free.

To the left of the stage area was a forested area that surrounded the racetrack to the north. For the entire Grateful Dead weekend, the US Army was doing training maneuvers of some sort and using the forest as a training ground. It was a dichotomy forming a paradox to say the least. We would sit in our lawn chairs being as groovy and as far out as possible and watch fully uniformed and armed soldiers slinking through the trees as if they were on patrol in a foreign jungle. Oddly enough, we did not see any Dead Heads mistakenly lose their way into the forest. Hats suggested we go ask the soldiers if we could join in on a game of capture the flag, but he couldn't find a buddy in RC, Ray, or me for the idea, so he tabled it without too much resistance. Road Trip Guiding Principles were in play, even in groovy land.

Right in front of us was the entrance to the hill that you needed to go over in order to watch the band. Only ticketed people could get behind the makeshift temporary fence that had been put up for the weekend. The fencing was the snow type fencing we see at home that arrived in rolls of red wooden slats, and they unrolled the fence and stretched it out and attached it to steel poles that had been pounded into the ground about eight feet apart. The purpose of the fence was to make sure only people with tickets actually got in to see the Dead play, and while you did need a ticket, this did not seem to deter some people from trying to go in without one. In other words, people would simply crash the fence. It was the most unusual and trippy thing to watch, and we watched it happen several times over the course of our hippie weekend. It came in waves about thirty minutes apart. It would start right after the band started in the afternoon when most ticketed fans were inside the grounds behind the fence. Security would be set up at the entrance and standing around the perimeter of the temporary fence, which was maybe a quarter of a mile long, with security people at about 20-foot intervals.

It would start with two hipsters coming together to form a team. The two would then start walking in a circle on the outside of the fence line with maybe twenty feet between the outside ring of their circle and the fence. As they walked their circle, more people would join them. They would do this for about twenty minutes, after which time they would have close to a hundred people going around. The security guys would watch the circle mob develop and would start to accumulate their own numbers on their side of the fence. At some point there would be a trigger of some kind, and the mob would break the circle and head towards the fence at a full run. The mob would jump over and through the fence, knocking the flimsy material down, and start running up the hill towards the band playing on the other side. Meanwhile, the fifty or so unarmed dime-a-time security officers would try to tackle the Dead Heads on their way up the hill. Some of the tougher security guys could tackle two or three stampeders on a good round. Once they were tackled, the marauding Dead Heads would walk back down the hill and outside the non-ticketed perimeter. It was as if there were an unwritten code of ethics that if you got tackled you had to go back to the starting line. This gave the security guys a fighting chance because they were well outnumbered, and even with these strict rules of engagement, at least ten or fifteen non-ticketed citizens of the Dead community would get into the show per wave of fence crashing. After the running of the Dead Heads ended, there would be peace for about ten minutes while the fence got resituated and until two people formed a new team and started walking in a circle. It was obvious to us that this whole process was clearly part of the Dead Head ecosystem.

Of course Hats wanted to join in on the game. "Come on, guys," he said. "It's a fucking combination of *Ring Around the Rosy* and *British Bulldog,* man! We learned this in kindergarten, lads! We got this, you bunch of groovy Dudes!"

RC and I were glued to our chairs. I don't think we could have stood up even if we had wanted to, let alone, stand up, run, and crash a fence. All the stimulation we needed was right in front of us; sometimes it's OK to be in the audience. You don't always have to be on stage as being on stage all the time can be exhausting. Many people have a curse because they feel they need to be center stage all the time. Taking a deep breath from the cheap seats in life can be a good thing, and that's what RC and I decided to do. Ray, on the other hand, decided to join Hats in his quest. I think he felt we had been shooting down all of Hats' recent ideas, which of course we had been, but in our defense, his recent ideas had clearly been unsafe and unwise. Nonetheless, Ray joined Hats in the game of Hippie British Bulldog. Good friends support each other's ideas even when there is undoubtedly a high probability of going completely and utterly sideways. Let's face it, life is about taking chances, life is about risk, so to sign up for friendship is to sign up for decisions that may have seemed like a good idea at the time.

Hats and Ray became a group of two to start a new circle. This was their first, but not last mistake. They had no local knowledge or inside information on their new sport, and this proved to be a bad move as you simply need to spend some time understanding a game before you try to lead it. Hats and Ray started the circle, and it did not take them long to get a good-size team going around with them. RC and I watched them walk in circles, and then looked at each other, wondering how it was going to end. Ozark sat quietly beside us and took in the spectacle as well.

Then the unknown trigger happened, and the group headed for the fence, including Ray and Hats. This was their second and last mistake. What the groovy Beaver Brothers didn't realize was that the security guys focus on the two hipster Dudes that start the initial circle. By focusing on them, I mean six or seven of the biggest security guys go after the two ring leaders. In this case, it was Hats and Ray. It's part of the rules of engagement. It's principle; a principle we had missed from our lawn-chair observations. So the minute Hats and Ray ran over the fence that was knocked down by runners in front of them they, in fact, got knocked down. Really hard, I might add. Ray was tackled immediately and landed on the fence that was lying on the ground. He hadn't made it anywhere. Hats made it about five feet over the fence line and was torn apart by four security guys who were clearly linebackers from some division-one university. They tackled him very professionally, and he literally flew head over heels and landed on his back. RC and I watched the whole thing in complete awe, and we were very proud of them when they came back and joined us in our lawn chairs. Hats was pissed and wanted to go again, assuming he had been screwed over by somebody or something, although he could not articulate exactly who or what had screwed him over. Ray declined the offer to run the fence again, so Hats stewed for a while and then moved on. Eyes forward was the theme of the weekend, with no regrets. Ozark licked Hats' face telling him he had given it a solid college try.

To the right of our lawn chair hangout was another very interesting activity. On a knoll in a field area were at least fifty people flying kites – real kites, not the kind bought in the grocery store. These were practically flying machines that the Wright Brothers would have been proud of. Some of them were almost glider size and required up to three light rope connections from the kite to the kite captain on the ground. All four of us were mesmerized, watching the kites ebb and flow with the wind currents. Ray and I both took our lawn chairs over to the knoll area and sat under the kites, where we met four very cool and cute kite Dudesses who let us fly their kites. RC and Hats saw what was going on and came to join us. Even though we had no aeronautical experience or knowledge, we were able to keep the kites in the air. Our new friends were good teachers and coaches.

Some people say that life is like a roller coaster ride, but I don't agree. I learned that day that life is more like kite flying. A roller coaster is a fixed structure, man-made, where all variables have been taken into consideration. The track is set and when you get on, you expect to get off safely, precisely because it has been engineered to have a happy ending. You can see and forecast the ups and downs, and you prepare yourself for what will happen next based on this visibility of the entire ride. You don't really enjoy the up as it's just what you need to do to get to the down ride, and the down is when you shriek with excitement and get the rush of the ride. When the ride is over you run around to the back of the line in an effort to get back on and do it again. This is not what life is like at all, at least not life for the Beaver Brothers. Life is more like flying a kite.

There is nothing predictable or stable about kite flying. If the conditions are not correct, you don't even get a chance to fly, and when the kite is in the sky, you never know what will happen next. Nature and circumstance have a vote in the outcome as one minute you are riding the wind up, and the next minute you are crashing toward the ground at full speed. You feel as if all is lost, and you try tightening the rope between you and the kite. Right at the last minute a small gust of benevolent turbulence comes to the rescue, and the next thing you know, you are on your way up faster than ever before. There is no track, no directional assurance, and no promise of a happy or safe ending. The ups and downs are equally invigorating but in such different ways as you don't know how long each up or down will last. So you attempt to prepare for a change in momentum at any time, then realize it's so unpredictable that you can't prepare at all, and you decide just to let it all happen. You go with the flow. Sometimes the kite just hovers in one place as if it's waiting for an external cue or trying to decide where to go next. Every movement or non-movement of the kite is a learning experience, and every time it takes on a crusade or maneuver you don't expect, you marvel and are bewildered all at the same time. You can feel alive with excitement and then absolutely terrified in an instant of change, and if the kite does come crashing to the ground, you just stare at in silence for a few minutes. Then you run up to see if it's OK. Did it survive the crash? Will it fly again? Should I fly it again even if it is able too? What if I crash again? What a ride! Life is no roller coaster experience. Life is a kite-flying experience.

We had a lot of fun flying the kites with our new groovy chick friends. We became close that weekend and coupled up and all sort of fell in love in a groovy way. It was our version of the summer or weekend of 1969 – our weekend of love. They were very cool Dudesses. They were smart, funny, confident, and cute as anything. Another thing about our groovy hippie chicks is that they could sing, which did not surprise us at all. It only supported that there was no such thing as coincidences any longer. Listening to our new friends sing was a big part of how we spent our nights during our stay at Laguna Seca.

USA

Summer 1983

Sam Comes Alive

SUMMER NIGHTS in California are pretty amazing, especially during a long weekend of the Grateful Dead. There is a world that exists at night that most people never experience, where subcultures and ecosystems exist, only coming alive at night. I suspect there is a reason why vampires and werewolves prefer night over day as there's a lot going on at night, and what is going on can be very, very interesting. Such was the case at Laguna Seca. What made it even more fun was that the Beaver Brothers' Barth became town central for the Dead Head night culture, although it all started very innocently.

After meeting our cute hippie chick Beaver Sisters, we invited them over to Barth for happy hour, which turned into dinner. After dinner and after dark, we got a great campfire going and sat around it, which led us to look up at the sky to marvel over the natural light show created by the stars dancing in the sky. At some point, the Dudesses started singing, and, completely appropriate to the circumstance, they had voices handed down from the angels. They started with *Twinkle Twinkle Little Star*, and it didn't take long for us to start singing the song in a *round*, with each of us starting a new round on the first *Little*

Star in the first line of the song. We only sang the first two verses, but that was enough to make us feel as if the entire world was fine and that Peace on Earth was achievable.

> *Twinkle, twinkle, little star,*
> *How I wonder what you are.*
> *Up above the world so high,*
> *Like a diamond in the sky.*
>
> *When the blazing Sun is gone,*
> *When He nothing shines upon,*
> *Then you show your little light,*
> *Twinkle, twinkle, all the night.*

Ray and RC grabbed their guitars from Barth and added the sounds of their strumming to the mix. Eventually other people found their way to our campfire and joined in on the fun and song. Every night that weekend was a clear black sky, and the stars were twinkling like diamonds. This just added to the brilliance of the moment. Ray really loved it. We all loved it. We were singing about the stars while watching a natural light show in the sky created by the sun's shining on the other side of the Earth.

After we finished singing as a group, Ray and RC started singing, and our hippie chicks and others joined in as well. That first night of music set the precedent for incredible and amazing weekend jam sessions. The boys played *The Weight, Ripple, Southern Cross, Blowing in the Wind*, and other songs that send shivers up and down your spine. Our Dudesses knew all the words and took the songs to harmony heights that had never been heard before, proving that the human being is capable of amazing and beautiful things when we choose to sing in harmony.

At some point that first night, Hats yelled across the fire at me, "Hey Sam, you wouldn't by any chance have a story you could tell us would you?" Well, I don't need to be asked twice, and before I knew it I was on my feet and reciting the poem of all poems. I was on stage – Sam on stage telling his story about Sam McGee.

"*There are strange things done, in the Midnight Sun,*" I started, and every person around the campfire started listening to me with undivided attention. They had obviously never heard the poem before, but they seemed very eager to hear a new tale, especially the tale of all tales. But here's where it got interesting. Ray decided that my simply reciting the poem was not going to be enough, that I needed a little visual support – a little improv acting to tell the story. So with that notion, Ray got up and walked around and stood behind me and put his hands above his head to form a big circle with his arms and fingers. He was the sun. He was the Midnight Sun. Oh man, it was so perfect. I just continued on with the poem and acted as if this were absolutely normal and all part of the Canadian Beaver Brothers Variety Show.

"*By the men who moil for gold,*" I continued, and Ray reached down and acted as if he were panning gold from a river stream. He would make the swooping down motion and then come up with his hands and his invisible pan. Then he would peer inside the pan, looking very hopeful that he would find gold, but his face would show absolute disappointment as he let the crowd know there was no gold in his pan. The audience of Dead Heads all gave him a look of sadness and consolation, and then they looked back at me to continue the tale of all tales.

"*The Arctic trails have their secret tales, that would make your blood run cold,*" I went on, and Ray started shaking his body as if he were shivering from the cold. He wasn't missing a beat. He had heard the poem so many times over the course of our lifetime that he knew it as well as I did, and he had the parts down pat. I carried on and tried not to look at Ray during his Hollywood Oscar-worthy performance. The group around the campfire was mesmerized, leaving no doubt that we had a captive audience.

"*The northern lights have seen queer sights, but the queerest they ever did see,*" I recited, and Ray grabbed a flashlight that was on our picnic table and started waving it in the air. It was the strangest of strange scenes. Somehow he actually conveyed the look of northern lights and queer sights, and I will readily admit that I have no idea what that even means.

"*Was that night on the marge of Lake Lebarge, I cremated Sam McGee.*" Well, with the ending of the opening stanza, Hats got up and joined Ray. Hats had decided that he was going to play the part of Sam McGee, and with that new entrance to the play, RC got up and assumed the role of Sam's mining partner, the poor soul who is cursed with the *promise made and the debt unpaid,* Sam's McGee's buddy, the nameless, faceless poem narrator who had to trek with Sam's McGee's frozen stiff corpse looking for a place to cremate his last remains.

The show went on. I continued to recite the poem of poems, and the boys continued to act out the story. Ray remained the Midnight Sun at all times but used shaking and pounding of his feet and the twirling of his arms and shoulders to exemplify who the hell knows what else in the poem. Hats, playing Sam McGee, sat in a lawn chair that we all presumed was the *sleigh that he was lashed to*. Ozark sat in front of Hats as the lead sled dog, while RC took up position behind Hats and acted as if he were laboring to push the sleigh through the heavy snow, showing clearly that the *trail was bad and he felt half mad*. It was, to say the very least, quite the show, and it did not end there.

Our new friends, our groovy, cool, far-out Dudess Beaver Sisters did not sit on the sidelines. They got up and joined the act, and even though they did not know the poem or the story, it didn't matter. It only resulted in a small delay between the verse of the poem and the corresponding action to support the verse. They would listen carefully to the words and then create a supporting gesture, and before we knew it, the girls were acting out images of mountains, frozen streams, huskies in a ring, and other images of all things Yukon and Gold Rush-related. Meanwhile, Ray, RC, and Hats all played the leading roles of the Midnight Sun, Sam McGee, and Sam's Promise Pal. Ozark excelled as the lead sled dog pulling Sam on his sleigh. We acted out the whole poem, and when we got to the end Hats decided to go for an Oscar performance.

"*And there sat Sam, looking cool and calm, in the heart of the furnace roar,*" I went on in my narration and Hats decided that as Sam, he really should be in the heart of the furnace roar, so he got up from his lawn chair makeshift sleigh and he walked over to the campfire and stood beside it and crouched down as if he were sitting in the fire.

"*And he wore a smile you could see a mile,*" I went on in my poem, and just as I was going to have my big finale, Hats decided to act out his own lines. He yelled out, "*Please close the door. It's fine in here, but I greatly fear, you'll let in the cold and storm. Since I left Plumtree, down in Tennessee, it's the first time I've been warm.*" Of course he made it his own version by adding an 'F' Bomb between *been and warm* in the last two words. He still wasn't through though, and just as he finished his lines his ass got so hot from the fire that he jumped ten feet in the air while letting out a scream that scared the hell out of every person who had congregated around Barth for the show. This included RC, Ray, Ozark, and me. We didn't know what had happened and thought it was all part of the act. It was a stellar performance.

And so this became the nightly routine during our stay at Laguna

Seca – Happy hour, dinner, Twinkle Twinkle Little Star, guitars, music, and a full production of Sam McGee. This routine was added to our daily routine of Army watching, fence stampeding and kite flying. What a time it was, but eventually it was time to go. We were one of the last groups of people to leave as verified by the fact that when we got Barth loaded up there were race cars going around the track. The field of grooviness had transformed itself into something very different within a few hours, and it was a lonely feeing. The energy was not the same; the people were not the same, it was still the same piece of ground, but it was a very different place. I guess something is only something for the time that it is that something, and then it becomes something else. This can produce a very lonely feeling when the something you wanted to remain is something that is now gone.

Saying goodbye to the groovy chicks was sad. What an amazing time we had had together, but we had to move on. They were going to follow the Dead to their next show in Oregon, and we were headed to Tijuana, Mexico. Oddly enough, we never kept in touch. In fact, I don't think we even traded addresses or phone numbers. It was as if our time together was supposed to be perfect, but finite, and that's exactly what it was. I guess maybe all relationships form and complete a full circle in the end, and some circles are supposed to be smaller than others. We didn't want to ruin that.

I often wonder where they are now. I hope they're happy and still flying their kites. I hope every once in a while they read the poem of poems and think of Ray standing up with his hands in a circle as he played the role of the Midnight Sun. I hope they're still singing to the twinkling stars in the sky.

I hope life has treated them well.

As we left Laguna Seca and headed back towards the Pacific Coast Highway I scratched a poem into the journal.

THE SKULL AND THE ROSE

The skull and the rose
An odd match I suppose
Cute little dancing bears
It's quite a strange trip
I really must admit
To be fuzzy yet so aware

The music and the sun
Our minds fast on the run
A north wind sails a kite
A gross lack of sleep
The basics seem so deep
And everything feels so right

We zoom and we peak
With color trails complete
Never worried about the cost
We walk, talk, and ponder
That not all those who wander
Are even remotely sad or lost

Ever grateful for our stay
The Dead had their day
It's time to head out to sea
Say good bye to new friends
All good things come to an end
I sure hope they stop following me

DAY 18
South Carolina

Tangled Up in Blue

TODAY IS A BLUE DAY. Sorry for adding complexity, but I had to develop a new day because I'm not green, but I'm not yellow or red either. I'm not angry or feeling anxiety, but I'm sure not feeling strong. It's more of a feeling of confusion and exhaustion; my brain simply won't slow down in its quest to generate thoughts – it's rapid-fire thought production, yet the thoughts are not always connected. It's as if my brain is a factory that produces thoughts, and the measurement system for success is thoughts per second, and there are no lunch breaks or shift changes. My brain is being paid by piece work and it's trying to maximize its daily paycheck, but quality of product does not seem to be part of the equation. It's a quantity game with no focus on quality. My brain is pumping out thoughts as quickly as it can, and it doesn't care whether the thoughts are helpful or logical in any way. It's all part of the survival mechanisms that are inherently part of a person's physical soul, where the brain feels it must constantly be scanning the environment for possible threats. It's as if my brain feels that as long as it is producing thoughts all will be OK. Good lord, I'd hate to be a brain, and I'd really hate to be my brain.

354

I'm feeling as if I'm so many different people these days. My conversations with Doc are one person, my conversations with Alec are another, my conversations or lack of conversations with RC, Hats, Ray, Sophie, and George are another person. I feel as if I should call the Judge but can't seem to pick up the phone. He's an old man in his nineties now, and he deserves a call from me.

My conversations with myself are another and another and another person. The private self is the hardest person to get to know, and no doubt there are other people inside me that I don't even know yet. I've decided it's hard being me. I wonder if all people find it this hard to be themselves. Could it be true that all people are suffering within their own skin? Yesterday I went for a walk on the beach but headed home after thirty minutes because I determined I had spent enough time with myself. The visit with myself was over. How do you reconcile that?

None of us is just one person. Instead, we are a hundred people at the same time, and the brain attempts to manage it all and has to work overtime to try to keep it straight. And then at times, it doesn't keep up and produces poor quality thoughts. When it produces poor quality thoughts it tries to compensate by producing at higher rates. It's as if the brain thinks it can get quality thoughts back on track by working harder and spitting out more orders. The brain continues to believe that economies of scale will produce quality. I'm so glad I'm not my brain. Just think of all the people it needs to keep tabs on.

First, there is the person I know I am and that everybody else knows I am; the public self, the transparent and obvious self. Then there's the person that I know I am that nobody else knows I am – the private and secret self. Then there's the person that others know I am that I don't know I am – the blind and ignorant self. And then lastly, there is the person that nobody else knows and that I don't even know yet – the future and potential self. And the brain is producing thoughts for all these people at lightning speed as it tries its best to keep it all straight. It's no wonder we are exhausted.

"Who is this thinking right now?" the brain has to continually ask itself. The brain is doing its own scanning and cataloging about what it needs to produce in thoughts. It's the management of the production schedule where tier-two secondary thoughts are required to produce tier-one primary thoughts, and I'm the customer for the output of this production process. It's no wonder entire religions and philosophies and *isms* have been created just to try to calm the brain down and get it to shut off for only a few seconds. It's no wonder so much addiction

356 DRIFT *and* HUM

exists as people just need the thought factory to shut down, and some drugs are very helpful with this. Too bad we couldn't outsource our brain functions to China and Vietnam as we have with all our other factories.

It's ironic that a Blue day is good for me. I truly believe it's a color on the road to recovery, and it's allowing me to be aware and enlightened as to what my brain is doing. I'm getting a handle on the tricks it's playing on me. For instance, I now know that my brain is not necessarily producing thoughts that are helpful from a big-picture point of view. There is a good chance my brain is not on my side all the time. In fact, at times, my own brain may very well be playing for the team on the other side of the red line. Maybe my brain is trying to score on my own net! How messed up is that!

It must be the hitchhiker, the ugly hitchhiker, the no-good hitchhiker, I curse the hitchhiker. But here's the secret. I have him figured out now, and I'm starting to use him to my own advantage. *Sure, man, hop in, Dude, do your thing, buddy, and watch what I do with it to turn it back on you, brother. You're not my friend so let's not pretend you are. I can see you now, pal!*

I figured out one of the hitchhiker's biggest feats. He's stopped me from growing up emotionally. My ability to think did not mature with each of my birthdays. Yes, I'm fifty years old, but my thoughts are largely those of a teenager. It's an odd situation when I look at fifty-year-old people: they seem old to me. I call them sir and ma'am. Respect your elders, right? I don't see myself as the same age. Even when I look in the mirror I see a teenager and not a man, but I know I look fifty to the outside world. My body matured through the years, but my brain did not mature at an equal pace. It stopped at some point in time. The hitchhiker put the brain-maturing button on pause, and I now wonder what exact day, many years ago, was the pause button actually pressed.

Some people think that feeling young at heart is a good thing. Perhaps it is, but being young at brain is different, and this is not a good thing. What is the point of living a long life if one does not seek and gain some wisdom along the way? What is the point of a life where you continue to make the same mistakes over and over? Is life not about learning lessons along the way and then in the end saying, "*I lived a good life. I learned a lot and became wise!*" The brain needs to mature in order for this to happen. We need to press *play* on the *mature machine* if the hitchhiker has somehow pressed *pause* at some point without our knowledge. A mature machine on pause allows the hitchhiker to play his music instead, where his favorite songs are played while we are in brain mature pause mode. And when in pause mode, he plays the rearview mirror like a finely tuned instrument. It's the hitchhiker's symphony of dissonance.

Yes, he plays the rearview mirror as a finely tuned and destructive instrument. *It's all right there,* the mirror will tell you. *It makes perfect sense* it will scream out. And your teenage brain in your fifty-year-old body will start to listen and actually start to believe the rhetoric. It's classic stuff like,

- Maybe I'm not cut out for marriage. And let's face it, marriage is not natural anyway, and being single again would be perfect!
- My kids will be fine with a broken home. Hell, my parents divorced and I turned out perfect!
- I was so in love back then and the partying and sex were so much better. If only I could go back and start up that relationship again, it would be perfect!
- Maybe I should just get in my Barth and tour the country just like the good ole days. I'll grow my hair long again, and it will be perfect!
- This working for a living is too conforming. Maybe I'll go open up a bar in Mexico, because that would be perfect!

What a barrel of lies and rationalizations. This is the hitchhiker trying to stay in control. The hitchhiker convinces us that the past holds the seeds for the future, when the only seeds the past holds are the seeds of wisdom. Take the lessons learned from the past, but eyes forward. No regrets...*Eat tree, Beaver!* There is nothing wise about a fifty-year-old man acting like an eighteen-year-old boy. To be sophomoric is to be a dumbass.

I've realized I cannot find peace of mind when I have the mind of a teenager in a fifty-year-old body. I need to get my brain and thoughts to be in sync and on a maturity par with my body. I need consonance in my symphony. My brain and the thoughts it produces need to be partners instead of working at cross purposes. I need to tell myself that *I'm fifty years old and I have experienced a lot and I know a lot and I'm going to use all of that wisdom to create an amazing life for my family and myself, and it will be perfect. This is what is important!*

I ended my day working on a song for Ray, or more of a poem. Either way, I think he will get a kick out of it.

MY BRAIN AND ME

I decided today
I need to find a way
To get control of my brain
It's got a mind of its own
Producing thoughts that are unknown
Until It decides to raise the cane

It loves living in the past
Enjoying the present never lasts
I question whether It's even my friend
It likes to focus on the bad
It's happy when I'm sad
It paints the future as a short dead end

I think I must have missed a meeting
Where my brain did some cheating
To get a new strategy passed
Where only It gets to decide
What thoughts will survive
And what images and feelings will last

It's a confusing situation
Worthy of pause and contemplation
To think your brain is separate from you
If this is the case
Which is a stretch to embrace
Then who is deciding what we do?

Like when It prefers to fixate
On something to hate
Instead of seeing the good
Or when you go through
With something you don't want to do
As opposed to doing what you should

It really can be a drain
Living with my brain
At times it's hard to be me
I'd really like to know
Who's actually the commander of the show
So my thoughts can finally be free

USA/Mexico

Summer 1983

Hey, Senorita

IT WAS NOT HARD to get back onto the Pacific Coast Highway, and we followed it south whenever possible, which was most of the time. Beach towns on the Pacific Ocean are very cool. The whole surfing vibe is a cool vibe. Let's catch some curls, Dude! Cool.

We were ready to drive, and relatively speaking Tijuana was a short drive. We did take a quick shot into Los Angeles, but oddly enough we did not stop, park, or even get out of Barth. It wasn't really our scene. The famous streets were neat to drive down and the big *Hollywood* sign on the hill was OK, but really the whole place felt somewhat pretentious and contrived. It felt like money and phony ruled the roost. I suspect in another time and place this might have been fun, but we were just coming off of an experience that was the exact opposite of what downtown LA was offering. I guess it's safe to say we were biased. Most important, though, is that LA was not a key destination on our BOP so we kept moving – guiding principles at play. Tijuana, Mexico, was the next stop.

We got south of San Diego and within a few miles of the US–Mexico border just before sunset. We went to the coast for the evening passing

359

of the sun, and it was exactly what it should be. It was spiritual as the Earth curved around the sun, and the sun appeared to be dipping into the ocean abyss. Ray just looked at us with his *See what I'm telling ya?* smile. Ray was onto something, and he had believers in his fellow brothers, Ozark included. We parked Barth in a parking lot at a public beach and sat in the beach sand and watched the sunset in the West. I suspect we would all be much happier if that's how we ended our days every day.

We moved on from the beach and parked and slept that night in a shopping mall parking lot close to the border. We hatched our plan for the next day as a team, and we were aligned that we did not want to drive Barth into Mexico. No offense to Mexico, but we just did not feel comfortable that it would turn out so well. In hindsight, I think this was a sign of the Beaver Brothers actually showing some ability to make a good decision. We also knew that on the other side of the border was Mexican tequila. That may have influenced our decision to be without Barth as well, so the plan was to walk over the border as pedestrians and take a Mexican taxi from the border station into the town center of Tijuana. The only problem with the plan was that Ozark could not come with us, so we needed to set her up for the day.

The sun and weather were working with us the next morning and allowed our Ozark plan to be executed. We parked Barth under a shaded tree by the border in a public parking lot and opened all Barth's windows to allow air to breeze through the inside of the vehicle. It was actually a reasonably cool summer day on the west coast, which helped immensely. We also left a small air conditioning unit on that was powered by our generator, although we argued about leaving the windows open with air conditioning going. In the end we agreed that windows wide open was the safest plan in the event the generator failed. We left Ozark lots of water, and Hats actually soaked down a t-shirt in a pail of water and put it on her so her front paws were in the sleeves and the rest of the t-shirt was over her body. She looked absolutely ridiculous, and when she objected, Hats argued that it would keep her core body temperature cool. He was in one of his moods so nobody argued any further, including Ozark. When we arrived back to Barth before suppertime that evening, Ozark was fine, cool to the touch, and very, very happy to see us. She was also not wearing the t-shirt, which actually had been torn to shreds. *Good girl, Ozark. Bad Hats.*

Getting over the border and into Mexico as pedestrians was easy. The Mexico–USA border is designed to keep people in Mexico, not out, so visitors with money to spend are welcome. We got over the border without incident and got into a cab that barely ran but was enough to get us to the downtown area of Tijuana. The cab driver asked us in broken English what were we looking for, and Hats replied, "Tequila and a new hat!" The cab driver said he knew just the place for the first item and that hats were available everywhere. He dropped us off at a very neat, rustic and non-touristy cantina. It was around ten o'clock in the morning and the place wasn't full, but it sure wasn't empty either. Likeminded people were already at it, and when we scanned the establishment we recognized that most of the patrons were Mexican locals. We were at the Tijuana Maple Tree Hotel Cantina.

"Perfect," Hats said as we sat down at a table and waited for service.

"Si, Senor," RC replied.

A very pretty senorita who was maybe twenty-five years old came over to us and asked us what we wanted. She had the most amazing look and beautiful accent. All four of us instantly fell in love.

"Margaritas!" Hats replied very confidently. Unlike in many parts of the USA, we were not asked to show our IDs.

"What type of tequila, Senor?" she replied in her Spanish–Mexican voice that made us fall even deeper in love.

"Well, I'm not sure," Hats replied. "How much is the cheap stuff and how much is the top-shelf stuff?"

The senorita gave us some prices in pesos, and we had no idea what it all meant. We also didn't have any pesos, so we asked how much it would be in American dollars.

"One dollar for normal tequila, two dollars for very, very not normal tequila," she replied, again making us fall even deeper in love with her.

"Well then," Hats answered back as confident as could be, "bring us the top-shelf stuff, Senorita!"

And with that, at ten o'clock in the morning Tijuana time, we started into top-shelf tequila in the form of salted-rim margaritas, a breakfast of champions to be sure. In pure champion Beaver Brothers style, we visited Tuneupville in Mexico, and for a day we renamed it Tequilaville. The cantina was renamed the Mexican Maple Tree Hotel, and we toasted the health of Vince and the Judge so many times that we actually came close to ruining our own.

The fame and recognition for tequila rests solely with the Mexicans. It is theirs and theirs alone. It is made from the blue agave plant, and some people will claim it is no different than any other alcohol. Then there are the rest of us that know differently. We know that as a tuning agent, tequila is more drug than drink. Ask anybody who knows, and my story will be corroborated. And anyone who says different is somebody who doesn't actually know. It's that simple. You either know or you don't, and you can only know from personal experience, as this is not something you read about in a book. You have to learn by doing.

We were well on our way to somewhere after our third or fourth round of margaritas. By that time, we had also made new best friends in the place and found the locals to be very inclusive and amiable. The weirdness and bad reputation of Tijuana certainly did not surface for the Beaver Brothers that day. Our cab driver did us well, and we spent the first part of the day eating and drinking local fare with local people. We were a band of tuned-up Beaver Brothers Gringos out on a mission to gain local knowledge, and that's exactly what we did.

There came a point in the early afternoon that was a point of no return of sorts. A tequila pivot point. Our senorita came over to our table and asked if we wanted another round. Instead of answering her on the drinks question, each one of us got on one knee and proposed marriage to her. In our own nonsense, blabber tone, all four of us competed for her hand and offered her the chance to live an amazing life in the land of the north. She smiled at us and asked again if we wanted another round. We all looked at each other, and without speaking, we knew the implication of the decision. If we said yes, there was a reasonably strong chance we would not make it back to the USA that day. This would be bad for Ozark, and bad for Hats as he wanted to get a hat. On the other hand, if we said no and got out then, we could still execute our plan with lots of time for walking around Tijuana.

"No, Senorita!" Hats replied for the entire team. "It is our duty to inform you that we must now vacate your fine establishment. And we love you!" The Mexican Beaver Brothers were a relatively mature bunch that day. We also knew we couldn't abandon Ozark.

We paid our bill and left a tip that was twice as much as the bill. We all scored a nice hug on the way out, and we headed out onto the streets of Tijuana in search of a hat for Hats. It's a strange feeling to be in a strange country and to leave an establishment in the early afternoon after a good session of margaritas. You roll out, look up at the sun, and hit the pavement as if you own the place. The streets are your world, and the world is your blue agave plant where all things are possible, nothing is impossible, and no idea is a bad idea. Self-confidence trumps doubt of any kind. This is your town! Tequila bent and Tijuana bound!

We hadn't even staggered down a full block when we walked by a tattoo parlor. RC looked inside the window of the place and walked in without even asking the rest of us. We all followed him without protest as we all knew that it was simply the right thing to do at a time when all things, and no things, were being considered based on merit of the idea. The four of us stood in the small shop and told the one guy in the place that we wanted tattoos.

In many countries it is unethical and actually against the law to put a tattoo on someone who has clearly been drinking too much. This makes sense because people will wake up the next day and wonder, *What the hell, man. What did I do to my body?* Therefore, in most cases, sobriety and good judgment are prerequisites to getting a permanent piece of art on your body. While this may be a practice in other countries, this was not the practice in downtown Tijuana.

"Si," our tattoo artist hombre replied. "What tattoo do you want, Senor?" he asked us in reasonably good working English.

"Hmm, well I don't quite know," RC said, really saying, *Oh crap, details. Like how is this actually going to work, and what will the actual tattoo be?*

Our tattoo artist friend's name was *Jesus*, but it was not pronounced the same way the famous Jesus pronounces his name. The J is said like an H. Ray thought this was perfect, and we asked Jesus if he could show us some ideas, whereupon he gave us some stencil books to look through. While we were doing that, he asked us if we wanted to upgrade the experience and have a shot of tequila with a Mexican beer chaser. We happily accepted the upgrade and told Jesus to have a round on us. He gratefully accepted the gesture of international diplomacy and brotherhood. Meanwhile, we looked through his big books of stencils, but nothing really jumped out at us. The books were mostly filled with USA-type eagles and naked women on motorcycles. After a bit of time, Hats brought us back to Earth and set the stage for the obvious.

"You got any stencils of a beaver?" Hats asked Jesus, really saying, *The search for the idea is over. We will be getting beaver tattoos today. Thank you very much, Jesus.*

"No, Senor Hats," Jesus said back, really saying, *Why in the hell would I have a stencil of a beaver, you dumbass Canadian!*

"That's OK," Hats replied. "I can draw you one."

At this point, Ray noticed a jar on the counter by the front door of the shop, and he asked Jesus what it was. "It is a jar of coin money, Senor Ray," Jesus answered in his broken English. "Many people sometimes leave me coin money for me to collect."

"Can I look in the jar?" Ray asked.

"Si, Senor," Jesus replied.

Ray went through the jar of coins that had been left by other international clients, and he found exactly what he was looking for. He retrieved a Canadian nickel from the jar and handed the nickel to Hats, who handed it to Jesus. "This is what we want!" Hats said to Jesus.

"Si, Senor Hats," Jesus replied.

With the template now in hand, we talked about what we wanted to portray permanently on our skin. We discussed the plan for fifteen minutes with Jesus offering some suggestions, and three hours later all four Beaver Brothers left Jesus and his tattoo shop with very cool tattoos on our left shoulders. Each tattoo is a beaver sitting on a rock, almost exactly like the image on the Canadian nickel. As well, there is a full-sphere yellow sun shining in the background behind the beaver. And in the middle of the sun is a perfect red rose – an Angel Rose. The tattoo was perfect. The tattoo is still perfect. That day in Tijuana produced something that none of us had any idea how much we would treasure. It means everything to us, it represents more than words can describe, it represents time and events, it represents friendship and family, it represents the past, present, and future, it represents body, mind and soul, it represents good and evil, and most importantly, it represents the Beaver Brothers.

The day was getting on, and with the tequila we had with Jesus keeping us going strong, we only had one more item to check off the list. We needed a hat for Hats, so we found an outdoor market that was loaded with stands and makeshift temporary shops that were selling all things Mexican to all people non-Mexican. It was a bazaar of gringo tourist trinkets on display and open for price negotiation, and in the end we walked away with a hat each, and Hats got one extra item. RC bought a very cool leather cowboy-style hat made of brown leather with a braided strip of leather around the crown. Ray and I bought the same style hats although they were not the same. The hats were made from suede leather and were a collage of multiple colors of small pieces of suede all sewn together. They looked like hats made from quilts of patches that had been cut up and put back together in a disorganized pattern. They were a bit smaller than cowboy hats but still had full crowns and full rims with flexible wire so we could change the shape. They were cool hats.

Of course Hats bought a full-size sombrero. I mean the biggest full-size sombrero available. It was burgundy and red and blue and fifty other colors. It had images of all sorts of stuff that none of us new anything about. It was pure Mexico. It was huge. It was pure Hats. To add to the look, Hats also bought a teal blue poncho. It was a blanket with a hole in the middle to put over the head of the wearer, which in this case was Hats. When he put on the whole outfit, he looked as if he should be in a *Spaghetti Western* with Clint Eastwood or a Canadian chocolate bar commercial.

RC said it first, although we were all thinking it.

"Hey, Senor Hats," RC said to Hats in a fake Mexican accent, "how do you like your coffee, Senor? Crisp?"

"Fuck off, RC," Hats yelled back as we were walking from the cab to the pedestrian walkway to get back into the United States.

"Nice hats, guys," the border patrol officer said to us as he stamped our passports to allow us back into the country.

"Thanks," we replied with complete pride and sincerity.

We got back to Barth, rescued Ozark, and walked the few miles west to watch another passing of the sun over the Pacific. It was a great day. The next morning we began another driving mission. The new plan was coast to coast without stopping for anything but gas and Ozark breaks. From the Pacific to the Atlantic – from where the sun sets to where the sun rises. It just made sense, and in the end we stuck to the coast to coast plan for the most part, although there ended up being one place that we couldn't resist a short stopover.

I was the last to go to sleep that last night in California. I spent some time with the journal. A short poem was the result.

HEY SENORITA

Hey Senorita
Ize sure is gonna miss ya
And da wonderful margaritas
Y'All mixed up in Mexico

Hey Senorita
Let's doa some more tequila
Before I gonna need to leave ya
Cause Hats needs a newa Sombrero

Hey Senorita
I really I think I love ya
But I'm getting kinda drunka
Thinking I should try to go

Hey Senorita
Can I just stay with ya
If not I'll need some helpa
Can't seem to find zee doo...r

Hey Senorita
Now I can't even see ya
I think I need to sleepa
Right here on da floor

USA
Summer 1983

A Fine Sight to See

IT'S NOT EVERY DAY you wake up on one coast of North America and decide to drive straight through to another coast. It's not a reasonable car commute. Our driving binge wasn't quite Los Angeles to New York, but it was close as it ended up being San Diego, California, to Charleston, South Carolina. We used the BOP and the string, and we figured it was close to twenty-seven hundred miles. We left early in the morning after our day in Tijuana and arrived in the Charleston area just shy of four days later. We made great time and only stopped for gas and Ozark. Well, almost only. It's not every day you go through Winslow, Arizona. It's not every day you can stop and stand on a street corner in Winslow, Arizona. It's not every day that you can stand on a street corner in Winslow, Arizona, and see if a few Beaver Sisters in a pickup truck slow down to check you out. Oh, ya. We stopped in Winslow, Arizona.

The Beaver Brothers Band plays and listens to and talks about and analyzes a lot of songs. But in the top three for sure is *Take It Easy*. What most people don't understand is the song describes a philosophy for living life. It outlines the steps to find peace of mind, and we were still searching, so we had a complete blast standing on a corner in Winslow, Arizona. We didn't stay long, but it was all we needed. Some checkmarks in life don't require extended time; sometimes it's not how long you were there – it's just the fact that you were there. Let's face it, a street corner is just a street corner after a few minutes of standing there, but the ability to say you stood on that particular street corner is a checkmark. Not surprisingly, stopping in Winslow created the dialogue and discussion for the conversation that took us across the country. We brainstormed through Arizona and New Mexico, we argued and debated through Texas, Oklahoma, and Arkansas, we agreed and aligned through Mississippi and Alabama, and then we confirmed and clarified our agreement and drew up the master plan through Georgia and South Carolina. By the time we got to Charleston, South Carolina, we had figured out the Beaver Brothers secret to *peace of mind*. This was the pivotal point in the trip where our creativity, constructive arguing, and ability to rally back together created the algorithm for our way forward. We developed our mantra – *Eat tree, Beaver!* and *Take time* to *drift and hum.* It was all too clear. It was all too easy. In our minds, we had it all figured out, and the summer was starting to pay dividends and produce what it was supposed to produce. We were all getting closer to some answers. Ray, in particular, was feeling better. We were all feeling better.

Our next road trip tollgate was Key West, Florida, but as the poem of poems goes, *a promise made is a debt unpaid,* so we wanted to make sure we paid our second debt before going too far down the road. Money was starting to get tight, and we wondered whether we could get all the way to Key West and up to Newfoundland and home without running out of gas. We had paid up on our promise to Vince in the Yukon at the signpost, and now it was time to meet our commitment to Judge Jeremiah. A man's gotta do what a man's gotta do, and we were trying to be men.

When we left home, the Judge pulled us aside and told us that if we got close, and if we could work it out, he would appreciate it if we would stop and say hello to his oldest and dearest friend. He made sure to tell us several times that it was *no problem if it didn't work out.* We decided on the spot that we would make it work out. The Judge gave us the name, telephone number, and address of his best friend, and we used the BOP to identify that his friend lived in the Charleston area, so that's where we headed first when we left the West Coast. When something is important to you, it's best to do it right away. That way the universal laws of entropy have less time to act upon your plans and make them fall apart. We could tell this was important to the Judge, and consequently it was important to us.

We got to the Charleston area and found a pay phone, and I called the number he had given us. Kees (Dutch for Keith, sounds like Case) answered the phone with a skeptical tone of voice at first, and after I explained who we were his tone changed and he sounded very excited.

"Of course, Sam," he said. "Betty and I were hoping we would get to meet the infamous Beaver Brothers!"

"Ahhh, thank you, sir," I said, really saying, *Wow, the infamous Beaver Brothers. I like the sound of that!*

"Where are you right now, Sam?" Kees asked.

"Downtown Charleston on Meeting Street," I replied.

"Well then," Kees said, "we need to get you out to Seabrook Island!"

"OK," I said, really saying, *Seabrook Island, wow, I really like the sound of that as well!*

I looked back at the boys in Barth who were watching me in the telephone booth and gave them the two thumbs up. Hats shot me the middle finger and silently mouthed you know what.

It took us an hour from the time we got Barth headed out of Charleston to the time we were at the guard shack that gate-keeps the entrance to the very luxurious Seabrook Island. It was a beautiful drive from the mainland onto Johns Island. Most of the drive was on Johns Island Road, which turns into Seabrook Island at the end of the road to the south. Equally beautiful, Kiawah Island is on the coast to the north. Large and small bridges connect all these islands together to form what can feel like one big island. Spectacularly amazing live oak trees stand very proud on each side of the twenty-mile road in from the mainland. The trees and their branches twist and curve and hang over the road to form a natural tree tunnel. This natural canopy goes on uninterrupted for what seems like miles. It's amazing in that it is so dense that the sun and rain can barely get through the canopy of branches. But the sun does get through enough to give you the essence of perfection and spiritual harmony. Ozark could not get enough of it. She would sit in the front passenger seat and look up and sideways and down and back up as she marveled at this tunnel we were driving through – a tunnel made entirely by nature.

Seabrook Island is now a private residential community, but it has a ton of history. The history dates back to when the world began and includes modern history with Native Americans, the American

Revolutionary War, slavery, religion, the American Civil War, and a whole bunch of contemporary stuff related to hunting, fishing, boating, and all things involving life around salt water. Known as the *low lands,* the whole area is one big ecological gold mine. This place is the perfect balance of sun and rain for all living things, so if you like nature you will like the low lands, and if you are a tree you will love the low lands.

Getting into the Seabrook community involves going past a guard shack. Hats was driving when we pulled up to the entrance gate, and he opened the driver's window to talk to the young man who was working in the booth. The young man phoned Kees from the shack, and we got the go ahead to enter. We were feeling a little bit like fish out of water: the whole scene was a little upscale compared to our road trip so far. This feeling continued as we followed the directions to Betty and Kees's home, which can only be described as a southern mansion on the beach. As we pulled into their driveway, all I remember is Hats looking at us from the driver seat with a big smile on his face as he said, "We have arrived, my fine rebel friends!"

Betty and Kees came out of their amazing home to greet us in the large circular driveway, and although we were essentially strangers their smiles instantly told us we were family. They both looked to be around sixty years old and appeared very healthy. The beach life can do this. Kees was a good-looking Dutch man who dressed impeccably, and Betty was a very good-looking Hawaiian native with gorgeous long hair and amazing bronze skin. We were all instantly in love with Betty and proud of Kees for his fine score. After we finished our initial greetings, Kees walked around Barth and complimented us on our touring machine. He noticed the broken bumper attached to the roof and asked if he could help us fix it. Betty, without remotely asking for permission, went straight into Barth and started to emerge with piles of our dirty clothes. Embarrassed, of course, we tried to tell her that her help was unnecessary, but she was not listening. She made at least two trips from Barth to their laundry room before she got wise and came out with a laundry hamper. We tried to tell Kees that we could do our own laundry at a laundromat, but he just laughed and stood in the driveway filling up the bowl of his pipe. He lit his pipe, and when we smelled the tobacco we all looked at each other and smiled. In that instant, all four us, plus Ozark, knew we were in good company. In that instant we also really missed the Judge, and we wished he could have been with us as we began our visit with his oldest and dearest friend.

We spent several days with Betty and Kees in their mansion on the beach, and I suspect we would never have left if the situation had been different. It was paradise. Each night Betty would come and get us from the beach and tell us, "Clean up and get ready for dinner, boys." We would then have a meal that could not be beat, always on their patio overlooking the Atlantic Ocean.

Our visit to Seabrook Island was pivotal in many ways. First, we learned a lot about the Judge. Second, I met Sophie. Third, and finally, was the event that resulted in our abrupt departure.

In Ray's Voice

THE DRIVE ACROSS the country from west to east was exactly what we needed. The drive and the conversation were the right drive and the right conversation at the right time. Going from state line to state line is such a neat feeling. In Canada, you can drive for a day and never leave a province, whereas in the USA you can drive through five states in a day, and each state has a new and unique vibe as evidenced by each welcome sign on the state line.

The USA truly is a republic of distinctive states. I love it.

Winslow, Arizona, was great. *Take It Easy* is our signature song because it describes all the things to do and not to do with life. Don't let the sounds and voices inside your own head drive you nuts, that's the real point of the song. Just chill out, lighten up your load a bit while you're still healthy and able, then find some spot that makes you feel good, feel really good, and *Take It Easy*. Life is too short not to accept this advice.

Winslow, *Take It Easy*, and our conversations while driving produced the creativity for us to come up with our new life mantra – *Eat tree, Beaver!* and *Take time to drift and hum.*

Once we figured it out, it just made sense, as this is the way of the Beaver.

Eat tree, then drift and hum.

Most people have no idea how incredible an animal the beaver is. For example, the beaver is the only animal other than the human being that can literally change and create new ecosystems. Because of this, other animals and plants thank the beaver for their homes. The beaver is the visionary, chief engineer, architect, and laborer that can create wetlands out of desert. The beaver's dam-building skills are unmatched by any other creature on the Earth, arguably even when compared to human engineers. Many Native American and Canadian First Nations people called the beaver '*Little People*'.

And yet are they considered hero to plants and animals and a pest to most humans? Why do they dam up streams and rivers and lakes?

Because the sound of running water drives them absolutely bonkers. The sound of a running stream is enough to send them to the looney bin, so they dam up their surroundings so the sounds of moving water won't drive them crazy. They work night after night building their lodges and their dams to stop that damn water from making that damn noise! Then when they are through, when they have single handedly built an entire new ecosystem, when not one drop of water is running, they go for a little vacation.

And while on vacation, they drift on their backs in their ponds, and they hum a little tune.

It's all true. The beavers stay busy and work hard eating trees all year to stop the sounds of the water, and when they have finished, they take a little vacation to reward themselves. Beavers will drift down a river or creek, or wander around through their local lakes, then eventually start heading back home, and this trip back home makes them feel really, really happy. This is when they hum and sing the most. They drift and hum and sing the most when they are swimming towards home.

In the end, they work hard to stop the sounds that drive them crazy, they eat trees and change their ecosystems to produce a safer environment, and when the hard work is done, they drift and hum.

And why do they eat trees? No reason other than that's what beavers do! Beavers Eat Trees! It's what they do best, so they do it!

Eat tree, then drift and hum. This is the secret to peace of mind. It doesn't matter where you are suffering, this mantra will work. Let's face reality: suffering can only take you to three distinct places. You are either suffering from memories of the past, or you are suffering in the present moment, or you are suffering from worrying about the future. Past, Present, Future – there are no other places you can be.

So if you are suffering in any of these places, here's some advice from the Beaver Brothers.

First: Don't let the sound of your own stream drive you crazy. And always remember, it's nothing but a stream that flows where you let it flow.

Second: Find your passion, seize the day, embrace the sun and nature, be who you are, leverage your strengths, and do what you do best because that's what you do! ... *Eat tree, Beaver!*

Third: Build a dam where you need a dam, change your ecosystem if required, change your surroundings if required, and in the process make the world a better place for you and others.

Fourth: After all this hard work, after feeling the pride of staying busy as a beaver, take time to be happy ... *Take time to drift and hum.*

This is the new way of the Beaver Brothers. *Eat tree, then drift and hum.* What a trip across the country that was for us. Sam and I turned our new mantra into a handshake. It's priceless.

Here it is. I hope I'm able to explain it.

While two people are facing each other, they throw their right hands towards each other with a flat peace sign being made out of their index and middle fingers. The knuckles on their hands are facing the sky while the two fingers are pointing towards the other person, allowing the fingers to represent the buck teeth of a Beaver. This is when they yell ... *Eat!*

Next, they put their left hands out in front of them with the palms facing up. Then they bring their right hands and arms up in a full circular action behind them and round-house so they end up slamming down on their left hands, making a loud slapping noise. This represents a beaver slapping its tail on the water to indicate action. When their hands strike each other, they yell ... *Tree!*

Next, and last, they put their right hands into fists and bump fists with each other. This fist shape represents the shape of a beaver lodge. At this point they yell ... *Beaver!*

Eat tree, Beaver! Do what you do, seize the day, live your life to the fullest. *Eat tree!*

Because that's what you do.

It's perfect, absolutely perfect.

USA

Summer 1983

Lots to Learn

KEES WAS A FOUNTAIN of knowledge to say the least – worldly, successful by all standards, articulate, and well read, and he had that *Je ne sais quoi* that makes somebody a person you simply want to be around. Some things can't be described, but you feel it when you are in its presence. It's just good chemistry.

Kees was born in Holland and was just shy of twenty years old when Hitler invaded Poland in 1939 to start the Second World War. He was going to join the Dutch Resistance, but his father convinced him to go to England and fight with the British forces instead, and so that's what he did. He had been educated as a mechanical engineer and was assigned to a platoon that was made up primarily of Canadians who had recently been dispatched from basic training in Winnipeg, Manitoba. Consequently, Kees and the Judge met and became instant friends as part of the same platoon.

One day their platoon was fighting the Germans outside of Antwerp, Belgium, and Kees and the Judge were both wounded with the same bullet. The German bullet went right through Kees's arm and lodged itself inside the Judge's leg. Their platoon survived this battle, and both

Kees and the Judge were sent back to London on a hospital boat. The next day their platoon was completely wiped out by the Germans. An indescribable friendship bond was forged by Kees and the Judge, and while it was clear they would not be sent back to the Western Front, they both stayed in England supporting the Allied effort for over five years. The Judge worked as an army barber and got his law degree at the same time, while Kees worked on engineering projects relative to the war's destruction and later on construction of electric power plants. Even though they were busy on separate projects, they were otherwise inseparable.

At some point during their stay in England, Kees received word that his parents had been killed in Holland in a house raid by Nazi sympathizers. His only sibling, a slightly younger sister, had survived and was being looked after by a relative. Kees and the Judge somehow went to Holland and rescued the sister and brought her back to London. Kees did not elaborate on any more details relative to the rescue, and the minute we even approached the topic, he became very quiet and clearly emotional. All he said when he concluded that part of the story was, "Boys, the Judge, your friend the Judge, is an extremely brave man. You have no idea how brave that man is."

The story goes on that Kees, his sister, and the Judge moved back to Canada at the Judge's urging. They all settled briefly in Chinook River, and the Judge passed his bar exams and opened up his law practice. He also married Kees's sister Johanna. Kees eventually took a job in Montreal with a big engineering firm that shipped him off to the Middle East to build oil and gas refineries required to meet energy requirements of the booming 1950s. While there he accumulated a small fortune in gold and gems, which he brought back to North America. He continued to work for various engineering companies, and along the way on one of his stopovers in Hawaii he met Betty. They married, raised a family, and ended up retired early and happy on Seabrook Island. The Judge raised his family with Kees's sister and has lived happily ever after in Chinook River.

By the time Kees finished the story, he had all four us, and Ozark, completely mesmerized. We knew the Judge was an incredible man, but our opinions were simply based on feeling, as we had no narrative or facts to back up what we believed intuitively, but now we had the data points to go along with our hypothesis. It's so interesting how the Judge never spoke a word about any of this to us over the years. Even though we always knew he was a private person, we never considered the extent of his humility. As the four of us sat at the kitchen table learning about the Judge, we all wracked our brains for signs of his past that we had missed. Collectively, we could come up with nothing.

"That motherfucker!" Hats said after Kees went silent, drank a sip of his port wine, and took a haul on his pipe.

"The Judge is a very, very modest man," Kees replied, ignoring Hats' colorful language skills for the moment.

"Did you know," Kees said, "that the Judge gave up a hockey career in the NHL to go to war?"

Absolute silence...I mean absolute, completely absolute, dead silence.

"Noooo?" RC replied for all of us in a long drawn out monotone nooooooo with the rhythm of a question right at the very end.

"Yes, boys, it's a fact," Kees went on. "While others were being drafted by the Canadian Armed Forces, the Judge was being drafted by the Detroit Red Wings. He would have preceded Gordie Howe by a few years, and if I have my facts correct, he would have still been there when Gordie had his rookie year in 1946. He chose to enlist in the army instead, and I personally thank God for that. Rumor has it he was one hell of a player."

"That motherfucker!" Hats said with such attitude and increased passion that we all knew he was really saying, *That old son of a bitch. I can't wait to get back home and kick his ass all over Chinook River!*

Nobody replied to Hats' comment, and what followed was a very appropriate moment of silence, broken only when Betty came out on the deck and asked if we wanted more sweet tea, which of course we did. Betty's sweet tea was better than beer, and believe me, I understand the magnitude of that comment.

And so went the week with Betty and Kees on Seabrook Island. We ate and drank sweet tea, and we talked about the Judge and Kees, and we walked on the beach, and we watched the porpoises in the ocean search for food. Ozark ran the beach every day as if she were trying out for the leading part in *Chariots of Fire.*

There was also another very nice thing about Kees and Betty's home. It was surrounded by other equally beautiful homes that housed very nice-looking and smart *Southern Belles,* and they liked to have evening campfires and get-togethers on the beach, which needless to say, the Beaver Brothers enjoyed as well. One night, in particular, was great for me because I got to meet Sophie.

In Sophie's Voice

THOSE BEAVER BROTHERS. Those funny, crazy Beaver Brothers. What a treat for all of us when they turned up in their motorhome that summer. We all knew this was a different bunch of boys the moment they walked over to our evening campfire. My girlfriends and I instantly looked at each other and smiled with the addition of their company. Of course the local boys didn't care for them much, but they didn't say anything. While the Beaver Brothers didn't come off as the tough sort, you could tell they could handle themselves physically. All four of them were clearly athletes and had a solid physical confidence within them. I learned later it was their hockey and their Krav Maga that gave them this persona.

Prior to the campfire, we had watched them swimming in the ocean. All four of them wore old *Levi's* cut-off shorts, and they would swim out beyond the surf and start fighting each other. Then at some point, one of them would yell, "shark," and each of the four would swing an arm around and hit the water surface really hard with his hand, after which he would dive deep into the ocean. They would only come up when oxygen was required. We had no idea what they were doing and later learned that they were imitating a beaver sensing danger, hitting the surface with its tail, and then diving deep towards the beaver lodge. It was absolutely hysterical.

My girlfriends and I promptly sized the four of them up. First was RC – tall and strong and handsome in a mature way. He was already a man even though he had not reached twenty years of age. Talkative, but not overbearing, he understood the essence of respect, and apart from his northern accent, he would have been a perfect southern gentleman.

Next came Ray. His long hair, his earring. He was handsome in a beautiful kind of way. So quiet in his demeanor; he only spoke when spoken to, and he had a sadness in his eyes that ran deep into his soul. We could all see it, we could feel it; we just wanted to hug him and tell him that whatever it is, everything will be just fine. His music was incredible. In all the summers I had been going to Seabrook Island with my family and all the campfires I had sat around, we had never had anybody play the guitar and sing the way Ray did. His music and lyrics were at times haunting, yet thrilling, and all in a fascinating way. He was extremely gifted, and we all knew it. He and RC would play duets and get us all singing as well. It was memorable.

Then came Hats. Good lord, Hats. He was loud, arrogant, and at times very rude from a South Carolina perspective, as his language was something we were not used to. He was also extremely cute, though. He was a strange stranger in our known land and this made him very appealing. His athletic body and his crude overconfidence made him hard to dislike, and even though my girlfriends and I tried our best to act indifferent, the truth is we all had a crush on Hats. It's hard not to love Hats, and the harder you try not to, the more you love him.

Last was Sam. My Sam – my cute, funny, poet Sam. He stole my heart the first night around the campfire when he recited his poem about *Sam McGee*. We didn't really understand the poem, but Sam's passion for the story bridged the gap. It was a pleasure to listen to him tell the tale; it was a pleasure to watch his three best friends and Ozark sincerely listen to the story once again, even though they'd heard it a thousand times.

We listened to the poem that first night while the southern oak was burning and crackling hot. The fire was much bigger then we normally built as a result of Hats' taking over the fire-building responsibility. It was a magnificent fire, and we thought Sam was going to jump right into the flames during his poem. It was a spectacle that none of us Southerners had ever seen before. It was my Sam, and we fell in love that night. I had no idea how it would all unfold, but I knew I wanted to be with him forever.

We loved our week with the Beaver Brothers on Seabrook Island. My girlfriends and I talked with them, walked with them, swam with them, campfired with them, sang with them, and even cuddled a little with them. They were not pushy in the slightest, though. They were true northern gentlemen, even Hats.

They were unknown to us, they were definitely interesting and mysterious, and they were the quintessential *boys of summer*. We privately hoped they would never leave, but they did, very abruptly I might add.

USA

Summer 1983

Late Night Phone Calls

WE GOT BACK LATE from the campfire on the beach with our new friends. Sophie and I were clearly falling for each other, and the other Beaver Brothers had small and convenient crushes happening. We were mostly a neat novelty to the young southern belles who would absolutely marry an appropriate southern gentleman one day. It's very important to keep traditions and wealth in the right places, although I thought I might have a chance with Sophie because she was actually a Texan who spent holidays in South Carolina.

When we got back to the house, Kees and Betty were waiting up for us. Kees told us that the Judge had just called and that we should give him a call, regardless of the hour. We asked Kees what was up, and he just told us to make the call. Hats volunteered to be the caller as he still had not given the Judge any grief for his non-communicated, completely secretive, almost professional hockey career. The rest of us, including Kees and Betty, sat at the kitchen table and watched Hats dial the number that Kees had written down on a note pad on the counter beside the phone.

The Judge answered the phone, and Hats started out with, "Hey Judge, you old Gordie Howe forward-line-playing *son of a bitch*!"

Then there was silence, and Hats' face took a more serious tone. He listened intently, breaking the listening to interject a "yes, sir" every once in a while to acknowledge receipt of whatever information the Judge was delivering. After what was only a few minutes, Hats hung up the phone and turned to face us to relay the information, his face as white as a ghost.

"Vince has had a heart attack," Hats said, his voice clearly quivering as he tried ineffectively to portray strength and calmness. "The Judge said that he is at Sacre Coeur Hospital and not doing so well. Apparently he is in and out of consciousness, and the doctors have him full of pain medication. The Judge said that Vince is asking for us and that we need to get home as soon as possible."

We all looked at each other and knew what needed to be done, and Betty and Kees, having only now spent a few days with us, knew as well. Betty got busy making sandwiches for us and built a lunch kit that would have fed an army for a month. Kees helped us gather our things, and we loaded Barth. Then, as we were putting our clothes into Barth and loading up Ozark, Kees asked the four of us to sit down at the kitchen table inside Barth.

"Boys," he said, "I know we have only just met, but I feel as if I have known you for years. The Judge talks about you more than you know, and has for many years. For some reason the Judge has kept large pieces of his life private, and I respect that. In any event, I was hoping you would stop and see us and I'm happy you did." At that point, Kees handed RC an envelope, and then continued talking.

"I have a lot of respect for you four," Kees said, his voice cracking ever so slightly with emotion. "I have respect for your friendship and I have respect for your having taken this trip together. I always wanted to do a similar trek when I was your age, but that was a different time and a different place, and it was not meant to be. I have a good life, though, and I have no regrets." At this point, he looked directly at Ray.

"Ray," he said, "I am so sorry for what happened to Rose and to your family. Even though I have seen evil up close and personal, I can still only imagine how you feel. Notwithstanding this, all I can tell you is that you cannot allow the unfairness in this world to tarnish your soul. The innocent victims of an evil deed need to stop accumulating at some point, and that point is now resting inside the coordinates of your heart."

We were all silent. At that point, we were all feeling the same thing, and RC grabbed Ray's hand with the hand that was not holding the envelope. Kees paused and then finished his goodbye to us. He pointed to the envelope in RC's hand and said, "I hope that will help you get home without having to stop for a part-time job."

An hour later when we were safely off Johns Island Road, RC opened the envelope. There was no note, no card, just twenty crisp one hundred dollar bills. We had no idea how Kees knew we were running low on money. Perhaps it was just obvious, perhaps he had pre-planned the gift to ensure we made it to the Florida Keys and then to St John's, Newfoundland. At this point, however, it was inconsequential, because we were heading home. Our road trip was in its final stage. Barth and the Beaver Brothers were now in expedite mode with Sacre Coeur Hospital in Chinook River as the destination.

In the Judge's Voice

THE BOYS ARE ON their way home. Kees is making sure they have the funds required to drive straight through and not worry about calling home for money. My estimate is they are halfway through their trip and all the way through their money. Boys will be boys. Kees and I had discussed the gift so they could finish their trip. I knew they would show up at Kees's home. I knew they would do the right thing. These boys live by principles even when they are making adolescent mistakes. I really wanted Ray to get to the Florida Keys, though. Maybe I will fly him down there after we deal with our current situation.

Kees has clearly talked to the boys about my past – about our past. I'm OK with this in that I suspect I gave Kees reason to believe it was his role to open the door. Maybe that's why I asked the boys to go see him. I struggle to share anything about my life, and even though I want the boys to be aware of what Johanna and I lived through, I have a steel door in front of many aspects of my life. My wife, Kees's sister, my beautiful, beautiful Johanna respects this part of me. There are some things we simply don't talk about.

War is brutal and the Second World War was the brutal of the brutal. You cannot describe the atrocities that were committed. It's simply impossible to believe that human dignity and respect can be suspended in such a way that good people follow sick and barbaric leaders in performing such terrible and inexcusable acts. To this day, I still do not understand that way of man, and I have become very discouraged wondering whether we have learned anything since those days.

I never questioned whether I needed to help Kees rescue Johanna. She was his sister, all he had left after their parents were murdered. Of course we would save her. There are some things you just do. It's principle. We thought she was safe with her parents, but of course that was untrue. Nobody was safe from the wicked, twisted, demented, and deranged ideologies of the Nazis. Johanna watched her parents be slaughtered, and was only allowed to live after having been violated herself. The sickness and cruelty of the pretend soldiers led them to believe it was more sadistic to let her live and be tormented with what had been done to her. Three of the four criminals were Dutch Nazi sympathizers who actually knew the family. Local boys being led and taught by one sick soldier. She watched the local boys kill her parents, and then she was treated like a worthless piece of garbage.

My wife is the strongest person I know, and I know a lot of very, very strong people.

Kees and I used all the underground resources we had to get into Holland to rescue Johanna. In war there are official processes and there are unofficial processes to get things done. We used the latter. We had connections, and we used every one of them. I owe those people everything. We were in and out of Holland within twenty-six hours. It would have been only sixteen hours if I had not tracked down and eliminated all three of the local boys who murdered Kees's family. The soldier got away. I have to live with only seventy-five percent of the job done. I don't like that much. I prefer one hundred percent completion when it comes to eliminating beings that are below maggots.

Killing the three local boys does not make me a hero. I am not proud of that act. Kees did not ask for it; Johanna did not ask for it; they would have been happy with leaving Holland immediately. Truth be told, they wanted to leave immediately, but that was not acceptable to me as my upbringing and value system demanded that I take care of business. You need to know, though, that my actions were not about hate. If I killed out of hate, I would be no different than the Nazis. No, this was not about hate; this was about principle. Those Nazi wannabes were not human beings. They were below shit on your boots, and they did not deserve to live. It simply needed to be done.

I'm smart enough to know it would get me nowhere. A tooth for a tooth is not the way, and I get that. But I was so sick from what had happened that I knew something had to be done. To seek and exact revenge is not a noble characteristic. I get that, but what I did wasn't revenge. Revenge is emotional; my actions were principled. What we learned back then is that evil actions at times require evil in response, so I became evil for ten hours while I hunted down and killed three parasites. And I would do it again. Some evil simply needs to be destroyed. This evil is the reason why the world will probably never live in peace. The idea of non-violence is shattered with one person committing one simple act of violence, and that one act of violence forces us to protect ourselves. Then the cycle continues, more violence erupts, and this will always happen because people are violent. I truly wish this were not the case, but I'm afraid this is the situation. A critical mass of the population is angry and violent. They always have been and always will be. Case closed.

I didn't even question my decision when I received the letter from the Detroit Red Wings. The United States was not yet in the war, but Canada was all in, and it was my responsibility and job to support England. This was just the way of the Canadian man. I burned the hockey draft letter before going overseas. Eyes forward, this is my way. I believe in principle-based decision making.

I knew I would never again skate well once I was wounded in my leg, so I never laced on the blades again. This is why the boys never suspected my youthful hockey experience. I miss playing the game immensely, but for some reason I can't bear to skate knowing what could have been, what might have been. I guess living with eyes forward can mean making harsh, one-way, and irrational decisions. Eyes forward can mean eyes never go backwards, and this can mean giving something up. Anyway, I get what I need from coaching the boys with Vince.

The situation with Vince is not good. Not good at all. It was last night, and we had just said goodnight to the last patron at the Maple Tree Hotel. I was hanging around to help Vince close up, as one of his bartenders had had to leave early. Vince leaned over to pick up a case of empties and fell over the case and onto his chest and face. I ran around to the back of the bar where he was sprawled out and I rolled him over. He had a look of surprise on his face, and I grabbed his hand while he stared into my eyes. His look of surprise turned to fear. He closed his eyes, and I felt his grip on my hand loosen. I asked Brigit, the last remaining waitress, to call 911, and I started giving Vince CPR. The ambulance was not long in arriving, and after some first response activities we rushed him to Sacre Coeur. I rode in the ambulance and just kept asking him to hang on. We got to the emergency entrance, and they rushed him into an examination room where I stayed with him as Dr. Tremblay and a few nurses came and did what doctors and nurses do best. They did everything to save Vince's life. I don't know the medical particulars of what they did, but the result was they revived him, stabilized him, and moved him into a longer-term room with a plethora of machines hooked up to his body. It was one o'clock in the morning by the time Vince and I were alone in his room. He was lying in the bed, and I was sitting in an armchair next to him.

I saw Vince's eyes flash open ever so slightly. After a few more efforts of lifting his eyelids, he finally kept his eyes open, and I moved closer to be with my friend. I grabbed his hand and he found the energy to pull me in closer. I have been in this position before, many times, in fact, during the war. It's a very interesting phenomenon that when a sick or injured person pulls your hand in towards himself, your first instinct is to lower your ear to his mouth, which is exactly what I did.

When I was close enough to hear Vince, he used all his remaining energy to tell me that he wanted to see the boys. I told him that I would make that happen, and he let go of my hand with an intended flinch, as if telling me to leave right away to find the boys, which is exactly what I did. I went to call Kees.

I ran into Dr. Tremblay while I was walking out of the hospital room. He asked me if Vince had any out-of-town family that needed to be contacted. The Doc knew that Vince did not have immediate family in town. I asked him if making contact with relatives would be necessary, and he let me know that Vince's situation was not good. I told the Doc that I was, in fact, working on getting in touch with the extended family. He told me that was wise and that they would keep Vince comfortable until the family arrived. I said that would be fine.

Thank God the boys were still with Kees. I have no idea how we would have reached them otherwise.

USA
Summer 1983

Head to the Sault

ONCE WE WERE IN drive mode, we had to rethink our basic guiding principles. Everything was different now. The first principle that went out the window was the rule about no interstates. We were now interstate bound because time reduction was the problem we were addressing. Ray used the BOP and determined we should take I-26 westbound to I-40 westbound to I-75 northbound. This would take us to the USA–Canada border crossing at Sault Ste. Marie. We could have crossed at International Falls, but for some reason, we wanted to get back onto Canadian soil. It added a little time to our trip, but we all agreed it made sense. Admittedly, there was also one other reason we wanted to go through the Sault. So the drive binge began, and needless to say, it was quite the trip.

We left South Carolina and ventured through the Smoky Mountains of North Carolina and Tennessee. They were amazing to drive through as the sun was coming up. When we hit I-75, we headed straight north through Kentucky and Ohio and into Michigan. Good ole Interstate 75. It starts way down in Florida just northwest of Miami and actually travels due west until it hits the Gulf of Mexico; then it turns north and heads up to Canada. At approximately eighteen hundred miles long, it finally ends at the USA–Canada border crossing at Sault Ste. Marie. The Sault is the end of the road as we know it. The only thing we stopped for was gas and Ozark, mainly because Betty had equipped us with enough food and iced tea to get us around the world twice. Well, gas and Ozark were almost the only thing we stopped for.

When we hit the perimeter of Detroit, Michigan, we made a strategic decision and headed into the heart of the city. Once in the city, we found the *Joe Louis Arena,* and while we were parked in front of the stadium RC and Hats ran into the open pro shop inside the home ice rink of the Detroit Red Wings. They bought two authentic NHL Detroit Red Wing jerseys, both with the name *Gordie Howe* and the number nine on the back.

"Why the fuck would you name an ice pad after a boxer?" Hats said indignantly when they climbed back aboard Barth.

"I don't like it either," RC added. "They should never have torn down the Olympia Arena. That's where Mr. Hockey did his best work. All the original-six temples are going down, boys!"

"Motherrrrr Fuckers," Hats said under his breath as he thought about the original-six NHL hockey arenas becoming markers in history.

Within twenty minutes, we were back on I-75 and heading north towards the Sault. A few hours later, we were going over the Mackinac Bridge (pronounced *Makinaw*). This is a very cool suspension bridge that feels as if it goes on for miles while connecting the upper and lower peninsulas of Michigan. You swear that the wind and the sway will lift your Barth right up into the air and land you either in Lake Michigan or Lake Huron.

While we were going over the bridge, Ray pulled out his guitar, and he and RC sang an amazing version of *The Wreck of the Edmund Fitzgerald*. Once again, it was incredible in a way I can't begin to describe. They were singing the ultimate song of the fury of the Great Lakes as we were traversing the almost six-mile-long *Mighty Mac*. The wind was trying to blow Barth right into the cold waters of the Great Lakes as they sang the haunting tale of icy water that never gives up its dead. When they were done, Ray said, "That was for Vince."

Things got a little quiet, and then Ray broke the silence with, "Hey guys, if you look west about fifty miles, you'll see *Beaver Island* in the middle of Lake Michigan!" We all looked over immediately, including Ozark. We couldn't see a thing.

"You're full of shit, Ray," Hats said really saying, *I hope he's telling the truth.*

"No, I'm not, Hats! It's really there!" Ray said back with complete conviction.

We all paused for a minute, and even though we could not see *Beaver Island* in the distance, we wanted to see it.

"Oh, ya," RC said first, I can see it now!"

"Me too," I added.

"Well what do you know?" Hats chirped, "There it is, Beaver Fuckin' Island. Who would have ever known, lads!"

We barely uttered a word for the next three hours as RC and Ray strummed on their guitars, Hats drove, and I worked in the journal. Ozark was at full attention in the passenger chair. All four of us were thinking about Vince, thinking about the last several weeks, and thinking about the last year in general. We heard only the sounds of the guitars and the road; no words were spoken until we reached the border crossing at Sault Ste. Marie, USA, and Sault Ste. Marie, Canada. It took us only twenty hours to get from Seabrook Island, South Carolina, USA, to the Canadian border at the most northern part of Michigan. While we never spoke of it, I know we were all feeling that somehow it only took twenty hours to go from one unique environment to a fundamentally different one. They were two completely different worlds yet not remotely worlds apart. RC calculated we were a little over halfway home.

Crossing back into Canada was uneventful. It was evening, not very busy, and we had nothing to hide. This was obvious to any onlookers. Our faces looked tired from travel and weary from worry. We had nothing to declare to the border agents other than two Red Wings jerseys, a few packs of Reds, a few cans of PBR and a little bit of Jack. They waved us through without even a blink of suspicion.

Getting back on Canadian soil was interesting. On the one hand, we felt morose because our trip was coming to an end. It's not that we were upset or feeling deprived in any way. Vince was far more important to us than the Florida Keys or Newfoundland. On the other hand, we felt proud and happy to be back in our home country. The Beaver Brothers, by nature and by nurture, were full-fledged Canadian boys. This was our land, and together we felt a sense of patriotism that we were home. Even Ozark seemed to perk up with the smells of good old fresh, crisp Canadian air.

While going through Sault Ste. Marie, we executed our intentionally planned event, and we purposely passed by the Sault Memorial Gardens. This is the now demolished hockey arena that had been home for the Sault Ste. Marie Greyhounds. It was built in 1949 as a war memorial. It's where Wayne Gretsky played as an amateur in the Ontario Hockey League during the 1977-78 season. He was sixteen. It's also where *The Great One* first started wearing number 99.

"Do you know how Wayne got to wear ninety-nine?" Hats yelled out, acting as if he were Vince telling us the Gordie Howe number nine story.

"No," we lied, just as we would with Vince.

"Well," Hats started, "when he joined the Sault Ste. Marie Greyhounds, he asked for number nine. He wanted Gordie's number. Mr. Hockey is the Great One's all time hockey hero. But nine was already taken, so he had to wear number fourteen. Then the coach came up with a great idea and told him to wear two number nines! 99! Two times Gordie Howe. How cool is that?"

"Very cool!" we answered, immediately thinking about Vince.

"You know what, though?" Hats went on.

"What?" we answered dutifully.

"The Great One never won a Memorial Cup as an amateur hockey player."

"Ya, but he's gonna win a few Stanley Cups. Just you wait, Hats," we answered on behalf of the Judge.

"I'm not fucking buying it," Hats responded after a slight pause. "Ya just gotta win the early stuff, boys!" Then he asked Ray a question, "Ray, who is your favorite player of all time?"

"Guy Lafleur. Five Stanley Cups," Ray answered without hesitation.

"What else did Guy win, Ray?" Hats asked, knowing the answer full well. He was already a practicing lawyer.

"The Memorial Cup, 1971," Ray answered reluctantly, allowing Hats an *I told you all so moment*.

We passed the rink to pay our respects and we drove on. The plan was to keep going until we got to the hospital to see our coach and friend. For the most part, we stuck to the plan other than one impromptu, unplanned stop I asked that we make.

Canada
Summer 1983

Last Notes

NONE OF US KNEW what we were heading into once we got home.
The Judge had clearly indicated that Vince's situation was serious, but
we had no idea how serious. Couple that with the inherent optimism
of the Beaver Brothers and you get the result of our simply assuming
that everything would be just fine. At least that was what we all silently
hoped for. It was very interesting that we didn't talk about Vince at all
other than the song dedication, and looking back, I think the trip from
South Carolina back to Canada was probably the quietest we had ever
been in our entire lives as friends – which was our entire lives.

I broke the latest round of silence when I told the boys what I
wanted to do. I had been writing in the journal the last few hours
while RC and Ray played their guitars and Hats drove with Ozark
riding shotgun. In a split second, I had a very funny feeling come over
me. It was a powerful sense, tantamount to the feeling of an epiphany.

"I want you three to write a final entry in the journal, and then I
want to bury it," I said out loud, jarring the silence away.

"What?" RC asked me in a curious tone.

"I want you three to write a final entry in the journal, and then I

392

want to bury it," I repeated myself, this time with an edge of more confidence and conviction in my voice. Practice was making perfect.

"Why?" RC asked.

Hats just kept driving, and Ray said nothing. I could tell Ray understood my suggestion, or at a minimum, he had his own reasons for understanding.

"Because I think we should bury the story of our summer. Someday we can come and retrieve it, but our writings need to stay buried for now," I said.

There were another few minutes where the only sound was the sound of the road. It was just after midnight and the road was dark and nearly devoid of traffic.

"When do you want to bury it?' RC asked, really saying, *I'm with you, but I need to learn more to know why I'm with you.*

"Between now and when we get home," I replied.

"Where?" RC kept going.

"Somewhere along the Chinook River," I said instantly as if it had been planned for years with every detail sorted out and previously agreed upon. After a couple minutes of silence, Hats yelled from the driver's seat.

"Fuckin' eh right, boys. Next stop is the Chinook River. I know just the spot!"

I handed the journal to Ray for his turn in writing some last thoughts about our summer road trip and life as we knew it at that point in our lives. RC went next, and then I took over driving so Hats could write his final thoughts as well. Hats also had a discussion with Ozark and wrote her comments down in the journal for her.

When we all had completed our writing, RC and I got the journal ready.

In Vince's Voice

I HOPE THE BOYS get here soon. I need to see them before I go. It's the last thing I need to do.

I know what the doctors are doing at this point. They are keeping me alive until my family arrives to say goodbye. What the doctors don't know is that the boys are my family, and the Judge, of course. I can feel the drugs they put into me to keep my heart going. I can also feel that my heart wants to stop. I know my time is up, and that's OK.

I wasn't surprised when my heart attack happened. I've been expecting it for years. You don't live the way I have lived and get away with it for too long. I didn't quite hit the average age for a man to go, but I also didn't live the average life. The human body can only take so much punishment, and Lord knows I punished my sixty-some-year-old body big time.

The Judge is such a good man. He has not left my side except to go find the boys. He said he found them, and they are now on their way home. I've been blessed to have him as a friend all these years. Blessed indeed. God bless the Judge.

It really is amazing how fast life goes; it seems as if it vanished right before my eyes. But I had a good trip. No complaints. There's no point in complaining anyway. I rolled the way I rolled.

That God damned Maple Tree Hotel. The bar killed my father and his father, and now it's taking me. It's a vicious cycle I need to stop, so it's going to stop now, or at least after one more party. All good parties need to come to an end at some point, and it's my job to end this one. Vince's last call to be sure.

I hope the boys are OK with my plan. I won't explain it to them, though. I'll let the Judge do that after I'm gone so I don't get any argument from them, especially from Hats. That kid is one royal pain in my ass. That little dumbass, he's the son I never had, and I'm really going to miss him. I'm going to miss all of them.

I know they are still just kids, but they can handle what I've laid out. I've set it up so they can also have some time to think about what they'll do. It's going to be really good. I hope somehow I get to look down and see how it all ends up. I really do hope there is something good after this life. If there isn't, then this whole thing called life is one sick joke.

The Judge asked if I wanted to talk to Preacher Pete, but I said no. I figure why start now. I may be a lot of things unholy, but I'm no hypocrite, and I figure I'm in good shape if that whole story pans out to be the truth anyway. I've lived a life of kindness, generosity, and hard work. I've been good to everybody but myself. That should earn my way into Heaven. I don't see why the entrance ticket should rely solely on believing. Isn't free will also about choosing what you believe and what you don't believe? No just God would punish a man for living a kind life and simply believing what he believes. Anyway, whatever happens, I just hope it's calming. I really just want a good long sleep.

If dying means you go nowhere and feel nothing, then I'm OK with that. Sleep is good.

I hope the boys get here soon. I need to see them. I need to talk to them.

Canada
Summer 1983

Book Burial

THE CHINOOK WAS OUR RIVER. We had canoed it fifty times if we paddled it once, so it just made sense to bury the journal around it somewhere. I have to admit, I really wasn't sure myself why I felt so adamant about burying the journal. I suppose something in my soul just told me it was necessary.

I gave the wheel back to Hats after he wrote his last entry, and RC and I got busy getting the journal ready for its introduction into the ground. RC grabbed a wooden box that we had with us to carry cassettes and eight tracks in. We dumped out the music. It was an old bullet box from World War II that he had bought at an army surplus store while on vacation one summer. It was perfect. It was thick hardwood with seriously strong hinges, and the strength of the box seemed appropriate for some reason unknown to each of us. While we did this, Ray strummed on his guitar in the background. He had gone very quiet since he wrote his last journal entry. It was as if he were trying out chord patterns for a new song. Ozark was back riding shotgun and navigating for Hats.

We lined the inside of the box with several plastic grocery bags in an attempt to waterproof it. Our plan was also to put the box itself in a green garbage bag prior to burial. RC was really getting into the mission with me. Once the box was lined we put the journal into the box, and then RC suggested we put a few other things into the box as well. Eventually the box contained the journal, the Book of Paths, a pack of Marlboro Reds, a half-bottle of Jack Daniels, and a handful of other trinkets we had managed to acquire along the summer tour. The bullet box, a time capsule in itself, was turned into a true time capsule. Unlike official time capsules, though, we did not have any preplanned date for its retrieval.

Hats eventually stopped at a remote spot on the river that we all knew well. It was our secret spot where we would put the canoes in while on a trip. We were now a couple of hours south of home, and the river flowed north from this point. The entrance was barely recognizable from the road, but Hats knew exactly where it was from our past visits. It was late morning now so we had enough sun to do the job, but what we didn't have was much time. All four of us knew we had to get to Vince so we wasted no time getting the box buried. We used some cooking utensils as makeshift shovels, and we dug into the ground in between two recognizable birch trees. Once the hole seemed big enough, we lowered in the green garbage bag with the box in it. It had a good two feet of clearance into the depth of the hole. It was above the frost line but we assumed the box would hold up. We pushed the dirt back over the box. There was no ceremony, no words of wisdom, no standing around the dirt wondering about the wonders of time. The whole burying affair took less than ten minutes. Once it was done, all three of the boys, and Ozark, looked at me for approval. I nodded that all was good, and we got back into Barth for the last leg of the trip home.

Canada

Summer 1983

Home

SEEING THE WELCOME sign to our hometown was interesting, and it meant home was less than an hour away. We had no idea exactly what time it was or what day it was, for that matter. For the last several weeks, we had been drifters with no need to pay attention to the realities of life. It was as free as free can get, but now we were home, and the reality of everything was settling in fast.

We got to Sacre Coeur Hospital and went straight to Vince's room. The Judge was there sitting in an armchair; he looked tired and haggard, and the stress showed on his face. Vince was awake and was clearly agitated and uncomfortable and was lying in his bed in a half-sitting-up position. The Judge got up from his chair and gave us each a hug. He then looked at us in a silent stare, peered straight into our eyes while his back was to Vince. His look was all we needed to understand the gravity of the situation, and our eternal optimism deflated in that moment. The Judge then moved so the four of us could approach Vince. Vince looked up at us and smiled. We could tell he was in immense pain while he reached out with his right hand and grabbed Hats' left hand. It was clear he found comfort in our being there. The

398

whole situation was moving way too fast for us, though, and it was hard to comprehend that this wasn't all some sort of a dream.

Almost immediately, Doctor Tremblay came into the room and asked if everybody Vince was waiting for had arrived. Vince nodded a *Yes*. The doctor then grabbed Vince's foot and took his pulse from the blood beating in the top of the foot. He asked Vince if he wanted some pain killers, warning him that they would put him to sleep. The two of them seemed to be having a conversation that was in code, and only they knew and understood the code. Vince said no to the drugs, even though he was in great pain. He didn't want to go to sleep yet because he wanted to talk to us. Doctor Tremblay left the room, and on his way out he told the Judge that he would be back in twenty minutes. The Judge nodded in agreement, once again, the known code being silently understood among the Doctor, Vince, and the Judge.

"Hi, boys," Vince said in a labored voice, still holding onto Hats' hand.

With that, we pushed in a little closer to Vince while the Judge sat back down in his chair behind us, giving us space.

"This is my last skate around the rink, boys," Vince said. "And I want you four to know how much I've appreciated having you in my life. It's been a great three periods and now it's time for me to head to the bench for good."

The four of us were stunned silent. We had no idea what to say, so I looked over at Hats and I could see that his eyes were starting to tear up. His grip on Vince's hand was becoming more firm, though trying to stay gentle with a caring touch. Hats was the first to speak.

"Come on, Vince. It's not that fucking bad, buddy," Hats said, really saying, *I know this is really, really bad, but I don't want this to be really, really bad. I don't want this to be happening. This can't be happening!*

Vince gave Hats a smile, really saying, *You are one of the funniest, strangest dumbasses I have ever met.*

"We all have our day of reckoning, boys, and today is mine." Vince continued with frequent grimaces of sharp pain shooting through his entire body. "Now, here's the deal, boys," he continued. "I have drafted up a last will and testament. The Judge is the executor of my estate, and he will be going through my will with you. I won't get into the details now, but suffice it to say that you are involved. I truly hope I don't put a burden on you, but I feel strongly about my wishes, and the cycle needs to end with me."

We had no idea what Vince was talking about. We were outside all normal protocols of life in that moment, and we had no idea how to process what was happening. Hats was clearly fighting back raw emotions, RC was standing strong for the team, Ray was looking lost, and I was feeling as if I wanted to run away as fast as I could. The Judge was looking sad and tired, and Vince was looking resolved in his situation.

Vince nodded to the Judge, and the Judge left the room and returned with Doctor Tremblay. Vince asked the doctor for some help with the pain, and as the doctor was preparing a solution connected to the IV beside the bed, Vince looked up at the four of us and said, "I love you, boys. I'm very proud of all of you."

All four of us felt our bodies rock with a feeling of fear and panic and sadness. Everything was moving at lightning speed and slow motion at the same time. Then all of a sudden Hats brought us back to some sense of reality.

"Wait!" Hats yelled, actually grabbing the doctor's hand to prevent him from releasing the drug that would put Vince to sleep. "We've got something for you," he said to Vince.

Hats went into the plastic bag he had carried into the hospital and pulled out the Gordie Howe–Detroit Red Wings shirt that we had bought for Vince at *The Joe*. He laid the shirt carefully over the sheet that covered Vince's chest. It looked as if he were wearing the jersey. Then Hats pulled out the second hockey jersey and threw it over at the Judge. He threw it hard, hitting the Judge square in the face with the shirt.

"We know a little something about you," Hats sneered at the Judge. "You old hockey-playing, World War–soldiering motherfucker, you!"

This actually got a big smile from Vince, even amidst the pain he was in. To this day, that smile is how we all remember that last day with Vince. This is the snapshot we all have ingrained in our minds as Vince's last moment on Earth. *Good boy, Hats.* The Judge got up and put his number nine shirt on over his argyle sweater. The doctor finished up his duty and nodded at Vince, who nodded back. The morphine drip was then opened, and the juice started to flow into Vince's bloodstream. This immediately brought Vince some relief from the pain.

The Judge took two steps forward and joined our vigil around the bed. Vince stared at us and gripped Hats' hand harder. This was his final act to say good bye, and within three minutes Vince was asleep. Within fifteen minutes, Vince was dead. His heart simply stopped. We watched his heart rate trail down on the monitor beside the bed. It was the scene we have all watched in the movies, where the heart rate machine slowly goes from a few a strong beeps to a few slower beeps and then to a straight line. The straight line and the accompanying sound are the visual and auditory confirmations that a friend is gone.

Doctor Tremblay returned to the room and patted the Judge sympathetically on the back. They nodded to each other, again talking in silent code. The Judge then asked us if we were doing OK, while a nurse came in to unhook all the wires and tubes that Vince had streaming in and around him. The four of us nodded to the Judge and moved away from the bed after what seemed like an eternity. Ray went to the window and looked blankly out into the parking lot while I walked up to a wall in the room and used it to support my weight. I put my hands to my face and slid down the wall knowing full well I was back in my bedroom as a thirteen-year-old boy. The Judge went up to Hats and gently eased the grip that Hats had on Vince's hand. He led Hats to the chair that he himself had been using for the last thirty something hours. Hats sat down and began to cry in an uncontrolled sob. The Judge stood by him with his hand on his shoulder, his Red Wings hockey jersey bulking his body. RC stood tall and strong in the middle of the room, circling his gaze to take in the entire situation; he was ready to support and protect whichever one of us needed him most.

Ten minutes later, we were back in Barth, and at the Judge's suggestion we drove to the Maple Tree Hotel. It was now mid-afternoon. We parked Barth and watched Ozark run into the bar. Curly was there to greet her. We all gave each other a look. It was a look that was the final confirmation that our summer road trip had come to an end and a look that told us life was now different once again. The pain of Rose. The pain of Vince. We knew what was behind us, but we had no idea what was ahead of us. It was as if we thought we were at the ending of some life tollgate.

Little did we know, in retrospect, that we were only mid-way through a beginning, as the next twelve months would unfold with events that nobody could ever have imagined.

Canada
Summer 1983

The Will

WHEN WE WALKED into the bar, it felt as if we were in some kind of surreal time warp. It was midafternoon, so the place was not that busy yet. After coming back to reality, we learned that it was Saturday of August Civic long weekend – one year to the date of our first big gig at the Maple Tree Hotel. We had been on the road for five weeks, and we were home four weeks early.

The Judge talked to the Maple Tree Hotel staff, and everyone became visibly upset. He then talked to the customers in the bar, and they too became visibly upset. The plan was that they would leave the bar after they finished their current drink. At the same time, one of Vince's bartenders worked the door and did not let anybody new in. The Judge had made the decision that the bar would be closed until Monday afternoon, when it would reopen for Monday night only, and after that it would forever be closed as a bar.

A sign was put on the door saying closed, and the bartender sat outside the door to communicate with would-be customers. The Judge sent the rest of the staff home and then asked us to sit down. We sat at a table that was away from the main entrance so we were not distracted by the stream of drinkers used to hitting the Maple Tree Hotel on a Saturday on a Canadian summer long weekend. It didn't take long for the word to spread around town that the bar was closed for the night because of Vince's death, but the bartender had a full-time job sitting outside the closed entrance for the entire night. People wanted to pay their respects by drinking at the bar.

The Judge grabbed a few OVs from behind the bar and brought them to the table. He pulled a formal-looking manila envelope out of a briefcase he had by his feet, put the envelope on the table, filled his pipe, and lit the bowl of tobacco. The smell of the bar and the tobacco was comforting to all four of us. I thought about the Judge, I thought about Kees, I thought about Vince, and I thought about Ozark and Curly nestled at the Judge's feet.

"OK, boys," the Judge started. "I believe in eyes forward, and there is no time like the present to get our eyes looking forward. Welcome home! I hope you had a great trip, and thanks for the shirt. So here's the deal. I am the executor of Vince's estate, and that means I will make all decisions and direct all activities regarding his estate and his wishes."

We were all silent, as we had no idea what the Judge was saying, and even if we did, we were emotionally drained. In some respects, I don't know why the Judge felt we needed to have this talk so soon, but it was his show, and we were going along for the ride.

"So," he continued, "here's the deal. Vince has created a trust, and he has named you four as the trustees. What this means is he wants you to administer and lead the decisions relative to the trust and the assets in the trust, which are sizable I might add. At a high level, we are talking about the Maple Tree Hotel, which is clear of debt, and there is a substantial amount of money in cash. Vince and his father and grandfather were proficient savers, and the hotel served a lot of drinks over the decades."

We had no idea what language the Judge was speaking. This was a foreign land for us, and we did not understand one bit of the culture or customs.

"Let me continue," the Judge went on, clearly seeing our discomfort. "Vince had some wishes he would like us to see through. The first deals with his funeral arrangements. He would like to be cremated. He thought Sam would like that, and he does not care what we do with the ashes. Together, we will come up with something. Regarding a funeral or service, he would like us to invite people to the hotel for a visit and a few final drinks, all on Vince of course. I suggest we do that on Monday. Then, after the doors close on Monday night, the bar will never see alcohol inside the establishment again. It will cease to be a drinking spot after decades of having been in business. When the doors reopen one day, it will be for some reason other than drinking. This is what Vince wants."

Silence

"What will it be?" RC asked the Judge for all of us.

"Ahhh, RC," The Judge responded, "that's the correct question, and this is where it gets interesting. What the Maple Tree Hotel becomes is entirely up to you four boys. Vince has left you the responsibility and task of deciding how the Maple Tree Hotel will make a difference in the lives of people other than as an establishment for alcohol."

Silence

"We have no idea what to do though, Judge," Ray spoke up for all of us.

"That's OK, Ray," the Judge said. "You don't have to decide right away. There's lots of money to pay the bills for a long time while you decide. Vince did not expect this to be an overnight decision. It may take years to figure it out, and in the meantime his trust will keep the building in good repair unless, of course, you decide to sell the building. In that case, the trust money and proceeds from the sale will be given to some charity of your choice. Either way, we don't need to decide this today."

Silence

"We need to keep the hockey team going for another generation," Hats said in an almost pleading voice.

"Of course, Hats," the Judge replied. "This is something you four can discuss and decide."

"It's already fucking decided! "Hats fired back, with a sharp tinge of anger and pain in his voice.

"Of course, Hats." the Judge replied patiently, ignoring Hats' emotion.

Silence

"OK, boys," the Judge continued, "I suggest you get home and say hi to your folks and get some rest, and then meet me here tomorrow morning to plan Monday's reception."

And with that, we finished our drinks, left the hotel, and loaded up Ozark and Curly into Barth. We didn't go home though. Instead, we spent the night at the Lodge. It seemed like the natural thing to do, as our parents weren't expecting us for several weeks anyway.

The Judge had told us to go home, and that's what we did. The Lodge was our home.

Canada
Summer 1983

Last Call

WE GOT BACK to the Maple Tree Hotel around ten o'clock the next morning, and the Judge let us in. Our parents were at the bar as well, as the Judge had called to check up on us and informed our parents about the situation. After a few hugs, the Judge went through Vince's will again so our parents could understand the circumstances. At this point, everybody was feeling honored that Vince felt we should lead the next stage of the Maple Tree Hotel. The Beaver Brothers felt an emotion that does not have a word to describe it. It was a mix of pride, surprise, curiosity, puzzlement, sadness, melancholy, responsibility, and accountability. There is no word that can adequately deal with all of those emotions.

Our parents decided to stay and help, and Vince's entire staff showed up as well. We got busy planning the reception for the next day. As per Vince's wishes, we kept it simple. We put the word out that there would be drinks and *together time* starting at four o'clock Monday afternoon. The bar would be open until last call. We also relayed that after the reception was over, the bar would be closed permanently as a drinking establishment. The plan was for the four Beaver Brothers to tend bar along with all the other staff. We decided that music was not required.

We wanted this to be about talking, telling stories, and spending time together as neighbors and friends. The only formality was the Judge asking me to write a poem for last call, and I agreed, recognizing for the first time that I had become the family funeral poet. *Eat tree, Beaver!*

We all slept at our respective houses Sunday night and got caught up with our families. Even though the reception was not starting until four o'clock, we were at the Maple Tree Hotel by ten o'clock in the morning. We wanted the place to be ready.

People started showing up before two o'clock in the afternoon. We let them in, and by four o'clock, the bar was full and the RCMP had cordoned off an area outside the bar so people could congregate there as well. This was, of course, breaking all Canadian drinking laws, and our assumption was that the Judge and the RCMP had made some executive decisions that day. In the end, the event was completely civil and exactly what Vince had wanted. It was not the calm before the storm, but rather the calming after the storm – the calm before the silence.

We had the bar set up for pouring drinks, and pour drinks we did. The Maple Tree Hotel was simply being the Maple Tree Hotel, where the only evidence that this was a wake for Vince was a picture, a shirt, and Vince's absence. The picture was a picture of Vince behind the bar, and the shirt was the Gordie Howe Detroit Red Wings jersey we had bought at *The Joe*. They were both hung on the wall that was covered with the annual pictures of the Maple Tree Hockey Teams.

Listening to the sounds of all the people was the best part of the celebration of Vince's life. So many amazing stories were told that night. Some were sad, some were historic, and many told of Vince's generosity. Other stories exemplified the hard-pounding life Vince had lived as an alcoholic owner of a bar. But mostly the stories were just plain funny, and between a few tears and some quiet moments there was uncontrollable knee slapping and belly-aching laughter. Everyone had a funny Vince story or one about an experience at the Maple Tree Hotel. From teenagers to ninety-year-old seniors, the stories flowed like the Chinook River, and for a few short hours that night hundreds of people became professional storytellers, gifted with the narrative. We were all talking, we were all listening, we were all laughing, and we were all crying – all at the same time. Together, as one family, we created one loud continuous white noise, yet inside the blare of the white noise you could hear the stories and the incredible essence of the life that Vince had lived. The stories solidified the place that the Maple Tree Hotel had played in so many lives. While working the bar,

I realized that the Maple Tree Hotel story was, in fact, our story.

I have no idea how many drinks we served that afternoon and that evening, but it was a lot. It was not from people taking advantage, but rather was from the aggregate number of people who came to pay their respects to Vince. Even the McMullen senior members showed their respect for Vince. They did this by leaving the younger generation at home, so we did not see Timmy or Joey that night, which was good for Hats.

People also did not overstay their visit. In fact, it was an interesting situation where the length of the stay for a patron somehow correlated with how much time they had spent in the Maple Tree Hotel over the years. It was as if an undocumented, unofficial tenure list existed, and your standing on the list drove your ultimate position at the bar. The more hours you had spent drinking at the Maple Tree Hotel gave you invisible stripes that were respected by all. It was a perfect system – a system that was not conceived or created by any person or process but was well understood without any rules or guidelines to make it understandable or manageable.

The Judge eventually gave the word that we should begin winding the reception down. At this point, there were no guests outside and fewer than fifty hardcore regulars left in the bar. It was late, so the Judge suggested we have last call and end the evening. This was my cue to deliver the thoughts I had written down.

With the help of the bar staff, we put out a shot glass for every person remaining at the reception. It was an eclectic group with random demographics, at best a motley crew. We poured a shot of the King's whiskey in each glass and each guest found his shot at the hardwood bar. We fell silent, one hand on our shot glass, the other holding onto the bar. The Judge thanked the group for coming, told them this was exactly what Vince had wanted, and then said that I had some thoughts I wanted to share. I came to life and stepped to the middle of the bar and asked the group to raise their glasses. All ears and eyes were on me, and all shot glasses were in the air.

I recited the poem I had written and easily memorized the night before.

LAST CALL

Pour us a drink, Vince
And don't you dare make us wait
Put the shot glass on the bar, Vince
'Cause you know it's getting late

Let's rise up our glasses, Vince
Let's rise 'em really high
Let's rise up our glasses, Vince
Let's try to touch the sky

Life is what it is, Vince
You taught us to take what we get
You lived each and every day, Vince
You lived without regret
So rise up your glass, Vince
As you rise to meet your fate
Rise up your glass, Vince
Because you know it's getting late

You did a great job, Vince
It was a wild and rowdy ride
Really, really great, Vince
You've left us filled with pride
So rise up your glass, Vince
Overlook any and all mistakes
Rise up your glass, Vince
Because we know it's getting late

It's time to close the bar, Vince
The day has turned to night
It's time to call last call, Vince
Your rest is within sight
But before you go, please rise up your glass, Vince
Please rise it up one last time
So we can say goodbye, Vince
So we can say goodbye

In complete unison, we all stretched our shot glasses as high as we could reach and drank the shots of whiskey. Then we slammed the shot glasses down on the bar in front of us. The sound of the glasses produced a symphony of time, and for that split second the acoustics in the Maple Tree Hotel would have been compared to Roy Thomson Hall. Even to this day, if there is one perfect sound that remains inside the walls of the Maple Tree Hotel, it is the sound of those last shot glasses hitting the hardwood bar. I love that sound.

The Judge gave me a look of approval, and the group began to leave the Maple Tree Hotel for the last time. There was no point in sticking around. What needed to be done had been done, what needed to be said had been said. All was complete.

The bar staff left and the Judge and the Beaver Brothers and our dogs left. The Judge turned off the lights and locked the door behind us, and we turned around and faced the bar from the street.

"I wonder what you boys will do with her," the Judge said to no one in particular as he puffed on his pipe and stared at the Maple Tree Hotel.

"So do we," all four of us thought without uttering a word.

As we walked away we did know, however, that we were walking away from a major chapter of our lives, and just like a book, the next chapter started immediately. Significant events do that to a story. Powerful events will accelerate the next series of powerful events. Emotion drives higher emotion. Speed drives faster speed.

Within a few weeks of saying goodbye to Vince and closing up the Maple Tree Hotel, I would be in South Carolina beginning my love affair with Sophie. Hats would be in Toronto beginning his love affair with the law. RC would be in college continuing his love affair with the RCMP. And Ray would be working up north on the pipeline beginning his love affair with heroin.

PART 3

Finding Warmth

BETTER WAY

There has to be a better way
Although I don't know what it is
But there must be a better way
'Cause this don't make no sense

Sam, Chinook River, 1984

DAY 19

South Carolina

Radar Up

TODAY IS A YELLOW DAY, although I can sense Red right around the corner. It feels as if something is brewing in my mind, like the grey of storm clouds prior to a storm. I'm easily convinced that today's Yellow is the calm before the Red Storm.

I went for a walk on the beach today but did not find any sense of peace because momentum and acceleration are in the air. I realize now that the near future will either have me moving forward or coming to a grinding and sudden stop.

We may need to hold on because things are probably going to start moving fast, and one way or another, some destination will be reached.

I have an appointment with Doc tomorrow, so perhaps it's just anxiety in anticipation of the meeting. I haven't talked to her in a few days as she has been giving me space to prepare for the final show-down. I know it needs to come eventually, so I may as well start the downhill slide – the snow has been building, and the mountain is ready to avalanche. Let the snow and show begin so that it can come to an end. If only some things could end without actually beginning. Maybe there are times when it should actually be about the destination and

413

not the journey. I often wonder why the journey gets higher billing than the destination. Some means don't add up in the end. Sometimes the beginning should be feared more than the ending.

Adding to my angst, a lot has happened over the last few days, mostly in the way of phone calls. First, Uncle Alec called and forced me to make a decision about the business. I continue to know what he is doing. He is my teacher, I am the student; but I am also aware when he is teaching. He wants me to come back to reality by focusing our conversations on reality. *Harsh realities first; then fix and repair.* There's something very simplistic and practical about this technique, so I told him to go ahead and find a buyer for the business. I'll admit I think he was somewhat surprised, but I also think he believes this may be the correct course of action. Knowing Alec the way that I do, I expect him to have a buyer by tomorrow. Prospectors always get it done. Hesitation and going slow drive him crazy. I'm lucky to have him in my life.

Next, Kees called to see how I was doing. Kees is now in his nineties. Both he and the Judge have defied all actuarial charts in spite of the fact that they both still love smoking their pipes. The pipe smoker is now a dying breed, no pun intended, but the Judge and Kees are helping bring up the average, if only marginally. What a couple of absolute characters. I'm lucky to have them in my life as well.

Kees and the Judge are truly from the greatest generation that ever lived. We will never have a generation like them; too much of whatever they have has been lost from one generation to the next. Young people these days simply don't have the gift – they did not receive it from their own parents or don't seem to have any inclination to find it. Societal entropy is still hard at work, and we don't seem to be putting reciprocating pressure on it to balance it out. When their generation is gone, we will lose the essence of their entire culture. That will be a sad day for the world.

Kees phoned because he prefers not to travel these days. He likes to stay out at his home on Seabrook Island, and even though I'm not far from him, it's hard for him to venture out. His wife Betty died over a decade ago. We all went to the funeral, and of course I wrote and read a poem for her. This is officially my job in the extended family now. *Eat tree, Beaver!* I feel as if I get called upon a little too much, though.

RC also called to see how I was doing, and he tried hard to be casual while asking about whether he and Hats could come down for a visit. I told him that would be nice. I told him I was good and that it would be great to see them both, although I could tell by his voice that he was only somewhat convinced I was doing OK. I really did try hard, but he knows me as well as anybody on Earth. You cannot fool people who love you, and if you think you can, it's only because they are allowing you to think that way. As Alec says, "There is a fool at every table, so if you look around the table and can't see the fool, you may just be the fool."

The last call was from the Judge, and this one struck me as strange. While it's not odd for him to phone me, I had not heard from him since I arrived here at the mental hospital retreat. I have received a few emails from him, but until now no calls. The emails were all upbeat and mostly sent words of wisdom from an old, wise, extremely accomplished and encouraging man.

Here's the deal with the phone call, though. I think he was saying goodbye. He's far too old-fashioned to say it directly, but I'm pretty sure that was what happened. I'm not sure why I feel this way. It's not from anything specific in the dialogue of the call but more of a feeling based on how the call ended. It just seemed more final then it needed to be. I don't know how I feel about this. I don't think I can think about it right now. It's one more rock in the glass jar that's already full. Eventually you have to stop putting rocks in the jar because all glass jars are fragile and will eventually shatter.

I can't shatter my jar right now.

I need to be ready for my appointment with Doc tomorrow. That means I can't add any more rocks to the jar.

In the Judge's Voice

I THINK SAM IS ONTO ME. I almost made it through the call right until the very end. That's when I had a small deviation from my master plan.

I asked RC and Kees both to reach out to Sam to judge his emotional situation. I needed to know whether I should even call, because the last thing I want to do is do more harm. That being said, both RC and Kees felt Sam was fragile but up to a call from me. So I phoned him.

I called him to say goodbye.

I'm an old man now. I've done everything I can possibly do in this life, and my work is complete to the best of my abilities. The doctors at the new hospital have informed me that I have cancer of the colon and probably cancer of the everything. These doctors look like teenagers to me now, but they are smart, really smart, although I do miss Sacre Coeur Hospital and Dr. Tremblay. They are both gone. That's the problem with living this long: you become the last person standing from your peer group, and you look down the line and there is nobody there. Oddly enough, Kees and Johanna are my only competition. They are survivors in so many ways. They have defied all odds, and I love them both so much.

At least Johanna and our children, grandchildren, and great grandchildren are all here still. I am very fortunate that my life has been filled with so many blessings, and all in the natural order of things. A parent should never have to bury a child. I think of Ray and Rose's parents often. While those events are now in the long-distant past, I remember them as if it were yesterday, and I now believe they have become more

416

significant to me and my life than the war. Truth be told, I won't allow the war that much power, and Johanna carries that torch enough for an entire village, so I am left with the memories of the Roses.

I don't plan to fight the cancer because it's just not worth it at this point. I would put up the good fight if I were a younger man, but I am an old man who needs to move on to the next stage of the overall universal journey. I also don't plan to let the cancer eat me alive. That's not fair to my family; no one should have to watch a loved one die a slow and inhumane death. That is not fair to anyone. Cancer is bullshit. Allowing people to be tortured by it is bullshit, and I have lived my entire life trying to instill some sense of stability, fairness, and justice in a world of chaos, injustice, and unfairness. I will go out on my own terms. No bullshit happening here. I'm not dying of Beaver Fever.

It is Wednesday today. This Friday, I will have dinner at our house with Johanna and all our family. Saturday I will spend time with my grandkids and great grandchildren. Saturday night I will have a quiet evening with Johanna, and then we will retire for the night. We will lie beside each other as we have for seventy years. I will hold Johanna's hand and look deep into her beautiful eyes. I will tell her that *we had a good run*. I will tell her that *she is the reason I was placed on this Earth*. I will tell her that *I love her*. She will smile back at me with a *don't be so silly smile* and squeeze my hand tighter. I will then go to sleep and not wake up. Sunday morning I will leave this earthly body.

I'm tired. I have done my job here, and my body, mind, and soul are ready to go. It's time.

My family will be fine. Yes, of course, they will be sad, but they are smart and logical people. We have been given a gift on this Earth with Johanna's and my health to this point. They know that, and they know it has to come to an end at some point for all of us. I am so proud of all of them.

Time goes so fast. It really does.

I mostly worry about Sam. He has been through so much lately, and I do not want to add to his burden. I know he loves me, but I also know his plate is full.

I may need to come up with a better plan than my phone call today as I don't want him receiving a phone call about me on Sunday. It could prove to be too much. I will call RC and come up with a better plan. I didn't do so well on the call today. I really wanted to get through it without sending any signals, and I was good until the very end. Yes, we had a nice visit right up until I started to end the call.

Right at the end, I said, "Sam, you are a good man, and your father is looking down on you, and he is very proud of you." At that point, I was almost through my words without unhinging, but then I lost my rhythm of emotional stability. I had shortness of breath, and I could feel my voice starting to shake and crack. A flight or fight adrenaline rush came over me as I could feel inside my own heart what I know these words mean to Sam in his heart. I know he never got over his father's death, and he has always been searching for his father to tell him that he has done a good job. There was a prolonged moment of silence on the call, and I was barely able to squeak out my last words with what breath I had left in my lungs. I almost broke down on the phone, and I finally ended the call with, "And I am proud of you too, Son."

I tried to be his father.

Sam did not respond. I could feel his energy and emotion through the phone, and there was a full minute of silence while neither of us could talk. Then he thanked me for everything I have done for him and the boys over the years. He told me that he loved me, and then our call ended almost as abruptly as it started.

I think he is onto me.

I'd better call RC right away. I need to come up with a better plan, because Sam deserves that.

Canada
End of 1983

Scatter

LIFE'S SERIES OF EVENTS moved at lightning speed from the minute we said goodbye to Vince until the end of the year. That's when things came to a grinding halt.

After saying goodbye to Vince, I immediately left for Sophie and South Carolina. Sophie was starting school in Columbia, and my plan was to get into school there as well. That is if you could call it a plan. I had no idea what I was doing. I had no idea how the rules worked or how much money I would need or how I would even get into the USA. All I knew was that Sophie wanted me and told me she would pick me up at any airport. Love is amazing in its flexibility. So I told my family my plan, and they told me I was crazy. They told me not to go, but I went anyway. I had some money that was put away for my college education, and my mother agreed to give me some of it, so I headed south. Eventually, I got all the country-university-bureaucratic-administrative issues taken care of, and Sophie and I settled into our undergraduate studies and our love affair. It was the real deal. It still is the real deal.

Hats left for Toronto and started his studies in Political Science, his precursor to law school. He knew what he wanted, and in his mind

419

he was simply executing the base plan that had been hatched in the Lodge when we were kids. I always envied Hats' ability to develop and execute a vision. I like a person who doesn't tamper with well laid out plans, and I've come to appreciate that the most successful people in life are those that simply stick to a basic plan.

RC ended up going to a local community college very close to our hometown. He had been disappointed, but not completely surprised, when he found out that he could not go from high school directly into the RCMP. The rules were changing literally as he began his drive to enter policing as a profession, and while the RCMP knew they wanted him, they could not make an exception. This was the downfall era where strict adherence to rules was trumping personal relationships and whom you knew. RC was fine with this. He always took everything in stride, and he began a two-year Police Foundations diploma at our local college, which would eventually lead to his acceptance into the RCMP, his basic training at RCMP Depot, and ultimately his becoming a Third Class Constable as an entry level position. He would later tell me that policing is not a profession but rather a craft. "A craft or trade that you can only learn on the road. Learn by doing," he would tell me. He spent a lot of time on the road, a lot of time "doing" over the years, making it so easy for me to be proud of him. As well as going to the local college, RC took care of Ozark and Curly while Ray made his own decisions. RC also helped the Judge coach the Maple Tree Hockey Team.

Ray decided he wanted to get out of town. He chose not to accept the Judge's offer for help with his education, and instead left for up north where he could get great pay working in oil and gas. Specifically, he made lots of money helping to build the pipeline that was being spread across Alaska and parts of Canada. This ended up being a defining decision for Ray and the rest of us. Everything was happening so fast with all of us that we never stopped as a team to know what was happening to any of us as individuals, and in this case, Ray simply headed out for the money in the far north. Unfortunately, this lifestyle was unique in that the work Ray was doing was about working hard and playing even harder.

Ray would go into the work camps and stay for weeks, working seven days during those weeks and as many hours per day as they would let him. He made a lot of money relative to what we were used to because of all the overtime he and the other men put in. Eventually, they would get some leave and they would fly to some city and get busy spending all the money. This meant spending the money on fancy hotels, nice restaurants, and lots of alcohol and other tuning agents. Unfortunately, though, Ray picked up the nasty little tuning agent called heroin, and it didn't take long for this to change his game fundamentally.

RC, Hats, and I knew something was going on with Ray because we didn't hear from him at all while he was working or playing. At Christmas that year we all got together in Chinook River, and we gave Ray a hard time for not communicating very well. We all had advice for him about how he should live his life. He listened and blamed his lack of communication on the nature and location of the job. Then a couple of things happened on New Year's Eve 1983 that brought more awareness of the real situation.

The first thing that happened was that RC received a phone call from Wi in Montana. Little did we know that Wi had been communicating with Ray regularly since the summer. They were writing letters to each other weekly and having occasional phone calls as well. Ray had been using the work camp mail system to carry on his correspondence with Wi. The problem was that Wi felt the letters were becoming somewhat odd as time progressed, and while he never missed a week, every so often Ray's writing would be disjointed. This was beginning to worry Wi. She knew we would all be together for Christmas, and she asked RC to make sure everything was fine with Ray.

The second thing that happened was significantly more *in your face* as they say. We were at Hats' place getting ready to get tuned up for New Year's Eve. The plan was to head to the Lodge and spend the night as a way for us to have a good visit and some laughs the old fashioned way – just the Beaver Brothers and their dogs, Ozark and Curly. Sophie had joined me for Christmas and met my family and the Judge, and then she had headed back south for the New Year. In retrospect, I suspect she was simply giving me some time with the boys.

We were getting ready to head out to the Lodge, and I went into the bathroom for a last pee before the walk. When I opened the door to the basement bathroom at Hat's house, I almost hit Ray in the head with the door. He was sitting on the floor of the bathroom, his right hand holding a syringe that was sticking into his left arm. I pretended I didn't see him shooting his heroin and acted as if he were being a pain in the ass because I needed to use the bathroom. To this day, we have never discussed my witnessing this. Ray played along for the rest of the time we were together that Christmas. We had fun that night at the Lodge, and I never noticed Ray acting any weirder than he normally would when we hang out together, which perhaps is a relative comment.

Shortly after the New Year, we all headed back to our new worlds, and Ray stayed behind, living at his folks' place. He did not head back to the pipeline, and this actually made us all feel more at ease. We hoped and assumed things would get back to normal, not that we knew what normal was. We only knew we did not like the current condition.

Unfortunately, we were incorrect in our assumptions that normal was going to become the future condition.

Canada
1984

Broken

NINETEEN EIGHTY-FOUR in Canada was quite the year. George Orwell's book had not been proven completely true, but it was clear the world was headed in that direction. Canada had three Prime Ministers in 1984, making it a year of happiness for anybody making money on elections. Trudeau began the year, Mulroney ended it, and Turner was the meat in the sandwich. In Quebec, a retired American soldier detonated a bomb in Montreal's central station, killing three and wounding at least thirty people. Nobody understood how to process this event. On the beverage scene, *Labatt Breweries* introduced the first twist-off cap on a Canadian beer bottle. This was seen by all Canadians as a bad move. On the music scene *Much Music* aired for the first time, showing television videos of the music of the 1980s. This was seen by most Canadians as a worse idea than the twist-off cap. We didn't care much, though, as we stayed loyal to our original bands and OV.

Hockey was a year of surprise and the expected. The surprise was that Canada and the USA placed fourth and seventh respectively in the Winter Olympics in Sarajevo, Yugoslavia. At the time, we thought that was the worst evil that would ever happen in Sarajevo. Oh man, were we wrong about that. The expected, and not surprising, was that Wayne Gretsky and the Edmonton Oilers beat the New York Islanders in the Stanley Cup Playoffs, ending one dynasty and starting another. All of our teams made it into the playoffs, but only Montreal made it through the first round. Things were different now. There were too many franchises, making it hard to be committed to original-six teams. Maybe Hats had it right by cheering for the Flyers.

On the local hockey front, RC and the Judge were coaching the Maple Tree Hockey Team. They moved the team back down to the Atom division and had a new group of young budding stars. Hats asked if they had "four Beaver Brothers" and the Judge answered, "Not a chance." Hats got to as many games as he could. In some ways, the year was settling into a new normal, but it did not last long as the year had other completely unexpected events.

I got a call from RC at the end of January. He had already talked to Wi, as well as Hats and the Judge.

"You need to come home right away, Sam," RC told me. "We're planning an intervention for Ray."

"OK," I said to RC. That was all I needed to be told. The call lasted ten seconds.

When RC picked me up at our local airport, he had Wi with him in the car. She had arrived that morning. Hats and the Judge were waiting for us with Ray's parents at the Judge's office. We also asked Preacher Pete of our church to help facilitate the intervention as he was trained in these types of engagements, and we thought it would be helpful. With our team formed, we headed to Ray's parents' place where we knew Ray to be. It was probably seven o'clock in the evening when the whole thing started.

The intervention was anti-climactic. Ray was surprised when we all walked in the house, but he was also genuinely happy to see us. In particular, he was happy to see Wi. Once the hugs were over, Preacher Pete sat us all down in the living room. I couldn't help but think about Ray's parents sitting in those same chairs while the RCMP informed them about Rose having been murdered.

"Do you know why we're here, Ray?" Preacher Pete started for all of us, his voice a little shaky on account of the fact that this was not a training course, but rather the real deal.

"Yes," Ray responded in a matter-of-fact way. "Because you love me, and I am an addict."

Silence, everybody not sure what to say, everybody feeling this is too easy.

"That's correct," the Judge said to break the silence. "And we have a plan for you to get clean, Ray. Will you allow us to help you?"

"Yes," Ray replied without missing a beat, and with that the intervention was over. This certainly was no made-for-television episode of reality TV. There was no screaming or accusations of this and that or anything said to be hurtful or to burn any bridges that had taken a lifetime to build. It was classic Ray. He had a problem, he knew it, and he wanted help to fix it. *Harsh realities first; then fix and repair.* Ray always believed all you needed in life was a few chords and the truth, so we provided the chords, he provided the truth, and he embraced the writing of the song. Ray is a true artist.

We all agreed that Wi and Ozark would stay with Ray and his parents that night, and in the morning, Wi, RC, Hats, and I would take Ray to a facility a few hours from home. The Judge had used his connections to get Ray the right treatment at the right time and in the right place. The new rules were broken and *whom you knew* was once again delivering the right answer. Everything had fallen perfectly into place.

Hats and RC stayed with me at my family home that night, and we had a calm night and got some sleep, having felt the effects of the long day. The sleep was short as the next day started with my home phone ringing around six-thirty in the morning. It was Wi calling. She was frantic and asked if Ray was with us. After doing a quick search, I answered no, and we all immediately headed over to Ray's house.

When we got to the house, Ray's mother was at the front door yelling to us that Ray and Ozark were gone. Wi said they had all fallen asleep on the two couches in the basement, and when she woke up, the two were gone. She searched the house and then woke up Ray's parents, whereupon the three of them searched the house again and then called us.

We huddled ourselves to think of where Ray could be, and then we divided to conquer. Hats and Ray's father headed to the Maple Tree Hotel, and RC and I headed to the Lodge. Wi and Ray's mother stayed inside to call the Judge and the RCMP.

RC and I made the hike to the Lodge faster than ever before. It was really cold, but we didn't feel the really cold. The snow was January deep, but it was hard so we could make good time without the support of snowshoes. We were hoping to see some tracks showing that Ray and Ozark had been there, but we couldn't find any. When we hit the tree line to begin the long walk, the sun was starting to become brighter, and by the time we got to the Lodge, the sun was up and the day had begun. The sky was blue, and the sun was bright. To the weatherman, it was a perfect northern winter day. A day where true northerners would embrace thirty-below weather to ice fish, snowmobile, cross country ski, or a host of other activities that define the healthy hobbies of the people of the north.

RC and I were not thinking about our hobbies.

The inbound path we chose to get to the Lodge brought us into the rear of the clearing where the Lodge stands. We walked up to the back of the Lodge, and we noticed some smoke coming out of Findley, although it was not a strong fire – more of a smolder from a solid fire that had previously burned. We felt a little sense of ease as we assumed Ray was passed out inside after having a solo tune-up session on his own. We calculated the worst case scenario was he would be a little weak, nervous, anxious, and maybe cold.

We headed around the Lodge to the front entrance, although we didn't quite make it before we saw Ozark lying by the woodpile. She didn't bark or make any sound. She simply lifted her head and stared at RC and me as we approached.

RC was the first to recognize that Ozark was lying across Ray's body in the snow. Ray was lying on his back in front of the woodpile that was stacked and suspended between our two big birch trees. RC immediately reacted.

"Oh my God," he said, his voice somewhere between a complete panic and a controlled take-action tone. "Oh my God, oh my God, oh my God, oh my God," was all he could say as we both ran to Ray. I followed RC, not knowing what to do, and desperately hoping he had all the answers to our next moves.

Neither of us had any significant medical training, but I believe it was clear to us in that first moment that Ray was dead. Even so, RC didn't waste a second before beginning CPR. Meanwhile, I ran into the Lodge to look for blankets, believing Ray needed to warm up so he would thaw out and come back to life. RC and I were both frantically doing anything we could possibly think of, including picking Ray up and moving him into the Lodge. I got the smoldering fire going stronger for heat, and RC yelled at Ray to wake up. I was still convinced we could bring Ray back if only he would embrace the warmth, and RC was convinced he could hope and scream Ray back to life. Both of us were wrong.

After what seemed like hours, RC and I finally stopped being frantic, and we started to understand what was happening. RC asked me if I was OK. I said, "No." I asked him if he was OK, and he said, "No."

Then we started to look around the Lodge to come to grips with the situation.

"Fuck!" RC said, as he stood up and picked up a dirty syringe that was on the table that we had played so many games of *Risk* on as boys.

"Fuck!" he said again. "We need to clean this all up, Sam," he said to me. "This can't be what people talk about. This is not the way this is going to go down."

We began to clean up the Lodge of any drug paraphernalia that existed, and we threw it all into Findley – all with Ray lying dead on his bottom bunk, his Dream Catcher earring shining at us, his eyes staring at the bottom of the top bunk. We cleaned up the Lodge, and this included going through his pants pockets, knowing the police would do the same. There was nothing in his jeans, but RC did find an empty bottle of prescription pills in his parka. They were strong pain killers of the generic valium type. The last thing we did in the Lodge was go through Ray's wallet that he had casually tossed on one of the chairs. Inside the wallet RC found several prescriptions for more pharmaceuticals. RC read them and then stuffed them into his own pocket as a hard look came over his face. It was a look I had never seen on RC before. It was a look of pure anger.

After the cleanup, we headed out to the spot where we had found Ray. Ozark stayed back in the Lodge with her head on Ray's chest. There was nothing incriminating on the snow for us to pick up. In fact, the only marking on the snow was the indentation where Ray had been. Once we focused on the ground, RC and I simply looked at each other in disbelief. There, on the ground in front of us, and what we were staring at, was the form of a snow angel. Ray had died with the morning sun shining on his face while he opened and closed his arms and legs in a gesture that would result in his making a snow angel.

"Fuuuuck," RC said in exaggerated lengthiness, all while really saying, *I can't believe this is happening, Sam. A snow angel? A snow angel, Sam? A fucking snow angel?*

We were both stunned into silence by the enormity of the situation, and then we were stunned out of our silence by the sound of a helicopter. We both lifted our heads to look at the sky and the RCMP helicopter hovering over us, and after a couple of moments of continued disbelief, RC waved at them to let them know they would need to find a place to land and come to the scene. They flew off toward the easiest place to land, which was our nearby Beaver Pond, the pond we had built so many childhood memories around.

RC and I did not return to the inside of the Lodge. Instead, we stayed standing in the sun beside Ray's snow angel. We were suspended in time, and neither of us had any idea how long it took for Hats and two RCMP officers to find their way from the helicopter landing spot to our Lodge. It may have been ten minutes. Hats was the first to come through the Lodge clearing with the very fit RCMP officers attempting to keep up behind him. Hats knew that Ray was dead the minute he looked at us. He was running towards us, and halfway from the tree line to where RC and I stood he was able to read our faces and eyes. He immediately collapsed in the snow, falling on his stomach with his face in his gloves, and he screamed into the snow below his face.

The RCMP officers quickly reviewed the situation by looking at RC and me and then went into the Lodge. Within twenty seconds, one officer exited the Lodge and went to work on his radio using the open air to gain better reception. Within an hour, there were easily ten people at the scene, including RCMP Constables, the Staff Sargent of our RCMP Division, the Judge, and Ray's father. Wi and Ray's mother were at home, not yet aware of the final outcome of the day.

"This is fucking broken, man," was all Hats said as we watched the Judge attempt to console Ray's father outside the Lodge.

"This is fucking broken, man," was all Hats said as the RCMP started to ask RC and me about what we had found upon our arrival at the Lodge.

"This is fucking broken, man," was all Hats said as they removed Ray from the Lodge.

"This is fucking broken, man," was all Hats said when we declined an RCMP ride home and we walked back with Ozark through the bush towards Wi and Ray's mother.

"This is fucking broken, man," was all Hats said as the RCMP Staff Sergeant, the Judge, and Ray's father tried to calm down Ray's mother in that God-forsaken living room above the basement where we had listened to the torment in her voice after Rose's death.

"This is so fucking broken, man," was all Hats said to Wi as we sat in the basement of my parents' house later that night and tried to figure out what the hell we were going to do.

And Hats was absolutely correct. It was totally fucking broken, man. Everything was just plain fucking broken. Entropy was alive, healthy, and in growth mode. Entropy was winning the game it was playing, and we had no idea whether there was even another team on the ice.

I left the group for a few hours and started working on my words for the funeral to come. Unfortunately, I could not find any words that would be suitable. I was not in control, and my brain created what it wanted to create. My art was no longer of my own doing. What went on paper came from some place that I did not know was in existence, and when I realized I had finished, this is what had been created.

BROKEN

I've seen broken
I've felt broken
I've heard broken happening
I've tasted broken
I've smelled broken
I sense when broken is coming
I've been on the start of broken
I've been on the end of broken
I've been in the middle of things breaking
I've lived the effects of broken
I've paid the price of broken
I've been the one doing the breaking
I've examined broken
I've analyzed broken
I've tried to fix broken along the way
I've cursed broken
I've embraced broken
I expect broken to show up today
I've learned to be one with broken
I've become accustomed to broken
I'm challenged with broken both day and night
I've made peace with broken
I've accepted broken
I realize broken is just a part of life

In Ray's Voice

OH, MAN, DID I EVER SCREW UP. I mean, I screwed up royally. This is the screw up of all screw ups.

Believe me. I had no intention of dying. I did not want to die. I truly did not want to die. Oh man, they are never going to believe that.

Oh, man, I have screwed up bad this time.

I need to relate the series of events. Rose's death did kill a part of me as well. I failed her as her big brother – I should have been there for her, I should have protected her, and a big part of me actually died the day she died. But meeting Wi helped with that. She filled some of the void in my soul, and I could feel over time that she could fill enough of that void for me to get through life. Meeting Wi this summer was not random, was not fate, was not chaos or predetermined happenstance. It simply was what it was, and it was perfect in all ways. I knew I loved her the moment I walked into her store and sat down in the chair to get my earring.

Vince's heart attack was another blow, but it actually helped me somewhat. Instead of feeling as if I would not be able to handle another tragedy, I realized that life is hard, life is tough, life is not fair, and life is really nothing but a series of events you react to in the moment. Real life is nothing but a series of moments and reactions.

So I went up north to work as a time-gap maneuver, a way to pass some time and take a deep breath and a break from the moments I was reacting to. The money up north was great, the work was hard, but equally rewarding from a physical point of view, and the tuneup scene was intense. In my mind, I was just getting some youthful energy out of my system. I knew I would eventually get back to reality, back to my love of music, and I would be with Wi. They are both my destiny.

Then one night in Vancouver I took a hit of heroin into my lungs. I *chased the dragon*. Then I took a shot of heroin into my blood. It was so good, so very, very good. I won't try to explain it for all reasons self-evident. If you've been there you know what I'm talking about. If you haven't been there, then my advice is don't ever go.

I knew I could not, and should not, continue with the drug for very long. It wasn't me, it wasn't Rose or Wi, and it wasn't the Beaver Brothers. Nothing about heroin was me other than that it eased some perceived pain I was walking around with. And it felt good. I don't know, I guess some things are just that simple, no real explanation required.

Oh, man, did I ever screw up.

Christmas and New Year's was brutal. I was getting high in spite of being with my family and Brothers. It was amazing to see Sophie and to watch the Judge and her talk about the common relationship in Kees, and even though I was high, they couldn't really tell. I was the great imposter. I had learned the mathematics of heroin. Yes, I had. Maybe you don't know this, but you can actually manage it if you put some rational intelligence into the irrational actions of being an addict. This is the irony of rational irrationalism, the irony of thoughtful addiction.

Then Sam busted me in the bathroom at Hats' house. He saw it, I saw it, we both saw that we both saw it, but Sam said nothing, and I chose to follow his lead. It was the path of least resistance, and let's face it, Sam has taught us all the art of management by avoidance. He began the art when his father died, and he has worked hard to perfect it over the years. Sometimes avoidance is arguably the right path. I told myself I would quit the moment Sam caught me and I saw how he decided to let it be. This was my free pass, and a smart person knows there are only so many free passes in life. Unfortunately, though, I wasn't quite able to quit. You see, addiction is a very powerful state of being. It has moments that are confusing to react to. Addiction can fight a formidable fight against music and love any day of the week.

I decided the easiest way to get clean was to not go back north, and this was a good plan until I needed a fix. Heroin is not so easy to score in Chinook River, so I went and saw an old-timer doctor in the next town over who is known for being an easy play for pharma synthetics. These are the pharma drugs that law-abiding people get prescribed in order to get through their own days of suffering. It was an easy score. I simply made an appointment, told him about Rose, and played up my pain. He acknowledged he knew about Rose and the crime, and then he prescribed me some good stuff. Hell, he gave me enough prescriptions to last a year.

The problem is the pharmas are not quite like the street drugs. Ironically, street drugs are much more stable and predictable. The pharmas made me act a little crazy, and my parents reacted by calling RC. Wi had also reached out to him. He came over to the house one night, and we had a good old heart to heart. I did not convince him. Then the Judge came over on his own, and that did not go so well either. After that, they both decided an intervention was required, which was all good. It was the perfect move by the perfect friends at the perfect time for a friend in need.

The intervention went as planned, and I will admit I was surprised and very happy that Wi was there. Just seeing Wi was all I needed to decide to get clean and get on with my life with Wi. After all, I was only a few months into the addiction, and I assumed there must be a ratio relationship between the length of the addiction and the length of time to sobriety – early in, early out.

Then I screwed up.

Wi and I fell asleep down in the basement. I woke up around three o'clock, and I couldn't get back to sleep, so I went upstairs to my bedroom and started the cleansing process while doing my best not to wake my parents. I gathered all the drug paraphernalia I had lying around. My intention was to throw it all away so I could start the morning off clean. I gathered and organized and then put it all in a pile in the middle of my bed. When I looked at the pile, I realized I had some real street heroin left over from Christmas. Then the addict took over. *What the hell,* I said to myself. *It would be a shame for this to go to waste since I'm quitting all of this in the morning. It would almost be an insult to the heroin. After all, the heroin worked hard to become heroin. Should it not be allowed to see its natural end?*

With that misguided notion, I packed a small bag, grabbed some warm clothes and Ozark, quietly left the house, and headed to the Lodge.

The walk to the Lodge was like a skip of joy with absolute thoughtfulness. I didn't feel the bitter cold and enjoyed every part of the walk. I purposely took a new path in order to follow my own rule of never leaving a trail. Man oh man, it was easy to be happy. I was walking with Ozark, my real friend, and my drugs, who were fake friends, but friends nonetheless. I was walking to a place where my real friends and

I always enjoyed ourselves. *Fake it till you make it* I told myself as I broke a new path through the winter terrain.

I got to the Lodge and got the Findley going. I was warm before I knew it, and I quickly began freeing myself of my fake friends. *See you later, buddy,* I told each fake friend as I puffed it, swallowed it, or shot it. It was a cheerful going away party for friends you hope never to see again in your lifetime. *See ya later, buddy! Not if I see you sooner, pal!* It was all good. It was a celebration gathering of absolutely sincere insincerity.

Then the sun started to come up, and I knew I would eventually need to straighten up and get back to the house, or at least show up at the house even if totally tuned up. I was heading to rehab, so I might as well show up in true style!

I had enough juice for one more hit and a few pharma pills left, so I decided to push it a little. It was my last venture after all, so I shot the drug into my arm, ate the pills, and then headed to get some wood for one last heat up of the Lodge before heading back home. When I got to the woodpile, the sun was streaming through the trees, so I decided to watch it bring in the dawn. This was my God telling me everything was going to be OK. So I lay down in the snow to look back up at the sun.

While lying in the snow, I started to feel the snow with the tips of my fingers. I did not have my gloves on. Then I started to kick a little snow with my feet and toes. I did not have my boots on either. Then I started to make a snow angel by spreading my feet and arms out in unison. I worked hard in the snow to build my angel, and it was an incredibly peaceful moment that I wished would last forever.

And then I died. It was very quick. My heart stopped just like that. It was the quintessential overdose.

I didn't freeze to death, although that's what the Judge will ask the coroner to tell my parents and the boys. My heart just stopped. I mixed the wrong drugs, in the wrong quantity, at the wrong time, and in the wrong place. I guess I wasn't as smart as I thought I was.

I screwed up bad.

But please believe me when I tell you that I did not want to die. I wanted to live. I wanted to embrace my talents and accept the Judge's offer to help me with my education. I wanted to sing and write and play hockey. I wanted to grow old with my Brothers, and I wanted to be with Wi.

I really screwed up bad.

DAY 20

South Carolina

Avalanche

"HI, DOC."

"Hi, Sam."

"You doing all right?"

"Pretty good, Doc. I appreciate the small break from our talks."

"Did it help?"

"Not sure. How would you define help?"

"Are you ready to talk, Sam?"

Silence

"Probably."

"OK, good. Where should we start, Sam?"

"Where do you feel we should start, Doc? You're the expert."

"OK, thanks for allowing me to lead. Let's talk about Sophie and George."

"What's to talk about? They left me. I'm here and they aren't."

"So that's how you see it, Sam? That they left you?"

Silence

"Yes, Doc, that's how I see it, and it's my fault."

"Sam?"

"Yes, Doc?"

"Why do you feel Sophie and George left you?"

"What?"

"Why do you feel that Sophie and George left you?"

"Because they did!"

"Sam?"

"Yes, Doc?"

"Where do you think Sophie and George are right now?"

Silence

"Sam, I need you to tell me where you think they are."

Silence

"Sam, do you think they're in South Carolina?"

"No."

"Do you think they're in the United States?"

"No."

"Do you think they're in Canada?"

"No, Doc, I don't think they're in Canada!"

"Then where are they, Sam?"

Silence

"Sam?"

"What?"

"Where are they?"

"I have no idea where they are, Doc!"

"Why not, Sam?"

"What do you mean why not?"

"Sam, I'm asking you why you have no idea where Sophie and George are."

"What?"

"You heard me, Sam."

Silence

"Fine, Doc. You want to know why I have no idea where they are? That's what you want to know, Doc?"

"Yes, Sam."

"Fine, fine, Doc. Just fine. I have no idea where they are because they're dead! They are dead and I have no idea where they are now that they are dead. Are you happy, Doc? Are you happy with your work now? Am I cured now, Doc? Can I go live a happy life now, Doc? My wife and child are dead, and it's all my fault. It's all my fucking fault, Doc!"

Canada
1984

God's Wrath

THE MOMENTUM of the chaos didn't slow down at all. The day after Ray died, we all met with Ray's father at the Maple Tree Hotel to discuss what would happen next. It was Saturday morning, and we were sitting at the same tables that people had crashed their shot glasses down upon while saying goodbye to Vince. We all wanted a drink, but no drink would be served in the bar.

Ray's mother was not with us. She was finished in every way, and this was the first day for her in an ongoing healing journey that would last the rest of her life. Ray's father told us that the RCMP had combed through Ray's bedroom and found some empty pill bottles that came from a local doctor in a small town one county over from ours. Apparently this doctor had lost his way from the Hippocratic Oath and had consciously or subconsciously become a narcotics dealer. Both the Judge and RC noticeably got their backs up with this information. The RCMP assured Ray's mother and father that the doctor would be investigated, although I'm not sure they cared either way. Dead is dead, and both of their children were now gone.

Ray's father then looked at the Judge briefly and then looked at

436

Wi and told her that Ray had frozen to death after over-drinking and passing out in the snow beside the Lodge. RC grabbed Wi's hand while she internalized the thought of his last moments, while Hats and I looked at each other with similar visions in our minds.

Ray's father said that Ray would be cremated and that we would have a small and closed ceremony Monday morning at the United Church presided over by Preacher Pete. Ray's father looked at the Judge again, this time with a look of appreciation, and told us no autopsy would be done and that the local funeral home would complete the cremation the next day, even though it was Sunday, a day they normally didn't work. We all nodded in agreement and appreciation for people we didn't know but who were now part of the process. The plans were not really open for discussion, and we were all fine with that. Of course, Ray's father asked me if I would say a few words, and of course I agreed. This was my role. *Eat tree, Beaver!* Our meeting lasted no more than twenty minutes, and Ray's father headed home to be with his wife.

After a few minutes of silence, RC banged his fist on the table and uncharacteristically ran out of the Maple Tree Hotel in anger. The Judge followed RC out, caught up with him, and ended up taking him to his house to calm him down. We did not see either of them until they arrived at the church Monday morning. They both clearly needed some space, as did I, so I found a quiet spot at the bar to attempt work on my words for Ray. Wi, Hats, Ozark, and Curly stayed with me at the Maple Tree Hotel, and Hats told Wi about Ray, Vince, the Maple Tree Hotel, and all our history. Wi listened with absolute concentration, breaking in only when she wanted more details or clarification on a certain story. When nighttime came, the three of us and the dogs spent the night at Hats' house. Sunday was a nothing day; we did not leave Hats' house. I worked again on my words for Ray while Hats continued to educate Wi on all things Beaver Brothers, each of us fully cognizant that across town Ray was being cremated.

Monday morning came, and the three of us and Ozark headed to the United Church, where Preacher Pete greeted us with his wife and led us to a small gathering room. It was prepared with chairs for no more than ten people. Ray's ashes were in a small urn on a pedestal at the front of the room. There was no picture or any identifying visuals relating to Ray, and in some way this made it easier for us to cope with the situation. I wondered whether Preacher Pete did that on purpose, or if Ray's father had something to do with it. Meanwhile, Ozark lay down beside the pedestal and ashes.

A few minutes later, the Judge, Johanna, RC, and Ray's father walked into the room. Ray's mother did not attend the service. This small group was the final quorum to say goodbye to Ray.

Preacher Pete asked us to sit down and began to say a few words, but nobody heard anything he said. I suspect he was trying to say something spiritual, something insightful, or something encouraging, but he was as lost as the rest of us. Once again, he was learning by doing. The whole time I was listening, but I was not hearing Preacher Pete talk. I was thinking about Bible verses he could have used for the day. There were so many he could have chosen from, and it was as if I suddenly remembered all the teachings we had received at Sunday school growing up. I felt my anger begin to grow, and I could literally feel my blood pulsing through my veins and arteries.

Come on, Pete, I thought to myself. *Don't leave out...*

Do not let your hearts be troubled. Trust in God; trust also in me. In my Father's house are many rooms; if it were not so, I would have told you. I am going there to prepare a place for you.

If we live, we live to the Lord; and if we die, we die to the Lord. So, whether we live or die, we belong to the Lord.

A good name is better than fine perfume, and the day of death better than the day of birth.

Even though I walk through the valley of the shadow of death, I will fear no evil.

My anger continued to grow as I started reciting verses in my head. I was still watching Preacher Pete talk, but I heard nothing that he said. His lips were moving and making no sound. I was completely disassociated from my surroundings. Then my thoughts took an even worse turn.

"*What about these quotes, Pete?*" my brain asked. *These should work pretty well for our little family gathering? How about a little:*

God is a righteous judge, a God who expresses his wrath every day.

Whoever believes in the Son has eternal life; whoever does not obey the Son shall not see life, but the wrath of God remains on him.

And if anyone's name was not found written in the book of life, he was thrown into the lake of fire.

I will execute great vengeance on them with wrathful rebukes. Then they will know that I am the Lord, when I lay my vengeance upon them.

The Lord is a jealous and avenging God; the Lord is avenging and wrathful; the Lord takes vengeance on his adversaries and keeps wrath for his enemies.

Then my anger turned on me, and I turned on God.

What's up anyway, God? Were you a little pissed off at Ray for believing in the sun? I guess your ego was a little damaged? Eh, God? A little sensitive are we? Or maybe a little angry? Just out of curiosity, God, what happened along the way that made you so angry at all of us? A little malfunction in the master plan? The whole freedom to choose concept didn't quite work out in the bigger picture? Or is the anger stemming from the whole Jesus dying on the cross thing? But wait, that was you, wasn't it? Ahhh, I get it now. Your own invention turned on you, and that really pissed you off. Sounds like a design flaw to me, buddy. Maybe you need to go back to engineering school? Don't you know the first design of something always has flaws? We call them failure modes. Did you skip class that day? Eh, God? Eh, God? Eh, God?

I finally came back to consciousness when I realized the Judge had grabbed my arm. Everybody was looking at me, including Preacher Pete, and it was clear I had been muttering under my breath loud enough for them to hear sounds but not the words making up those sounds. And it was now my turn to speak, although I will readily admit I was not in a good spot emotionally.

I smiled and tried to appear normal. I'm not sure I fooled anybody, certainly not myself anyway. I walked up to the podium and stood beside Ray's ashes and Ozark, and I pulled my notes out in order to read what I had finalized the day before as it was not possible for my brain to memorize the poem. I said nothing as an introduction, I simply read the title of the poem, and silence and my quick departure were the only indications of the ending when I finished.

I simply read my words and talked to Ray.

MEMORIES OF TOMORROW

*Reflecting with a friend
Is it the right thing to do
Should memories be left behind
Will skeletons crash through
We're only ages once
Regrets can be forgotten
Is childhood overrated
In a place that seems forsaken*

*I must believe in you
Your stories are mine to tell*

Without a sense of pride
Thoughts will feel like hell
Those times that seemed confusing
We made decisions that seemed best
No one craves the dark side
Some don't pass the test

Take a good look at me now
Completely lonely but not alone
Wondering about days to come
From actions the past has grown
Where would I be without you
The push to just move on
Can I still count on your support
When my road gets too long
Have you ever lost yourself
When searching for the same

Memories will always surface
With the mention of a name
Who knows what tomorrow holds
It's a waste to live in fear
As daybreak arrives
Only friendships are held near

Would you change the times we had
Given that "ifs" were true
Would I agree with your changes
Is that what I would do
So many questions unanswered
Using precious time
Also answers questioned
There is too much yet to find

Did we make a difference
To the surroundings in our path
If our sticks had not turned the soil
Would fond memories still last
I can't believe this to be
As our walks made who we are
I needed you to show me the way
When memories of tomorrow seemed so far

I walked out of the church immediately after reading my poem. I simply walked out without making eye contact with anybody, and I waited outside for the group in spite of the cold temperatures.

And to this day, I have never again set foot in the Chinook River United Church, or any other church for that matter.

1980   1990   Present

DAY 21
South Carolina

Failure Modes

I'M SITTING IN MY little room in my little hospital whose purpose is to make me sane. Yet my peace of mind seems farther away today than it has ever been. The Doc finally threw out her clinch move, and I took the bait. I suspect I was ready, though, and now I have to relive everything in order to live with a few things. I have to relive the past in the present to live in the future. It's time travel without any hope of advancement, and the very best we can hope for is just to get to some place that is acceptable for existence where there is no prize for success. Where there is only punishment for failure – all pain and no gain. Not so perfect.

Well, there is no time like the present to work on the future. So here's the story.

March of two years ago was Sophie's forty-seventh birthday. George was just learning how to be a teenager, and I had big plans for Sophie's birthday for the Friday night of her birthday week. We loved birthdays. They were important celebrations, and we enjoyed celebrating how happy we were together. Our love for each other and for George only grew as we grew, and birthdays were an objective measure of this growth.

442

I was working in New Orleans that week. We had a large convention organized, a very successful event, but it meant I had a lot to do. I got caught up in my work and missed my flight home for Sophie's party. *This was failure mode number one.* This was the critical root cause of the series of events, and this was entirely my fault. This was all my doing, and there is no one to blame but myself.

Instead of sticking to my priority of getting home, I called Sophie with a wonderful idea. *This was failure mode number two.* The idea was to charter a plane for her and George to come to New Orleans the following morning. It was extravagant, but they could avoid all the post-911 air travel headaches, and we would have a wonderful birthday weekend together in a very cool city. Sophie and George thought this was a fantastic idea, so I had my office set it up while I got back to work, knowing they would leave home on a private charter the next morning before the sun came up.

The wheels of *entropy, brokenness, and Godlessness* were set in motion.

Sophie and George arrived at the airport in South Carolina and boarded the small aircraft. I had splurged and chartered a jet, which meant two pilots. *Safety first!* It was still dark; the pilots received information from air traffic control, and they took off for New Orleans. Their cargo was two people I loved more than life itself. Thirty seconds after takeoff the airplane crashed into the forest at the end of the runway. The plane burst into flames and all four on board perished. My Sophie and George were killed. Just like that, they were gone.

I found out about their deaths on cable television. That's right. I was in my hotel room getting ready to go meet them at the executive airport in New Orleans, and I had the television playing in the background. A *breaking news* story came on the screen and caught my attention. The Talking Cable Heads are very good at getting one's attention. It was a small aircraft accident. I stopped what I was doing and stood in front of the TV. The accident had just happened. The Talking Cable Heads were all over it because this was what they live for – a small aircraft crash is like a wet dream for them. A large commercial aircraft accident is like a two-month orgy.

I don't know why, but I instantly knew it was Sophie and George, even though the Talking Cable Heads got it all wrong. They had the originating airport wrong, but I knew it was Sophie and George. They had the destination airport wrong, but I knew it was Sophie and

George. They had the make and model of the aircraft wrong, but I knew it was Sophie and George. They had the name of the charter company wrong, but I knew it was Sophie and George. In fact, the only piece they got right was their opinion as to whether there were any survivors. I knew Sophie and George were gone as I watched the images of the smoldering aircraft.

I have no recollection of what I did or what happened next. At some point, I received a call on my cell phone. I answered it. It was Alec calling me via the Judge calling him via Kees calling him. I later learned that Sophie had put Kees' name and number down on a form asking for a *non-family member* to reach in case of an emergency.

Alec was vintage Alec. He does not mince his words.

"Sam," he said, "Sophie and George have been in an aircraft accident, and there are no survivors. Sam, Sophie and George have been killed. Sam, I am so, so sorry, son, but we will get through this. Now please do exactly what I tell you to do." I listened, and I followed his instructions, as there are times in life where you simply have to put trust into the people you trust, into the people who have your back, into the people who love you.

I was handled by my employees and without complaint was put on a chartered jet that flew me to Sarasota, Florida, where I was picked up by Alec and taken to his home on Siesta Key. After I had been at Alec's house a few hours, a doctor arrived. I was sedated, and I stayed in that state for over two weeks. In the end, I spent over two months at Alec's before returning to our home in South Carolina, before returning to the world, although saying I returned to the world would actually be a stretch. I returned to the world by avoiding my home, by focusing on my work, by continuing to build my business. I lost myself in a blurred reality.

The first few days at Alec's are a crazy, hazy image in my mind's eye. I did not go to the funeral for Sophie and George. Alec, the Judge, and Kees made all the arrangements; RC, Wi, and Hats provided support along with Sophie's friends. I was later told that hundreds of people showed up, including all the young people from George's school, where there was an outpouring of grief and support. Oddly enough, I did write a poem for Sophie and George, although nobody has ever seen it. I guess some habits never die; I guess we just have to *Eat tree* when that's what we are made to do.

I slowly pieced the series of events together while recovering at Alec's, mostly with the help of Hats, who was coming to Sarasota regularly and spending days at a time with me. Hats believed the only way for me to get through the tragedy was to re-channel my energies largely through understanding facts and getting angry, so I signed up for his style of therapy. Anger was easier to embrace than any other option or alternative emotion.

This is what I learned through the fact-finding process.

The pilots took off on the wrong runway. *Failure mode number three.* The runway they used was too short for that particular jet. *Failure mode number four.* The airport was under construction. *Number five.* The air traffic controller was tired and half asleep and did not continue to watch where the plane taxied while heading to the wrong runway. *Number six.* According to the law, there were supposed to be two air traffic controllers in the tower, but there was only one. *Number seven.* The maps the pilots were using for the airport and runway layout were out of date and inaccurate due to the construction at the airport. *Number eight.* The lights, numbers and visual cues on the runways were all in varied states of disrepair. *Number nine.* The pilots were talking about the latest football game while taking off as opposed to following "sterile cockpit" rules. *Number ten.* At the end of the runway the jet clipped some parked construction equipment with its landing gear while trying to rotate and get airborne once the pilots realized the runway was too short. *Number eleven, twelve, thirteen.* There was more fuel on the plane than there should have been, which made the plane heavier, making it harder to take off, all because the gauges on the fuel contractor's pumps had not been properly maintained. If only the fueler had flicked the plastic of the gauge with his finger to make sure the needle was moving. *Number fourteen, fifteen, sixteen.* The trees at the end of the runway were taller than they were supposed to be by Federal Aviation standards, making it even harder for the plane to clear the forest. *Number seventeen.* The numbers of the two runways at the airport were 31 and 81, making it easy to mix them up in the dark. *Number eighteen.* The short runway the plane took off from serves no useful purpose for any aircraft today and was supposed to have a concrete barrier across the entrance, but the barrier had never been put in place. *Number nineteen.*

The world is broken, and there is no God. *Number twenty and twenty-one.*

Hats wanted to sue everybody. He wanted to sue the pilots, the airline, the airport, the FAA, and the US government. I told him that I did not need that type of energy, and he started threatening to sue them anyway. The airport authority responded with threatening to counter-sue the estate of Sophie and George. Their lawyer claimed Sophie and George contributed to the negligence of the accident because they should have been aware that the airport was under construction. Hats was furious and leaked this information into the community, where-upon the lawyer quickly backed down. However, the damage had been done, and in my shared anger with Hats, I signed over power of attorney to him and told him to do whatever he wanted. I told him I didn't want to know any of the details and that any money he collected should go to the Maple Tree Foundation. My sense is he went after everybody. You don't mess with Hats, especially when he is angry and believes he is right, which is pretty much all of the time.

And that is the story. I lost my family, I lost my life, and to cope I lost myself inside my work, and it actually appeared to the world that I was going to survive the tragedy. The great imposter called Sam was alive and well, that is, of course, until I went back to New Orleans recently.

You know that part of the story.

I've never shared the poem I wrote for Sophie and George. I carry it in my wallet, written on the same piece of old paper I grabbed from a desk in Alec's house during my first week after the accident. I re-read it often.

You will be the first people I have ever shared it with.

Please treat it with respect.

PLEASE DON'T TELL ME

Please don't tell me
that you can imagine how I feel
Unless you've been where I am now
You can't know how I feel
I am so sad, I am so mad
I just don't understand

Please don't tell me
that you can imagine how I feel
How can you know
when I don't even know myself
I pray I will wake soon
realizing this is but a dream
and that my world has not changed

Please don't tell me
that you can imagine how I feel
But please stay by my side
Your presence comforts me
I feel so all alone
Yet I sense that you are close
I know I need you

Please don't tell me
that you can imagine how I feel
Time will not heal my wound
It does not know what I've lost
Although I may laugh again
Things are different now
Life will never be the same

Please don't tell me
that you can imagine how I feel
I truly hope you can't
For you are my friend
and as my friend
I wish you will never face
The pain I feel today

Please don't tell me
that you can imagine how I feel
Tell me about the past
Of the memories and love I've known
Tell me about the future
How my memories of love
Will somehow make me strong

In Sophie's Voice

MY POOR SAM. I feel so terrible for my Sam. How I wish I could tell him that everything is fine.

But I can't reach him. Only Ray is able to get through.

His heart was in the right place. All he wanted was for George and me to be with him for my birthday. His heart is always in the right place; all he has is his heart; he wears it on every part of his being.

He was incapable of coming to our funeral, but he wrote to me, and I could hear him and his words. But he doesn't hear me because his anger will not allow it. Anger is the most powerful negative force in the universe, so powerful that the darkness of anger needs to be overcome before the light of love can shine through. Anger and hate can, in fact, be more powerful than love. This is the one secret people need to learn and find a solution for.

I wasn't surprised when he called with a new plan for my birthday weekend. I knew he was exceptionally busy in New Orleans. He had spent months getting ready for the convention, and it was one of his biggest turnouts to date. It validated that he was helping people and that he had a mass following, even though Sam would never allow himself to accept that people wanted to follow him. Sam is not ready for that responsibility, and that is noble, that is the modest heart that drives Sam. Both George and I are so proud of Sam.

The idea to spend the weekend in New Orleans was a great plan, and George and I were both excited. The charter of a jet just added to the excitement. Sam's business was doing well, and we were starting to enjoy some of the benefits of success. I believe people need to enjoy the results of hard work. I believe this is important.

I didn't know anything was wrong until it went all wrong, and I had no way of knowing all the universal entropy that was in motion that morning. It made the concept of the perfect storm look more like a light rain. I guess you never know. I guess only the universe itself knows even though the universe is part of its own momentum. The universe is the cause of all actions, and it is also the result of those same actions. You see, the world is not cause and effect. Y is not always a function of X. Sometimes the Xs are dependent on the Ys. It is not always inputs driving outputs as outputs can, in fact, drive inputs. Causation is not binary, cause and effect are not linear. It is all one. Everything is one, and this is the Great Mystery, where the only real question is, *What is the origin of everything being one*? The Great Mystery – a mystery that will not, and should not, ever be answered by people while they are alive on the Earth. You have to be patient to find out the answers to the big questions.

My first instinct of doom was when we abruptly left the runway. The wheels of the small aircraft hit something that created a thundering noise, and the plane began to shake. At that point everything went into quantum slow motion.

I knew in that instant the plane would crash. I also knew we would not survive, and with this deep knowledge I only wanted to comfort George, so I grabbed his left hand with my right hand and I told him everything would be fine.

Time continued to slow down, but it was still moving forward. A second felt like a year.

We didn't participate in the ultimate impact of the crash. We didn't feel pain and we didn't suffer.

At some point, time stood still. At some point, time actually stopped.

I felt a presence, a presence that was a hand taking my left hand, and I looked towards it and knew my Poppa was with me. Then I saw him. I looked at him. He was young, strong, and healthy. He smiled at me. He talked to me.

"It's OK, sweetie," he said. "We're here."

"OK, Poppa," I said, as I squeezed my father's strong hand. The feel of his hand was familiar; it was comforting, and it was safe.

I looked at George in the seat beside me. I was still holding his left hand.

Ray was holding his right hand. Ray, looking just as I remember him

– gentle, beautiful, wearing his Dream Catcher earring – was holding onto George's hand. He leaned over and talked to George.

"Hi, George," Ray said, his voice sounding like the voice of an angel. "Everything is fine, son. Your Grampa and I are here for you and your mom."

"Who are you?" George asked.

Time did not exist; any understanding of earthly rotations had disappeared.

"I'm an old friend of your father," Ray said to George.

"Are you Ray? George asked.

"Yes," Ray answered.

George smiled.

"Are we going with you and Grampa?" George asked.

"Yes," Ray answered.

And then we went with my Poppa and Ray.

On Earth, time and the laws of entropy continued on.

Canada
1984

The Foundation

WE HEADED BACK to the Maple Tree Hotel after Ray's intimate service. It was the Judge, Wi, RC, Hats, Ozark, and I. We picked Curly up on the way. Ray's father had gone home to be with Ray's mother – another first day of their long journey. Ray's father is a good man.

We sat down at our regular table. Silence overtook the atmosphere, and the Judge lit up his pipe, allowing the smell of the tobacco to soothe the air in some strange respect. RC, Hats, and I did not smoke any torpedoes. Something was missing; Ray was missing. We changed a lot of our habits that day. Certain Beaver Brothers traditions have lived on, but others died with Ray. I suspect the torpedoes were a good one to leave behind.

Wi broke the silence by asking about the Maple Tree Foundation. She was asking questions for clarification on what she had heard from Hats the day before, and she had new inquiries to help her better understand the wishes that Vince had left behind. We talked for over two hours, the Judge explained details even the boys and I did not fully appreciate from the conversation we had had after Vince's goodbye celebration.

451

We then resumed our silence.

After a few minutes with all of us in private thought, Wi broke the silence again.

"Can I ask a question?" she said, her soft and gentle voice making it impossible for any caring human being to deny her the request.

"Yes?" The Judge asked, really saying, *Wi, you can ask any question, any time, any place.*

"Could you turn the Maple Tree Hotel into a place for kids to come and be with other kids? And maybe have some counselling and coaching available? Maybe focus on underprivileged and *at risk* teenagers? Maybe even work closely with the Aboriginal and First Nations community, or try to help with the abuses of drug addiction and alcoholism?"

We all allowed this idea to register in our minds, quickly generating all the uplifting possibilities. Then we all looked at the Judge to see if this would pass the test of Vince's wishes for the foundation. A huge smile came over the Judge's face as he took a puff from his pipe and adjusted his posture before answering the question.

"I think that is the type of idea that would line up congruently with what Vince wanted," the Judge said in a formal tone of voice, really saying, *God bless you, Wi. God bless you, my child. That is the perfect idea.*

RC, Hats, and I did not speak. Ozark and Curly were both asleep and lying beside Wi. We fell back to our silence to imagine visions of what Wi had suggested until Wi broke the silence for the third time.

"Can I stay and be part of it?" she asked us, really saying, *I want this to be my home. I want this to be my life. I want this to be how I make a difference in the world.*

Without hesitation, we said yes to Wi's request, and for the next ten hours there were no more moments of silence. We spent that entire day and evening planning the future of the Maple Tree Foundation. In the end, the Maple Tree Hotel would be turned into exactly what Wi had described to us in her initial question. Wi would stay and be the full-time managing director, and she would be paid a salary through the foundation as the first full-time employee. The Judge said he would take care of any Canadian immigration issues that Wi would need taken care of. He then taught us about some of the Foundation formalities that were required, and from that we had to vote in a Board of Directors. RC was voted in as Chairman, the Judge accepted the temporary role as Treasurer to sort out the money processes, and Hats and I were voted in as Active Board Members. We both knew we were going back to our studies and therefore could not accept a position that would require local presence to keep things going. Ozark and Curly were listed as non-voting board members.

Hats was the only one who had a request that added to Wi's vision of the foundation.

"I think we should change the Maple Tree's hockey uniforms to reflect the colors of the Detroit Red Wings," Hats threw out on the table.

"Done," the Judge said in an instant, slamming his coffee cup down on the table as if it were a gavel and he were on his bench.

"Good," Hats replied back, really saying, *You're fucking right we will use the Red Wings colors.*

We were close to being done with the plan for the Maple Tree Foundation. There was only one thing left to accomplish.

"What will we call it?" The Judge asked us as a group.

Once again, and without hesitation, we all turned to Wi as she was now our idea person. In the last twelve hours she had proven herself as a visionary, a strategist, an administrator, and a leader. She was our managing director, our friend. Wi, whom we had only met a few months earlier, but now with whom we had a lifelong bond, our trusted friend Wi, who came all the way from Montana to help save Ray. Our little but strong Wi – beautiful in body, mind, and spirit. Our Wi, our Sunshine. Our Wi, our Sunshine who we knew had been in love with Ray.

There were a few moments of silence while we gave Wi some time to think.

"How about *The Ray and the Rose?*" she asked us in her quiet voice, as her match to Ray's Dream Catcher earring dangled from her right ear.

RC, Hats, and I all stared at the floor while Ozark popped her head up as if telling us she understood the significance of the suggestion. We continued to stare at the floor. We knew that if we looked at each other we would break down. We knew that if we looked at the Judge, we would break down.

"Done!" the Judge said with absolute passion, again slamming his coffee cup down on the table as if it were a gavel and he were on his bench. He did not need to seek our approval. He knew as well as we did that it was the perfect name.

Having been saved by the Judge, we raised our heads from our floor gaze. Ozark got up from the floor.

"Done!" we all said in unison, and RC stood up and walked over and gave Wi a huge hug. Hats, the Judge, and I then did the same. Ozark went to Wi and put her head on her lap. Curly wagged his tail.

"Good," the Judge said. "All business has been taken care of. We can rest now. Vince, Ray, and Rose can rest now. True healing will begin."

What a day we had been through. We said goodbye to Ray in the morning and we said hello to *The Ray and the Rose* that night. We were emotionally and physically exhausted. It was time to go home, so the seven of us left the old Maple Tree Hotel, now *The Ray and the Rose,* and we started heading down the sidewalk towards the parking lot where the Judge and RC had parked their cars.

It was late on a Monday night so there were not a lot of people out, but there were a handful of people heading in and out of the Empire Hotel, the new watering hole for local drinkers. Other than that, there was no one out other than an RCMP cruiser with two constables in it. It was their standard work for Monday night to park in front of the Empire Hotel in order to let people know there was no point in trying to drive impaired. Getting caught was a certainty.

There was an unfortunate lack of timing: just as we were walking by the Empire Hotel entrance, Timmy and Joey McMullen were walking out of the bar with three of their cousins, all around the same age as the dumbass twins.

We were so exhausted that we didn't even notice Timmy and Joey, although that didn't stop them from noticing us. Our two groups passed each other without confrontation, and when Timmy was about five feet behind us, he turned around and yelled, "Hey, Beaver Brothers, your new bar sucks! A closed bar with no booze? That's fucking brilliant, Beaver Brothers!"

We didn't even stop. We had no intention of getting involved. We were done with those morons. Too much had happened; we had matured ten years in the last six months, we had matured another ten years in the last forty-eight hours, and we were tired. In fact, even Hats was too tired to get involved. *Good boy, Hats.* We were all so very tired.

As we kept walking, Joey decided to support his brother. There was a space of twenty feet between the two groups now, so Joey had to yell loudly. "Hey, Hats," Joey screamed at us. "I hear your buddy Ray can't handle the needle or the spoon too well!"

We all heard it loud and clear, every word of it; even the constables in the cruiser heard it. My blood started to boil with anger, but we didn't look back, and we kept walking. We were above anything the dumbasses could say to us. We kept walking. Even Hats brushed it off and kept walking – that is, right up until he did not brush it off and he stopped walking. The rest of us were five steps ahead of Hats when we realized he had stopped walking. Only Ozark and Curly were by his side. We stopped, turned around, looked at Hats, and saw the look on his face. There was no point in arguing with him about what would happen next. Sometimes Hats simply needs to be Hats. Sometimes a man simply needs to be a man. Sometimes what is right is simply doing what is right, and I was in full agreement with his decision. It was time. *Good boy, Hats.*

The Judge, always thinking ten steps and five years ahead, told RC and Wi to go into the RCMP cruiser that was parked on the street. The two constables were totally engaged in the situation at this point and were going to take the Judge's lead. The constable riding shotgun got out and opened the back door for Wi and RC, and while RC complied you could tell he was not very happy about the Judge's orders.

I joined the Judge, and we walked up to Hats. Timmy and Joey and their three inbred cousins were stopped on the sidewalk, dumbass grins on their faces, waiting for our response.

"You boys got this?" the Judge asked, looking at both of us, but specifically talking to Hats.

"I got this," Hats replied, really saying, *I fucking got this, Judge.* Hats then looked at me and said, "Sam, you can go wait in the cruiser if you want. I'm OK here."

"I'm not going anywhere, Hats," was my reply. The Judge nodded his approval and walked back to the cruiser where he joined RC and Wi by getting in the driver's side rear door of the police cruiser. Ozark and Curly stayed beside Hats the entire time.

Hats and I didn't waste any time developing a plan. We simply turned around and started walking towards the McMullens. They started walking towards us. It didn't take long to close the gap, and before we knew it we were facing each other with no more than a foot between the two of us and the five of them. I was standing on the left of Hats. The McMullens formed a straight horizontal line in front of us. Timmy was on our far right, Joey right beside him, and the other three to Joey's right completed the team of five, which coincidentally was their combined IQ.

I briefly looked back to the cruiser and could see the Judge putting his hand on RC's shoulder. While I could not hear them, it was obvious he was telling him to stay in the car. I saw Wi say something to RC, which I assumed was her asking RC to listen to the Judge. I quickly came back to the situation at hand.

I had no idea how this was going to play out, but I did know that I was filled with emotion, mostly in the form of anger, and it was flowing through my veins, so I was ready to get busy and use some of the Krav Maga we had learned over the years due to our friend Ray. That being said, Hats was the director of the play, and I fully intended to wait for his lead relative to the first move, which not surprisingly didn't take long to make itself evident.

Hats was standing directly in front of Joey with Timmy only an elbow to the left of his twin. All Hats said to Joey was, "What did you just say, Joey?" He then gave Joey absolutely zero time to answer. "Fuck it," Hats said after only half a second. "I heard you the first time." And with that, Hats threw a punch with his right hand and crushed Joey's face. Every ounce of Hats' immense strength was in the punch, and Joey fell to the ground in an unconscious crumpled ball.

The three cousins at Joey's right assessed the situation and decided I was the weak sheep in our flock, but still not taking any chances two of them came at me at the same time. They were both my size or bigger, but my confidence and anger level were higher. Hats did not move in to help me, as he kept his eye on Timmy the entire time. Besides, Hats knew I was as pissed off as he was.

The cousin on my left threw the first punch with his right hand. It was way too wide a throw, and I blocked it easily with my left arm. Remembering our training, I then followed up with a kick to his groin. When his face was on the way down because of the kick to his nuts, my right knee met his jaw at the halfway mark to the pavement. The contact was perfect. He was out, his jaw clearly broken. My knee felt as if it were crushed as well, and I wanted to scream in pain but did not allow myself to show any sign of weakness.

Within a split second, the cousin to my right did the exact same thing in a mirror image of the first cousin's attempt. Obviously left handed, he threw a punch that was once again far too wide, so I blocked it with my right arm, then kicked him in the groin and met his jaw with the same right knee while he was on the way down. He fell on top of his kin. I was proud that they were both TKO, but my knee felt as if I had suffered as much damage as their jaws.

At this point, there were two of them left and the two of us. Ozark and Curly were ready to engage as well, but really it was now about the Hats and Timmy Show.

"OK, Jackass," Hats said to Timmy, "let's get some closure on this game and finally shut down this overtime period with a little sudden death!"

Timmy didn't answer. He mostly looked puzzled. Yet with so many options available to him, what he decided to do was pull a knife from his pocket. It was a jackknife, and a good-sized one with at least a five-inch blade. He opened the knife and stood with it in front of Hats, and I will readily admit that he stood with a reasonable amount of confidence.

Hats just stared him down. Timmy didn't say a word; the knife was supposed to speak for itself. I looked back over my shoulder to the RCMP cruiser and noticed the constable who was the wheelman was opening the door of the car in order to approach the situation. I also noticed the Judge leaning forward from the backseat to put his hand on the constable's shoulder asking him to sit down and let the overtime period proceed. I could see the Judge holding RC back as well. *The show must go on* was the thought that went through my brain in that instant. The Judge knew this finally had to end, with Hats conducting the ending.

"OK, Jackass," Hats said to Timmy, "this will work fine, just fine." Hats then took off the thick leather jacket he was wearing and wrapped it around his left arm, creating a shield of sorts, presumably to protect himself against the blade of the knife. I couldn't remember learning that particular technique in our classes, and as I watched Hats I could not help but notice that he was now a man. He was athletic, he was strong, he was tough as nails, and he was really, really pissed off. Once again, I was very proud to be a best friend of The Hats.

While I was standing there being proud of Hats, I was also adding nothing to the battle. The leftover dumbass cousin still standing was equally doing nothing. This was the Hats and Timmy show, and Hats decided to get the last act under way. Shakespeare himself would have been delighted by the performance.

"You know your mistake here, Timmy?" Hats asked.

"What's that, Hats?" Timmy replied.

"You brought a knife to a fist fight, dumbass," Hats said, and then Hats threw his jacket-covered left arm into the air in a forward motion towards Timmy's right ear. Timmy, the inexperienced knife fighter, the infinite dumbass, took the bait and decided the arm was the target. He feebly threw up a potential stab at the jacketed arm, playing right into the plan, and Hats seized the moment and crushed Timmy's face with a right hand punch. Timmy fell onto Joey and the twins became a pile of morons.

Hats and I both looked at each other, and without speaking, we both remembered the day the Soup Man died and the hockey game we played that evening so many years ago. It was a strange feeling. So much had happened since that day.

At this point, Joey and Timmy were out cold, and my two related nemeses were still on the ground, moaning while holding their nuts and jaws. This left Hats, me, Ozark, Curly, and the last cousin. The cousin assessed the scene to the point his small brain could process reality, and he quickly decided running was the best option for his particular circumstance. He headed at full speed down the side of the road, coincidently heading right towards the RCMP cruiser. I once again noticed the wheelman constable moving to get out of the car, and once again, I observed the Judge calming him by putting his hand on his shoulder, asking him to sit back down behind the wheel. The main event wasn't over yet.

The cousin was at full speed running down the road and was quickly nearing the RCMP cruiser, and it appeared as if he would pass the cruiser and run his way back to the bush where he came from. The cousin was just about even with the hood of the cruiser, and when the timing was impeccably perfect, the Judge rammed his passenger door open. The colliding energy of the door moving one way and the cousin moving towards that way proved to be a Hollywood moment. To this day I'll never forget the look on the face of the moron cousin as he hit the cruiser door and slid vertically down to the pavement in a ball of dumbness.

Hats and I watched the whole track meet, and when the cousin hit the pavement, Hats looked at me and threw his hand up and we did our *Eat tree, Beaver!* handshake. "Now that's fucking Philadelphia Flyer Hockey, brother!" was all he said as we completed the handshake with the Beaver Lodge fist pump.

The constable riding shotgun got out of the cruiser, and when he got out we could see that he was a big man. He walked around the cruiser, picked the dumbass up off the street, literally put him over his shoulder, and carried him like a sack of potatoes, only to drop him in the pile of morons on the sidewalk. He then went back to the cruiser, and the cruiser was put into drive. RC, the Judge, Wi, and the constables pulled up to Hats and me. "We have an errand to run," the Judge said to us, yelling over RC and Wi through the opened passenger window. They then headed down the road, and Hats, Ozark, Curly, and I headed to Hats' place with me limping the whole way. We would finally fall asleep that night after a few good-size shots of the King's whiskey.

The next morning RC and Wi came over to wake us up, both of them still running on the adrenaline from the night before. RC told us that they had spent the night with the Judge and Johanna. He also told us that after they left in the cruiser they headed out past the town line where the McMullens have their family compounds and various business ventures.

"It was priceless," RC started telling us.

"We were in the cruiser not knowing where we were going," RC continued, "but the Judge and the constables knew exactly where they were going. We ended up at the house of the patriarch of the McMullen clan – the oldest, smartest of the uncles. When we got there, the Judge asked me and the senior constable to join him to go meet Old Man McMullen. He told the junior constable and Wi to stay in the car."

"Really?" I said, really saying, *Good God, RC, what the hell happened next?*

"So we banged on the door and the Old Man answered," RC went on. "He was standing in the doorway, and he and the Judge gave each other a nod that suggested they knew each other well. It was eerie. They didn't shake hands, but there was some sort of mutual respect that existed between the two men. The Judge told the Old Man that he needed to go clean up the street in front of the Empire Hotel. He then told the Old Man that he expected Timmy and Joey to be gone from our county within twenty-four hours."

"Really?" I said again, not knowing what was coming next. Hats was just listening to the story with a big smile on his face. I noticed the knuckles on his right hand were badly bruised.

"Yip," RC said.

"Then the Old Man said, 'No fucking way. I ain't sending any more of our boys outta here, Judge. You gotta just deal with 'em from now on. I'm sick of this bullshit!'"

"Really?" was all I could continue to say. Smiling was all Hats could continue to do.

"Yip," RC said back to me.

"So then the senior constable said to the Old Man, 'OK, then. Tomorrow we will be back with warrants and we will tear up every aspect of every criminal activity on this compound. And believe me, we will enjoy every minute of it!'"

"Really?"

"Yip."

"So the Old Man thought for a minute and then said, 'OK,' and headed to his pickup truck to go to the Empire Hotel. We turned around and headed back to the cruiser."

Hats and I were silent as we digested the story. RC and Wi were glowing in the pride of being part of the night's event.

"Holy shit," Hats said, breaking the trance we were in. "The Judge actually told the bad guys they have twenty-four hours to get out of town?"

"Yip," RC said, "or at least the twin brother dumbasses. The rumor is they were sent to Southern Ontario so they could be closer to Kingston, which is no doubt where they will live a ten- to fifteen-year stretch at some point." We all had a laugh at this comment, as we knew Kingston was home to a majority of Canada's penitentiaries.

"That Judge is one badass son of a bitch," Hats exclaimed to end the story, really saying, *I totally love that guy.*

And with that, our Tuesday morning turned into planning what the day would bring. I made my plans to leave to get back to school, and Hats did the same. We tried to have a visit with Ray's parents, although we were only able to see his father. We then talked to the Judge and Ozark and jointly decided Ozark and Curly would stay with Wi at the Judge's house while she found a place to live in town. RC made his plans to get back to his college course in Police Foundations.

I was back with Sophie in South Carolina by late Tuesday night.

I received a phone call from RC on Wednesday afternoon. He read me three articles from the Chinook River weekly paper. The first was a short article on Ray's passing. It was a little more than an obituary, but was still short on detail. It talked about Ray's musical abilities, his hockey playing, and his great work as a student. It did not talk about the cause of his death. We assumed the Judge had written the piece for the paper.

The second article was much larger and was about the Maple Tree Foundation and the plans for the hotel. It announced *The Ray and the Rose.* It introduced Wi. It was an excellent and upbeat piece. We assumed the Judge had written the piece for the paper.

The third article was completely unexpected. The article was a short blurb about the passing of a doctor in a neighboring town. He was found in his office, and the police reported that he had died of a heart attack and was found by an RCMP officer who was making a call on the doctor's office. What the article didn't say was that the doctor was the narco, drug-dealing, non-doctor that had sold Ray the not-so-legal part of his final concoction.

"I'm not sure how I feel about that," I said to RC.

"I know, Sam," RC said back. "The Judge told me that apparently the doctor knew the jig was up and that the police would be coming. According to the Judge, this is what caused the heart attack."

"Maybe he killed himself and the papers are lying," I said to RC.

"Maybe," RC replied.

"Anyway, what does it matter?" I said. "Dead is dead, and dead is too good for him."

"I hear ya," RC said back.

We finished our phone call, and I was weak beyond measure, as the events of the last week hit me like a lead balloon.

I needed to lie down. Every part of me felt as if I had been run over by an eastbound Canadian National train.

DAY 22

South Carolina

World of Red

EVERYTHING IS RED. It's not just in my mind now – it's everywhere. I'm colorblind in that I only see one color, and that color is red. The walls are red, the beach is red, the sky is red, and only one shade, a shade of bright red. Yet what I'm feeling is not a normal feeling of anger. I would actually welcome that right now, as to be angry is to feel only one emotion.

I am mixed up with emotions. I am completely mixed up.

It's all out there now. The Doc has done her job. It's all up to me now; however, I don't feel as if this was a turn in the right direction. I feel as if I turned down the wrong road, and I am now on the final dead end road that I have been slowly navigating towards.

This afternoon I could not help myself, so I turned on the television to feed my addiction. I listened to the Heads for three hours. I was manic and frantic. I changed the channels incessantly, never staying on one story for more than ten seconds. I finally turned off the box and tried to sleep, but my thoughts started racing at lightning speed. My brain was like an engine that has the throttle stuck at full speed. I had no control at all.

Death, Terrorism, Disease, Dead White Girl, Dead Black Girl, Car Wreck, Washington Broken, He's Lying, She's Lying, Go to War, Come Home From War, Thieves, Stealing, Chasing, Kidnapping, Spin, No Spin, Up Is Up, Down Is Down, Up Is Down, Down Is Up, The Left Is Right, The Right Is Wrong, Racism, Who Will Win, Who Will Lose, Don't Eat That, Do Eat This, Red Pill, Green Pill, Orange Pill, Cop Killers, Killer Cops, Muslim Radicals, Priest Pedophiles, Brave Soldiers Coming Home, Wounded Warriors Need Money, Economy Bad, Corruption Everywhere, Everyone Needs Money, God Is Good, God Is Dead, Global Warming, Snow Storms Looming, Climate Change, Weather Is Bad, Hurricane Winds, Take Shelter, Take Shelter, Take Shelter, Take Shelter, Take Shelter, Take Shelter, Take Shelter, Take Shelter.

At this point I don't believe I will make it, and I'm now convinced I don't want to make it. Why is living so important to everybody anyway? Why is death considered such a tragedy? You know you will die! Nobody gets out alive, so what does it matter when you die? A hundred years from now, what will it matter! And what if everything you lived for is gone? What is the point then?

It will be easy. I have ample depression meds left from past doctors' failed attempts at trial-and-error medicating – one water glass of whiskey with a chaser of meds and it's good night, Sam. My mind will finally stop producing thoughts, the hitchhiker will be tossed overboard, and to quote the poem of poems, before nightfall a corpse is all that will be left of Sam.

I need this. One way or another, I need relief. So it's time to cash in this trip I guess.

Sophie, if you and George can hear me, please hear my words.

COMING HOME

This morning when I woke up
Everything was changed
Morning is supposed to bring a fresh look
But all it brought is pain

This isn't just another event in life
Or a lesson along the way
I won't be made any stronger
Don't call this a simple twist of fate

Sophie, my Sophie, please tell me it's not true
Sophie, my beautiful Sophie, I can't stand losing you

Sophie, my Sophie, there's something you both must know
Sophie, my one and only Sophie, you weren't supposed to go

The days are relentlessly passing by
While I pray to hear your voice
Or your footsteps coming down the hall
To tell me I had a choice

The chaos and the breakdowns
Leaving everything in flames
My sadness turned to anger
As I realized I'm to blame

I go to bed this evening
Knowing I won't wake from my sleep
I've decided it's time to come to you
My life and soul are yours to keep

DAY 23

South Carolina

All Colors

I WOKE UP THIS MORNING with my life changed in two ways. The first, and most obvious, is that I am still alive. The second is that I have calmed the storm in my mind. Yes, my anger has left my body. I can see color for the color that it is. The sky is blue, the sun is yellow, the clouds are white, the morning sun passing emits shades of red, but it's a nice soothing red.

I feel different. I am different because Sophie saved my life.

Last night I prepared my party favors for the big one-person Saturday night bash. I had more than enough meds, and I had a nice big bottle of bourbon, top-shelf small-batch whiskey no less. You can't be frugal on your suicide whiskey; it's too important a decision. I still have the bottle.

I sat down at the desk in my small room. I reached out to Ray, and we wrote a song together for Sophie. I read it to her. I asked if she could hear me, and she did not respond. I then laid out all the pills in front of me. I built a pile that could be picked up in one big handful. I filled a water glass with whiskey. I picked up the glass and held it to the ceiling. I said a cheers! to Ray. I assumed he was with me.

I did not hear from Ray.

I then confirmed in my mind that I would, in fact, kill myself. I was certain it was the right decision, and then in the instant of that decision, my anger disappeared. You see, it was no longer required. Everything I was angry about did not matter any longer. It would all be in the past and I would not be in the present for it to screw up my future. It was ideal. I did not require anger to fuel me any longer. This was the one trip the *Hitchhiker* was not invited on, and knowing I would soon die allowed me to find the peace of mind that I had been searching for my entire life. I was at peace with Rose, Vince, James, Ray, Sophie, and George. I was at peace with the Soup Man. I was at peace with myself.

There was nothing to worry about; my rationalization was easy, and it went like this. If there is something after this life, then I would experience it. On the other hand, if there is nothing after this life, then it did not matter. A sleep-like state of nothingness would be a gift as compared to living like this. I had nothing to lose or gain, and that allows peace of mind.

Completely free from basic human emotions, I grabbed the handful of pills. Then Sophie spoke to me.

She told me she heard the song. She told me she and George were OK. She told me they were not ready for me yet. She told me to be happy. She told me to smile. She told me to write. She told me to love. And she told me to live.

She told me to live.

And so I live. And I am ready to leave this place.

I talked to the Doc this morning and told her I was ready to hit the road. She looked at me and saw the change. The eyes tell all as they are the gateway to the soul.

"Great," she said. "I'll take care of the paperwork."

The Doc also told me the timing was perfect because she had received a call from RC, and apparently he and Hats would be coming to the hospital to visit me that afternoon. I went out and spent some time walking the beach and eventually came back to the room and called RC on his cell phone. He and Hats were in a rental car they had just picked up at the Charleston airport and they were heading towards me.

"Where are you staying?" I asked them.

"Out with Kees," RC replied.

I told them to go straight to Kees's and that I would meet them there.

"You OK, Sam?" RC asked, really saying, *I was expecting you to be all messed up but you don't sound all messed up!*

"I'm good, RC, really good," was my response. I hung up and prepared to leave by plugging in the television. I turned on the Talking Cable Heads. I had no reaction. I saw it all for what it is.

Beaver Fever. Plenus Excrementum. Good boy, Hats.

I grabbed my things and silently thanked Uncle Alec for previously having my car placed at the hospital. He wanted any part of normal life to be in place for me when I got normal. I got into my car and headed out to see Hats, RC, and Kees.

When I got to the house, Kees, RC, and Hats were sitting in the late afternoon sun out on the deck. The ocean looked and smelled beautiful. They all got up, and I embraced each of them individually. I could tell RC was watching me; he was assessing my situation. He has been a Police Officer for over twenty-five years. He can spot crazy, and we caught eyes, me catching him watching me, him catching me catching him, and we both smiled. I punched him in the shoulder. Hats smiled at that and harnessed enough self-discipline to refrain from punching one of us.

We sat down with a cold beer. The sun felt good, the beer tasted good, it was all good. RC continued to watch me, and then he decided I was going to be a survivor.

"You're OK, Sam!" RC said as a statement and not a question, really saying, *Yes, we made it through this. Thank God we made it through this. I could not have handled not getting through this, Sam.*

"Yes," I answered.

"Good, Sam. Well not to possibly turn a good situation bad, but we have some news," RC said.

"I know," I replied. "The Judge has passed away."

The boys were not surprised by my knowledge. The Judge had said goodbye to RC personally, Hats and Kees by telephone; and the Judge had told RC that I was probably onto him. I got up and walked over to Kees.

Kees got up and I gave him another hug. "He was the greatest man that ever lived," I said to Kees.

"The greatest and bravest," Kees replied.

We planned our trip back home to attend the Judge's funeral. Of course the Judge had asked RC to assess my situation and if appropriate to ask if I would write and read a poem. I gladly accepted. *Eat tree, Beaver!* Hats called and arranged with Alec that we use his jet to get

Kees to the service, and Alec said he would pick us all up the following morning at the Johns Island executive airport. He would also join us on the trip to attend the service. Vintage Alec – one class act of a guy, one of the good guys.

We had a light dinner that night and Kees went to sleep early in order to be rested for the next day of travel. He is an amazing man, and I hope he and Johanna both see their 100th birthdays. We'll throw a great party, and I'll write something fantastic for that get-together.

With Kees in bed, RC and Hats and I strolled out onto the beach. We took a small cooler of beer and some firewood, and I brought my bottle of would-be suicide whiskey. We got a fire going in the fire pit on the beach. It was the same fire pit that shared its warmth of flames the night I met Sophie. Knowing this made me feel good, and I sent Sophie a thought, and she responded in kind. She was there with me. It felt really, really good.

We got the fire going and the three of us started talking about our lives. Our lives that were heavily integrated, but now at age fifty we all had stories that the others had not heard before. We talked about all the good in our lives, and we talked about all the entropy that had happened as well. It was clear there was an equal share of both and that perhaps it all averages out in general, with some of us getting a little more than our share of the entropy. People that have lived a life with limited tragedy should thank a person who took a few too many for the team.

Our conversation naturally took us to Ray, and we told stories and laughed about all the amazing and crazy times we had had. We talked about growing up, all the hockey games with the Maple Tree Hotel, the Lodge, the fires, the music, the tuning-up sessions, Vince, Rose, the Judge, and of course our road trip. We almost died laughing when we remembered the Hats reincarnation as a chicken in the gazebo in Banff.

Then we started to talk about the day Ray died and the subsequent events. At one point, I looked over at RC and I could see that he had gone quiet and was staring at the ground. He then put his face in his hands and started mumbling. His six-foot-six frame looked small as he curled himself up tight into a ball.

I walked over to RC, and going down on one knee, I put my arm around him. Hats came closer and knelt in front of RC as well. "What's going on, man?" I asked.

There was a pause, and then RC started mumbling in his hands. "I killed him," he said.

"What?" I said "You didn't kill him, RC. He died from an accidental overdose. It was nothing but an accident!"

"I killed him," RC said again, now raising his face from his hands so he could look me in the eyes. Hats then spoke.

"Are you sure you want to do this, RC?" Hats asked, really saying, *RC, this is a point of no return. Once the ship sails, there is no going back, brother!*

It was clear to me that whatever RC was about to tell me had already been shared with Hats at some point.

"Yes," RC said to Hats. "Sam has a right to know."

All of a sudden I felt my fears, anxiety, and anger coming back. I felt Sophie leaving me. I was scared beyond belief. I spoke to RC in a very matter-of-fact tone. My sanity and life were at risk in the next minute.

"What are you talking about, RC? Tell me right now what you're talking about!"

RC looked at me, and then at Hats, then back at me.

"I killed him," RC said.

"Who?" I begged. "Who the fuck did you kill, RC?"

"I killed the dope-pushing doctor who killed our friend Ray."

In the Judge's Voice

EVERYTHING WENT AS PLANNED. My family came to visit, and I saw everybody. I said goodbye to Johanna, and I went to sleep. At my age you can do this. Once your work is done in one place, you can will yourself to a new place. It was hard to say goodbye to Johanna, but I take solace in knowing the separation will be temporary.

I had a nice call with Hats. That kid, that pain in my ass for my whole life kid. I love that kid. I knew he would make a great lawyer. He allowed me to coach him somewhat over the years, but mostly he did his own thing. That's Hats. It didn't help him in his marriages, but I guess every strength must have a corresponding weakness. Hats is a superb father, though; terrible husband, but a great father.

It makes me proud to think about what he built – law offices in multiple countries specializing in criminal and environmental law. What the hell kind of firm does criminal and environmental? I believe the criminal law was for him and the environmental was for Ray. Hats has put a lot of money into *The Ray and the Rose* over the years, and I always suspected he took the profits from the environmental work and handed it over to Wi. That would be typical Hats. The criminal law was all him, though. Criminal law *Philadelphia Flyer Broad Street Bully* style. The phone call with Hats was nice. We said a proper goodbye. He told me he would make sure the Maple Tree Hockey Team won next year. He said the win will be in my name. I bet you the little turkey will figure out how to make it happen. I'll be watching.

470

I met with RC in person. I needed to see him. I needed to know he is good. I love that boy as if he were my own son.

He has made us all so proud with his career. Policing is not easy. Only unique people can even do it, much less do it well. The average human being has no idea what Police Officers do each day. I was with RC every step of the way as, unlike Hats, RC accepted coaching, accepted my advice and my help, but he also worked his ass off and earned everything he has.

We were so proud of him when he finished Police Foundations. The RCMP scooped him up eagerly, and he began his ten years of working in different towns in different provinces. Behind the scenes, I was always trying to get him home to our divisional detachment. It took a while, but finally he came, first as a Corporal, then a Sergeant, and then a Staff Sergeant. He is the boss now. In fact, he is youngest, biggest, and smartest boss in the history of the division, maybe the entire force. Yes, I'm very aware of my bias. The thing about RC is he embraces the very essence, culture, and history of the RCMP. Some of the proudest moments of my life were the ceremonies where he received his Boots, Breeches, and Red Serge.

He also brought home his beautiful wife, although he got some flak for that. The local girls were not very appreciative of a beautiful and smart woman coming into town with the guy they were all hoping to end up with. Johanna loves her, though. RC and his wife are perfect together, and their four children are good citizens of the Earth.

When I think of RC, I mostly think of his ability to make good decisions, like bringing Clive to *The Ray and the Rose*. I was more than a little leery. It had been two years since the boys had met Clive somewhere in California, and the whole rolling-crucifix part of the story had me more than a little concerned. Clive had called RC and asked him if he was serious about helping him get into Canada. RC came to me for advice and help, and he also told me Clive would be perfect for *The Ray and the Rose*. I was more than skeptical so I called in a few favors and got an American background check done on Clive. It came back as RC had described – a soldier, a very brave soldier, who had lost his way after the war. This holds a lot of weight in my books, so we got Clive to town legally, and he has been working with Wi ever since. Clive was full-time employee number seven, and his dog Oscar was dog number three behind Ozark and Curly. We now have forty-five full-time employees at the *The Ray and the Rose*, and Clive is excellent with the teenage boys. They call him Rambo behind his back.

They call him Sir to his face, because they know Clive does not mess around when it comes to addiction and our young people.

"This is serious business, Judge," he once said to me in such a way that it sent a chill through my spine.

Mostly, though, I needed to talk to RC once more about the events surrounding Ray's death. While I feel good that we are in a good spot, I think RC just needs to get a few things off his chest with Hats and Sam, and then he'll be fine. He knows in his brain that he did nothing wrong, but in his heart he feels guilt, which I suspect he will have forever, but he has learned to harness it. I had the same struggles from my years during the war.

I did not allow RC to fight the McMullen twins that night. That could have ruined his future career, and besides that, Hats and Sam had it taken care of. That being said, I did take RC with the senior constable and me when we went to talk to Old Man McMullen. It was a coaching session, although RC had no idea what was going on. The senior constable did, though, as his primary job is to coach his rookie wingman. I also wanted the constable to see how well RC would stay calm during the discussion. He would one day put in a good word for RC.

Truth be told, I liked the Old Man, and I wanted RC to see that. In a different place and different time, the Old Man and I could have been friends. He was too young for the war, but I suspect that had he served it would have changed who he turned out to be. The Old Man was smart. He was hard working and he cared for his family, but some series of events resulted in his running a criminal organization. Bootlegging, drug dealing, and gold high-grading were their favorite business models, and because of this the Old Man and I crossed paths on several occasions.

I wanted RC to see how the law really works, that relationships exist, that a moral code exists, that power exists. I wanted RC to see this so one day he would use this knowledge while building his career. RC is the best Police Officer I know, and that's because he understands the rules and regulations, but he also understands people. Policing is about people, where a bad cop is one who knows a lot about the rules and nothing about people, where a good cop is one who knows enough about the rules and a whole lot about people. Cop stands for *Corporal on Patrol*, and being on patrol is about being with and engaging with people.

RC was very mad at me when we saw Timmy pull the knife and I called down the Constable. He told me I'd better run and hide if Hats ended up getting stabbed. He was serious. I took him seriously, and

I secretly prayed that Hats would do exactly what he did. RC has a temper that only I know about. It's only flared up once, and I was the only one to witness it.

It happened at the Maple Tree Hotel the day after Ray died. I saw the rage in his eyes, and I know that rage because I've harnessed that rage in my life.

I followed RC out of the Maple Tree Hotel as he ran to his truck. I ran to stop him but couldn't keep up. He didn't even notice me. Rage does that. So I got in my car and drove in the direction he was heading. I knew where he was going, and thirty minutes later I pulled into the small parking lot of the office of our local dope-peddling doctor. We knew all about this guy, and he was a few weeks away from being arrested. He was done in all respects – career, relationships, health, moral fiber – it was all gone. That's why he was peddling prescriptions, and that's also why he was in his office on a Saturday afternoon all by himself with a closed sign on the door. I don't believe RC expected the doctor to be there. I always believed he was just going to smash the place up a bit. RC is not a killer.

The office door was open and I raced into the reception area. I then found the doctor's personal office, and when I entered he was standing behind his desk, and RC was standing in front of it. RC wasn't yelling at the doctor, he was just staring at him, and to this day I have no idea if words were ever exchanged. The doctor looked terrified enough though, with absolute fear and the recognition of his own failed life clearly evident on his face. RC did not notice me. He was in a fixed trance, a place somewhere deep in his soul where he was deciding what to do. Many years ago, I was in that exact situation, a point of *Go or No Go*. Back then, *Go* was the right choice for me; it needed to be done. But for RC, *No Go* was the right choice.

I walked up behind RC, and the doctor saw me. We knew each other. He looked at me, then at RC, who was just silently glaring at him, then looked back at me. His whole life flashed in front of his eyes – good decisions, bad decisions, happy times, sad times, bad times. And then he had a heart attack and died.

RC watched the doctor drop to the floor and came out of his silent rage, and watching him made me relive my own experience. I was on a military airplane with Kees and Johanna when I finally snapped back to reality. I remember Kees's shaking my arm, asking me to focus on his words. It had been a full two hours since I had put the final bullet through the sick skull of the last evil Nazi sympathizer who had killed and violated my new family. Even though my actions were principle based, you do not take care of serious business without shifting to a different gear in your mind, and gearing down from that acceleration takes time.

It was over, and RC was safe. I grabbed him by the shirt and got him into his truck and sent him to my home. I then called the Staff Sergeant of the RCMP and waited for him to arrive. We knew each other well. I told him the truth. We knew all about this lost doctor's activities, and he agreed that RC was fine. As far as we were both concerned, the old doctor got off easy. After all, he was killing our kids.

I raced home to make sure RC had followed my request. He was sitting with Johanna at the kitchen table when I arrived. She was consoling him. He was visibly upset, and we talked for hours and then got some sleep. We woke up early on Sunday morning and talked some more. We talked all day and into the evening and then got a good night's sleep. On Monday morning we headed to Ray's service.

We made a promise to each other that Sunday. We made a promise about how RC would deal with the event going forward. We made a promise that he would only talk to Hats and Sam about it, and only once, and only at an appropriate time. We made a promise that RC would not allow that doctor to destroy another one of the Beaver Brothers. We made a promise, and RC has kept that promise.

That's what makes a promise a promise. That's what makes a man a man.

RC is a real man.

DAY 24
Canada

The Hike

WE LANDED AT OUR hometown airport a little after lunch on Monday afternoon. Travelling on Alec's private jet allowed Kees to enjoy the trip. The irony of the jet's being so convenient and luxurious was not lost on me, but life goes on. I was going on. Sophie was smiling with me. I could feel her.

RC was doing great. He had rid himself of the one secret he had ever kept from Hats and me. He simply needed it off his chest, and we finished the night with his telling us the entire sequence of events while we finished my bottle of potential suicide bourbon. The re-living of the story was complete for RC, and we all agreed we would never talk about it again.

Services for the Judge were scheduled for Tuesday and Wednesday, Tuesday for visitation and Wednesday for the funeral service itself. Preacher Pete, now in his late sixties and retired, was going to preside over the service. My role was on Wednesday, and I spent some time on the flight getting my thoughts together. I completed a draft and showed it to Kees, and he said it was perfect. Little did I know, he would leak some of its contents prior to the service. In the end, I was ready to make the Judge proud.

It was clear that the United Church would not be big enough for the services, so they moved the venue to the Sportsplex just outside of town, which was fine with me as I had not made peace with the church. The Sportsplex is a fancy new facility built about ten years ago. It houses three ice pads, one curling rink and an Olympic-size swimming pool. The town is justifiably very proud of the venue, and the young players on the Maple Tree Hockey Team enjoy winning games there. The facility was built with public and private money. I know I gave some, and I think Hats gave lots. Wi also uses the facility often for events delivered through *The Ray and the Rose*.

Once on the ground, we headed to RC's house so I could see my two Labs, and we also had an equally nice reunion Monday afternoon with Johanna, Wi, and Clive. My hug with Wi felt good. She never married and never had a family of her own and has always said *The Ray and the Rose* was all she needed.

I stayed with my mother, now in her seventies, and my brother, sister, nieces, and nephews were all arriving from various cities. It was nice to spend time with my family, even though I was embarrassed that I had not been very communicative with them since Sophie and George died. Truth be told, I was probably not very communicative even before that, perhaps ever since my father's death so many years ago.

On Tuesday morning Hats, RC, Wi, and I had breakfast with Ray's parents at Frank's Diner. The first thing we noticed was that everybody is getting old. We all laughed about that, and it was amazing to hear Ray's mother laugh. She's doing OK and has been working as a full-time volunteer for the last fifteen years at *The Ray and the Rose*. Wi was the one who finally coaxed her out of her house and out of her depression, and as a result, she and Wi are very close friends. Ray's father is doing great because Ray's mother is doing OK. I guess life is relative at the best and worst of times, but to be sure life does go on even within the boundaries of relativity.

Preacher Pete chose the main ice pad that had the most seating around the ice itself and put a false floor over the ice for chairs. It's the rink used for any big game, the one that feels like *The Montreal Forum* to all local people. The Judge was cremated, and his urn was on a pedestal on a temporary stage right where one of the goalie nets would normally be. They put his pipe on top of the urn, and there was a piano beside the pedestal. There was a camera that projected the urn and the stage onto two big video screens. The time clock and Canadian flag were right above the stage high up on the wall, and they had the clock ticking in seconds and minutes in an upward sequence. Time was not running out; new time was being created. Even though the rink was now a church, it smelled and felt like a rink, and we knew the Judge would like that. Being inside the rink made me realize how long it had been since I had laced up my own skates, and I made a promise to myself that I would join RC and his old-timers' league. It was time to get back on the ice.

Three other items hanging over the stage from the ceiling completed the transformation of hockey rink to memorial. The first was the Detroit Red Wings jersey that we had bought for the Judge so many years before on our rushed trip home to see Vince. *Gordie Howe number nine.* The second item was a large picture of a young hockey player on the ice, leaning forward, staring at the camera, with his stick on the ice. The classic hockey pose. The player was big and strong looking, and it was obvious that it was a picture of the Judge. Below the picture in bold black numbers were the years he played for that particular team, 1935-1937. A decade before Gordie Howe would be in Detroit and a million years before the Great One would be in Edmonton, but only two years before Canada would join England in the Second World War, join England and the world in order to fight an evil the world had never before known.

Completing the bookend, on the right side of the picture, hung the actual jersey the Judge was wearing in the picture. The jersey was from the Winnipeg Monarchs, and its number was nine.

"That motherfucker!" Hats yelled out far too loud under the circumstances. "The Monarchs? 1935 through 37? Number nine? What the fuck, man! That's two Memorial Cups! Two fucking Memorial Cups! Are you hearing me, boys? That son of a bitch! That no good, number-nine-wearing, Memorial Cup-winning son of a bitch! It's a good thing he's already dead because I'd be kicking his ass right across this rink!"

Ya just gotta love Hats. It struck me in that moment that we had never pursued finding out about the Judge's hockey career. He never brought it up, we never asked, and we never thought it was appropriate to find out on our own. If the Judge had wanted us to know, he would have told us, and if he didn't want us to know, then we also did not want to know. This is living by principles. This is what we learned from the Judge.

The turnout for the visitation was totally overwhelming. The Judge was 95 years old, and he had impacted a lot of people along the way, so we were not surprised, but we were proud. There was representation from the law community, police forces, fire departments, military, social services, friends, family, government, diplomats, and probably a hundred other groups or associations that the Judge had impacted over the course of his life. People came from all over Canada, and many others came from the USA and Europe. We had no idea where everybody was sleeping, and the rumor on the street was that Preacher Pete had organized a billeting program where people all stay at local family homes, similar to what is done to facilitate large hockey tournaments.

After paying our respects to the Judge's family, we headed to *The Ray and the Rose*. Wi showed me around, and I was amazed by what they had accomplished. Maybe lots of *good* can come from lots of *bad*. They have made great use of technology and the latest trends to engage young people. The place looks hip, and I thought that George would have loved it. They're using rooms in the upper level that had had no useful purpose during the last several years that the bar was just a bar. Wi has her piano on the main level, along with other instruments that the kids can play, and I recognized several guitars that I know belonged to Ray. The best part for me though is the three centerpieces on the walls of the main level of the hotel. The first is an up-to-date series of annual pictures from the Maple Tree Hockey Team. RC and Hats are in each and every one. I knew that RC and some local parents are doing the coaching, while Hats is moral and financial support and shows up for important playoff games and team-picture day. When you scan the pictures, you eventually come to the years the Beaver Brothers were on the team. The pictures are classic – the four of us standing in full gear with tough looks on our faces, Vince and the Judge looking proud as they stand behind us. In a couple of the pictures, Ozark and Curly actually found their way into the frame. In the pictures we're in, the team uniforms are Toronto Blue; in the pictures post-Beaver Brothers, the uniforms are Detroit Red. *Good boy, Hats.*

The second centerpiece on a wall is the Gordie Howe jersey we purchased in Detroit so many years ago. Wi has put a great picture of Vince on the wall beside the shirt, and I couldn't help but think of Ray singing the sinking song as we went over the Mackinac Bridge while racing to get to Sacre Coeur Hospital to say goodbye to Vince. Looking at the picture, I was reminded of the day we dealt with Ray's and Vince's ashes. Two years after Ray's death, the Judge arranged an air charter to take RC, Hats, Wi, Ray's father, the Judge, and me to Churchill,

Manitoba. Of course we took Ozark and Curly as well. We sprinkled both sets of ashes into the Hudson Bay. We sprinkled them when the fourteen-foot tide of the bay was falling. Rising tides are good for long hellos, and falling tides are good for short goodbyes. We hoped the ashes would find their way to the entrance of the *Northwest Passage*.

The last visual on a wall is a new painting created for *The Ray and the Rose*. I learned that Hats drew the picture and a local artist painted the image. It's on the wall right behind the stage where the Beaver Brothers Band once played *Tommy Weeks the Carpet Man*. In the foreground of the picture is a large creek that leads to a pond. The creek is painted to look about twenty feet wide and narrows as it flows to the pond at the back of the landscape. Trees and forest surround the creek and pond. At the far end of the pond is a conical beaver lodge with the unmistakable logs and branches forming a dome above the water line. In the middle of the pond, there are four beavers swimming. They're swimming on their backs and look happy, as if they're smiling, singing, drifting, humming a tune. Behind the pond, on the land behind the beaver lodge, is another lodge, a log cabin built for people by people. There's a hint of smoke coming from a pipe in the roof, and behind the cabin, above the tree line and in the middle of a blue sky, is a full yellow sun. The sun is shining on the four beavers drifting in the pond, and painted in the middle of the full yellow sun is a beautiful long-stem red rose – an Angel Rose.

I stared at the image until RC interrupted me to get us moving on with our day.

We still had most of the afternoon available to us so I asked RC and Hats if they would join me for a hike. They were happy to oblige and we went to RC's to pick up my two Labs for the walk. It had been nice to see Texas and Georgia when we arrived the day before. Getting reacquainted was vintage Labrador. They immediately poured unconditional love my way, and a hike into the woods was going to be too good to be true.

"Where to?" RC asked.

I answered the question, and the three of us and the two dogs headed out to the Lodge. It was mid-August and mid-afternoon, fall was looming in the north, and it was a beautiful summer day. It was perfect.

The bush looked different. Old trees are gone, and new ones are in their place, new housing developments have encroached on our typical trail head, and if you didn't know better you would never know the land had ever been different than it is today. We parked the truck on the side of a new road and started walking into the bush. While concrete was certainly moving into our town, it was not long before we were in the deep woods. We were headed to the Lodge, recognizing silently that none of us had ever returned since we found Ray there. Truth be told, I had only been back to Chinook River a few times since his death. In my mind, I had abandoned my boyhood town. It had let me down too many times.

I'd like to think I would have easily found the Lodge site, but I'm not sure I would have. RC, on the other hand, is a scout and pioneering master. He leads the search and rescue operation's team for our RCMP region. RC was clearly the leader, but Hats assumed the lead position, even though he would look back every few seconds to get a directional queue from RC.

At one point, RC yelled up at Hats and asked, "Hey, Hats, how cold is a witch's tit?"

"Really fucking cold, RC!" Hats yelled back without missing a beat.

We laughed for the next ten minutes as we hiked through the woods remembering all the times and circumstances we had walked the walk in the past.

The Labs stayed close, but not that close. Mostly they were weaving in and out of the trees at full speed. I couldn't help but think about Ozark as I watched them. Ozark has been gone for a long time now. Wi took excellent care of Ozark and Curly right to the end. Wi called both Hats and me when Ozark was ready to be put to sleep. She was thirteen, her hips had failed, and it was time for her to move on. Hats and I both flew home to join Wi and RC at the vet. It was one of the hardest days of our lives. Ozark was cremated, and Wi still has her ashes, along with Curly's and Oscar's. We had dinner with the Judge and Ray's father that night at the Judge's house. The Judge poured a round of Irish whiskey and toasted, "To Ozark," as we lifted our glasses, took the shots, and slammed our shot glasses down on the Judge's hardwood dining room table. I still love that sound.

Thinking about Ozark made me remember the poem that I wrote after she died.

If a gentle north wind blows
When a summer sunset glows
A watchful eye might see
Ozark running through the trees

I'm convinced I saw her run across our trail a few times that afternoon, and I believe Hats and RC were thinking the same thing.

RC finally brought us into the clearing of the Lodge site. "That was a path we had never taken before," he said.

"Good," both Hats and I replied.

What once had been the Beaver Brothers Lodge was now gone. There were remnants of the walls and roof, but they were not structurally together. It was as if the roof had collapsed onto the walls and then over time the walls had fallen. Looking at the Lodge made me realize it had been over thirty years since we had last been there.

"I told Ray his roof plan sucked!" Hats said, and this brought a smile to RC and me. Surprisingly, it did not feel as if anybody had been to the site, either to use it as their own or to vandalize it out of kicks. Perhaps it was just too remote.

"I told you my site selection was perfect!" Hats added, taking credit for RC's work from thirty years ago.

Not knowing what to do with the Lodge, we walked over to the two birch trees that had formed the bookends for our woodpile so many years ago. The trees still stood, and you could see evidence of rotten split wood that had now become a compost mound on the ground. We turned our attention and looked to the spot where we had found Ray. In our silence, I know each of us wanted to find something special. We wanted to see special flowers and a solitary sapling growing strong. We wanted to see an indentation of a snow angel. We wanted to see a permanent mark of Ray made by the sun.

There was nothing physical to see. The ground was grown over, and there was no evidence of human or spiritual interaction with the natural elements of the soil. Nobody besides the three of us would ever know that our best friend took his last breath on that very spot, childishly and innocently making a snow angel while looking up to the sky – up to his God.

We headed back to the Lodge site after an unrehearsed moment of silence. We were able to move a few logs and one of the steel roof panels, and this allowed us access into one half of the Lodge. Once inside, we were able to use upward leverage to throw the remaining rooftop off to one side. We were now standing in the square of the Lodge with no roof over us at all. We started to look around. It became clear that nothing had survived completely intact, but there were relics to be seen. The outline of the bunks and table, some old dishes, utensils, and other articles made from metal or plastic could be seen, and rotten fabric from sleeping bags and old clothes still existed.

We would point to something, identify it, and then tell a story about it.

At one point, Hats bent down and picked up a little piece of red plastic. It was a single army from our Risk game. He put it in his pocket. We couldn't find the *Risk* board itself; no doubt it had decomposed over the years. Moving my attention away from Hats, I could see RC digging in the ground in one corner of the Lodge. He was moving leaves and dirt and branches away from the area.

"It's the stove!" he yelled. "It's Findley!"

Hats and I went over and helped him dig the rest of the stove up from its not-so-final resting place. It had obviously fallen on its side when the roof collapsed. The stove pipe was no longer attached, and one hinge on the door had broken off. Other than that, Findley looked perfect. We looked at the stove and instantly remembered the trip to get it to the Lodge and all the nights it kept us warm.

"We're taking it home," RC said, really saying, *I'm taking this thing home if I have to spend two days carrying it myself!*

"OK," Hats and I replied without hesitation.

We said goodbye to the Lodge and spent the next two hours lugging Findley back to the road. It was hard, hard work. We had moved it in using a tripod and wheel as our friend, but this was pure manual labor. Watching us carry the stove through the woods would have competed with any long lost episode of the Three Stooges. We argued about what the best technique was, and we experimented and tried new carrying approaches. At one point, Hats was so pissed at our lame ideas on how to carry the thing that he said, "Fuck it, man, I'll just carry it myself!"

RC and I stood back and told him to have at it. You never get in the way of a man on a mission. Hats bent down and picked the stove up the same way an Olympic weightlifter would do the *Clean and Jerk*. He got the clean part pretty well, and he even accomplished the jerk in that he got the stove over his head, although it didn't stay there long, and Hats started weaving and staggering and eventually fell over with the stove into a pile of brush.

It was hilarious, and RC and I laughed hard. "Fuck off," was all Hats said to us. Some things never change.

Once on the road, we put Findley in the back of RC's truck, loaded up the dogs and went to RC's to unload the stove and the dogs. I then headed home to have dinner with my family.

It had been a long day, and I was ready for sleep.

DAY 25
Canada

Goodbye, Judge

THE FUNERAL WAS at ten o'clock in the morning. It was the funeral of funerals, and I'm sure the attendance was measured in the thousands. The agenda was thoroughly thought through. Bagpipers started the service with *Amazing Grace*, an armed guard walked Johanna and her family into the arena, and eulogies were given by a retired Provincial Premier, the current town Mayor, Preacher Pete, and RC. RC did not speak about his personal relationship but rather from the point of view of a senior member of the police community. We listened to RC on the stage from our seats behind Johanna and her family. We were beaming with pride the entire time. He was in full formal RCMP dress, and he looked just as I had imagined him so many years ago while we were saying goodbye to Rose. In the end, the list of speakers was perfect, each eulogy noting a unique aspect of the Judge's contribution to the community, to the province, to the country, and to the world.

The Judge had outlived all his friends other than Kees and Johanna, so it was particularly moving when Kees got up to speak. He did not look like a man in his nineties as he walked to the podium. He was too proud to look old, and his words were as powerful as words could ever be.

"*My friends*," Kees started, "*today we say goodbye to my best friend. My best friend and the husband of my dear sister Johanna. When I look out, I see many young faces at this service today. Many of you only know about your history through books or stories that have been passed down to you. Many of you do not know the sacrifice that so many others have made so we can be here together. So we can be here free to congregate, free to worship, free to say goodbye to a great man. I know how we all feel today. I can personally feel the collective emotion of this entire congregation. And I can tell you it is overwhelming to try to absorb the totality of the impact of this one man's life. This one man, my best friend, was the bravest, the most principled, the most courageous man who ever lived. And so I implore the young people here today, do not take for granted what this man and so many others fought and died for. Do not squander the freedoms that most of us cannot fathom will ever be taken away from us. Live a life of courage, and be brave to do what is right and to fight against what is wrong. Make your world a better place to be, and in doing so, make my best friend proud.*"

Because we were in a hockey rink, nobody really understood funeral protocol, but nobody really cared either. Kees received a standing ovation, hockey arena style, and Preacher Pete had to eventually ask everybody to sit down so Johanna could say a few words.

Johanna, with her large family all looking on from the front row, was very poised and was as classy as an elderly lady has ever been. She thanked everybody for their support, and she thanked our town and community for the life it had provided her and the Judge. Johanna also received a standing ovation.

Preacher Pete got up to start to bring the service to a close. There were only two official items left. He let the congregation know that the family would be dealing with the ashes as a private matter. I would later find out that the ashes were spread at a gravestone in our local cemetery and specific locations in England, Belgium, and Holland. Preacher Pete then introduced me to read my poem. Hats, RC, Wi, Clive, Alec, Kees, Johanna, Ray's mother and father, Hats' and RC's families, and my family all gave me a look that told me they were proud of me. I looked at all of them and realized I had an amazing extended family. The years had dealt us tragedy but had left us with a group of people who loved each other, and in the end we had each other, and that was all that mattered.

I went to the podium and read my poem.

JOURNEY

to begin your life on Earth,
is to begin a precious journey
throughout which you laugh
and you cry
you live, and you die

to learn of your mortality,
is to learn about life
a fragile, finite cycle
to be cherished along the way
offering complete respect
for each and every day

to question your mortality,
is to question your surroundings
using the gift of thought
feeling spirituality
deciding who you are
and who you can be

to understand your mortality,
is to understand yourself
allowing hard times
to remain in the past
leaving fond memories
in a place where they last

to fear your mortality,
is to fear separation
not being surrounded
by family and friends
all those you love
from beginning to end

to accept your mortality,
is to accept who you've become
the progression of age
and the changes it brings
to body and mind
in all living things

to end your life on Earth,
is to end a precious journey

and everyone you touched
will laugh and cry
happy that you lived
sad that you died

I finished my poem and received a standing ovation from the large congregation. I wondered what the ovation was for exactly. I suspect the standing ovation was for the Judge, as we needed to be on our feet celebrating his life every chance we could.

Preacher Pete then got up to end the service. He asked Wi to come up on the stage, and he told the congregation that Wi was going to play a song as a final goodbye for the Judge. Neither RC, nor Hats, nor I knew anything about this part of the program.

Wi went onto the stage and sat down at the piano and started to play. She played beautifully, and we recognized the song immediately. She was playing *Let It Be*. Not only that, she began to sing the words with the voice of an angel, because she is an angel.

Not one person in that arena that day made one noise until she finished her song. Every single person just let the music flow through their entire being as the music provided a rapture of emotion for thousands of people with thousands of individual thoughts. Then the music ended.

The loudest sound ever recorded in a hockey arena was in 1954 when Tony Leswick of the Detroit Red Wings scored the winning goal, in overtime, in game seven of the Stanley Cup playoffs. The game was played at the Olympia in Detroit, Michigan, when they beat the Montreal Canadiens. Gordie Howe skated with the Stanley Cup around the arena, and the roof almost came off the building. Perhaps that's why they needed to build The Joe.

What happened in Chinook River after Wi stopped playing her piano made 1954 in Detroit sound like a whisper. We went wild. It was as if every single person in the place just needed a good release, so we cheered to break all sound barriers. Johanna stood up and clapped her hands while her family joined her and screamed at the rafters. Preacher Pete, still on stage, was jumping up and down and pounding his fist in the air as if the Judge himself had just scored an overtime game-seven goal. Kees, bouncing on his ninety-year-old feet, was pointing to the Judge's young hockey picture with a look on his face that said *great job, my friend, great job!* He turned and gave Alec a warm embrace while Ray's mother and father stood tall and held hands and pointed their joined fist at the

Canadian flag flying proudly from the ceiling. Clive ran up and down aisles fist bumping all the young people he was helping at *The Ray and the Rose*; the bagpipers started blowing their pipes in random bursts; Wi stayed at the piano and pounded on the keys as if she was performing a recital to join a carnival; and RC, Hats, and I did *Eat tree, Beaver!* handshakes until our hands were sore. We were tearing the barn down.

And just when I thought it could not get any louder, the most amazing thing happened. The bagpipers, who were blowing in random bursts, noticed many people pointing to the Canadian flag hanging from the rafters, so they started playing the tune to O *Canada*, our national anthem.

There we were, saying goodbye to the Judge in our hometown hockey rink, and we ended the funeral with the loudest rendition of O *Canada* ever heard. People sang in English and French, and we sang with all the accents that exist in a town filled by people with rich and varied backgrounds.

We sang so the Judge could hear us.

O Canada!
Our home and native land!
True patriot love in all thy sons command.
With glowing hearts we see thee rise,
The True North strong and free!
From far and wide,
O Canada, we stand on guard for thee.
God keep our land glorious and free!
O Canada, we stand on guard for thee.
O Canada, we stand on guard for thee.

Judge, if you can hear me, and I believe you can, you need to know something. You stood on guard for us, Judge. You stood on guard for your family, for your town, for your province, and for your country. You stood on guard for the world.

But not only that, Judge.

You stood on guard for me.

For me and my best friends.

For those very interesting Beaver Brothers.

Thank you, Judge.

Thank you for standing on guard.

DAY 26
Canada

Afternoon Road Trip

THERE WERE MULTIPLE receptions in the Judge's honor around town, but we decided to pass on attending. Alec drove Kees back to the Judge's house where he and Johanna would have a visit before Alec got him home the following day, and we knew we would visit with Johanna when the time was right and she had rested.

I told my family I would see them for dinner, and Hats and RC and I went to RC's house. We were exhausted as well and needed an hour to breathe. After a visit with RC's family, we sat outside on his porch. It was another beautiful northern summer day, but I struggled to decompress from the morning's events. I had something on my mind.

"I have one more thing I would like us to do," I said to no one in particular.

"Sure, Sam," RC replied for both of them.

"I would like to go get the journal," I said.

After a micro-second, RC jumped up and said, "I thought you would never ask! Let's go, Beaver Brothers!" And he abruptly left us and went into the detached garage behind his country home. We didn't know what RC was up to, but it didn't take long to figure it out. After only a couple of minutes, the overhead door to the garage opened, and Hats and I immediately recognized the sound of Boomer. You just never forget the sound of an old Volkswagen Micro Bus. RC had poured time and energy over the years to make sure Boomer was in tip-top condition, ready for a road trip when the time presented itself, and the time had now presented itself.

Hats and I took a minute to admire Boomer, which led us to think about Barth. We knew Barth was gone, as Ray's father had sold him after Ray's death. We were not involved in the decision but would have agreed with it had we been consulted. Sometimes the need to move on means ridding yourself of physical images of the past. I often wonder where Barth is today. I wonder if seeing Barth would bring me more pain than joy.

Boomer brought more joy than pain.

RC had done a great job keeping Boomer in working order. His attention was all on the engine and other powertrain parts of the bus, although he had not touched the interior or the outside paint job. The side of the bus still has *Beaver Brothers* painted in yellow on the two front doors, and when I opened the middle door I immediately recognized the bench seats. The smell of the vehicle had not changed. It's a perfect smell, and our tools of the trade were still all in the back of the bus, including the old hockey Mik-Maq sticks we had used to perfect the art of cleaning eavestroughs. Here's the best part, though. Ozark hairs still plastered the seats. Man, oh, man. That dog sure could shed her fine white and brown fur.

We loaded up in Boomer, grabbed Texas and Georgia, and headed out towards our launching spot on the Chinook River. RC drove, Hats rode shotgun, and I sat in the middle of the front bench with Georgia and Texas on either side of me. Within five minutes, I had Ozark hairs all over my clothes. I had Ozark on me and loved it.

It took us a couple of hours to get to our destination, and every minute of it was spectacular. We played our old cassettes and even drank a couple OVs. RC drove and navigated, and he remembered exactly where to go. We got there with ample daylight left, and when we arrived at the clearing RC walked us to precisely the spot where the journal had been buried so many years ago.

"That's interesting, RC," Hats said to him, really saying, *That was a little too easy, buddy. What gives?*

RC simply said, "Let's just say I've been out a time or two to make sure everything was OK."

Hats and I looked around and saw evidence of a bench that had been built and a small campfire pit.

"Really?" Hats answered back, "and what exactly does that mean?"

"OK, fine. I took my kids canoeing when they were younger. I figure this is as good a spot to put the canoes in as any other spot!"

"Oh," Hats replied after a short delay, really saying, *RC, maybe you ain't as tough as you want the world to think you are!*

We used a shovel from Boomer, and Hats dug in the area that RC suggested we dig. It was clear RC had never tried to find the box; nevertheless, we hit the old green garbage bags after a few minutes and pulled the treasure up. We sat down on the ground and opened up the old bullet box, and to our surprise everything was perfectly intact. We laughed and talked about each trinket as it came out of the box. We went through the Book of Paths, our BOP, and laughed about the roads we had chosen on our quest for peace of mind. We took a deep breath when Hats took the journal out and gently put it by his side, all three of us intentionally playing it cool that it had been retrieved from the box. We continued to pull out little gems from so long ago, and then getting to the bottom, RC pulled out an undeveloped roll of 35 millimeter film.

"What's this? RC asked in general, really saying for all of us, *We don't remember leaving a roll of film behind. How did this get into the box?*

We sat puzzled for a minute and broke the silence by deciding we should get back on the road, so we headed home, having spent less than an hour at the journal burial site. Two hours later, RC dropped me off at my mother's house.

As I got out of Boomer at the house I grew up in, Hats looked at me and said, "Sam, are you forgetting something?"

I turned around and Hats handed me the journal through the passenger window. I smiled, grabbed it, and headed into the house.

It was well past dinnertime when I got home, but my family had waited for me, and we had a nice dinner together. It was good to visit with my mother, brother, and sister in the home the three of us grew up in. After dinner, I talked with my mother and asked her if I could stay with her for a while until I found a place to live. She told me I could have my old bedroom, and I asked her if I could put up my *Lynyrd Skynyrd* and *Eagles* posters. We had a good laugh, and I realized I looked forward to conversations and visits with her over the next few years. Perhaps I'll even find the courage to take her to the United Church on Sundays. I know she would be pleased if I escorted her, and I'm thinking this would be appropriate.

After visiting with my mother, I went to my bedroom and stood in the middle of the room, which was virtually frozen in time. I looked at the red maple bed that the boys had hidden under the day my father died. I looked at the corner of the wall that I had pushed myself into while trying to escape the reality of the news my mother had just shared.

Then I walked over to my bookshelf. All my books were still there, and I took my favorite one from its spot – *Collected Poems of Robert Service*. I opened the inside cover to read the inscription and poem that I knew was there – *To Robert, Love Dad, 1965*. It was a gift to me from my father, given to me on the day I was born, and below the inscription is a short poem, a poem handwritten by my father.

SETTING THE BAR

A Father's job is never complete
It begins again with each new feat
To recognize the true north star
To calm the pace and set the bar

I thought about all the times I had relied on the book to memorize the poem of poems. I thought about all the times I had opened the cover after my father died, just to read the inscription, to read the poem he had written for me.

And I thought about why I had left the book behind when I departed for South Carolina so many years ago.

I sat down at my old desk, opened the journal, began to read, and six hours later finally put my head down to get a couple of hours of sleep. I had what I needed from the journal. I had what I needed in order to put my thoughts together. I had what I needed in order to write this story.

To write this story for you.

And for me.

I had what I needed to know that I am a survivor.

DAY 27
Canada

Warm Again

RC PICKED ME UP around ten o'clock for breakfast with Hats, Kees, and Alec. Kees and Alec would be leaving that afternoon after the laying of the Judge's ashes at the local cemetery. We met at Frank's Diner. I didn't need to look at the menu. I knew exactly what to order.

I was tired but feeling good, and I talked to Alec over breakfast about our business. On the way up from South Carolina he had told me he had a buyer. In vintage Alec form, he had brokered a deal so my employees could buy the business. All they asked was that I be available to consult and participate in the bigger events. Over breakfast, I told Alec to do the deal. I was ready to sell but also ready to work a little bit as a consultant. I asked him to structure the deal so my portion of the money goes to *The Ray and the Rose*. I have enough money; not Alec money, not even Hats money, but enough to live a good life and help my family out if required.

From breakfast, we headed out to the cemetery as Johanna had asked Kees to ask Wi and us to join the private ceremony. Wi drove on

492

her own, and when we arrived we were amazed by how big the Judge's family is – multiple generations of great people. Exponential growth is an interesting concept.

Preacher Pete said a few very nice words and then Johanna and the Judge's children sprinkled some ashes over the headstone. It was a nice headstone, not too small and not too large; it was perfect. It had both the Judge's name and Johanna's name on it. His dates were filled in; of course her final date was not. There was a short epitaph that read, *leaving fond memories in a place where they last,* a line from my poem.

We said a temporary goodbye to Johanna and her family and walked Kees and Alec to their rental car. We all gave Kees a big hug. He told us we were welcome to stay with him anytime, and we knew we would definitely take him up on the offer.

I then asked Hats and RC and Wi if we could go for a walk. RC and Hats knew what was on my mind but they did not vocalize it. RC understood too well, and he silently led the way to my father's grave site. It was a nice granite headstone, and while staring down at it I couldn't remember the last time I had been there. I realized the answer was maybe never. There were two well manicured blue spruce trees, one on each side of the headstone, making me wonder who had done all the work to keep the site so well maintained. Then I looked up at RC and did not wonder any longer. He simply shrugged his shoulders when I looked up at him. Hats punched him in the arm.

I looked down at the dates on the stone. He was forty-four when he died, six years younger than I am today. It occurred to me that I am his elder, that I could be his coach, that I could offer him advice.

In that instant, I saw my father in a different light. For years I only saw him through the lens of a thirteen-year-old boy, a little boy frozen in time, frozen on the day his father died, and I had spent thirty-seven years constantly seeking my father's approval in this frozen state, constantly wondering whether he thought I was doing well, constantly wondering whether he was proud of me.

Standing there, for the first time, I saw my father through the lens of a fifty-year-old man, a man who has struggled to find his own peace of mind for so many years. Through this lens, I wondered what my father had struggled with, I wondered how he dealt with those struggles, I wondered if I could have helped him somehow, I wondered what it was like to be him.

Doing some quick math, I realized my mother had been in her thirties when my father died, in her thirties with three kids and no husband; she was just learning about life herself. I thought back to the day she had to tell me that my father had died, and how it must have been so hard on her as well. I don't remember thinking about her feelings that day, and now I can only imagine it must have been torture for her.

My mother was so mad at me when I started calling my father the Soup Man. She believed it was disrespectful to the memory of her husband and our father. I didn't care, though, as in the same way that I did not consider her feelings she struggled to understand mine. Mourning is a selfish act and so it's hard for us to have empathy while mourning.

I had to call my father the Soup Man. I had to dehumanize his memory. I had to put a barrier up to guard against my biggest fears, to guard against the idea and possibility that my father had been an alcoholic, to guard against the idea and possibility that my father had loved his addiction more than he had loved his family, to guard against the idea and possibility that his addiction had killed him, and to guard against the idea and the possibility that my father hadn't loved me.

I looked up from thought and saw Wi, RC, and Hats looking at me. All was good, so I told my father I would be back soon, and we headed to the cars. We walked with Wi, and before she got into her car I asked her if she had an entry-level role I could play at *The Ray and the Rose*. She smiled at me, and raising herself on her tippy toes, she gave me a very soft kiss on my lips. Then she whispered in my ear, "That's from Sophie." She turned and got into her car without saying a word.

We started walking back to RC's truck, and Hats looked at me and said, "Nice kiss, Romeo," and then punched me on the arm. I punched him right back, and he punched me back harder. It hurt. RC then used both his hands and all his strength and shoved Hats in the chest, hard enough to send Hats flying backwards into a set of bushes on the side of the walkway.

"Fuck you both!" Hats yelled as he got himself out of the hedges and started chasing RC and me as we all ran at full speed to the truck.

We went back to RC's house and spent the rest of the afternoon outside with his family and the dogs. You just have to take advantage of the northern summer nights because winter is coming soon. Nighttime came, and we could see that there would be a dash of Northern Lights in the sky. The dancing colors are a beauty that calms the soul.

RC suggested that the three of us sit by the fire in his backyard, and Hats and I thought that was an excellent idea, so RC led us out to his spacious backyard, where the forest surrounded us on three sides. The night sky was alive with the images of the north, and when we got a little deeper into the backyard we saw what RC had in mind. He had set up three Muskoka deck chairs for us to sit in, and he had also set up Findley from the Lodge. In typical RC fashion, he had also repaired the broken hinge on the door. The stove was right in the middle of his lawn with the three chairs pulled up in front of it, the fire was burning, the door of the stove open to show the colored flames. Findley offered soothing warmth as the smoke rose to the open sky through the hole in the top that was missing its stove pipe.

We sat down, and RC went into a small bag he had brought with him. He pulled out a six-pack of OV and the half-bottle of Jack and the pack of Reds that were buried in the journal box. The Torpedoes were stale as could be but still excellent, even though it had been a long time since any of us had smoked a torpedo. Not since we quit at the Maple Tree Hotel the weekend Ray died.

We sat in our chairs, and RC looked at me and asked, "Did you bring it, Sam?"

We spent the night reading the journal and being old friends. We read the journal by the natural lighting of the northern sky while the flames and sounds of Findley kept us company. We stayed up until there were signs that morning was coming, and I suggested that it was time for us to get to bed so we could get up with RC's family in a couple of hours.

"I'm ready if you are, Sam. Are you ready, Sam?" RC asked.

All three of us thought about the question. We all fell silent for several minutes, the fire burning hot with the flames flowing out the front door of Findley. I was thinking about the question, I was thinking about everything, and then I started thinking about the most amazing poem ever written. All my life, I have pondered so many questions about the poem of all poems.

Why did Sam allow the spell of gold to turn his life into a cold living hell? And if he was on a great adventure, why did he give up? Why did he quit so easily? And what about Sam's friend, the nameless, faceless prospector who so unselfishly promised to cremate Sam after his death? Why make such a promise when you know the hardships that meeting the promise will bring?

I was lost in thought, thinking about the poem of poems, and then I thought about RC's question again. *Are you ready, Sam?*

I went back to my poem, and I silently recited the ending in my mind.

And there sat Sam, looking cool and calm,
in the heart of the furnace roar
And he wore a smile you could see a mile,
and he said: "Please close that door."
It's fine in here, but I greatly fear, you'll let in the cold and storm
Since I left Plumtree, down in Tennessee,
it's the first time I've been warm."

I stood up and looked at my two best friends.

"Yes, I'm ready," I said.

I walked up to Findley and placed the journal into the heart of the furnace roar. I closed the door to the stove.

We walked up to the house to start a new day.

"Fucking right Sam's ready," Hats said quietly to himself as we walked to the house, all three of us smiling, while silently saying thank you to the lights in the northern sky.

In Ray's Voice

WELL, I GUESS OUR WORK is done here. Thank you for sticking with Sam. He needed you, and having you with him made all the difference. Support is required to navigate a world of entropy.

Sophie and I were very worried last week. Sam needed to hear from Sophie, but he was not open for dialogue. His anger was too powerful, so I helped him write a song that night for Sophie. It was our last attempt. We had to take him right to the edge and hope he would create a small window for Sophie to break through.

It worked. Sophie and I are all good now.

George and Rose love playing with Ozark, Curly, and all the other furry creatures. But mostly they enjoy listening to Vince, the Judge, Grampa James, and Sam's dad debate how Hats will go about winning next year's hockey championship. Sam's dad argues all Hats needs to do is put Sam in as coach. All is good.

Did you hear Wi play and sing at the Judge's funeral? She is an angel. I look forward to being with her again one day. Not too soon, though.

I also look forward to the boys getting that roll of film developed. I hope it's not ruined. It will take a few days before RC gets it back, but they're going to love some of the shots I got on our trip. I can't tell you about them as that would not be fair to the boys. OK, I'll tell you about one. There is a beautiful picture of Sam and Sophie sitting by the fire on Seabrook Island. It's the night they met, the night Sam recited the poem of poems to Sophie. They are young, they are healthy, they are beautiful, and they are in love. You can see it in their eyes, because the eyes tell all.

I wish I could give you some idea of where your journey will take you next, but I can't. That wouldn't be right. I can tell you one thing though. It's not what you think. It's not any of the stories that people believe, not even close. It's so much better than any of that. The Great Mystery is better than anything people have ever imagined.

I guess I can tell you that the sun is not the ultimate God, but the sun does play a big role. A key role actually, and that makes me very happy.

I noticed Sam didn't share all our songs. There is one important one you should have. I wrote it in the journal as my last entry right before we buried the journal in the bullet box. I hope he gives it to RC to put it to guitar. Maybe Hats can even bang out some percussion. It only needs a few chords because it already has the truth.

I'll leave it here with you. I hope you like it.

Bye for now, my friends. I hope you have a good life. We will see you one day.

In the meantime, don't let entropy and the sound of the stream drive you crazy.

And always remember, make sure you take time to drift and hum.

DRIFT AND HUM

I've been searching for a long time
For a little peace of mind
Not seeing what's worth seeing
As I'm trying to chase a dime

Take time to drift and hum, my brother
Find the time to drift and hum
Dam up the noises from the stream
Work hard then drift and hum

Busy means we're on the trail
Too often though it feels like hell
Searching for what can't be found
Trying to buy what no one sells

Past and present in my brain
The future drives me more insane
My head's a forest that's on fire
And the forecast it ain't got no rain

Maybe rain ain't what I need
It's getting clear I now can see
The answer is within my grasp
The answer's easy, just be free

The good news is I may be done
The search is now where it began
Full circle to know what to do
I'm taking time to drift and hum

51788345R00279

Made in the USA
Charleston, SC
27 January 2016